LETHAL IN A KILT

Hot Scots, Book Seven

ANNA DURAND

JACOBSVILLE BOOKS JB MARIETTA, OHIO

LETHAL IN A KILT

ISBN: 978-1-949406-20-7 (paperback)
ISBN: 978-1-949406-19-1 (ebook)
ISBN: 978-1-949406-21-4 (audiobook)
Library of Congress Control Number: 2020902211

Manufactured in the United States.

Jacobsville Books
www.JacobsvilleBooks.com

Publisher's Cataloging-in-Publication Data
provided by Five Rainbows Cataloging Services

Names: Durand, Anna.
Title: Lethal in a kilt / Anna Durand.
Description: Marietta, OH : Jacobsville Books, 2020. | Series: Hot Scots, bk. 7.
Identifiers: LCCN 2020902211 (print) | ISBN 978-1-949406-20-7 (paperback) |
    ISBN 978-1-949406-19-1 (ebook) | ISBN 978-1-949406-21-4 (audiobook)
Subjects: LCSH: Man-woman relationships--Fiction. | Scots--Fiction. | Americans--Fiction. | Highlands (Scotland)--Fiction. | Spies--Fiction. | Single mothers--Fiction. | Romance fiction. | BISAC: FICTION / Romance / Contemporary. | FICTION / Romance / Romantic Comedy. | FICTION / Romance / Workplace. | GSAFD: Love stories.
Classification: LCC PS3604.U724 L48 2020 (print) | LCC PS3604.U724 (ebook) | DDC 813/.6--dc23.

Chapter One

Logan

I tapped one foot on the elevator floor and wondered for the hundredth time this morning how having killed people made me qualified for a job at a tech company. My cousin Evan swore he'd found the perfect position for me here at his company, Evanescent Security Technologies Limited. He made security and surveillance devices, but I knew nothing about that. Back when I'd served in the Secret Intelligence Service, I'd used the devices provided to me, but I didn't understand how they were constructed. Since leaving the SIS, I had worked as a bricklayer.

Why was I here? In America, in Evan's building, for a job interview. I'd never heard of Carrefour, Utah, until Evan moved to the city. I scratched my head. Evan had insisted on flying me here from Scotland in his private jet. He was up to something, that much I was sure of.

The elevator doors opened, and I stepped out into the hallway. Evan had said to turn left and go to the end. I strode down the hall, past closed office doors and open ones, nodding to anyone who glanced my way. The hallway dead-ended at a reception area. Evan's closed office door was on the other side of the desk occupied by his executive assistant.

I paused at the periphery of the reception area to drink in the sight before me.

Serena Carpenter was bent over at the waist tinkering with a paper shredder. She'd removed its top and was trying to pull scraps of paper out of the many blades that spun and shredded when the device was turned on. The power cable stretched toward a wall outlet, but she'd unplugged it.

The paper shredder didn't interest me. I was fascinated by the sight of her erse and the way her tan skirt stretched tight over those round cheeks when she bent over, not to mention the way her hips shimmied as she struggled with her task. Since she stood at a diagonal to me, I got a glimpse of her breasts, thanks to her white blouse sagging away from them. A lacy white bra partially covered those apple-size mounds.

Ah, how I loved those breasts. I'd never seen them bare, never touched them either, but I'd fantasized about her tits on a regular basis for eight months.

Serena, engrossed in her battle with the shredder, growled at the machine. Though a clip held her toffee-brown hair away from her neck, strands of it had come loose. She blew them away, but they fell back onto her cheek.

I sauntered up behind her and laid a hand on her erse, molding my fingers to its shape. "Need a hand?"

She jerked, letting out a sharp squeak, and popped upright to glare at me over her shoulder, squinting her gray eyes. "Ugh, you. I'd hoped Evan was kidding when he said you were coming in for a job interview today."

Her lip curled slightly every time she spoke to me. I'd gotten used to it. Oddly, her disdain for me made me want to shove her skirt up and have her on the desk.

She slapped my hand away. "I don't need a hand from you. Ever."

"Liar." I knelt and freed the scrap of thick paper that had gotten stuck in the shredder, then snapped its top back on and straightened. "There. It's fixed."

With her brows furrowed, she contemplated the shredder.

I patted her bottom. "You can thank me later. When we're naked."

The lass growled at me this time and pulled away from my touch. "Sit down and shut up. I'll see if Evan's ready for you yet."

Sighing, I ambled over to the quartet of chairs placed against the wall opposite Serena's desk. I dropped onto one of the them. To my right lay the door to Evan's office.

His executive assistant settled her bum onto her chair and wheeled it forward until her legs were tucked under the desk. She eyed me, her lips puckering. "Why aren't you wearing a tie? This is a business meeting."

"I don't like ties." I'd worn a suit, but with a kilt instead of trousers. The plaid was cut from the MacTaggart clan tartan, the blue-and-green pattern belonging to my family. Women loved me in a kilt, but naturally, Serena had to be combative instead of admitting she liked it.

The lass punched the button on the intercom on her desk. "Evan, your nine o'clock appointment is here. Should I send"—she threw me a sharp look—"your cousin into your office yet?"

Evan's voice resonated through the intercom. "Yes, Serena. I can hear your scowl. Do try to be polite and professional."

The humor in his tone was unmistakable.

One side of Serena's mouth twisted upward. "Yes, sir, Mr. MacTaggart, sir."

I raised one brow. "Do you always talk back to your employer?"

"Evan doesn't care, and he's being snarky anyway." She waved toward the office door. "Go on. Get out of my sight as quickly as possible."

I walked to her desk and leaned in to level our gazes. "You've missed me, haven't you? Don't worry, I plan on seducing you soon. How's tonight for you?"

Her lips compressed, a breath hissed out of her nostrils, and she flattened her palms on her desk. "I hate you."

I tapped the tip of her nose. "Hate and lust often go hand in hand."

Without giving her a chance to respond, I marched into Evan's office and shut the door.

My cousin relaxed in the chair behind his desk, one elbow propped on the chair's arm, twirling a pen between the thumb and forefinger of his raised hand. "Have a seat, Logan. I'm glad you finally took me up on my offer."

"I'm humoring you," I said as I sat down in one of two chairs positioned in front of his desk. "I've even adopted your absurd tradition of wearing a kilt every Monday. Whatever job you mean to offer me is a farce, I'm sure. You and the rest of our cousins have developed an unhealthy obsession with meddling in my life."

"What farce do you think I'm acting out?"

"One that I'm sure involves getting me married off." I braced my ankle on the opposite knee, a pose that would've seemed inappropriate if a woman had been in the room, considering I was wearing a kilt with nothing on under it. "I'm not the marrying kind."

"That's what I thought about myself until I met Keely."

I made a rude noise. "Ever since the MacTaggarts started marrying Americans, all of you pod people have decided I need to be initiated into the cult."

"Make up your mind. Are we alien pod people or cult members?"

"Both. Aliens took over your bodies and formed a love cult."

"I'm offering you a job, not a wife." He dropped his pen and folded his hands over his belly. "Serena is bonnie, though."

On the inside, I was growling and glaring at Evan. On the outside, I stayed calm and unaffected. "Your executive assistant is a right bitch. If your plans are to have her ensnare me, you and your wife are wasting your time. Serena dislikes me as much as I dislike her."

"Then why do you flirt with her every time you see each other?"

"It's habit." I dropped my foot to the floor. "Besides, I wouldn't mind fucking her once."

Evan sighed. "Really, Logan, you're even stranger than I am. At least I was nice to Keely when I ruthlessly pursued her. You treat Serena like the enemy."

That woman *was* my enemy. She made my balls ache and my fists clench. I couldn't decide whether I should shag her or spank her. Maybe both.

I gave Evan my best disinterested look. "Let's stop talking about that woman. Tell me about this job you claim to want me to take."

"All right." He sat forward, arms folded on the desktop. "You will be the chief of security for the American headquarters of Evanescent Security Technologies Limited. You'll also oversee security at our subsidiary, Vic's Electronics Superstore."

The firm he'd bought from Vic Bazzoli, his wife's employer. My cousin had relocated to America, not because Keely expected him to, but because he'd wanted to do it. For a woman, he'd left his home.

No one would catch me doing anything as barmy as that.

"There's a problem with your plan," I said. "I'm not a security expert. You are."

"I know how to design and manufacture devices and software for security systems. What I want you to do is make sure our facilities are secure." He tilted his head to the side, smiling. "You're a former MI6 agent. Surely you can handle this job."

"Unless you want me to spy on your employees"—*or kill someone* —"I won't be much help. What do I know about security? In MI6, I had other people to handle the technology, and I only had to know how to turn the bloody things on. For the past three years, I've been a bricklayer. That makes me supremely unqualified for the job you're offering."

Evan's smile faded. "I need someone I can trust, Logan. After the incident last year with Ron Tulloch, I know I can trust you. Please, take the job for a while as a favor to me. If after a few months you still feel it's not the right fit for you, I won't stop you from leaving."

Ron Tulloch. Aye, I remembered that scunner. Tulloch had been the head of Evan's accounting department back in Scotland, but secretly he'd been embezzling from the company and blackmailing Evan with anonymous text messages. The bastard had threatened the lives of everyone Evan loved, including Keely. Our cousin Iain had called me in to help, but all I'd done was waylay Tulloch's cohort and scare him into telling us Tulloch's plans. Keely had stabbed the scunner, and that was one reason why I liked Evan's wife so much. She had the heart of a warrior.

"I didn't do much," I told Evan. "You and your wife did most of the work."

"Are all spies as modest as you?" Evan shook his head. "Take the job, Logan. Give it a go, what have you got to lose?"

"Your executive assistant might drive me to commit murder."

He chuckled. "It's more likely you'll be under her skirts inside of a week."

Working here would give me more opportunities to seduce Serena and get her out of my system. Since the first time we'd met, I'd known I would need to fuck her once or risk going insane. A woman with a body like hers had to be a bitch. It was a law of nature.

I rose and approached Evan's desk, holding out my hand. "Have it your way. I'll take the job."

He stood and shook my hand, grinning. "Keely will be happy to hear it. And by the way, you're coming to our house for dinner this evening."

I groaned. "I landed on this continent yesterday. Can't you give me one more night to settle in before you throw me into the wolves' den?"

"Are you calling my wife a wolf?"

"No, Keely is an angel." I squinted at Evan. "But I have a suspicion I'll turn up at your home to find Serena Carpenter there."

Evan gave me a solid deadpan look, but it didn't fool me one bit. "Would I do that? I'm a recluse, you know."

Not anymore, he wasn't. He'd been inducted into the love cult last year. These days, he spent more time with our other cousins than even Aidan, who had always been the most sociable.

"Like hell you're a recluse," I said. "And like hell Serena won't be there tonight."

He shrugged, then pulled a manila envelope out of his desk drawer. "All the papers you'll need to fill out to start your employment are in here." He offered me the envelope. "Bring them back tomorrow at nine o'clock. That's when you'll have your employee orientation."

"Orientation?" I narrowed my gaze on him again. "And who will be in charge of that?"

His deadpan expression returned. "Serena Carpenter, of course. She is my executive assistant, and I wouldn't trust anyone else to help my new chief of security get oriented."

The only orientation I wanted was to get Serena horizontal under me. Up against a wall might do, though. Actually, any position would work.

By my estimate, I should be able to quit this job within forty-eight hours.

I took the papers from Evan. We said goodbye, and I agreed to be there for dinner tonight, then I walked out into the reception area.

Serena fixed me with a cool look. "I hope you turned down the job."

"Afraid not." I ambled up to her desk and leaned over until our faces were millimeters apart. "You'll be seeing me tonight at dinner and every day after, starting tomorrow when you give me orientation."

"Evan," she hissed. "That bastard."

I chucked her under her chin. "Cheer up, lass. You've always wanted an opportunity to get your hands on my *slat*. Now you can fondle it anytime you want."

"You are disgusting."

"Do you know what *slat* means?"

"Erica and Calli clued me in to all the dirty Scottish words. For one thing, I know you're cursing when you say *bod an Donais*, which means the devil's penis. As for *slat*..." She drummed her nails on the desk. "I will never, ever, ever lay a finger, much less a hand, on your dick."

My cousins' wives had told her what *slat* meant. Those women blethered too much.

Serena focused on the papers on her desk, shuffling and reshuffling them.

I walked past her desk, heading for the hallway, but stopped. How could I get Serena naked? That question had tormented me since the day we'd met eight months ago. Once I'd had her, I could forget her. Now I only had to answer the question of how to make that happen as soon as possible.

Don't let her dismiss me, that was how.

I stomped back to her desk.

She gasped, her eyes flying wide.

I planted my hands on the back of her chair at either side of her head and lunged in to press my lips to hers. Soft, warm lips. Slick with lipstick. Yet they tasted faintly of strawberry.

I pulled back, gratified by her stunned expression and the way her lips parted as if begging for a deeper kiss. Not today. Not yet. If I wanted her in my bed, I needed to seduce her. And that took time.

Without a word, I strode away from her.

And *bod an Donais*, I still craved her.

Chapter Two

He had kissed me. The disgusting, vile, rude, obnoxious man had kissed me. What was Logan MacTaggart up to? He wanted to fuck me, that's all I knew. Never going to happen. I'd sleep with a serial killer before I'd do the bump-and-grind with him. Of course, he might be a serial killer. Nobody knew much about what Logan had done during his time as a spy for MI6.

"The Secret Intelligence Service," he'd corrected me the first time we'd met, at Keely and Evan's wedding, when I'd tried to start a polite conversation with Logan by asking about his previous career. He just had to correct me, explaining, "The official name is Secret Intelligence Service or SIS. Most people call it MI6, though."

"Is that like the CIA in America?"

"Yes, it's similar."

"What was it like being a spy?"

His gaze had drilled into me, like he was an assassin sizing up his target. "Most of the work I've done is still covered by the Official Secrets Act. I can't talk about it."

At that point, he had walked away without offering even a half-assed excuse.

Keely and Evan's wedding had been a low-key affair with everyone wearing casually dressy clothes, though the Scotsmen had all worn kilts. Logan had arrived wearing the requisite kilt—the MacTaggart tartan consisting of light blue and green with orange lines—and a navy-blue, long-sleeve shirt with a black suit jacket. He'd looked every bit the sophisticated and deadly spy. He always had that glint in his eyes, the one that sent a shiver down my spine and made me feel like I should back away slowly. Maybe knowing about his previous career had influenced my reaction to him. Or maybe he was just…strange, and it unsettled me.

Still, I couldn't deny he was hot.

But I would never, never, never have sex with him.

Logan was crude and bizarre. I often wanted to deck him. And sometimes I wanted to drag him into the nearest private room to—No. Oh no-no-no, never in a million years. I hated him. Never in my life had I hated anyone, but I despised Logan MacTaggart. Every time I saw him, he told me he wanted to fuck me or shag me or poke me. Maybe it was "have a poke," not just "poke." I couldn't keep those Scottish sayings straight.

Shortly after Logan left the vicinity of my desk, I barged into Evan's office without knocking and marched straight to his desk.

"You," I said, pointing an accusing finger at him, "have explaining to do, young man."

He was thirty, and I was forty-two. Sure, he was married to my best friend, but I still had the right to call him "young man" when he'd done something boneheaded.

Evan rocked his chair casually, hands clasped over his belly, his lips curving into a slight smile. "You seem to have forgotten the rules, Serena."

"Maybe you should call me Mrs. Carpenter from now on. Reminding you I'm a widow might hammer it into your head that I am not interested in your disgusting cousin."

His lips twitched, a sure sign of amusement. I'd worked for Evan for nine months, and I'd spent plenty of time around him outside of work too. I recognized his expressions and what they meant.

"What is it you think I've done?" he asked.

"You hired Logan as part of a matchmaking scheme dreamed up by you and Keely." My fingers crooked toward my palms, but I stopped short of fisting my hands. "Maybe once your baby is born, the two of you will stop meddling in my life."

"I doubt it." He sat up straight, his hands on the desk. "I hired Logan because he's the best man for the job. If you fall in love with him, it won't be my fault."

Fall for Logan? Had he lost his ever-loving mind?

"I hate Logan," I said, emphasizing each word by smacking my palms on the desk. "He is the most repulsive, obnoxious man I've ever met."

"He is a wee bit odd." Evan pushed his glasses up. "But he's not that bad.

Give him a chance. You'll be working closely with him, anyway, so you might as well get accustomed to him."

"Working closely? I have nothing to do with security."

Evan adopted a look of pure innocence that he could pull off only because he had the face of an angel and the eerie silver eyes of one too. "Logan needs someone to get him settled in here and show him around. I need my most trusted employee to conduct his orientation." He pointed a finger at me. "That's you, Mrs. Carpenter."

"Yeah, Logan told me as much, but I figured you had to be pulling his leg."

"I'm not joking." Evan stood, his fingertips resting on the desktop. "You are Logan's liaison for employee orientation and anything he might need after that. I'm counting on you, Serena."

And he was my boss. I couldn't say no.

"Yes, sir," I said and spun on my heels, marching out of his office.

When I sat down at my desk, my gaze wandered to the chair Logan had occupied earlier. The dark-blue jacket he'd worn had accentuated every muscle, and the white dress shirt had clung to his body. The top two buttons, unhooked, had revealed a tempting wedge of skin dusted with dark hairs. I remembered his eyes too, with their warm, golden-brown color.

My body awakened at the memory, at the vision of his muscular form sprawled in that chair. His casual posture belied the vigilance he always conveyed, like he was on guard at every moment for bad guys who might attack. These days, the focus of his vigilance seemed to be me.

The idea made me wet. Not because I wanted Logan, but because I'd never been the sole focus of anyone. It had nothing to do with him. Nothing at all.

I forced myself to concentrate on work, but after twenty minutes, my phone rang. My cell phone, not my work phone. The screen announced, "Chase calling."

"Hey, honey," I said, answering the call. "What's up?"

"Aw, Mom," he whined like the teenage boy he was. "Stop calling me stuff like that. I'm not a kid anymore."

"You're fifteen. That makes you still a kid, and besides, you will always be my kid."

He grumbled. "Can I go to the store? Keely says they've got a new shipment of games. My friends want to meet me there."

With my son, "the store" always meant Vic's Electronics Superstore, where Keely worked. She was vice president of the company.

"Sure," I said, "you can do that. Will you be going anywhere else after?"

"To get burgers." He paused and added in a long-suffering tone, "Am I allowed to do that?"

"Yes, honey, you are."

"Cool." He paused again, but this time he sounded sneaky when he said, "Keely told me Logan's moving here to work for Evan. Guess that means you'll be working with him too. Sounds awesome."

My son had become infatuated with Logan after their first meeting. Logan was a former secret agent, and that was all it took for a teenage boy to idol-worship him. I'd tried to dissuade Chase from his awe, but there seemed to be nothing I could do about it. My son thought Logan was the coolest guy on the planet.

Probably because Logan was much nicer to Chase than he was to me, and he never said anything lewd in front of my kid. I supposed I had to thank Logan for that.

Not likely.

Keely and Evan had invited Logan to our little dinner party tonight, but I'd had to learn that fact from Logan. I would have to see him this evening, and I'd have to see him tomorrow for his orientation. Hell, I'd be seeing that man every day with my luck. I had no hopes he might stay away from the top floor since this was where his cousin worked. As Evan's executive assistant, I had to be here at this desk five days a week. Shit. Evan had done this on purpose. He hired Logan to push us into each other's orbits, and I had no doubts whatsoever that Keely had conspired with her husband.

"Mom, you still there?"

"Yes, but I have to go. Lots of work to do."

"Guess I'll see you at home." His voice took on that sneaky tone again. "Keely said Logan's coming to dinner tonight."

"I know. Goodbye, sweetie, I have to get back to work."

Yes, I hung up on my snickering son. Keely had probably roped him into her plot to meddle in my life. A blissfully happy marriage had turned both her and Evan into a pair of pests.

A wave of melancholy crashed over me, making me sag into my chair. I'd been that happy once upon a time. So damn happy. Rob Carpenter had been my everything, until our son was born. All I'd needed was the two men in my life. Anything else seemed like icing on the best cake ever. Sure, we'd had problems now and then. No marriage was perfect, but I preferred to focus on the good parts and not dwell on the four tours he'd served in Iraq. I wished he'd never enlisted in the army. I wished...

Wishes didn't matter. They were wisps of smoke blown away on the breeze.

My mind started to flash back to the day when I'd been informed of Rob's death in combat. I squeezed my eyes shut, fighting against the memory.

The intercom buzzed.

I jerked. Wiping tears from my eyes, I punched the intercom button. "What do you need, Evan?"

"The production reports."

Damn. He'd asked for those ten minutes before Logan showed up, and I'd forgotten thanks to the aggravation of seeing that infernal man. "I'll email those to you right away."

I needed a distraction from the memories, but emailing the reports took up all of thirty seconds.

Rob. His smile. His laugh. The way he used to pick Chase up and spin around and around until Chase was shrieking with glee. How could I ever want to love anyone else? I didn't want to. The fact I'd endured my most vivid flashback in years right after I saw Logan MacTaggart did not mean anything.

I would never love another man.

Especially not Logan.

Chapter Three

Logan

I arrived at Keely and Evan's house two hours before the dinner party was set to begin. Since I couldn't move into the apartment Evan had chosen for me until next week, I was stuck in a hotel. Loitering in my room proved too mind-numbingly boring. How long could a person watch bad television shows before he went insane? Though the hotel offered pay-per-view "adult entertainment," I couldn't get interested in that either. My thoughts kept spiraling back to Serena in that skirt, bent over, wrestling with a paper shredder.

Sometimes, I wished she wasn't such a bitch. I'd enjoy having a poke at her a lot more if I could like the woman, and not just her body. But she insisted on scowling at me, cursing at me, calling me every synonym of the word disgusting. Why did the lass with the most sensual body I'd ever seen have to be a harpy?

I still planned to fuck her. Once, and only once.

The house where Evan and Keely lived was enormous. It had two stories, an attached two-car garage, and a large backyard with a patio. I parked my hired car in the drive as Evan had instructed. The cars he and Keely drove were in the garage. At the instant I rang the bell, Evan swung the door open like he'd been waiting for me to arrive.

Grinning, he slapped my arm. "Glad you came, Logan. Keely's excited to see you again."

"Your wife saw me yesterday."

"And she'll be happy to see you again." Evan swung the door open wider and adjusted his glasses. "Come in, Logan."

I crossed the threshold.

Evan shut the door and clapped a hand on my shoulder. "Don't worry. Serena and Chase will be here soon."

"Am I meant to be excited at the prospect of seeing that witch again? I last saw her spawn at Aunt Aileen's birthday, when he was shoving an entire Scotch egg into his mouth. I hope he's matured since then."

"Chase is fifteen. So you don't need to worry he'll spit up all over your posh jacket."

I'd worn a suit without the tie, though a different jacket and shirt than earlier today and with trousers instead of a kilt. "Is there food yet? Or are we required to wait until the evil queen arrives before partaking?"

Evan sighed and led me through the foyer, past the wide staircase that led to the second floor, and straight through the kitchen onto the patio.

Keely was reclining on an outdoor chaise, her hands clasped over the top of her very round belly. She had her eyes closed, a delicate smile on her lips. Her raven hair draped over her shoulders.

"The guest of honor is here," Evan said, moving toward his wife's chair. He perched on its edge beside her and patted Keely's thigh. "Wake up, *gràidh*."

He always called her darling or some other endearment in Gaelic. All my married cousins did the same, and all of them had married Americans too.

Why was I the guest of honor? Evan, who'd once been standoffish, had become the most annoyingly cheerful person in the family. Even our cousin Aidan, previously the king of good humor, had trouble competing for the cheeriness throne these days.

Keely opened her eyes, smiled sweetly at her husband, and aimed her striking green gaze at me. Her smile broadened. "Logan, I'm so glad you're here."

She tried to get up, but her husband stopped her. "Logan can come over here to hug you."

Naturally, Evan had become not only a doting husband but an overprotective one too. Like all the married MacTaggarts of our generation, he wouldn't let his pregnant wife do anything. Unlike the other wives, Keely was over forty, so her husband might've had valid reasons for fussing over her. Pregnancy at that age had more risks. I knew that because, while I was captive in the car with Evan the last time he visited Scotland, he had told me everything I never wanted to know about pregnancy.

I gave Keely a quick hug.

She kissed my cheek.

For the next two hours, I helped Evan set up the banquet, dragging tables out onto the patio and pushing them together to form one long table. We set out the silverware too, along with plates and glasses and everything else. By the time Serena and her child arrived, Evan and I were starting to bring out the food. Serena, who wore a red dress with slim straps and a frilly hem that swished around her knees, helped Keely get up from the lounge chair and take her seat at the head of the table. Evan would sit at the opposite end.

Serena sat next to Keely.

When I tried to grab a chair at the other side of the table from Serena, Evan pushed me in the opposite direction. He pointed to the chair next to hers.

I frowned at him.

He smiled and gave me a light shove toward the chair.

"Doesn't Chase want to sit by his mother?" I asked.

The teenager shook his head. "You should sit by Mom."

"It was Chase's idea to seat you there," Evan said. "Don't let the lad down."

Ah, the dirty tricks had begun. My married cousins would do anything, probably even commit felonies, to get me married off next. The American Wives Club, as the Yankee partners of my cousins called themselves, had made me their official mission. Gavin Douglas, the only American man in the lot and my cousin Jamie's husband, had betrayed his gender and sided with the American Wives Club. The head of that group was Emery, the wife of my cousin Rory. The lot of them were spearheading the mission to jam a ring onto the third finger of my left hand.

That would never happen. As long as they didn't rope my sisters into their scheme, I'd get through it unscathed, and unmarried.

I watched Chase taking his seat on the other side of the table and then glanced at Evan. "Won't the lad be lonesome over there by himself?"

"No way," Chase said, grinning. "I'm cool here. Besides, you and Mom can talk easier when you're both over there. Right, Evan?"

"Yes, definitely," my cousin said, winking at Chase.

Strategic surrender was my only option. But before I took a seat, I leaned in close to Evan and hissed, "Enough matchmaking."

"No idea what you're talking about."

"*Pòg mo thòin*, Evan."

"Wouldn't you rather Serena kissed your erse?"

My ice-cold stare didn't faze him, so I gave up and sat down.

"So, Logan," Chase said, "were you, like, really a spy? Like James Bond?"

I opened my mouth but didn't get a chance to speak.

"Oh please," Serena said. "Nobody in real life is like James Bond. He probably decoded boring messages or something."

Was she dismissing me as no one of interest? I stiffened and clenched my fists on my lap. "I was a field agent, not a cryptologist. So yes, in a way I was like James Bond."

Better to have the boy think I was a superhero secret agent than a useless bore. Neither was entirely accurate, but I wouldn't let Serena paint me as a human paperweight who held down a desk for a living.

She flashed me a sharp look, her lips pinched.

I moved my hand onto her thigh and gave it a squeeze.

The bitch shoved my hand away.

We proceeded to ignore each other throughout dinner, despite valiant attempts by Chase, Evan, and Keely to start a conversation between me and Serena. Once we'd finished the main course, Keely tried to get up, but Evan jumped out of his chair to lay a hand on her shoulder and stay her movement.

"What are you doing?" he asked.

"I'm going to help clear the table and clean up."

"No, you are not. You're pregnant, Keely."

"Which does not make me an invalid."

He touched her cheek. "You need to rest, *gràidh*. I can handle the clean-up."

"I can help," Serena said.

Chase pushed his chair back and stood. "Let me do it. You can stay here."

Serena's eyes narrowed, but she said nothing.

Like she clearly had, I realized the lad was attempting to play matchmaker.

"That's a wonderful idea," Keely said. She batted Evan's hand away and got to her feet, despite his frown. "Relax, honey. I can dry dishes without straining myself."

He seemed dubious but nodded anyway.

What did he expect? He'd married a feisty woman, the sort who would stab a villain if the need arose. He couldn't honestly have believed she would become a loafer because she was having a baby.

I started to get up, but Evan shook his head. "No, Logan. You're a guest."

"And so is Chase."

"Stay where you are."

With a heavy sigh, I dropped back onto the chair.

The three matchmakers disappeared into the house.

Serena glanced at me sideways. "You know what they're doing."

"Aye. Marriage has made Evan a nutter." I slouched in my chair. "He's become a matchmaker, and he treats his wife like she's made of glass."

"Evan loves Keely. It's sweet." Serena slouched in her chair, letting out an exasperated sigh. "He went on the internet and read about all the possible pregnancy complications for a woman over forty. Now he's obsessed with making sure Keely does nothing more strenuous than lifting a napkin."

"Like I said, marriage has made him a nutter."

"Maybe we should scream at each other over dessert so they'll stop trying to set us up."

"Aye, and you can claw my eyes out. That ought to set them straight."

She plucked at the tablecloth absently. "I don't think anything short of murder would convince Evan and Keely to stop trying to shove us together."

"Your son seems to be in on the conspiracy."

"Chase thinks I need to get married again." She looked at me sideways, and her lips formed the smallest of smiles. "He thinks you're James Bond and Superman rolled up in one kilt."

"Don't think either one of them wore a kilt. I love to wear those, since I have wonderful legs."

"And such humility too."

I eyed her sideways. "You do realize we're having a civil conversation."

"Guess I'd better smack you again. I hate you, remember?"

The soft tone of her voice didn't convey hatred. Her words had sounded almost sultry.

My pants grew tight in the groin. I remembered the night she'd smacked me at Aunt Aileen's birthday party in Scotland. I'd asked if she wanted to go into the cloakroom and have a poke. Her response had been one sound slap to the face.

The memory made my cock twitch.

I cleared my throat and pushed my chair back, rising to stretch and yawn. "Sitting all evening is making me want a lie-down. Better get a bit of exercise. This yard is large enough for a wee stroll."

"Yeah, I could use one too." Serena got up and stretched her lithe body. "I'll join you."

We ambled around the yard for a few minutes without talking. I admired the way her erse moved under her red dress and the way the neckline exposed an enticing glimpse of her cleavage. The second time we passed the oak tree in the farthest corner from the patio, Serena stopped to lean back against the trunk.

She gazed up at the sky. "What a lovely night it is."

"Aye, it is bonnie." I let my focus wander down her body, along her slender legs to her ankles that had a sensual curve thanks to her modest heels. "Very bonnie."

Her attention swerved to me, those gray eyes trained on my face.

I was staring right back at her, while the blood rushed out of my extremities and straight into my cock. Her lips obsessed me, and all I could think of was how badly I wanted to kiss her.

As if she'd heard my thoughts, her lips parted. Her breaths seemed to grow heavier, and she flattened her palms on the tree trunk, fingers curling into the bark.

Kiss her. The need to claim her mouth seized me hard.

I stalked up to her and slapped my palms on the tree at either side of her head. Her mouth opened just enough to give me a glimpse of her pink tongue. A glimpse was enough. The lust she always inspired in me surged through my body.

And I mashed my mouth to hers.

She went perfectly still, not responding but not pulling away either.

My pulse pounded in my ears, and I fought the nearly overpowering impulse to hike up her skirt and fuck her right here and now.

Her body relaxed. She moaned, the sound almost imperceptible, and opened for me.

I thrust my tongue between her lips. Christ, the taste of her. It inflamed me to the point I had to dig my nails into the tree bark to keep from seizing her hips and doing the thing I'd burned to do since the first time I'd seen her. Taking her in the backyard of my cousin's house while he, his wife, and Serena's son waited inside would be too wrong even for me. Instead, I devoured her. I swiped my tongue around hers, teased the roof of her mouth, plunged deeper and more wildly until she grasped my shoulders and moaned again.

With a guttural groan, I plastered my body to hers and shifted one hand to palm her breast. The silky fabric of her dress only made me crave her more, made the need to rip the bloody dress off her more intense, almost irresistible.

Laughter coming from the house roused me from the spell cast by the enchantress in my arms.

I tore my mouth away from hers and stumbled backward a few steps. My breaths came sharp and fast. This woman drove me insane. What was it about Serena Carpenter? Why did I need to fuck her more than I'd ever needed to fuck a woman in my life?

Her cheeks were dusted with pink, her lips swollen.

She looked beautiful that way, her expression soft and hungry at the same time.

Bloody hell, MacTaggart, get a grip on yourself. I stalked back to the table and collapsed onto my chair. At least the table would hide my flaming erection.

Serena shuffled up to her chair and dropped onto the seat. Her eyes were slightly glazed, and she still breathed more roughly than normal.

Evan, Keely, and Chase arrived with dessert.

When Evan walked me to the front door later, to see me off, he set a hand on my shoulder and whispered, "What happened earlier? Between dinner and dessert? You and Serena looked like you'd either run a marathon or..."

Evan lifted his brows.

"We argued, what do you think?" I lied. Luckily, my years with MI6 had taught me how to lie with ease.

But my cousin wasn't convinced.

He lifted his brows again. "That must have been a right rammy to have you both so...stimulated. I would've expected to hear shouting."

"Go pester your wife, Evan. I'm sure she's feeling neglected. It has been more than thirty seconds since you fussed over her." I glanced across the foyer at the siren who had bewitched me, if only for a moment. "Serena is a witch."

"Not a bitch anymore, eh? Witch seems like a step up."

"That woman is a she-devil."

Evan chuckled. "Whatever you say, Logan."

He patted my shoulder, still chuckling.

I stomped out the door.

Chapter Four

At precisely nine o'clock, Logan sauntered up to my desk. This time, he approached the front of it rather than sneaking up behind me to cop a feel of my ass. I was sitting down, but still, he would've tried it. Dressed in a charcoal suit and white shirt without a tie, he looked both professional and sexy. Like yesterday and last night, he had the top two buttons of his shirt undone to reveal a mouthwatering glimpse of his skin and the fine hairs that dusted it. His lips curved into the barest of smiles, the closest I'd ever seen him get to expressing a positive outlook.

He set his palms on the desk and leaned into them. "Good morning, Mrs. Carpenter. You are as bonnie as ever today."

What was his game? Complimenting me had to be part of some nefarious plot.

I glanced up from my computer, feeling my forehead tighten as my brows cinched together. "Thank you. Good morning, Mr. MacTaggart."

"What's the agenda for today, Mrs. Carpenter?"

The way he spoke in a level tone and kept his gaze trained on me was unnerving. Why did he keep calling me Mrs. Carpenter? It was weird. Especially after last night. Kissing Logan had been a huge mistake.

The memory of his lips on mine rushed through me complete with sensations and sounds. I'd moaned when his agile tongue invaded my mouth.

I cleared my throat, pushed my chair back, and stood. "Evan expects me to show you around and tell you all about the company. How we do things. Stuff like that."

He straightened and spread his arms. "I'm all yours, Mrs. Carpenter."

"Just call me Serena."

"All right, but only if you call me Logan."

"Fine, whatever."

Had I ever used his first name when I was looking at him, speaking to him? I didn't think I had. That made his request seem bizarrely...arousing.

I grabbed a folder off my desk, the one emblazoned with the logos of Evanescent Security Technologies Limited and its American subsidiary, Vic's Electronics Superstores LLC. Vic's still had only one store, but Evan and Keely planned to expand it into a chain. I offered the folder to Logan. "Here's your orientation packet. It includes a map of the building, names and extensions for all the people you might need to contact, and some other stuff."

"Other stuff?" He leaned his hip against my desk. "Do tell, Serena. I'm already mesmerized."

So that was his game. Pretend to be nice while inserting the occasional sarcastic jab. At least, I assumed he was being sarcastic with his "mesmerized" comment. What exactly did he hope to accomplish? Driving me nuts would only drive me to murder him.

"The other stuff," I said, "is our dress code and rules of conduct, plus our policies concerning sexual harassment, ethics, and the handling of sensitive information."

"I imagine I've already violated some of the rules." He glanced at the folder in his hand but didn't open it. "Never been terribly concerned with propriety."

No shit. "What rules do you think you've broken?"

He came around the desk to me and leaned in a little. "I've been sexually harassing you, haven't I? And I plan to keep doing it."

"What if I sue you?"

"Go on. I don't mind."

I shook my head. "You don't mind being sued? What about losing your job?"

"Lawsuits don't frighten me and losing this job wouldn't devastate me." He traced a line down my jaw with his fingertip, the touch delicate. "Seducing you will be worth any legal annoyances."

Who called getting sued a legal annoyance? He seemed genuinely unfazed by the prospect.

"You won't be seducing me," I said. "I will never sleep with you. Get that through your granite skull. No sex. Not ever."

He took half a step back. "Kissing is acceptable, though."

"No, it is not."

"You not only let me kiss you last night, but you kissed me back. Passionately."

"I was—Never mind. Follow me." I spun on my heels and headed for the hallway. "This is your official tour of Evanescent's US headquarters. Listen up, keep your trap shut unless you have a relevant question, and do not stare at my ass."

"Afraid I can't adhere to any of those rules." He caught up to me and squeezed my bottom. "Feel free to submit a sexual harassment complaint to the CEO."

"Complaints go to human resources."

"Send it there too." He walked alongside me, his gaze steadily on my face. "I'm working here because Evan asked me to. The job has nothing to do with seducing you. I'll be doing that either way."

"Do you not realize how obnoxious that sounds?"

"I'm telling you what I want and what I intend to do. Why does that fash you?"

"Oh, you can't confuse me with your Scottishisms. I know what fash means, and I am not bothered at all."

"Glad to hear it." He cupped a hand over my bottom and held it there. "That means everything you've said to me was flirtation, even when you called me disgusting."

I swatted his hand away. "You *are* disgusting, but it doesn't bother me. I can handle your crude, obnoxious behavior."

"Good."

We reached the first doorway, and I stopped there to explain. "This is the copy room. There's one on every floor. To make photocopies, you need a code that you type into the keypad on the machine. Your code is in the folder I gave you. Would you like me to demonstrate how to use the copier?"

"Yes, please do."

I couldn't decide if he was being sarcastic, or if he really wanted me to show him. Since I couldn't decide, I went for the safest option. "Come on, I'll show you how it works."

Well, I hoped it was the safest option.

Swinging the door open, I walked over to the big copier. Metal shelves lined the walls on either side. Gesturing toward them, I told Logan, "The paper reams are kept on the shelves, inside their wrapping. Do not unwrap one unless the copier is out of paper. If it needs new toner, call me or one of the janitorial staff. They know how to switch out the toner cartridges."

Logan leaned against the shelves, thumbs hooked inside the waist of his pants. "I know how to change a toner cartridge, Serena, but thank you for providing all that scintillating information."

"Yeah, sure." My skin had started to itch, but I fought the urge to scratch. I wished to hell I knew what he was up to with his polite routine. "Let me show you where to enter your code."

"Please. I'm waiting with bated breath."

Ignoring his comment, I faced the copier and pointed to a keypad attached to its corner. "This is where you enter the code. Type it in and press enter."

He strode up behind me, peering over my shoulder at the keypad. "Sounds reasonably simple. Shall I give it a go?"

"Um, sure." The scent of his cologne, spicy and earthy, surrounded me. "Just type—"

"Yes, I understand the concept." He reached around me, his arm brushing mine, and typed the six-digit code into the keypad, then hit enter. "Mission accomplished."

I twisted my head around to see him. "How did you know the code? I never saw you open the folder I gave you."

"While you had your back turned, I found the code and memorized it."

"Oh. You, uh, have a very good memory."

"Photographic." He plastered his body to mine and bent his head to whisper in my ear. "Anything you say or do will be engraved in my mind forever."

"I guess that's handy for a spy, but you're a civilian now."

"A photographic memory is handy in any walk of life." He nuzzled my neck, his breaths tickling my skin. "Particularly when it comes to seduction."

His lips vibrated against my skin when he spoke, and the soft rumble of his voice made all the fine hairs at my nape stiffen. I should've pushed him away, but I couldn't make myself do it.

"What I want," he said, sliding an arm around my waist, "is to fuck you on this copy machine. Right now."

He dragged his mouth up my throat, licking at my flesh as he moved.

A warm, liquid tingle rushed over my skin and settled between my thighs.

Logan backed away. "What's next on the agenda?"

Speechless, I shuffled around to face him. Though I opened my mouth, no words would come out. Everything south of my waist had awakened at the sensation of his body so close to mine, his lips grazing my skin, and his heated breaths tantalizing me. The sexy rumble of his voice had only made things worse. Looking at him, with his casually dressy clothes and those hazel eyes fixated on me, I wanted him to do exactly what he'd said. Fuck me on the copy machine. Right here, right now.

I gripped the copier with both hands.

"Shall we get to it?" he asked, his voice deeper and rumblier.

"What?"

He gestured toward the door. "Shall we get on with the tour?"

"Oh, that. Yes." I straightened and rolled my shoulders back. "Follow me."

For the next two and a half hours, I showed Logan around the building. We visited every floor, and I introduced him to every department head so he would know to whom he should speak if security problems arose in any part of the company. I introduced him to the janitorial staff too, and anyone else who might have a need to interact with Logan. Maybe I went a tad overboard. Maybe I hadn't needed to introduce him to the cafeteria ladies or the accounting interns. And maybe, just maybe, I was going overboard because I desperately needed to have other people around us to keep myself from begging him to kiss me again.

No, I would not beg. I might order him to do it, but I would never plead for a kiss.

Probably not.

Once he'd met everyone, I had no choice but to take him back upstairs to the secluded room that housed my desk. I laid a hand on the back of my chair but did not sit down.

Logan leaned against the corner of my desk and watched me.

A hot little shiver sidled down my spine.

The door to Evan's office hung wide open. Inside, I could see him gathering papers into a leather binder. Keely had given him that binder. She had one just like it.

Christ, they were too cute for words.

Not that I was jealous. That would've been petty, and besides, I was happy for the two of them.

Evan strode out of his office and pulled the door shut behind him. His gaze flicked from me to Logan and back again. "I'm away for a meeting at Vic's. Don't forward any calls to my mobile unless it's urgent."

I nodded.

"And Logan," Evan said, approaching his cousin, "do try not to incite Serena to murder you. It would be hell getting the blood stains out of the carpeting."

"I'll do my best." Logan shot me a snarky glance. "But don't blame me if the woman can't control her passions."

Evan patted Logan's shoulder and left.

Logan and I regarded each other in silence. He smirked. I scowled. He casually scratched his cheek and let his gaze wander down my body, his tongue slipping out to wet his lips when his attention paused on my breasts. He adjusted the bulge in his slacks.

My breasts tingled and tightened.

"What's next on the agenda?" he asked in the sexy tone that unnerved and excited me.

Oh lord, why did the hottest guy I'd ever met have to be such a jerk? If he were a normal person, I could have sex with him and get this lust out of my system. We would have good sex for sure, potentially great sex. I mean, with a body like his…

I let my gaze wander over him. My God, all those muscles. Whenever he moved his arms, his biceps flexed and bulged, straining his suit jacket. When he walked, those charcoal slacks stretched taut over his glutes with every step he took.

My focus landed on the bulge in his pants. How big was his dick? The size of that lump suggested he was well endowed, to say the least. What would it feel like to have him inside me, filling my body in the most delicious way, pushing in and pulling out, his shaft glistening with my wetness, and—

"Serena," Logan half growled.

His rough voice jerked me out of my fantasy. I made the mistake of looking at him. His pale-gold eyes shimmered with desire, and every time he moved his head the slightest bit, the light glinted on the emerald flecks in those irises. With his lips parted, he gazed straight into my eyes.

"Stop staring at my cock," he said, "or I will fuck you right here on your desk."

My cheeks grew hot, my sex too. Between my thighs, a molten slickness burgeoned.

I grabbed the first sheet of paper I saw on my desk, cleared my throat, and announced, "I need to make copies of this. It's urgent. Stay here."

Whirling on my heels, I stalked off to the copy room.

Logan strolled into the room a few seconds later.

I stifled a groan. Why oh why hadn't I shut the door and locked it? I had the copier's lid up, but I couldn't seem to get the paper positioned right. It kept slipping out of my grasp, sliding across the clear glass surface.

Logan laid a hand over mine, stilling my frantic movements. "Let's get it over with. We'll both feel better after a good, hard poke."

My throat tightened, but my mouth watered. The slickness pouring out of my sex soaked through my panties and dribbled down the insides of my thighs. A good, hard poke, he'd said. My nipples shot erect. Logan fucking me. I squeezed my eyes shut but couldn't shake the image of it.

He snatched the sheet of paper off the copier's glass and flipped it over to read what was written on it. A soft chuckle tumbled past his lips. "You urgently need to make copies of your grocery list?"

"Um, yeah." How stupid did I sound? The mature single mom had reverted to being a dumb, lust-drunk teenager. "I have stuff to do. Go away."

"The stuff you need to do would be me."

I snorted, though it came out sounding more desperate than sarcastic.

"Aye," he murmured, his lips suddenly poised so close to my ear they brushed against the lobe when he spoke. "Ye want me. I want ye too. Let's just do it."

I couldn't speak. Could hardly breathe.

He moved behind me, his hands on my hips and his erection scraping against my backside. "Say yes, Serena."

Oh, the way he spoke my name. His voice rough. His words strained like he couldn't wait another second. The lust that always seized me whenever I was around him gripped me so hard I almost whimpered, and I spoke the words I'd sworn I would never say to him. "Fuck me now."

He shoved my skirt up and yanked down my panties. The harsh sound of him unzipping his pants echoed in the room. With one foot, he kicked my feet further apart, opening me to him.

Cool air rushed over my flesh, from my entrance straight down my thighs. Had I ever been this wet before? No, I hadn't. What was it about Logan MacTaggart that made me crazed with need?

I heard rustling, then the distinctive rip of a condom packet. He walked around with a condom in his pocket? At work?

Logan grasped my hips, tilting them back, and plunged inside me.

The fullness of him felt so damn good. While he thrust in and out, hard and fast, I gripped the copier's edges, my hands at either side of the still-open lid. The sensation of his cock gliding in and out, the slapping of his balls on my ass, the sucking noise of my outrageously aroused body…It was all so fucking hot. I threw my head back and moaned, my eyelids drifting half shut.

"Yes," I groaned. "Oh yes, harder, please, faster, more."

He tightened his hold on my hips and plowed into me faster, deeper, harder. The angle of his thrusts grew more oblique, putting pressure on parts of me that didn't want to be pressed on.

"Ow," I said, shifting my hips in an attempt to ease the discomfort. "Ow, Logan, that's—Ah!"

I kicked his shin.

He jerked and muttered something that must've been a curse, given his tone of voice, but I didn't recognize the words. Must've been Gaelic, but phrases the American Wives Club hadn't taught me yet.

"What was that about?" he asked. "You kicked me on purpose."

"Yeah, you big oaf. Didn't you hear me say ow? You were hurting me."

"*Mhac na galla*," he hissed. "I'm sorry."

That curse I knew. It meant son of a bitch.

Despite the pain, my body still craved release. Craved it like crazy. My clitoris throbbed, my sex burned, and I couldn't catch my breath. "Please, just get it done."

"All right." He pulled out. "Turn around. I cannae get the right angle this way."

I turned to face him.

He lifted one of my legs and thrust into me. His hips pistoned in time with his grunts. I locked my leg around him, freeing his hands to hold on to my hips while he kept pounding away, the slick glide of his cock pushing me higher and higher toward orgasm again. My head fell back, my mouth open as moans and gasps spilled out of me. My fingers clenched the copier's edge so fiercely it almost hurt. I bucked my hips into his thrusts. So close, almost there. Every muscle in my body started to tense in anticipation of climax. I let out a sharp cry and slapped my palms onto the copier's glass surface.

Logan punched into me with such force the copier shifted.

And the lid slammed down on my hands.

I cried out, though not from the bliss I'd been waiting for. Pain stabbed through my hands.

Logan froze, then heaved the lid off my hands. "Are you all right?"

Hissing from the pain, I nodded.

"Bloody hell," he growled as he pulled out of my body again and clasped my wounded hand in both of his, sandwiching it between his much bigger palms. He ran his hands lightly over mine like he was searching for serious wounds. Seeming satisfied I hadn't broken any bones, he cupped my hand in one palm while with the other he traced slow circles on the back of my hand. "I'm sorry. I've never had anything like this happen before."

"Let me guess. You always rock the bedroom."

"Aye." Head down, he rolled his eyes up to look at me. His lips kinked upward the tiniest bit. "Not always in a bedroom, though. This was my first attempt at fucking a woman against a copy machine. Maybe that's why I bollocksed it up so badly."

"Maybe we just aren't compatible. Sexually." I bit the inside of my bottom lip. "Or in any other way."

His erection had gone limp. He stripped off the condom and tossed it into the nearby trash can.

I pushed away from the copier.

Logan took hold of my hand again, rubbing those slow and gentle circles on the back. "Does it still hurt?"

"Some, but I'll survive."

He raised his head, his golden eyes zeroing in on me. "You should see a doctor."

"No, I'm fine. I used to be a nurse, so I'm qualified to assess my own injury." I studied his face, the tightness etching faint lines across his forehead and around his eyes, and I realized something shocking. Logan was worried. Genuinely worried. About me. I wrestled my hand free of his. "Thank you for your concern. I'm okay, really."

"If you're sure." He lifted my hand to kiss it in the softest, sweetest way. "I could get you an ice pack."

What else could I do but gape at him? I couldn't move a muscle, not even to blink. His tenderness both surprised me and gave me an odd pain at the back of my throat. Until a few seconds ago, Logan had shown me nothing but arrogance and lust, with crude humor thrown in for good measure. At this moment, gazing into his worried eyes, I wondered if I might have misjudged him.

"Do you want the ice?" he asked, his voice as gentle as his hands that still held mine.

"No," I said, my voice barely a whisper. "I'm okay. The pain is almost gone."

He kissed my hand again, then released it and walked to the doorway. He grasped the knob as he glanced back at me. "I'll do better next time."

I intended to tell him there wouldn't be a next time, but my voice refused to function.

Logan pulled the door partway shut, his body half out of the room. "I'll shut the door in case you need to rub one off. I won't be offended if you do."

With that, he left and closed the door.

"Rub one off" meant getting off the solo way. I knew that much, but everything else I'd thought I knew about Logan MacTaggart had crumbled to dust in the past few minutes. How could the man be such an ass ninety-nine percent of the time, only to turn around and be sweet and tender? Most men would've gotten embarrassed and irritated if they mucked up sex. Some wouldn't care as long as they got their rocks off. I'd assumed Logan would fall into the latter category. Instead, he occupied a category all his own.

I had no frigging idea what to make of him.

Our encounter had started out so hot, so good, then…disaster. Was fate warning me not to get involved with Logan? I'd never believed in fate. I still didn't. Like I'd told Logan, we simply weren't compatible.

But at first, when he'd been thrusting into me, it had felt so damn good to have his thick cock inside me. And that kiss last night. Holy heaven, it had been the best kiss I'd had in years.

We were not compatible. End of story.

My body thrummed at the memory of both encounters.

I groaned. Maybe I did need to rub one off.

Chapter Five

Logan

After the disaster in the copy room, I meant to wait for Serena at her desk. I couldn't help myself, though. Would she rub one off to relieve her needs? I lingered by the closed door, listening. After a few minutes, when I was about to give up and go away, I heard heavy breathing punctuated by the occasional grunt. I pressed my ear to the door. No, I really shouldn't be eavesdropping on Serena while she made herself come, but I couldn't force myself to walk away.

The feel of her body surrounding my cock…It had been intoxicating. She'd been so hot and so wet. Serena was the sexiest, most erotic woman I'd ever fucked. Or tried to fuck. *Mhac na galla.* "Son of a bitch" did seem like an appropriate curse since Serena was a bitch. Most of the time.

But in that copy room, with our bodies crashing together, Serena hadn't seemed like a she-devil. She'd been soft and willing, eager and hungry, begging me to take her harder and faster.

Inside the copy room, Serena's heavy breathing became panting. She let out a strangled cry.

Silence.

With my ear to the door, I waited for more noises, but she seemed to have finished herself off. I wanted to be the one making her come. I'd wrecked that, hadn't I? Now she thought we were sexually incompatible. Somehow, some way, I had to prove she was wrong.

The door swung inward.

I stumbled and grabbed for the jamb to keep from colliding with Serena.

She looked startled for a second, but then her mouth tightened. "What are you doing out here? Spying on me?"

I opened my mouth to deny it, but realized I had no reason to pretend. Leaning against the jamb, I crossed my arms over my chest. "Yes. Was it good for you?"

"The fantasy of you is so much better than the real thing."

She must've hoped I'd be insulted, my manly pride wounded. But I heard what she'd said between those tart words. "Ahhh, so you fantasize about me when you rub one off."

"I—" She lifted her chin, straightening her skirt that was slightly askew. "Only because you were just in there with me, trying to do something you clearly have no idea how to do."

"What might that be?"

"Showing a woman a good time."

I swung forward, penning her to the opposite side of the jamb with my hands above her head. "You have no concept of the kinds of pleasure I could give you. We had one bad moment. That's all it was, and you know it. Next time you beg me to fuck you, I'll do it right. No copy machines involved."

"There won't be a next time."

"Of course there will." I skated my lips over hers, gratified by her sharp intake of breath. "And next time, you'll tell me the real thing is better than a fantasy."

"I would never say such a thing."

"We'll see."

I licked at the seam of her lips, loving the way she tasted. The flavor was beyond description, but it made my groin tighten and my breaths shorten. Why did she taste so good? When I'd been devouring her mouth last night, the flavor of her had made me drunk with lust. I couldn't think straight, see straight, or stop myself from plundering every corner of her mouth while wondering what other parts of her might taste like. I wanted to shove my head between her legs and sample her desire.

Maybe I could in a different way. Only a moment ago, she'd been pleasuring herself with those long, elegant fingers. Though we hadn't spent a great deal of time together, I'd noted a number of facts about Serena Carpenter. For one, she was right-handed. Women most often used their dominant hands to masturbate.

I captured her right hand, lifting it to sniff her skin. The scent of her arousal lingered on her flesh, a musky, heady scent all her own. No two women smelled the same, but the aroma of Serena affected my body in ways no other woman's could.

"What are you doing?" she demanded.

"Tasting you." I slid four of her fingers into my mouth and sucked, rewarded by her soft little gasp and the way her eyes widened a fraction. I released her fingers one by one. "Mm, you taste as good as I thought you would."

"My skin does not taste good."

"Ah, but it does." I held her hand to her groin. "Your fingers taste like your cream."

Though she maintained a haughty expression, her cheeks were speckled with a delicate shade of pink. She caught her upper lip with her teeth. "How would you have any idea what I taste like? We barely had sex, and all you cared about was getting your dick in the right orifice."

Her claim stung a little, but I'd had far worse insults aimed at me over the years. Besides, I knew she was lying. Another thing I'd learned about Serena was that when she lied, she bit down on her upper lip right before she spoke the untruth.

And she'd done that a split second before announcing all I cared about was getting my dick inside her.

I raised her hand to my mouth again and gave the tip of each finger a slow, sensuous lick. "You're a liar, Serena. You wanted me as much as I wanted you, and you couldn't wait for foreplay any more than I could. The second I suggested sex, all you wanted was my cock inside you."

She bit her upper lip again, about to spew another falsehood, and even opened her mouth in preparation for speaking.

Then she hoisted her chin to glare at me over the bridge of her nose. "You are the most arrogant, obnoxious, disgusting, vile, loathsome man on the face of the earth."

I chuckled. "Have you memorized a thesaurus? I'm sure you can dredge up a few more synonyms for disgusting to lob at me."

She exhaled a sharp huff and stomped off down the hall.

Deciding she needed time to consider what we'd just done, or almost done, I headed to my new office on the first floor. I had a secretary, a perky young woman who dressed like an uptight librarian but acted like an overly cheerful college student. Delilah Williams and I had spoken for a grand total of thirty seconds during Serena's whirlwind tour of the building. Now, Delilah smiled brightly at me.

Evan had jumped the gun on hiring my secretary. Delilah would have nothing to do, since no one would be calling me or visiting me at my office yet.

"Mr. MacTaggart," she said in her cheery voice, "welcome back. Are you starting work today?"

"Yes." I paused at her desk. "Call me Logan, please. I don't care for formality, and it will get confusing if you call both me and Evan Mr. MacTaggart."

"Sure, I get it." She blushed a little. "Is there anything I can help you out with, Mist—Logan?"

"Thank you, no. Not yet." I needed to figure out what the bloody hell my job was and how on earth to do it. Delilah couldn't help me with that. "I'll let you know when I need something."

Delilah nodded.

I started to walk away, but hesitated. "Are you Canadian, Delilah?"

"My family moved to America when I was sixteen. How did you know?"

"It's the way you pronounce certain words."

As I headed into my office and shut the door, I wondered why Evan got a mature executive assistant, but I got a lass who looked like she'd graduated from college yesterday. Delilah was bonnie, but not my type. Evan got to admire Serena Carpenter's perfect erse and kissable lips all day long. Not that he gave a whit about her looks. Evan had eyes only for his wife.

I dropped into the leather executive chair behind my desk. Large windows offered a view of downtown Carrefour. Since Evan had built the tallest structure in the city, like any self-respecting billionaire would, I had a panoramic view that extended all the way out to the hinterlands. Though I gazed out the windows, I didn't see the view. My mind rewound to the time I'd spent in the copy room with Serena, and I relived every sensation, from her wet heat around my cock to the smell of her hair and the sounds of her soft gasps and hungry little moans.

My phone rang.

I glanced at the landline phone on my desk, but then realized it was my mobile ringing in my pocket. Digging it out, I answered. "Aye."

"Lohhhhgannnn," a feminine voice purred into the phone. "You're being a bad boy, aren't you? Wish I may, wish I might, make Logan MacTaggart take a wife."

"Excuse me? Donnae be casting your rubbish spells over me, Isla. I'm immune to witchcraft." I swung my legs up to brace my feet on the desk, ankles crossed. "Besides, the words might and wife don't rhyme."

"Sure they do. It's called assonance. Rhyming vowels, Logie."

I rolled my eyes, but she couldn't see it. Or maybe she could, with her witchy vision. "Did you ring me for a grammar lesson?"

"No," she said with a delicate, almost ethereal laugh. "I'm checking in on my baby brother. A little birdie flew into my bedroom this morning and whispered all your secrets to me."

Serena thought I was strange. She ought to meet my sisters, the Witches of Ballachulish.

"My secrets," I said, "are covered by the Official Secrets Act. That little birdie will need to be executed immediately for treason."

Isla laughed again. "After all these years, how can you still not believe in magic? It's the power of the human mind and the eternal soul. Wicca is very popular these days. Step into the twenty-first century, Logie."

I growled under my breath. "Would you cease and desist calling me that? I hated it when I was a wee laddie, and I hate it even more now."

"You are so uptight," she said in a chastising tone. "Serena has you tied up in double knots, doesn't she? Why donnae ye just shag her and get it over with?"

Well, I'd tried…

I froze, gripping the phone tighter. "How do you know about Serena?"

"Witchy, witchy powers." She lowered her voice to a melodramatic whisper. "Are you starting to believe after all these years?"

"Absolutely not. You, Kirsty, and Elspeth do not have mystical powers." I grunted. "Though the lot of you do have the uncanny ability to annoy me."

"All right, have it your way." She paused, and I could hear her disapproval in her voice when she said, "By the by, your way is very boring and not at all fun. I spoke to Keely and Evan yesterday. They filled me in on you and Serena. I did your horoscopes, and you two are perfectly aligned in the zodiac. Of course, the best method for determining your true love quotient is by reading tea leaves, but you would need to swirl the tea for that to work. Although you could take a picture of the tea leaves and text it to me…"

Tea leaves. Zodiacs. Aye, this had been my life ever since my three sisters had become fascinated with Wicca. Ten years of listening to them prattle on about auras and spirit guides and whatever other nonsense they read about in a book. I loved my sisters, but they were the barmiest of the barmy.

I had Evan and Keely to thank for Isla's call. Once my sisters got an idea in their heads, especially if it pertained to my personal life, they would not let go of it.

"You'll see," Isla said. "Soon, you won't be able to deny that Serena is your one true love."

"Sorry to burst your bubble, *gràidh*, but Serena hates me. I'm not fond of her either."

"Ohhhhh, that's no impediment. Once you get to know each other better, you'll see the real Serena and she will see the real you, our sweet and snuggly Logie."

There was no point in reminding her I disliked that nickname.

"I was a spy, Isla," I said. "I've killed men. Sweet and snuggly is not an appropriate description of me."

"Donnae forget I knew you before all of that. My sweet little brother is still in there."

"Was there a legitimate reason for this call? I have work to do."

I had no fucking idea what that work was, but I needed to get on with figuring that out.

And I needed to shut my sister up.

"Oh, Logan," she cooed, "you are so pent up these days. Cousin Rory used to be the one with a caber up his erse, but now it's you. Let Serena dislodge that thing with a rollicking shag."

I covered my face with my free hand. "Yes, I enjoy talking about my sex life with you almost as much as I enjoy your palm readings. That means I don't like it at all."

"When did you become a prude? Honestly, Ma and Da always encouraged us to talk openly about sex."

Too openly at times. I really had not needed to know when my sisters lost their virginity and whether they had liked it.

"Ma and Da," I said in the calmest tone I could muster, "meant that we shouldn't be ashamed to ask them questions about sex. They did not intend for my sisters to divulge every last shred of information about their sex lives to me."

She said nothing for a few seconds, giving me the false hope she had nothing left to say. "Logie, are you impotent? Is that the issue keeping you from admitting you like Serena?"

"Impotent? Conversation over, Isla. I have to get back to work."

"You're right, I pushed too far. I'm sorry. I do it only because I love you."

"Aye, but sometimes I wish you didn't love me quite so much."

"No, you don't. Think about what I said and have a good day. Blessed be, Logan."

I grunted. "Goodbye, Isla."

Shoving my phone back into my pocket, I surveyed my desk. It looked like any other desk in any other office. I had a computer, a phone, a desk calendar, and a holder full of pens. Aye, I had all the appropriate tools. Now, if I could figure out what a security chief did...

My thoughts returned to the copy room and Serena, and the flavor of her lust.

Chapter Six

Serena

I stared blankly at my computer screen. The document displayed on it had blurred into a meaningless blob. I would've preferred to think I'd developed a sudden vision problem, or maybe I was having a stroke, but I knew the truth. Logan MacTaggart had me distracted and flustered. Why did I let him do this to me? The man was loathsome. He couldn't honestly believe talking dirty would make me want to try sex with him again, not after our disastrous encounter in the copy room.

Except it kind of had worked.

The proof was my distracted state, the fact my brain insisted on reminding me of those moments in the copy room every five seconds, and the fact my panties had been damp ever since.

I did not want to want Logan. I didn't want to think about him or see him. Yet I was now forced to bump into him every day, five days a week. Maybe he would avoid me. *Hah.* Like that would happen. He enjoyed tormenting me. Logan had a sadistic streak, I'd decided, because he took pleasure in making me squirm, snarl, and finally give in to this inappropriate lust.

Slumping in my chair, I rubbed my eyes in hopes of clearing my vision. Clearing my head.

No more Logan fantasies. No more, do you hear?

Did my brain listen? Of course not. The second I issued the silent command, my mind conjured a memory of Logan sucking on my fingers. Those hooded eyes locked on me. His cheeks caving in slightly. His faint groan of pleasure. I'd gotten wetter watching him do that, and I'd been seconds away from dragging him to the floor and riding him like a sex-starved cowgirl.

"Is the report ready?"

Evan's voice jerked me out of my fantasy—literally. I jumped and yelped.

He raised a brow at me. "Are you all right, Serena?"

"Yes, fine, yes." Sure, that didn't sound pathetic at all. I clumsily shuffled papers on my desk in a pointless effort to look like I'd been working instead of imagining all the ways I might hump Logan. "Uh, the report is, um, right here."

I shuffled with a bit too much vigor, and papers slid off my desk onto the floor. Mumbling a curse under my breath, I gathered them up in my hands. My hair had fallen over my eyes while I was bent over doing that. I straightened and blew the hair away with a noisy breath.

Evan's lips twitched, a sure sign he was struggling not to laugh. He bent over my desk and pointed at the computer screen. "Isn't this the report you're looking for?"

Shit. Of course it was. Damn that Logan.

"Oh yeah," I said with a nervous laugh. "That's the one."

Evan studied me with an infuriatingly calm expression, the light glinting on his glasses. "Could you please print it out for me? I'm away to another meeting in five minutes and need that report."

"Yes. Right away."

"Thank you."

He ambled back into his office, and as he shut the door, I heard a soft chuckle.

Damn, damn, damn that Logan. He'd turned me into a moron. A sex-obsessed, lust-drunk, clueless and senseless moron.

I printed out the report and handed it to Evan when he exited his office a few minutes later. He tried hard to suppress his smirk, but it tightened his lips and his eyes. Once he'd left, I slumped into my chair again. I needed a drink. Something hard like bourbon or maybe vodka.

Or Logan MacTaggart.

Yes, he was hard in all the right ways. When he'd penetrated my body, it had felt better than anything I'd experienced in years. If things hadn't gone awry, I had no doubts he would've given me spectacular orgasms.

Bourbon. I needed bourbon.

I winced. Evan might've been a very understanding boss, but I doubted even he would overlook a tipsy executive assistant. What else could I do to relax?

Let Logan finish what he'd started in the copy room.

"Gah!" The exclamation exploded out of me, and I smacked my hands down on the desktop. I muttered, "Stop thinking about him, you idiot."

A glance at the clock on my computer told me lunchtime had arrived. Thank heaven for that.

I got up and stretched.

"What an enticing view."

Logan's voice shivered heat through me.

I turned toward him and wished I hadn't.

He leaned against the wall at the entrance to my little domain, one hand in his pants pocket, his gaze sliding over me with unmistakable interest. "Stretch again, Serena. I love watching your body move almost as much as I love feeling it move while I'm inside you."

"Forget it, Logan. Whatever that was in the copy room, it's over and done."

"Is it?"

"Yes."

He sauntered up to me, caught my face in both hands, and touched his lips to mine. "We'll see."

Then he left.

I gaped at the empty space where he'd stood a minute ago. What the hell? He'd stopped by to kiss me? It hadn't even been a hot kiss. Chaste seemed like the best description.

What game was he playing now?

Somehow, I managed to reassemble my wits enough to go downstairs and grab lunch in the cafeteria. I didn't see Logan there. After eating too much, including two brownies, I left the cafeteria and got into the elevator with three other people.

Logan ducked inside a second before the doors slid shut. He hung back, leaning against the rear wall.

I faced forward, separated from him by two other bodies, and pretended not to notice him. Had I reverted to high school behavior? Ignoring the boy I liked. Pretending I didn't like him.

Because I did *not* like Logan. This wasn't childish behavior. It was self-preservation. I despised the man, but he seemed to know every erotic button to push to make me wild with lust.

One by one, the other people disembarked.

When Logan and I were alone in the elevator, as it rose toward the top floor, I tensed in anticipation of another sneak attack. No, not in anticipation. That was not excitement fluttering in my belly. I dreaded the moment when he might try to kiss me again. Dreaded, not anticipated.

He stayed where he was, still leaning against the wall. The blasted man didn't even speak.

The elevator stopped. The doors opened.

Relief rushed through me, sagging my shoulders, as I stepped out of the elevator.

"Serena."

Instinctively, I turned toward the man who'd spoken, toward Logan.

He surged forward and planted a firm but brief kiss on my lips.

As the doors slid shut, he ducked back inside the elevator.

I stayed there, frozen and not really seeing the closed doors in front of me, for several seconds before I summoned the wherewithal to move. When I got back to my desk, I stared at the computer screen. What was Logan up to? He must've followed me upstairs in the elevator for the sole purpose of kissing me. Why? He hadn't even stuck around to taunt me with sarcasm or dirty talk about what he'd love to do to me.

The man was insane. No other explanation fit his behavior.

I got back to work, doing my damnedest not to think about Logan.

My efforts paid off for about an hour.

That's when Logan strolled into my domain again, spun my chair around, and planted another solid kiss on my lips. He pulled away almost as quickly as he'd swooped in, then he ambled off down the hallway out of my sight.

He did this three more times before Evan got back from his meeting.

I must've looked dazed or harried or something that wasn't like me because Evan halted halfway past my desk and scrunched his eyebrows at me.

"Are you not well?" he asked. "You're behaving strangely today."

Blame your cursed cousin. I cleared my throat and straightened in my chair. "Everything's fine. I'm tired, that's all."

"Go home early. I can handle things on my own for the rest of the afternoon."

"That's not necessary."

It was three fifteen, and I usually left at five. Evan accommodated my single mom schedule, though, letting me leave early or come in late whenever I needed. I did not abuse his kindness. Only for good reasons did I leave early or show up late, and only with prior notice. I couldn't take off because Logan had me in a tizzy.

Evan patted my hand. "Go on. I insist."

"Okay. Thank you, Evan."

"You're family, Serena. No need to thank me."

Giving my hand a quick squeeze, he walked into his office.

I logged out of my computer and filed away all the papers on my desk before I left. At least Logan couldn't sneak up behind me to kiss me at home. Locked doors and windows prevented that. Since he was a former spy, I couldn't help wondering if he knew how to get past locks. What if he crept into my house in the dead of night and crawled into my bed to—

For pity's sake, woman, cut that out.

Yes, I should cut that out right this minute. No fantasies of Logan breaking and entering for the sole purpose of seducing me. Never mind that the idea got me hot and bothered.

What did he look like naked?

I headed for the elevator and punched the button. While I waited for the car to arrive, I imagined what all those muscles might look like. I'd felt them around me when he'd had me up against the copier. To see those muscles, to fondle them and lick them...

"Hello again, Serena."

That was not Evan's voice.

I squeezed my eyes shut and compressed my mouth, praying I'd imagined hearing Logan's sexy voice behind me.

The elevator doors slid open. No one was inside.

Had it been too much to hope for a car full of people? I needed a buffer between me and the sinfully hot man behind me.

I had no choice. I shuffled inside the elevator and faced the front, faced Logan.

He stepped inside, standing next to me, and folded his thick arms over his broad chest.

The moment the elevator started to move, he grasped my shoulders and rotated me toward him.

"Logan, you shouldn't—"

He pulled me into his firm body and mashed his mouth to mine.

I held motionless, stiff and unyielding—for about three seconds. Though he didn't invade my mouth, the pressure of his soft, warm lips and the sensation of his muscular body against mine did things to me. My body softened without my permission. When I exhaled the breath I hadn't realized I'd been holding, it emerged as a moan. He withdrew his lips just enough to glide his tongue over the seam of my mouth, then fastened his lips to mine again.

And I melted into him.

The elevator doors opened.

He stepped back, his face blank. The way his Adam's apple bounced when swallowed told me he wasn't as unaffected as he pretended to be.

I stood paralyzed, my lips parted, my body thrumming with desire. I wanted more. Kissing, touching, more of everything.

The doors started to close.

Logan thrust out a hand to stop them. "You wanted out, didn't you?"

I blinked several times, rolled my shoulders back, and nodded. "Yes. Thank you."

"No need to thank me for the kiss. I enjoyed it too."

"I meant thank you for holding the door open."

He swept his sizzling gaze over me. "I'll hold anything you like for you."

"The door is all I need."

I hustled out of the elevator and did not look back. I traveled three steps before Logan's voice made me pause in my flight.

"You want more, though. A lot more."

Without glancing back, I hurried out of the building.

Chapter Seven

Logan

For the rest of the week, three entire days, I continued my kissing campaign. Sometimes I wondered why the hell I was doing this. Mostly, I relished every opportunity to confound and arouse Serena, loving the way each time I kissed her she started out stiff and unyielding, but soon dissolved into the kiss. Her lips tasted different from her body, though no less enticing. Why did this woman feel, smell, and taste so much better than any woman I'd known before? She was just another female, not a sensual goddess descended from the heavens.

Except she was.

Your bum's oot the windae, MacTaggart.

I was talking rubbish for certain, if only to myself. I didn't mind, though, since I'd been off my head for some time before I met Serena Carpenter. My family would attest to that. Logan the strange. Logan the standoffish. Logan the man you called on when you needed a tangled mess undone and didn't care how it got sorted. My family never said those words. They didn't need to. I understood what I was and what my limitations were. I would never become best mates with my cousins.

They should be grateful for that.

On the day after I'd begun my kissing campaign, Serena hunted me down and cornered me in my office. I'd been standing at the windows gazing out on the city when she stormed in and slammed the door.

She marched straight up to me and set her hands on her hips. "What is your game, Logan?"

"I like poker, five-card stud."

"You know what I mean." She bent toward me a touch. "You can't waltz up to me in the middle of the lobby and kiss me."

"I did, therefore I can. It was a good-morning kiss, *gràidh*."

Why had I called her darling in Gaelic? I never called women that unless they were my sisters.

Serena huffed. "'Sexual harassment is not a greeting."

I shrugged one shoulder. "It's only harassment if you don't enjoy it. Which you do. Besides, aren't you the woman who begged me to fuck you in the copy room yesterday?"

"Wrong. I didn't beg, I ordered you to do it."

"Your body begged me." I took hold of a lock of her hair, twirling it around my finger. It was soft as silk. "Your noises begged me too. Face it, Serena. You can't control your lust for me."

She glowered at me for a couple seconds, then stabbed a finger into my chest. "No more kissing bandit. Understand?"

"Not really. Try speaking proper English instead of the American version."

"Right, because Scots speak proper English." She crossed her arms over her breasts, and her lips curved up at the corners a little, no more than a hint of a smile. "Donnae, cannae, willnae. Have a canary, have a poke. Fash, fankle, haver. Get your head in your hands to play with." She shook her head. "I still don't get how that one means to punish someone."

"Maybe it's because if you don't do your job properly, you'll lose your head." I made a slashing movement across my throat with my hand and made an appropriate noise to accompany the gesture. "Then your head'll be in your hands to play with."

"If you're dead, you can't play with your own head."

"Sure you can." I leaned in and spoke in my best menacing voice, tempering it for the lass. My full-on menacing voice would've sent her running. "Haven't you ever seen decapitated chickens running around? Blood spurting from their severed necks?"

Her lip curled. She drew her head back. "You are insane."

I leaned back against the window frame. "Well, I suppose insane is better than disgusting."

"You are insanely disgusting."

A chill trickled down my spine. This time, she wasn't calling me disgusting because her lust for me fashed her. No, this time her discomfort was genuine. I'd gone too far, showing her the side of me none but my enemies ever saw. She thought I was insane, not as a euphemism but as the bald truth. I'd known for a long time other people didn't understand my sense of humor, so why had I inflicted it on Serena?

And why did her reaction fash me?

I turned away from her, toward the windows, pretending to admire the view. "Go. I have work to do."

"Logan—"

"Go."

I kept my gaze glued to the view while I listened for the click of the door that indicated she had left the room.

The scent of her lingered. That indefinable, feminine scent unique to her. It filled my senses and awakened parts of me I'd thought died years ago, the part that wanted…something. I couldn't name it or describe it, but I wanted more than the solitary life I'd convinced myself I needed and even cherished.

By the time my lunch break arrived, I'd shaken off the disquiet my conversation with Serena had triggered. I felt like myself again, for better or worse, and I re-instituted the kissing campaign by sneaking up behind Serena while she stood in line at the cafeteria counter. I tapped her shoulder.

She turned to look at me.

I stole a kiss, quick and chaste.

The lass growled at me.

Holding back a chuckle, I winked, then went to the end of the line before anyone could whinge about me jumping the queue.

For the remainder of the week, I kissed her as often as possible without impinging too much on the hours I was supposed to be doing my job. I spoke to the man whose company had installed the building's security system and learned how the bloody complicated thing worked. I explored every nook and cranny of the building hunting for weak spots. I questioned department heads and lesser employees to learn what security precautions they took to safeguard private information and proprietary processes.

Christ, it was dull as dirt.

Laying bricks started to sound like the more exciting and challenging career choice. Maybe I wasn't cut out for the civilian life. Maybe I'd become a kissing bandit to spice up my mind-numbing existence. Maybe Serena spiced up my life all on her own.

Aye, that would explain my obsession with kissing her, flirting with her, and antagonizing her.

Evan and Keely insisted I come over for brunch on Saturday. I realized they would make certain Serena turned up as well, but I agreed anyway. Did I want to see Serena? I'd been seeing her all week—seeing, kissing, imagining her naked body and all the ways I'd prove to her our debacle in the copy room had been an aberration. I didn't need to see her on the weekend too.

Why, then, did I spend an hour choosing my clothes on Saturday morning? I never spent more than thirty seconds contemplating my wardrobe. Today, I changed my outfit three times before I walked out the door of my hotel room.

I had even shaved, which I never did on the weekend.

We gathered in the dining room of Evan and Keely's house this time, rather than on the patio. It was a bonnie day full of sunshine, but according to Keely, brunch belonged in the dining room. When I'd pointed out the day was plenty warm enough for an outdoor meal, she shook her head.

"No, Logan," she said, "brunch is indoors. We may have hosted a brunch outside last year when my family visited, but nowadays it's an indoor activity."

"But bonnie women deserve to be seen in the sunshine."

Keely kissed my cheek. "You are such a sweetie-pie in disguise."

I decided not to question her statement. It was ludicrous, calling a spy a sweetie-pie, but she meant well.

Serena arrived with her son a few minutes later.

I kissed Serena's cheek in greeting. And then I wondered why I'd done that. It had been instinct, I supposed, nothing more and nothing less.

The lass gawped at me like I'd pulled out a gun and aimed it at her face.

Her son thrust his hand out to me.

I shook it. "Good morning, Chase."

"Good morning. It's way cool you're here. Mom didn't tell me you would be."

"Because I didn't know," Serena said, now eying me sideways.

She must have suspected, but maybe she'd hoped to be wrong about how meddlesome Evan and Keely were.

Evan popped out of the kitchen and trotted toward us. "We have a wee bit of an emergency. I forgot to buy maple syrup."

Keely emerged from the kitchen moving much slower than her husband.

"You forgot?" I said, giving Evan my hardest stare, the one that usually convinced men to confess everything. "You expect us to believe you accidentally neglected to buy syrup."

"Aye," Evan said, unaffected by my attempt to intimidate him. "I forgot. It happens, Logan. Would you like to check the cupboards?"

I studied him for a moment. "No, I believe you."

"Keely and I will go to the store." He looked at Chase. "Why don't you come with us?"

Now that was a purposeful act. He might have honestly forgotten to buy syrup, but his suggestion the laddie go with them to the store was pure conniving.

"Can I, Mom?" Chase asked.

"When have you ever voluntarily gone to the grocery store?" She threw a furtive glance my way. "Fine. Have a blast shopping for syrup."

"Awesome. Thanks, Mom."

Evan, Keely, and Chase left in the Porsche SUV owned by our hosts.

Serena and I were alone. In a large house. With five bedrooms, two sofas, and various other pieces of furniture that would work nicely as locations for a good poke.

I tore my gaze away from the large, well-padded sofa in the living room. I tried not to look at Serena, but my eyes had a different idea. They gravitated to her like she was a black hole dragging me into oblivion.

She shrugged out of her jacket and hung it on the rack beside the door.

Bod an Donais. The woman wore a short denim skirt that exposed most of her shapely thighs and a sweater that clung to her body, accentuating her breasts. The neckline dipped low enough to grant me a glimpse of those lush slopes.

My cock woke up.

Serena swept her gaze over my entire body. She drew in a slow, deep breath while her tongue darted out to moisten her lips.

I focused on the wall and coughed into my fist. "What should we do while they're gone?"

"Please fuck me, Logan."

Her request stunned me to the point of paralysis. I couldn't blink or move my eyes, and I certainly could not speak. My muscles refused to function, my brain too. All the blood in my body flooded into my *slat.*

"Did you hear me?" she asked.

"Aye." Women had propositioned me before, many times. Why did her request leave me speechless and frozen? "I heard, but I'm half convinced it was an auditory hallucination."

Why had I said that? A dead stupid confession.

Serena stepped in front of me, her gray eyes sharp and clear and focused on me. The stiletto heels of her shoes elevated her to near my height. "I want you to fuck me, Logan. Is that real enough for you?"

"You said it would never happen again."

"I changed my mind." She inched closer, so near to me that her breasts nudged my chest and I could feel their hard tips. "Every night I have vivid dreams about you doing all sorts of naughty things to me, and I wake up wet and tangled in the sheets. I've had to create my own happy ending every night. Last night, I did that four times. And it's all your fault."

"My fault?"

She nodded solemnly. "That's right. I can't get a good night's sleep because of you, so it's your responsibility to make sure I can get some shuteye tonight."

And she thought I was insane? Serena had a bucketful of screws loose inside her head.

What are you complaining about? She wants you, so fuck her, man. Do it now.

This was what I'd wanted since the first time I'd seen her, more so since our aborted attempt in the copy room. Serena's offer had stunned me, but I would rise to the challenge.

I was rising right now. Rising and throbbing.

"Where do you want it?" I asked.

"Anywhere you want." Her lips curved into a teasing smile. "We should probably avoid office equipment, though."

I swept her into my arms and carried her into the living room. When I dropped her onto the sofa, she let out an oddly adorable squeak of surprise. I straddled her legs.

She glanced at the bulge in my trousers and licked her lips. "We probably have fifteen minutes until they get back from the store. Better skip the foreplay." She smiled again in that teasing way. "Not that you worried about that the first time."

Her reminder of our first awful encounter made me want to prove to her I wasn't a selfish prick, the sort who cared about his own pleasure and didn't give a toss about his lover's satisfaction. I needed to prove it to her. My stubborn side demanded it, but the time restriction made that difficult.

We had to do this fast. Maybe we should've waited until a better time, but the second she'd asked me to fuck her, my cock had shot hard as steel. I couldn't wait. My breathing was labored, my entire groin ached for her, and I was…shaking. What the hell? I didn't quiver with need, not for any woman.

But Serena wasn't any woman.

"Hurry it up," she said with a hint of annoyance. "We don't have much time."

I pushed her skirt up and dragged her knickers down to her ankles. The scent of her desire flooded my senses. I hauled in a deep breath, savoring the aroma, hungering to taste her. No time for that. I undid my trousers and pushed them down enough to free my cock. When I dug a condom packet out of my pocket, Serena snatched it away.

"Let me do that," she said, her voice husky and her breathing heavy.

She ripped open the packet and slanted closer.

I watched her hand, my focus riveted to it as she rolled the condom over me. If I'd had any self-control left before she did that, it disintegrated at the sensation of her long, elegant fingers sliding up my shaft.

A deep groan resonated in my chest.

She lay back on the sofa, arms crossed above her head, breasts heaving. The blush of desire tinted her cheeks, and when she spread her thighs, the sight of her glistening pink flesh took my breath away.

I grasped her hips, lifted them, and thrust inside her. Even with a thin layer of latex between our bodies, the feel of her hot sheath penetrated into me. God, she felt good. Incredible. Perfect. I held still for a moment, our bodies merged, reveling in the sensations and the vision of her face tight with need and her nipples jutting against her sweater. As badly as I wanted to tear off her clothes and suck those nipples, we didn't have time for it.

She locked her legs around my hips. Her stilettos dug into my erse at the exact moment when she clenched her inner muscles around me.

"Fuck," I snarled, then I pulled my hips back and drove into her.

Her neck arched. Her back arched. She gripped the sofa's arm above her head, her nails scraping on the fabric. "Hurry, Logan, please."

My name tumbling from her lips pushed me over the edge.

I pumped into her fast and hard, relentless in my need to make it to the finish line this time. I braced my hands on the sofa's arm and punched into her over and over and over until the slapping of flesh and our fevered grunts became a cacophony of lust. Her stilettos bit into me hard enough to leave bruises, I was sure, and still I fucked her with a mounting intensity.

The sofa thumped and shook.

Serena's cries echoed through the room.

I swung a hand down to rub her clit.

"Logan!" she screamed as her body convulsed under me and her sheath pulsated around my cock.

My body went rigid. My back bowed, and I came with a blinding power. By the time my senses started working again, Serena lay limp beneath me.

I gaped down at her for several seconds, unable to move, before my muscles gave out and I collapsed on top of her. With the last iota of energy I had left, I turned sideways to avoid crushing the lass. I wound up half wedged between her body and the sofa's back, and half sprawled over her.

She held the back of her hand to her rosy cheek. Between gasping breaths, she said, "That was definitely an improvement over the first time."

"An improvement?" I lifted my head off her shoulder. "I made ye come so hard ye screamed my name. Ye writhed like a wild thing."

"Yeah, okay, I did that." She wriggled away from me to sit up. "You'll be out of my system now. We can go back to our normal lives."

Out of her system? Like hell. Having her once, making her come for me, had taken the edge off my need but hadn't gotten rid of it. I still wanted her. And I was sure she wanted me too.

We needed to do that again. Aye, another time would get rid of the problem.

Serena stood and righted her clothes, then wandered over to the nearest window.

Twice we'd had sex, and I still didn't know what she looked like naked. Those luscious breasts couldn't be as perfect as I imagined. Maybe that was why I still craved her body, because I hadn't seen all of it yet. Aye, that explained it.

Serena gazed out the window with the slightest smile curving her lips. Her hair shimmered a lustrous toffee brown in the sunlight that filtered through the windows, and her gray eyes seemed bluer in the soft light.

The woman was bonnie. Her mouth was the problem, or rather the words that came out of it.

Her eyes went wide. Her jaw dropped, and she whirled around with her shoulders bunched.

I sat up. "What's wrong?"

"They're back." She twitched her head like she couldn't decide in which direction to look and flapped her hands at me. "Get off the sofa and cover yourself up. They're pulling into the driveway."

The pitch of her voice rose with every word she spoke.

I got up, stretched, and stripped off the condom. Zipping up my trousers, I glanced around in search of a trash bin but couldn't find one. "Do you see a bin?"

"A bin of what?" she almost shrieked.

"The kind that holds trash."

"I don't see a trash can." She frantically patted her hair. "Do I have sex hair?"

Since I had no idea what "sex hair" looked like, I shrugged.

The lass ran up to me and pounded her fists on my chest. "They'll walk through the door any second."

I stuffed the used condom in my pocket. "Sit down, Serena. If we're on the sofa having a blether, no one will think we just fucked."

She gnawed on her lip.

"Have a seat, Serena." I sat down, hoping to encourage her.

Gingerly, she lowered her bum onto the sofa, leaving a distinct gap between us.

I laid an arm across the sofa, angling toward her.

Evan, Keely, and Chase entered the house and spotted us in the living room.

"There they are," Evan said, smiling as he spotted me and Serena.

Keely smiled at us too. "And they haven't killed each other."

Chase grinned.

The five of us headed into the dining room. Naturally, Evan and his wife had conspired to seat me beside Serena. Evan took the chair at the head of the table while Keely and Chase occupied the seats across from me and Serena. Our brunch consisted of pancakes, sausage links and patties, biscuits, blueberry muffins, bacon, waffles, eggs, and toast. The eggs came in three varieties—scrambled, fried, and hardboiled. They'd even supplied a few Scottish favorites like Lorne sausage, tattie scones, and fried tomatoes.

Once the feast was laid out on the table, I arched a brow at Evan. "This is enough food for the entire MacTaggart clan. I know teenage lads eat a lot, but this seems like overkill for one boy."

"Chase doesn't eat like that," Serena said, smiling at her son across the table. "He's the most civilized teenager you'll meet, and the sweetest."

The lad in question rolled his eyes. "Mom, jeez, don't wreck my rep. I'm not sweet or civilized, I'm a badass."

"No cursing," Serena said in the stern tone every parent seemed to learn the second their first child was born.

Chase rolled his eyes again.

Evan leaned back in his chair, hands linked over his lap. "We need all this food for the other guests who haven't arrived yet."

I squinted at my cousin. "What other guests?"

"You'll see."

The table did have three other chairs, one at the end opposite Evan and one on each side next to me and Chase. Three chairs. Three. I stared at the vacant seat at the end of the table, the number three echoing in my brain.

Why did the number three set my stomach to churning?

The doorbell chimed.

Evan sprang up from his chair and flashed me a sly smile. "They're here."

I didn't get the chance to ask who was here. Evan took off through the dining room door and out of sight. I swung my attention to Keely. "What has your husband done?"

She feigned innocence, even batting her eyelashes in the attempt. "What do you mean?"

Feminine laughter echoed through the house.

My spine snapped straight. My gaze shot to the doorway. I knew that laughter. I'd heard it all my life.

Evan ambled into the dining room and moved aside. He spread one arm to indicate the three women who followed him into the room. "Our guests have arrived."

Isla, Elspeth, and Kirsty stepped across the threshold.

"Logie!" Isla exclaimed, throwing her arms out as if she intended to hug me from halfway across the room.

Elspeth and Kirsty shouted "Logie!" too, and all three descended on me. They flung their arms around me, and I could no longer see anything through the wall of lavender-scented bodies. They kissed my cheeks and ruffled my hair. Isla cooed sounds that might have been words, but in her baby-talk voice none of it made sense. Elspeth called me her "bonnie sweet Logie."

Kirsty whispered into my ear, "Donnae be angry. It was their idea, but I agreed we needed to come and check on you."

As the middle sister, Kirsty had always been the mediator between Elspeth and Isla. She was the most level-headed of the three, aside from her insinuations that she had psychic powers. It made sense Kirsty hadn't come up with this ridiculous ambush scheme.

But I was certain Evan had conspired with them.

My sisters stopped suffocating me and each took a small step back.

Their gazes landed on Serena—and they rushed at her.

Bloody fucking hell.

Chapter Eight

Serena

Three beautiful women swarmed me, firing off so many questions I couldn't sort out who'd asked what or how to respond. Who on earth were these women? They knew Logan, that much was clear. They'd called him "Logie" and fussed over him like he was their child. All of them were too young to be his mother. Very young aunts? Maybe sisters?

Logan pushed his chair back and stood, clearing his throat. His expression had reverted to his usual unreadable state.

"Serena," he said, nailing his gaze to mine, "meet my sisters. Isla, Elspeth, and Kirsty."

He pointed to each sister as he named them, but I couldn't get a clear view of them, what with the MacTaggart ladies surrounding me. They touched my hair and cooed about how soft and bonnie it was. They admired my clothes, telling me how "posh" I was. They giggled and whispered things I couldn't understand, maybe Gaelic. I knew a little bit of the language, but not enough to keep up with what they were saying. Their cheerful banter and laughter filled the dining room.

A sharp whistle pierced the din.

Logan's sisters fell silent, straightened, and faced their brother.

He was just removing his fingers from his mouth.

"What's wrong, Logie?" one of the sisters asked, her expression full of genuine innocence.

"You are suffocating Serena." His voice held no censure, only a hint of affection that matched the tiny upward tick of his lips. "If you kill her, you can't conspire to get us married off."

"Good point," the sister he'd spoken to said. She nodded to the other two. "We're being rude, aren't we?"

A chorus of ayes followed as each sister repeated the affirmation multiple times.

Logan's sisters backed away from my chair, and a different one spoke this time. "Serena, would ye mind awfully standing? It's hard to do a proper introduction at the table."

How did this woman know my name? I doubted Logan talked about me to anyone, and he clearly hadn't known they were coming. I imagined Evan had told the sisters all about me. Well, Evan and Keely. My best friend was currently giving me a sheepish look, her shoulders hunched.

I shook my head at her and pushed up out of my chair, turning to face Logan's sisters.

The one who'd asked me to rise clasped my hands. "Please forgive us, Serena. We're so happy to meet you, we couldn't hold it inside. Logan's very skilled at that, but we're more...outgoing."

"Don't worry about it," I said. "I've met lots of MacTaggarts, but not you three. It's about time we got acquainted."

"I'm Isla," she said. "And aye, it is time we met. My sisters and I always seem to miss you at family gatherings."

Since I hadn't attended a lot of MacTaggart events, that was hardly surprising. Still, I wondered why Logan hadn't mentioned his sisters. As I took in the full picture of them, I began to get an inkling.

Isla wore a black blouse with long lace sleeves, paired with black slacks that flared out around her ankles and a black beaded choker that featured one large jet stone as the centerpiece. Her earrings consisted of slender metal dragons that pierced her lobe and curved up the shell with their heads hanging down from the top.

"This is Elspeth," Isla told me, gesturing at another sister. "She's the baby of the family, and she's partially deaf in her left ear. So if she doesn't answer when you speak, make sure you're talking to her right side. Kirsty is number three in the family. I'm the oldest, by the way, and Logie is number two."

I glanced at Logan and caught him wincing. He must not like being called Logie. Big surprise. He did not seem like the easygoing type, or the type who tolerated silly nicknames.

Elspeth had dressed in a scarlet tunic with long, puffy sleeves and a Mandarin collar, with ornate metal clasps instead of buttons. Her wide-leg pants flared out even more than Isla's and had a gauzy black layer over the solid black fabric. Her boots were scarlet too, with flower-festooned pentacles painted on them that matched her pentacle earrings. While Isla told me the third sister was Kirsty, I admired her slightly less Gothic clothing. Her dark green, crushed-velvet dress draped halfway down her thighs while the sleeves covered her arms down to the wrists. She wore simple black boots and a cute necklace featuring a black cat and a crescent moon.

I noticed Isla and Elspeth had hazel eyes like Logan, but Kirsty's were pale blue. Elspeth's eyes were a shade darker than Logan's, but Isla's mirrored his in color and in the way the green highlights in them glittered in even the subdued lighting in the dining room.

"What a cute necklace," I said to Kirsty. "Very Halloweenish."

"Thank you," Kirsty said with a smile. "We do love Halloween, though we prefer to call it Samhain, since we're practitioners of Wicca."

"Wicca?" Sure, I'd heard the word and thought I knew what it meant, but I didn't want to insult these lovely women by getting it wrong.

"They think they're witches," Logan said from behind me on the opposite side of the table. "They're barmy, in case you hadn't figured that out. At least they don't have a cauldron, but watch out if they offer you a pentacle. They might be cursing you."

"Oh tosh," Isla said with a dismissive hand gesture. "Donnae listen to Logan. He doesn't believe in anything he can't shoot with a gun or beat with his fists. The pentacle represents the five elements."

"Five?" I said. "I thought there were four."

"Traditionally, yes, but in Wicca—"

"Enough," Logan announced in a stern tone that probably cowed many people, male and female, though it seemed to pass right by his sisters. "May we eat brunch with no talk of magic or pentacles?"

"Of course, Logie," Isla said. "Whatever my wee baby brother wants."

Logan was not wee in any sense of the word. He was big in every way, from his massive shoulders to his powerful thighs, and especially in reference to his manly equipment. A sensuous warmth shimmered through me. We'd had sex twice, but I still hadn't seen his naked body, only that impressive dick. Maybe we should try it again, strictly so I could satisfy my curiosity about what the rest of him looked like.

"No magic," Isla said, drawing a cross over her heart with one finger. "We promise."

Kirsty and Elspeth crossed their hearts too.

We all took our seats with Isla at the end opposite Evan, Kirsty beside me, and Elspeth beside her brother. If Logan was harried by his sisters' arrival, he didn't show it. At least, not much.

He flashed me a tight smile.

I angled toward Kirsty. "So, how long will you girls be in America?"

"As long as it takes." She threw her eldest sister a sidelong glance, but Isla was focused on Logan, who grimaced at something she'd said. Kirsty returned her attention to me. "That's what Isla said. We should come here and stay as long as it takes to get Logan in order."

"In order?"

"Donnae ask me. This was all Isla's idea. Well, hers and Evan's."

"Yeah, I think Keely had a hand in it too."

She absolutely had. Evan and Keely made big decisions as a couple, and conspiring to push me and Logan together was their biggest idea yet.

Kirsty's expression turned pinched, and she whispered to me, "I think Isla wants to maneuver you and Logan into…um…"

"Wedded bliss?"

She nodded. "I'm sorry."

"It's okay. My best friend is in on the conspiracy too." I hesitated, then said, "I'm afraid Logan and I aren't compatible."

Kirsty tipped her head to the side, her eyes alight with curiosity. "Aren't you? I see the way Logan looks at you, and the way you look at him."

"No offense, but you three arrived two minutes ago. You don't know how we look at each other."

"Logan is talking to Isla and Elspeth, but he's looking at you."

I glanced across the table toward his chair.

Logan was watching me even as he muttered something to Elspeth.

When ours gazes collided, a sensuous warmth rippled through me.

"See?" Kirsty whispered. "The sparks are practically setting the room on fire."

Maybe we did have sparks. That did not equate with compatibility. So what if I couldn't tear my gaze away from his, and so what if I'd experienced a tingly anticipation all week wondering when he might kiss me again.

"You still don't believe it," Kirsty said. "Trust me, it's true. Isla did your horoscopes, and they showed you and Logan are compatible. I can do a tarot reading for you later, but I think deep down you already know what you and Logan have is more than sex."

I whipped my head toward Kirsty. "What makes you think we're having sex?"

Her cheeks dimpled as her lips tightened into a knowing smile, but she said nothing.

Oh God. Was it that obvious? I looked at Chase, who was having an animated discussion with Evan. Had my son noticed what Kirsty seemed to think was obvious? What if he figured out I'd done the deed with Logan? Chase would be thrilled, I had no doubt about that. He worshiped Logan the ex-spy. I hadn't been exaggerating when I told Logan my son thought he was James Bond and Superman wrapped up in a kilt.

I slumped in my chair. Chase would be devastated when he realized Logan and I were not a couple and never would be. I had to stop this thing, whatever it was, between me and Logan. No more kissing bandit. No more screwing Logan. No more, period.

What kind of example was I setting for my son? Ever since Rob had been taken from us, I'd engaged in the occasional fling, but nothing more. Now I was having sex with a man I didn't even like and letting Chase get attached to him. Logan would move on eventually. He hadn't really wanted the job Evan gave him, and he didn't seem like the settling-down type.

Not that I wanted to settle down with him. Hell no.

"You're a worrier, aren't you?" Kirsty said.

"Huh?" I blinked a few times, trying to clear my mind of thoughts of Logan. "No, I'm not really a worrier."

"Don't fight it, Serena. Logan is a good man."

I opened my mouth, prepared to spout something about how I'd never witnessed any good behavior from him, but I stopped myself. His sisters didn't need to hear that. They seemed like sweet, if odd, women. I liked Kirsty after spending a few minutes with her. How could Logan's sisters be so different from him?

Maybe I had witnessed his good behavior. That day in the copy room, when the copier lid had slammed down on my hand, he had been genuinely concerned. My gaze wandered to him.

Logan was smiling at his sister Elspeth. He had an arm draped across the back of her chair. The affection on his face infected his voice too as he told Elspeth about his new job and how he didn't have "a bloody clue" what he was doing.

Seeing him this way, relaxed and chatting with his family, something inside me warmed and softened in a way that had nothing to do with lust.

Kirsty wore that knowing smile again.

When I glanced at Keely, she gave me a similar smile.

Across the table, Chase grinned at me.

Oh shit. Everyone thought I was infatuated with Logan MacTaggart. They were wrong, dead wrong, but no one would believe me if I denied it.

To hell with what everyone thought. I knew the truth.

No way would I ever develop feelings for Logan.

Chapter Nine

Logan

After brunch, my sisters insisted on washing the dishes despite Evan and Keely's proclamation that guests did not have to clean up. Evan hadn't spent much time around my sisters, so he still suffered from the delusion he might talk them out of something they'd set their minds on doing. Isla was too bloody-minded for that. Elspeth and Kirsty went along with her. That was how my sisters wound up in the kitchen washing dishes and silverware while Keely and Serena retreated into the living room, with assurances my sisters would join them soon. Chase's friends had picked him up for a trip to the shopping mall.

I cornered Evan in the study.

He seemed to think he might get away from me by hiding in there with the door closed. What a dafty. Only a fool could think I wouldn't barge into the study to confront my meddling cousin.

Evan, reclining in a puffy leather chair, paused in sipping a glass of whisky to look up at me. "What's fashing you, Logan? You look ready to pummel someone."

I bent over his chair, my hands on its arms. "You conspired with my sisters. Why in heaven's name did you drag them here?"

He took another sip of whisky, his expression bland. "Isla called me yesterday and announced she and the rest of your sisters were coming here to see after you. Isla seems to think you're in denial about your feelings for Serena."

"Donnae be ridiculous. I do not have feelings for that bitch."

I developed an odd queasiness when I called her a bitch. I'd said it before, many times, but today I didn't feel right about referring to her that way. Because my sisters were here, that's why. It had nothing to do with what Serena and I had done in the living room earlier. That had been a release of pent-up sexual tension, nothing more.

Why, then, did I keep wondering what she might look like naked? Why did I remember with vivid detail the look on her face when I'd been inside her and the sensual sounds she'd made?

"You're thinking about Serena, aren't you?"

I tugged at my collar, trying to scratch an itch, but it wasn't on my skin. It was inside me. "Of course I was thinking of her. You just mentioned the woman."

"Ah, but you're having misty-eyed thoughts about her, not evil-bitch thoughts."

"You're daft."

My cousin hooked his ankle over the other knee and studied me while tapping one finger on his whisky glass. "Why are you determined to dislike Serena? The real reason, Logan, not the tired line about what a rotten harpy she is."

I glowered at him, but Evan only chuckled.

Feminine laughter echoed in the hall outside. My sisters had finished their cleanup, which meant I had a chance to corner Isla and demand she explain herself.

Or I could stay here and interrogate Evan, who seemed disinclined to admit wrongdoing. Nothing short of torture seemed likely to make him confess, but torturing my own cousin would make the entire family think I'd gone off my head.

"*Bod an Donais*," I hissed as I stalked out of the study.

I shut the door as Kirsty and Elspeth walked into the living room on the opposite side of the entryway. Isla was following them, so I snared her arm and towed her down the hall into the kitchen.

Releasing her, I slapped my palm down on the granite island. "What the bloody hell do you think you're doing, Isla?"

"Looking after you, Logie."

"I don't need my sister looking after me."

She gave me a pitying look. "You need a lot of help. That bonnie, sweet woman likes you, and from what Evan told me, you treat her like your enemy." Isla tsked. "That's not the Logie I know. What's wrong with you?"

"Would you stop calling me Logie? I'm not a bairn."

The boy she'd known had died years ago. Taking lives changed a man. Watching others die at the hands of terrorists, saboteurs, and traitors had made me less than trusting of anyone. I couldn't fault Isla for wondering how I'd become such a bastard.

I scrubbed a hand over my face. "Isla, I can't change what I am. Being a *bod ceann* is my nature these days."

"You are not a dickhead." She patted my cheeks with both hands. "You're a good man, Logan. Whatever you went through in the army and the SIS hasn't changed who you are deep inside. Stop thinking you don't deserve happiness, because you do."

How did she know I felt that way? I hadn't realized it until she suggested it. Isla had always been the most perceptive of my sisters, the one who could guess my feelings even when I tried to hide them. But to know how I felt before I did… Maybe she had supernatural powers after all.

Bullshit.

"Come," she said, grabbing my hand. "Kirsty, Elspeth, and I have a surprise for you."

"Another one? Your arrival is all the surprise I need today."

She rejected that statement with a sharp hiss and a wave of her hand.

And she towed me out of the kitchen, down the hall toward the study. The door hung open, and Evan was in the hallway talking to my other sisters. When he saw me, Evan nodded to Isla.

"The study is yours," he said, and left the vicinity.

I couldn't blame him for wanting to escape my sisters. I loved them, but they'd gone barmy with this Wicca nonsense.

Then again, Evan never seemed bothered by my sisters. No one other than me seemed to mind their strange behavior.

Isla ushered me into the study and to the sofa. She gave me a little shove. "Sit, Logan."

At least she'd stopped calling me Logie.

"Why should I sit?" I asked.

"Because I said so," Isla said, as if I'd asked a silly question.

"You are my older sister, not my mother."

"Didn't Ma always tell you to mind me?"

"I definitely mind you ordering me to sit."

Kirsty shut the door as she and Elspeth entered the room. The three of them swarmed me in a semicircle, giving me three choices—push past them, stand here and glower at them, or sit down.

With a long sigh, I dropped onto the sofa. "If the lot of you are planning to lecture me about the way I treat Serena—"

"No-no," Elspeth said, "we have a surprise for you. Didn't Isla mention it?"

"Aye, but I informed her I don't want a surprise."

"Tosh," Isla said. She sat down on the coffee table in front of me. "We're giving you a wonderful gift."

Kirsty and Elspeth seated themselves at either side of me.

"All right, sisters," Isla said "It's time to cast a love spell on Logie."

"Like hell you will," I said. "Ye cannae make me love Serena by waving your hands around and chanting meaningless phrases."

"Of course not," Isla said. "Silly Logie, this isn't that kind of love spell. The one we have in mind will make you more open to the possibility of love, that's all." She bent forward to pinch my cheek. "You're so uptight these days. You need all the help you can get."

Elspeth and Kirsty murmured their agreement.

Whenever the three of them got together to conspire to interfere in my life, I was doomed.

I let my head fall back against the sofa and made a go-on gesture with my hand. "Get it over with."

While they began waving their arms slowly and chanting in hushed tones, I closed my eyes and fantasized about Serena's naked body.

Chapter Ten

Serena

Monday morning, I arrived at work early so I could catch up on the tasks I'd neglected to finish last week, what with Logan the kissing bandit distracting me. That infernal man was driving me bonkers. Our interlude in the living room at Evan and Keely's house hadn't helped. Memories of it kept flashing through my mind, complete with sensations and sounds and scents. Logan had smelled of spicy cologne and that indefinable essence of man. I remembered the scent of my arousal too. God, I'd wanted him so much he must've noticed the aroma. And the look on his face, so full of lust and determination and…something else I didn't dare examine too closely.

Something that had seemed dangerously close to tenderness.

I did not want Logan developing tender feelings for me. We were so completely wrong for each other that we should've had signs on our chests announcing, "no romance here, dead-end ahead." Maybe that would've deterred our friends and family from trying to maneuver us together.

No, it wouldn't have. They were all hell-bent on forcing a romance.

Seated at my desk again, with my plastic cup of takeout coffee in front of me, I felt in my element. Work had always been my safe place. No matter what was going on in my life, getting back to work eased my anxieties. I logged on to my computer and browsed my emails, trying very hard not to think about Logan. Seeing him with his sisters had been an eye-opener. Isla, Kirsty and Elspeth were a bit odd, but in an endearing way, and their love for their brother showed in their smiles and their gestures when they spoke to him. Kirsty would touch his arm and say something to tease him. Isla pinched his cheek and called him Logie, which always made him grimace, though his affection for his sisters was clear. All the MacTaggarts were a little strange, but I'd come to appreciate their unique traits. I admired their loyalty to each other and the way they would always step up to help a member of the family.

Logan had stepped up in a big way for Evan and Keely. I'd heard the story of how he belly-crawled through the woods to sneak up on the bad guy's car when it was coming up the long driveway. Keely had told me Logan threw a knife to puncture the car's tire while it was still moving. He'd then collared the cowardly villain and smacked him around until the guy fessed up to where his cohort was hiding. Later, the local cops had let their buddy Logan have a chat with the main bad guy, a chat that ended with the man confessing everything. They said Logan hadn't laid a finger on him. He'd simply stared at the man and said who-knew-what to him.

A thrill rushed through me, awakening the hairs on my arms. Logan could make a man confess with only a steely glare and a few choice words, spoken in a tone I was sure would've sounded menacingly sexy.

The email I'd been perusing had become a blur on the screen.

Oh for heaven's sake. I was too damn old to go gaga over a guy. Menacing was not sexy. Logan was hot, for sure, but I did not like dangerous men. Or men who liked danger. I'd had enough of that in my life. No more.

I blinked several times until I could focus on the computer screen again, then I took good swig of my coffee and got back to work.

Ten minutes later I'd gotten in the zone, whizzing through email replies with the keyboard clacking furiously as I typed at my top speed. I sent a reply to Tamsen Spurling, who was one of two vice presidents at the UK arm of Evanescent, then I opened an email from a new client. He asked a question that required me to skim his contract again before answering. Luckily, I kept contract files close by, in a cabinet up against the wall behind my desk.

I pushed my chair back and headed for the file cabinet. This client's name started with W, and the drawers were alphabetized starting with A through D in the top drawer. I had to half kneel and bend over to reach the drawer with the W's in it. My skirt didn't look overly snug when I was sitting or standing, but kneeling made it stretch too tight for me to get all the way down to the level of the bottom drawer. I had to bend over too. These file drawers held the folders sideways, so I had to angle myself to the cabinet in order to flip through the files.

That's how I spotted Logan loitering near the juncture where the hallway opened into the reception area. He leaned against the corner with one ankle hooked over the other. He was smirking, of course. And of course, he looked delectable in a finely tailored charcoal suit jacket with a pale blue shirt and no tie, not to mention the kilt that showed off his muscular calves. Logan had clearly taken up his cousin's habit of wearing a kilt every Monday.

Logan's short, dark hair glistened in the glow of the natural-light bulbs. His hazel eyes glimmered too, their green highlights sparkling in the warm light.

No fluorescent bulbs here. Evan hated them.

Logan roved his gaze over my body, where I still hunched in a bent-over, half-kneeling position. "I always enjoy the view when I visit you, Serena."

The way he spoke my name made every hair on my body shiver and stiffen. Once upon a time, he'd said my name with a slight snarl, or maybe a touch of sarcasm. Ever since our quickie in the copy room, he wrapped his voice around my name like a warm, silken scarf dragged across my bare skin.

"Good morning, Logan," I said. Snatching up the file I'd been looking for, I straightened and kicked the drawer shut. "Why aren't you in your office downstairs?"

"I'm feeling disoriented." He pushed away from the wall and moseyed toward me. "That's your job, isn't it? To orient me."

In typical Logan fashion, he made the word orient sound dirty.

"Check your orientation packet," I said, holding the file folder to my chest. "It has all the information you need."

"Evan said I should come to you for all my needs."

Shit, he was right. Evan had commanded me to help Logan get settled in.

Logan moved closer, narrowing the gap between us to no more than two feet. "I need you, Serena. I'm lost in this vast building."

He managed to smirk and sound huskily erotic at the same time.

And I tingled all over, including deep inside my most private regions.

"Uh-huh," I said. "I'm sure you're helpless. If you can wait a few minutes while I finish answering emails, I can give you the grand tour. Again. Or if you have specific questions, ask away."

I hurried to my chair and dropped onto it, determined to avoid looking at him. Setting the file folder on my desk, I flipped it open.

Logan planted his hands on my chair's back and leaned over my shoulder. His mouth hovered a hair's breadth from my ear, his breaths tickling my skin and exciting the hairs on my neck. "I have a specific question."

"What is it?"

He nuzzled my earlobe. "Could you show me how to use the copier again? I've forgotten how it works."

Like hell he had. He'd told me he had a photographic memory, so he probably remembered his high school locker combination and the phone number of the girl he dated in eighth grade.

"The instructions," I said with deliberate calmness, "are in your orientation packet. They tell you step by step how to use the copier."

"I seem to have left my orientation packet in my office." He moved his mouth closer to my ear. "Would you have me slog all the way downstairs just to retrieve it? I'll be too knackered to work after that."

"We have this crazy new invention called the elevator. Try it."

"You'll have to show me how that works too. All those buttons confuse me."

Sure, I'd believe that when I saw neon-orange pigs flying over downtown Carrefour.

"Please, Serena," he murmured in my ear, "I'm desperate and in need of personal assistance."

I cleared my throat, because it had suddenly gotten dry and tight. My nether regions, however, had grown slick. "Fine, I'll show you the copier again. But that's it. Instruction on how to use the machine, no hanky-panky of any kind."

"Thank you, Serena."

Christ, I wished he'd stop saying my name that way.

He backed away from my chair.

I got up and led him to the copy room. This time, I left the door wide open. Would that deter him if he got naughty ideas in his head about how to use the copier? Probably not. But at least I would be able to run out the door more easily.

Right. Like I'd tried to get away the last time we'd been in the copy room.

Once I reached the copier, I turned to the side so I could see Logan. He liked to sneak up behind me, or linger behind me in this case. Having him there, feeling him there, made me antsy. Or maybe excited. No, annoyed was more like it.

Yeah, sure. This dampness between my legs resulted from annoyance. It wasn't fair for an obnoxious man to be so sexy.

Logan watched me without expression.

"Okay," I said, laying a hand on the copier. "Here's how you make photocopies with this machine. Maybe you should take notes, so I don't have to explain this again."

"I'll remember."

"You claim to have forgotten what I showed you last time."

"I was distracted. This morning, I'm concentrating on every word you say. Concentrating on you."

To his credit, he kept his focus on my face instead of poring over my entire body the way he usually did. His expression stayed bland too.

What was he up to? He couldn't actually be fascinated with the workings of a photocopier.

I went through the same spiel I'd given him before, demonstrating what each button did. Last time, I'd barely gotten started with the instructions when he shoved my skirt up and nailed me to the copy machine. I shivered at the memory. I liked the occasional fling, but I had never screwed a guy at work or had sex in a place where I could easily get caught. Never. Not until Logan.

Which meant nothing.

By the time I finished explaining the copier to him, Logan was standing beside me, staring down at the clear glass of the scanning surface like it contained secrets he needed to extract from it.

"Well," I said, "that's it. You should be a photocopying expert now."

He turned toward me, his body inches from mine. "Thank you, Serena. I appreciate your patience with me."

"Uh, sure. You're welcome, I guess." Whenever he acted like a normal person, it made my skin itch. "I should get back to work."

"Walk me to the elevator. I might get lost without you."

Since his request seemed innocuous enough, I gave in and accompanied him to the elevator. I even punched the button to summon the car. The doors slid open a couple seconds later.

Logan tipped toward me in a partial bow, lifted my hand to his lips, and kissed it. "Until we meet again, Serena."

With that, he strode into the elevator and hit a button.

The doors glided shut.

I stood there in front of those doors for several seconds, confounded by the man who'd kissed my hand. He loved to say crude things to me—let's have a poke, touch my *slat*, et cetera—but lately, he also said civil things to me. On occasion, he even sounded sweet.

He had to be up to something. Nothing else explained his behavior.

What exactly was he plotting? Politeness as a means of…what?

Oh God, woman, stop thinking about him.

I returned to my desk.

Five minutes before my lunch break, my cell phone rang. Chase was calling.

"Hi, sweetie," I said. "What's up?"

"Summer is boring. I miss school."

A laugh snorted out of me. "Is this the same boy who swore he'd die if he had to go to one more day of algebra class?"

"Yeah, I don't miss *that*. But there's so not anything to do in this town." He sighed with melodramatic flair, the way only a teenager could. "How many times can we go to the movies? They show the same ones for months. And the arcade gets old too. Keely's store is cool, but my allowance isn't enough to pay for any new games."

Ah yes, here came the angle. My son wanted more money.

"Your allowance is plenty," I told him. "Try doing something outdoors. You know, exercise. I always liked playing hide and go seek."

"Jeez, Mom, that's so third grade. I'm fifteen."

The clock on my computer read noon precisely. I logged off and slung my purse over my shoulder while I said, "How about you stop making me guess. What is it you want, Chase?"

He made noncommittal noises, a sure sign he knew what he wanted but was positive I'd say no.

Rising from my chair, I headed for the hallway and the elevator. "Spit it out. I may have eyes in the back of my head, but I can't read minds."

"Grandma and Grandpa want me to spend the summer with them."

I stopped halfway to the elevator. All the blood seemed to have gushed out of my body, leaving me cold and numb. Chase meant his other grandparents, not my mother and father. Rob's family. They'd been pestering me, in a polite and almost hesitant way, about letting Chase visit them this summer. And last summer. And the summer before that. For ten years, the Carpenters had asked every summer. They always invited me too, but I always said no, for myself and for my son. First, I'd convinced them it was too soon after Rob's passing. Then, I'd decided Chase was too young. Eventually, I had stopped making up excuses and just kept saying no.

Chase was fifteen now, a levelheaded and well-adjusted kid who never did anything bad. Not once in his entire life had I grounded him or chastised him. I hadn't needed to. He minded me, even when he complained about it. Maybe I owed him a little leeway. Rob's parents had come to see us here in Carrefour at least a few times over the years. They lived in the same lovely house on a lake in Vermont where they'd lived for two decades. Rob had grown up here in Carrefour, like me, but his parents had retired up north not long after we got married. I'd been to their house a few times, with Rob. Maybe Chase deserved to see their home too.

My throat constricted. I gripped my purse's strap so hard my fingers hurt.

"The answer's no, isn't?" Chase asked. "I'm not a baby anymore, you know. I can fly on a plane all by myself."

"I know." My voice came out hushed. Tears stung my eyes.

"You okay, Mom?"

Straightening, I wiped the tears away with the heel of my hand and cleared my throat. "Yes, I'm fine."

"Can I go? To Vermont?"

The hopefulness in his voice tugged at my heart. Let my baby go far away all on his own? I wanted to say absolutely not, but I knew it was time to let go. Maybe I couldn't stand to face Rob's parents, afraid I'd break down when they started talking about him, but I could no longer deny my son the chance to spend time with his grandparents. I had no valid reason to say no.

Even if the thought of not having him with me tore at my heart.

I cleared my throat again and sucked in a fortifying breath. "Yes, you can visit your grandparents for the summer. I'll call them tonight to arrange everything."

"Awesome! Thanks, Mom. I'm so stoked about this."

The excitement in his voice made me smile even while I sniffled. New tears burned in my eyes.

I said goodbye to Chase and dumped my phone into my purse, then shuffled down the hall to the elevator. It took a minute or two after I pushed the button before the car arrived. I spent those minutes getting hold of myself, using redness relieving eyedrops, and fixing my makeup. By the time I walked out of the elevator into the lobby, I felt reasonably recovered.

Logan got up from the chair where he'd been sitting and approached me. "May I buy you lunch, Serena?"

This time, hearing him say my name did not make me weak in the knees. I still had a balled-up tissue clenched in my hand.

And of course, he noticed it. "Are you all right?"

"Yes, fine, great." That was what they called trying too hard. Damn, I needed to get a grip. "I was going to grab a protein bar or something. Not very hungry."

Why did I blab that to him? He didn't need to know. So what if I was a little nauseous, my throat hurt, and I wanted to lie down on the floor to have a good cry? It was dumb and none of his business.

He closed his hand around mine, the one clutching a dirty tissue. "Let me buy you a good lunch, and dessert too. You look like you need it."

"That's sweet, but—" Had I called Logan MacTaggart sweet? I resisted the urge to glance around and make sure the world hadn't flipped upside down. "I-I really don't want a big lunch. A protein—"

"You need a good meal." He pried my fingers open and tossed the tissue into a trash can fifteen feet away, hitting it dead-on. "I'm starved, and I hate to eat alone."

"Since when? The way I hear it, you eat alone every day, in your office."

"A man can change his ways, can't he?"

Had I embarrassed him? It didn't seem possible, but the signs were there. He wanted to have lunch with me, and I realized I kind of wanted to have lunch with him.

"Okay," I said. "Let's go eat a big, politically incorrect lunch."

"No vegan, eh?"

"Absolutely not. If you try to feed me hummus, I'll deck you."

"That won't be necessary." He settled a hand on the small of my back and guided me toward the automatic doors. "What's your pleasure?"

Oh, now there was a loaded question. Maybe a quickie with Logan would perk me up.

No, I needed food. Red meat. Butter. Sugar. All the decadent things talking heads on TV told us never to eat. Still, even the richest food couldn't compare to the most decadent thing of all.

Logan MacTaggart.

Chapter Eleven

Logan

Lunch with Serena was…different. We didn't argue or insult each other. We talked about work and commiserated over the annoying way our loved ones insisted on playing matchmaker. We also agreed there would never be a romance between us. Neither of us wanted that, and besides, we were wrong for each other. When it came to sex, we were compatible. In every other way, we had nothing in common.

Sex was enough for me. I didn't need or want to get entangled in a relationship.

Why was I taking Serena to lunch, then?

By the time dessert arrived—something known as double chocolate lava cake—Serena had relaxed. When she'd stepped out of the elevator earlier, I'd seen the signs of sadness, from her faintly red eyes to the puffiness under them and the tissue crushed in her fist. She'd been crying, for sure, but made a valiant effort to hide it. Seeing her that way had made me want to hunt down whatever bastard had made her cry and batter him into the ground. I briefly wondered if I might've been the cause of her distress but dismissed the idea.

Throughout lunch, I fought the impulse to ask what had upset her. It didn't matter. I shouldn't care. We were fucking, not forging a lasting bond.

Over dessert, I seemed to lose all my good sense.

Serena plunged her fork into her piece of lava cake, tearing off a chunk of the darkest, moistest cake I'd ever seen. Chocolate liquid oozed from its center. She slipped the fork between her lips and pulled it free, moaning as she chewed the confection.

I wanted to drag her onto my lap and do things to her that would get us both arrested.

My fantasy wasn't the moment when I lost my good sense, though. That came next, when I asked, "What was bothering you earlier? You seemed upset."

She swallowed her bite of cake and stopped blinking. "What makes you think that?"

"I'm a spy. Interpreting body language is a requirement for that sort of work."

"Thought you weren't a spy anymore."

"You never really stop. It stays with you for the rest of your life." I rested my elbows on the table. "Tell me what upset you."

She consumed another bite of cake. "It was nothing."

"You're lying."

"I suppose you won't give up until I tell you." My expression must've confirmed what she'd said, because she set down her fork and took a swig of her water. "My son wants to visit his grandparents in Vermont for the summer."

"And?"

She huffed, snatching up her fork only to smack it down again. "And it's upsetting."

"Why? You're going with him, aren't you?"

An odd sensation gripped me, something like a cold sweat with a touch of nausea, but without the actual sweat. The thought her leaving town shouldn't affect me. It didn't affect me. What did I care if she went away as long as I got to screw her one more time before she left?

Serena bowed her head, gazing down at her lap where she'd placed her hands. "Chase is going alone."

"Why?" The better question was why I kept pushing for an explanation. "Do you not get along with your parents?"

"He's not visiting my parents. Chase is going to stay with Rob's parents."

"Rob?"

She grabbed her glass and downed the rest of the water in one large gulp. "Rob was my husband. He passed away eleven years ago, killed in the line of duty in Iraq."

Everything inside me froze. I stared at her blankly, having no bloody idea what to say. I'd heard her husband had died, but no one had mentioned his military service. Why would they? I wasn't in a relationship with Serena. Neither she nor her friends had any reason to share that fact with me. At least now I had an idea of why she'd been upset earlier.

She raised her face to me, looking remarkably composed considering what she'd shared with me. "Rob's parents invited me to go with Chase for the summer. I can't do it. I mean, I have a job here. But I know Evan would give me the time off, so mostly, I can't face them right now. They have visited me and Chase here, but lately they keep talking about the anniversary of Rob's passing, and how we should do something to commemorate it. They wanted to do that last year, the tenth anniversary, but I couldn't. Still can't. The last thing I need is to relive losing him with his grief-stricken parents standing beside me."

I still had no idea what to say. Anything I spouted would sound hollow and pathetic.

"Don't get me wrong," she said. "They're wonderful people. I love them. But it's too much right now."

"Why do you keep saying 'right now'? Has something changed lately?"

She stopped blinking again. Her jaw fell open, but she clapped it shut. "No, nothing has changed. It's the same old stuff."

It hadn't sounded that way. But then, what did I know about these things? She must have loved her husband very much, and that was why she had trouble talking about what happened to him. Rob Carpenter must've been the love of her life. Aye, there was a subject I knew nothing about—love, the romantic and everlasting kind described in books and films. No woman ever had or ever would feel that way about me. I understood that, and I'd accepted it.

My sisters never would.

Serena wolfed down three more large bites of cake while studying me. After finishing her third mouthful of dessert, she pointed her fork at me. "What was all that bullshit earlier about you being confused and lost?"

"What do you mean?" I could feign innocence rather well when the situation called for it, but based on the way she squinted her eyes, I was failing miserably with Serena. None of my usual tricks seemed to work with her. Either I became a daft moron in her presence, or she was exceedingly perceptive. It had to be the latter.

She jabbed her fork in the air in my direction. "Come off it, Logan. There's no way you are helpless. So why were you pretending to be?"

I sat back in my chair, suddenly uninterested in my dessert. "To tease you. I've been bored out of my skull with this job."

"Not enough excitement for you?" She set down her fork. "Or is it the danger you miss?"

"What are you talking about?" I knew damn well what she was talking about, but evasion seemed like the best option. Discussing my covert past impressed some lasses, but Serena wasn't like any other woman.

Her lips thinned into a sharp line. "Don't get coy with me. Considering we've had sex twice, the least you can do is tell me the truth. I don't like secrets."

Then you're with the wrong man, lass.

We weren't together, though, not in the traditional sense. Maybe it didn't matter that I was exactly the wrong sort of bloke for a woman like her, because what we shared was purely physical. She didn't need to know my life was a tangled mess of secrets and lies.

She tilted her head, studying me with more intensity. "How long ago did you quit being a spy?"

"Intelligence officer. I resigned three years ago."

"And then you started working in construction. For your cousin Aidan, right?"

What was this, the bloody American Inquisition? "Aye, for Aidan. I'm— I was a bricklayer."

"Now you work for Evan."

"You know that already. What is it you're really trying to ask me?"

She picked up her fork, tapping it on her plate. "The question you wouldn't answer before. Do you miss the danger and the excitement of being a spy?"

"Intelligence officer," I all but snarled. What was wrong with me? No one got under my skin. No one except Serena Carpenter.

"A few minutes ago, you called yourself a spy. Now it's an insult?" She made a noise best described as a huffing pig snort. "You're full of shit, Logan. Either you start telling me the truth, no evasion, or you will never have a poke at me again."

Not even the daftest dafty could've missed the sarcasm in her voice when she said the phrase "have a poke."

I slumped against my chair and rubbed my eyes with my thumb and forefinger.

"What's wrong with you?" she asked. "Is telling the truth so painful? Normal people have no trouble with it."

That was total bollocks, and I was sure she knew it, but her hostile reaction to my evasions was beginning to rankle. Other men must've lied to her before, about stupid things, but I kept secrets for a damn good reason.

Mostly.

I dug my wallet out of my pocket and slapped several bills on the table, more than enough to cover our meal and the waiter's tip.

"Those are British pounds, not American dollars," Serena pointed out.

Cursing under my breath, I rooted through my wallet until I found American money. I'd exchanged my pounds for dollars when I arrived in the US, but clearly, I'd overlooked a few.

"Some of those pounds look funny," Serena said, peering at the money on the table.

"They're Scottish notes, and the others are Bank of England notes." I slapped the dollars on the table and swiped the pound notes off it. "Lunch is over. We need to get back to work."

"Fine." She jerked her chair away from the table and got up, lifting her chin and squaring her shoulders. "Trying to be friendly with you was a mistake, anyway. You are—"

"Disgusting, vile, loathsome, obnoxious, et cetera. I'm aware of your opinion of me."

I jumped up, clamped my hand around her elbow, and all but shoved her in the direction of the exit.

We went back to the office—our separate offices, on separate floors—and ignored each other for the rest of the day. After work, I sequestered myself in my hotel room with a bottle of whisky I'd bought from a store down the street. Slouched in a chair by the windows, I propped my feet on a table and sipped my whisky. The American brand wasn't as good as Ben Nevis or Talisker, but it would do.

Why had I let Serena get to me? I rarely lost my temper, and never with a woman. She seemed to know exactly where to dig her nails into me for maximum discomfort. Other women had called me much worse things than disgusting or loathsome, but I didn't let it fash me. It must've been the new job, the new life in a new country, getting to me.

For the hundredth time today, I wondered why I'd accepted Evan's job offer.

My mobile phone rang.

I snagged it off the table and answered.

"Logan, mate, how's it going?" said a cheerful British voice. "Are you really in America? I heard the rumor from a friend of a friend of the Mac-Taggarts."

"Friend of a friend?" I chuckled halfheartedly, in no mood for this call, or any call. "Alex Thorne, is that you? I'm surprised even a distant acquaintance of the MacTaggarts would speak to you after the way you threw Catriona over."

"The throwing over was mutual. But if I'm still persona non grata in the Highlands, why haven't you hung up yet?"

"I've always formed my own opinions." I swallowed the last of my whisky and set the glass on the table. "Why are you calling me, Alex? We haven't spoken in years."

"Need a favor, of the Logan MacTaggart variety. You were quite helpful last time."

"Sorry, I don't do that anymore."

"This is an emergency."

"I've heard that before. You like to exaggerate the severity of a problem to get me to do what you want." I glanced at the whisky bottle, three quarters empty, afflicted with a sudden urge to pour the entire contents down my throat. "Not interested in whatever trouble you've gotten yourself into this time. Besides, if I helped you, Catriona would not be pleased."

"And you always do what your cousins tell you."

"Cat is a sweet lass, and you hurt her badly. I may not have been there when it happened"—and I hadn't been close to Catriona until recently, a fact Alex didn't need to know—"but I heard about it. Helping you would mean betraying someone I care about."

Alex fell silent for a moment. His tone was more serious when he spoke again. "I know you don't want to hurt Catriona, and I respect that. But you helped me with a problem after Cat and I parted ways, so I'm guessing you don't hold a grudge."

"Doesn't mean I trust you." I fingered the whisky bottle, considering whether to pour another dram into my glass. Maybe several drams. "Last time, you told me it was a simple little job. It turned into a right mess."

"Everything worked out in the end, though. And I paid you extra for the trouble."

"Not interested, Alex."

"You haven't even heard the details. Let me explain before you say no."

I let my head fall back, my gaze landing on the ceiling where the intersecting lines of white tiles laid out a geometric pattern. "Not interested."

"Let me text you the details. You can decide later."

Alex had not mellowed in the three years since I'd last seen him. He still had the doggedness of a bloodhound. I'd admired his determination back then. Tonight, it irritated the hell out of me. If I could've shoved my arm through the phone to strangle him, I might have done it.

Too tired to argue, I said, "Fine. Text it to me. No promises."

"Of course not," Alex said in a tone that implied he was certain I'd say yes eventually.

My curiosity got the better of me, and I asked, "Are you still in America?"

"Yes, I've been here for fifteen years, since before I met Catriona."

"Still teaching?"

He said nothing for so long I wondered if we'd gotten disconnected. "These days, I'm the curator of a museum at a modest-size institution of higher learning."

Ah yes, I remembered how cagey Alex could be. He didn't want to tell me where precisely he worked, not yet, so he gave me vague clues that might lead me to the wrong conclusion, the conclusion he wanted me to reach because it benefited him. Alex Thorne was no con artist, but he did know how to maneuver people to end up exactly where he wanted them. The term modest size could have meant almost anything. Did he want me to believe he worked at a well-known, but not large, university? Or did he hope I'd assume he worked for a wee college attended by students of lesser academic talents? I could've searched for him online, and perhaps found out where he worked, but I wouldn't bother.

Where he worked didn't matter. I was not taking the job.

"Tell me, Logan, how long have you been over here on this side of the pond?"

Alex's words pulled me out of my contemplation of his previous statement. "Slightly more than a week."

"You must be knackered from the time change. I'll say good night."

I wasn't tired, but I was ready for this call to end. "Good night, Alex."

We hung up, and I permitted myself one more dram of whisky. As the liquor slid down my throat, I wondered about Alex. I still had contacts inside various government agencies, both in the UK and here in America, as well as some shadier acquaintances. He must've realized I would check up on him in my own, very thorough way. Maybe he wanted me to do it. I couldn't decide if that was good or bad.

Didn't matter. I would not get entangled with Alex Thorne again.

Chapter Twelve

Serena

The day after my lunch with Logan, I still couldn't figure out what to make of him. After months and months of speaking to me only when he made lewd advances, he'd finally shown me what I took for his human side. Wrong. It must've been a scam, all that niceness and hand-kissing, because at lunch yesterday he'd turned back into Logan the obnoxious. Was telling the truth so difficult? Instead of trusting me, he treated me like the enemy.

Maybe being a spy had trained him to mistrust everyone.

No, I would not give him the benefit of the doubt. He needed to earn that.

I was at my desk, poring over emails, when Logan walked up behind me. I knew it was Logan, though I couldn't see him. The scent of his cologne wafted over me before he reached my chair. Somehow, I thought I kind of maybe felt him approaching too. Which was crazy. I did not feel him. Sure, I liked to tell my son I had eyes in the back of my head, but that was strictly parental psycho-manipulation.

Logan bent forward, but I still couldn't see him, what with his head several feet above mine. His shadow fell over me, alerting me to his position.

"What do you want?" I asked.

He lowered his head until it hovered beside mine and swung his arm in front me, a bouquet of pink roses in his hand. "I need to apologize."

"For what? You've done so many rude things, it's hard to keep track."

"Yesterday, I behaved like a *bod ceann*. I'm sorry." He set the bouquet on my desk, right in front of me. "I feel awful about it. Will you accept my apology?"

He felt awful? That meant guilty. Guilt was something I'd never dreamed I would hear Logan admit to experiencing.

I examined the roses, tracing the delicate lines of their petals with one finger while I tried to figure out what on earth to say to him. "Uh, fine. I forgive you."

A sigh rushed out of him, almost like he'd been holding his breath. "Thank you, Serena."

"Sure, whatever." I squirmed in my chair. "I have work to do."

"Of course. I'll let you get back to it." He kissed my cheek. "I won't pester you for sex anymore. If you don't want to speak to me again, I'll understand. I'm sure you'll be glad to have me out of your hair, not fashing you on a regular basis anymore."

Logan walked away.

I twisted in my chair to watch him vanish around the corner. He hadn't pestered me for sex in days, so he had no reason to tell me he wouldn't do it anymore. I, not Logan, had initiated our liaison at the brunch on Saturday. Everything he'd said and done a minute ago seemed an awful lot like a goodbye. He had mentioned being bored out of his mind here. Maybe he found another spy job.

Did I care if he left? Absolutely not.

I punched the intercom button.

Evan answered right away. "Yes, Serena?"

The words I'd been about to say got stuck somewhere between my brain and my mouth. "Uhhhh…"

"Should I call an ambulance for you? Sounds like you might be having a stroke."

His sarcasm snapped me out of my mental freeze. "I'm fine, thank you very much. Is your cousin quitting?"

"Quitting what?"

"His job here."

"Not that I know of," Evan said carefully. "Did he say something to you about resigning?"

"Not exactly."

The intercom clicked off, and the door to Evan's office swung open.

He walked up to my desk. "I'll speak to Logan."

"Why did you come out here to tell me that?"

"I'm going to speak to him in person." Evan smiled and touched my hand. "Don't worry. I'm sure he's staying here with us."

"Not worried. Confused." I fiddled with the papers and pens on my desk. "Your cousin is a very strange and confusing man."

"That he is. But so am I, and you've gotten used to me."

Before I could say anything, he hustled off toward the elevator.

I got back to work. Or pretended to get back to work. What Logan had said shouldn't bother me. I had trouble concentrating on my job because…I was tired. Yeah, that was it. I hadn't slept well last night, and I was wiped out. Nothing more going on here.

Oh great. I was making excuses for why I didn't care what Logan did, exactly the way Keely had done with Evan last year. She'd tried her damnedest to not fall in love with him. I slumped back in my chair. Maybe I was making excuses, but not because I felt in danger of developing romantic feelings for Logan. No way in hell would I ever fall for him.

And that was exactly what Keely had said about Evan.

I growled under my breath and grabbed a pen, gripping it tightly like I was about to write something of world-shattering importance. What had I intended to write down? I slid a small yellow notepad into position and tapped the tip of my pen on it. Something incredibly vital. I'd been about to write…

"Ugh," I grunted, tossing the pen onto my desk. "You're too damn old to be acting this way."

"What am I too old to act like?"

Evan's voice made me jump and yelp. A tiny yelp. Hardly a yelp at all, really.

I spun my chair around to see Evan standing ten feet away. Sitting up straighter, I smoothed my blouse. "Nothing. I was talking to myself."

He gave me an odd look, almost like he thought I might turn into a ravening vampire at any moment. "Maybe you should talk to Keely."

"Relax, Evan, I'm not going to attack you. Talking to myself is not a sign of raving insanity."

"I know. But your conversations with Logan seem to upset you, and Keely is your best friend."

That was true, and normally I would discuss the Logan thing with Keely. Not that there was a Logan thing. Sheesh, I was doing it *again*. Deny, deny, deny. Nobody seemed to buy my denials. Maybe I'd avoided talking to my best friend about Logan because I knew what she'd say. Maybe I was afraid she was right. But I barely knew Logan, and I could not have feelings for a man I'd had a few brief conversations with and screwed twice.

"Did you talk to Logan?" I inquired, having no frigging idea why I asked.

"No, he wasn't in his office. I'll see him later." Evan headed for his office but stopped at the threshold. "Talk to Keely."

He disappeared into his office, shutting the door.

For ten minutes, I scrutinized my desk calendar without comprehending anything that was written on it and chewed on the end of my pen. Finally, I picked up the phone and called Keely. We agreed to meet for lunch at our favorite Mexican restaurant.

I arrived as Keely was clambering out of her car. Though I offered to help her, she waved me away. "I'm pregnant, not incompetent."

"There's nothing wrong with accepting a hand."

Keely shut the car door. "I appreciate your concern, but I'm getting plenty of help from Evan, whether I want it or not."

"I'm surprised he didn't drive you here."

"He tried to, but I scowled at him until he gave up on the idea."

The affection in her voice was unmistakable. Her husband might've been driving her nuts, but she loved him for it.

Rob hadn't been half as anxious about my pregnancy as Evan was about Keely's, but then, Keely was over forty. I'd been twenty-seven when Chase was born. Pregnancy over forty brought a host of potential complications, and though Keely had evidenced none of those, Evan had reason to be concerned for the health of his wife and child. He did go a touch overboard with it, but only because he loved his wife so deeply.

"Serena," Keely said, her tone sharp.

I blinked rapidly. "What?"

"You were daydreaming, weren't you? About Logan, I hope." Her lips curved into a sly smile. "He's jalapeño hot, isn't he?"

"Hm, I don't think a married woman should be salivating over another man."

"Admiring a sexy man is acceptable, and Evan knows I don't want anyone else." She bumped her shoulder into mine. "But I think you're doing more than admiring Logan's hot body. Am I right?"

I took hold of her elbow and urged her toward the restaurant's doors, pretending I hadn't heard her question. "Let's go inside and get a table before the lunch crowd descends. I'm famished."

"Sure you are." She waggled her eyebrows. "For something Scottish, I bet."

"Honestly, woman, you are too old to be talking like a teenage nymphomaniac."

Keely let me shepherd her into the restaurant, and a waitress took us to a booth, handing us menus before she left. We sat on opposite sides of the table, which I decided had been a mistake. Every time I glanced up, Keely was smiling at me in that annoyingly knowing way. If she'd been sitting next to me, I could've avoided looking at her.

Since I couldn't do that, I held the menu in front of my face to block my view of her.

The waitress returned to give us glasses of ice water.

Once the waitress had toddled off again, my best friend cleared her throat deliberately. "For the record, no woman is too old to salivate over a MacTaggart man. They're the brawniest, sexiest men you'll ever meet. And those accents? No heterosexual woman on the planet can resist a sultry Scottish brogue."

I set down my menu, remembering the way Logan spoke my name. Sultry. Yes, that described it perfectly. Brawny? He was that, for sure. As for the other part, I had done the deed with him twice, so I guessed that answered the sexiness question.

Feeling suddenly warm, I swigged a mouthful of ice water.

Keely examined me with her keen gaze, her lips puckering on one side and then the other, back and forth, puckering and unpuckering.

"What?" I demanded, sounding testier than I'd intended. I took a slow breath to calm myself. "You're staring at me like I've mutated into a hairy, bug-eyed monster from another dimension."

Keely laughed. "Hairy, bug-eyed monster?"

"Chase is into cheesy old sci-fi movies at the moment."

She laid her menu on the table and spread her palms over it. "I think it's time you tell me about you and Logan. Evan thinks you're having panic attacks about it."

"Panic attacks?" I collapsed back against the booth. "Your husband needs a new hobby, since he sucks at amateur psychoanalysis."

"I've known you for a long time, sweetie, and I've never seen you act this way before."

"I've never been this way before." I rubbed my forehead and moaned pitifully. "Logan drives me crazy. I can't figure out what his game is. I mean, he can't be…interested in me."

"Why not?"

The waitress came back to take our orders, giving me a few moments of peace before the best friend interrogation started up again. Once the waitress had left, and we were alone in our secluded corner of the restaurant, Keely repeated her question.

"Why couldn't Logan be interested in you romantically?"

"Because he's obviously not that kind of man." I gulped down a too-big mouthful of water and spluttered when it went down the wrong way. Once I'd recovered, I said, "But if all he wants is sex, why does he keep hanging around? Making up excuses to see me?"

Keely screwed up her mouth, considering the question, then that knowing look returned. "You've slept with him, haven't you?"

I snatched my napkin off the table and pretended to concentrate on placing it on my lap.

"You did," Keely said, sounding far too pleased with the idea of me having sex with Logan.

"Maybe," I mumbled. "Twice."

Keely tipped forward but couldn't lean over the table very far with her big belly. "Maybe twice? If you slept with Logan, there's no need to be shy about it. You're an adult, he's hot, and I'm your nonjudgmental best friend."

"I have a teenage son who thinks Logan MacTaggart is the coolest guy in the universe, like he's James Bond and Superman put together."

"What's that got to do with you and Logan tangling in the sheets?"

"There were no sheets either time." I propped my elbows on the table and bowed my head. "Yes, Logan and I had sex."

Christ, I swore I could feel her smiling. When I glanced up at her, she was grinning.

"It's not a good thing," I said. "Well, it was good, but—Ugh. You know what I mean. Logan and I are complete opposites, and I do not want any kind of relationship with him. Most of all, I do not want my son to get attached to Logan and think we might get married or whatever."

"Would that be so awful? Maybe you and Logan can work as a couple."

"No." I shook my head, my throat going dry and tight before I even spoke the next words. "It can't happen. I had the love of my life, I lost him, and I will never love anyone else."

"Did you ever think you might get more than one love of your life? For different times in your life?"

I gulped more water, chomping on an ice cube. "You don't get it. Even if it were possible, I don't want to do it."

"Do what?"

"Fall in love again. I'm done with that shit."

Keely observed me in silence, her expression no longer shrewdly certain, but instead filled with empathy. "Oh sweetie, don't push Logan away because you're scared. I know how hard it was for you when Rob died, but—"

"Rob was a wonderful man. Logan is…weird."

"I know you loved Rob, and he was a good man in general. But come on, I was there. I know how much he hurt you when he—"

"Stop." I held up a hand to emphasize how much I needed this conversation to end. "I don't want to talk about this anymore."

Keely watched me some more, until the waitress arrived with our food.

We didn't say much during our meal, but on our way out of the restaurant, Keely stopped me with a hand on my arm.

"You say you don't want to have feelings for Logan," she said, "but I think it's too late. You wouldn't be this upset if you didn't already feel something for him."

"I'm not in love with Logan."

"No, not yet. But you're afraid you might fall for him."

God, I hated it when she understood me. How could I hide my fears from myself if I couldn't even fool my best friend?

"Do me a favor," Keely said. "Let yourself consider the possibility you might not actually hate Logan. Maybe you're afraid to like him."

I shut my eyes for a moment, pulling in slow, deep breaths. "Fine. I'll consider it."

"Good."

We said goodbye, and I drove back to the office. For the rest of the day, I did not see Logan. And every so often, I took my best friend's advice. I let myself think about Logan MacTaggart, and I considered the possibility that maybe, just maybe, I didn't despise him. Even considering the idea felt like a betrayal of Rob, of everything we'd had together, but that was the fear talking. I forced myself to entertain the possibility I could develop some sort of feelings for Logan.

Maybe I liked him. A teeny bit. Somewhere deep down in my psyche.

Thinking about it scared the hell out of me.

Chapter Thirteen

Logan

For two days, I stayed away from Serena. I moved into my new apartment, but unpacking didn't take long since I'd brought only two pieces of luggage. The rest of the time, I slouched behind my desk in my office and stared out the windows in between pretending I knew what the fuck I was doing here. No one at this company needed my advice on security issues. They'd been vetted and signed nondisclosure agreements. Evanescent designed and manufactured security devices, and the specifications for those were proprietary information. After the Ron Tulloch incident last year, when Evan's lead accountant had embezzled from the company and blackmailed Evan himself, the company had instituted new security measures. It all involved technology. I knew next to nothing about that.

Which begged the question of why I hadn't resigned and gone home.

Evan had offered to buy me lunch today at his wife's favorite restaurant, which served Mexican food. Keely had stayed home, feeling tired after her outing yesterday with Serena. So I endured the male version of girl talk with my cousin, with no one else there to serve as a buffer. I liked Evan, but his attempt at matchmaking was making me seriously consider assassinating him.

The small talk ended once our appetizer arrived. The waitress delivered a bowl of queso and a larger bowl overflowing with tortilla chips. Evan consumed three chips dripping with cheese before he laid into me.

"It's time you asked Serena out on a proper date," he said in a tone that reminded me of my father when he'd found out I'd failed a math test. "I know you had lunch with her on Tuesday, but it's time to step up. Take her to dinner."

"Why?"

Evan consumed another cheese-laden chip. "Because you want to woo her."

"Woo? Does anyone call it that these days?"

"Nice evasion, Logan, but you're not fooling me. You like Serena."

"You make it sound like we're children." I snatched up a chip and crumbled it with my fingers. "Maybe I should pull her hair to let her know I like her."

Evan grinned. "You admitted you like her."

"I—You tricked me." Grumbling, I dunked a chip into the queso and shoved it into my mouth. Chewing gave me an excuse to not talk for a few seconds. "No more manipulation, Evan. You and your wife can't maneuver me and Serena into a relationship neither of us wants."

"Keely and I are doing no such thing." Evan leaned back, the fingers of one hand tapping on the tabletop. "I thought you and I were having a conversation, that's all. Why are you so sensitive about the idea of dating Serena?"

"It's ridiculous. Having sex with her twice doesn't mean we have anything in common." Maybe I'd spent the past two days thinking about her to an almost obsessive degree, but that meant nothing. I liked fucking her, period.

Evan's face lit up. "You had sex with Serena?"

Bod an Donais. I hadn't meant to let that slip. Did it matter that Evan knew? Serena might have told Keely about our liaisons, but being a good friend, Keely hadn't told her husband.

I shoved another loaded chip into my mouth before answering. "Aye, we had a poke or two. I'm sure you'll read deep meaning into those two brief encounters, but it was strictly sex."

My cousin adopted his analytical expression, the one I'd seen many times before, a sure sign he was trying to dissect me psychologically. "One of those encounters happened at my house, right before your sisters arrived. Correct?"

Sometimes I wished Evan wasn't quite so clever.

"That's right," I said. "It happened on the sofa in your living room."

Evan took his glasses off and examined them, as if he were looking for stains. "You can't keep your hands off Serena, can you? That means you—"

"I do not like her, not the way you mean. She might not be the bitch I thought she was, but we will never become more than colleagues who occasionally have a poke. End of discussion."

Evan slipped his glasses on again. "All right, no more talk of Serena."

The waitress brought our food, granting me a reprieve that lasted about thirty seconds.

The second our server left, Evan said, "I need you to go to Seattle tomorrow."

"Why?"

"To attend a conference. I don't want to leave Keely right now, so I need two of my top people to go instead."

I stabbed my knife into the burrito I'd ordered, my focus on my plate and the food I no longer felt like eating. "What is this conference about?"

"Technology, of course. We are that sort of company."

"Evan, I know nothing about that."

"You know how to take notes, don't you?"

I sawed on my burrito with my dull knife. "Send someone who knows what to make a note of."

"You're going to force me to order you to do it, aren't you? Well, all right." He set his hands on the table, leaned forward, and spoke in his CEO voice. "I command you and Serena to attend this conference."

The knife tumbled out of my grasp. "Me and Serena? Bloody hell, Evan, this is nothing more than another attempt to push me into dating your executive assistant."

"No, this is your employer ordering two of his best employees to attend a work-related conference." He affected a nonchalant attitude, like this wasn't an underhanded scheme at all. "If ye cannae keep your hands off each other, that's not my fault."

"It's bollocks, Evan. You and your wife cooked up this barmy plot to push me and Serena together."

He took a bite of his food, chewing it slowly. "As a new employee, you need to learn more about the business. A conference is an excellent way to do that."

I muttered a curse in Gaelic and hacked at my burrito until it resembled a dismembered corpse.

"You have no choice," Evan said. "Unless you want to resign. Serena thinks you mean to quit, and I gather she's a wee bit upset about that."

Upset? At the idea of me resigning? Impossible. The woman wanted me gone.

Of course, she had asked me to be honest with her, to tell her about my past. Maybe she did want me to stay. I'd never given up on a mission before, and I didn't like the idea of giving up now. I would stick with this boring, pointless job for a while longer—only so I could get her naked and satisfy my curiosity.

"I'm not resigning," I said. "And if you insist on sending me to Seattle, with Serena, I will obey your command. Donnae be surprised if one or both of us doesn't survive the trip."

"You won't kill each other." Evan picked up a chip, twirling it between his fingers. "You'll have all weekend to get better acquainted."

"All weekend? I assumed it was a one-day event."

Evan pulled a brochure out of the inside pocket of his jacket and handed it to me. "The conference starts at noon tomorrow and ends Sunday evening. You're not obliged to attend every session. I'll leave it up to you and Serena to decide which ones are important."

Nearly three entire days with Serena? No meddling friends or relatives. No teenage son. Just the two of us. I'd promised not to pester her for sex, and I meant to keep my word, but I'd be essentially alone with her all weekend. Not long ago, I'd planned on seducing her at the first opportunity. What had changed? Why had I made that promise to her?

I pictured Serena in her red dress, the one she'd worn on the night when I'd first kissed her. That body. Those lips. Her silken hair brushing my skin. In the copy room, I'd finally taken her, and at the Saturday brunch I'd learned what it felt like to come with her body enveloping my cock. The memory of being inside her tormented me, but I still hadn't seen her without clothes. A full weekend alone with her would offer plenty of opportunity to strip her naked and explore every inch of that sumptuous body.

But I had promised. Though I might've been a bastard, I had enough honor to keep to my word.

Her soft lips. Her slick flesh. Those gasping moans.

Mhac na galla. One whole weekend of pure temptation. My *bagais* already ached at the thought of her. By Monday, my balls would have turned to stone.

If I accepted the job Alex Thorne had offered, I could get out of this mess I'd gotten myself into with Serena. I wouldn't need to see her again, ever.

Since when did I run away from a complicated situation?

One weekend. I could handle that. If we accidentally had sex, so be it.

I snorted at my own thoughts. Accidentally had sex? I'd become as witless as my cousins, and over a woman, no less.

"You leave at six a.m. on the company jet," Evan said. "Feel free to join the mile-high club."

"Stop it, Evan. I'm not touching Serena again."

"We'll see."

Somehow, I survived the rest of lunch without assassinating Evan. I returned to my office, but immediately got called to the third floor for a pointless meeting with the head of R&D, a man called Marvin Wilson. He claimed to want my input on how to keep their already secure rooms more secure. The R&D teams worked in areas protected by doors that required a code to unlock them. What could I contribute to their security? Nothing. I was an expert on keeping secrets and wheedling them out of other people. I knew nothing about keypads and electronic locks.

Wilson was professional and friendly, but I was certain Evan had arranged this meeting. He wanted to convince me I performed a valuable service here. His effort had failed. My meeting with Wilson only reinforced the fact I did not belong at this company.

Yet I was traveling to Seattle for a tech conference.

After my pointless meeting, I headed for the elevator. While I waited for it to arrive, I skimmed through the information Alex Thorne had texted me—for the tenth time since I'd received it. Alex had a unique definition of "details," which meant he provided very little in the way of actual specifics about the job. Still, his offer was intriguing. Excellent pay, an enticing mystery, the chance to travel. I had no real ties here in Utah. I could accept Alex's offer.

What about Serena?

As if on cue, the elevator doors slid open to reveal Serena inside.

When her gaze met mine, she blinked several times quickly. "Logan. It's you."

"Glad you remember my name."

She looked spectacular, in a cream-colored pantsuit that hugged her body without being overtly sensual or inappropriate. Her hair curled around her face and tumbled over her shoulders. I wanted to tear the clothes off her body and pin her to the wall of the elevator car.

"What are you doing here?" she asked.

"I work in this building. Why should you be surprised to bump into me?"

She laughed nervously. "I'm not surprised."

"You gawp at everyone, then?" I stepped into the elevator and hit the button for the first floor. "What are you doing away from your desk at two in the afternoon?"

She made an exasperated noise. "I have meetings too, you know."

"Of course you do." I moved over a little, enough to let me admire her body while the car began its gradual descent. "I'm sure Evan told you about our business trip."

"Yes," she said curtly. "I'm seriously considering sneaking poison into his coffee."

"Don't do that. How can I fuck you again if you're in prison?"

"You're obsessed with sex." She toyed with the cuff of her shirt, where it poked out of her jacket sleeve. "I...thought you might be quitting. After what you said the other day."

"What did I say? Don't recall telling you I wanted to resign."

"You apologized for being evasive and said you wouldn't pester me for sex anymore. You also said you understood if I didn't want to talk to you." She glanced at me sideways. "It sounded like a goodbye."

"It was goodbye—for the moment." I studied her facial expression and her nervous movements, the way she fingered her cuff and then fussed with her collar, repeatedly. Could she have been worried I would go back to Scotland? Did she want to have me around? I edged closer to her until a space of inches separated us. "If I meant to leave the country, or even the state, I'd tell you. And I wouldn't leave it open to interpretation. You would know for certain."

"Sure, whatever." Another nervous laugh bubbled out of her. "It's not like I care what you do."

Ah, but she did care. Everything about her demeanor and her tone of voice attested to that fact. Did I want her to care whether I stayed or left? Damned if I knew. Since the day I'd first met Serena Carpenter, I'd been sure of nothing. If she'd told me she was quitting her job and moving to another city or state or country, how would I feel about that?

My throat tightened. My skin went cold.

I took two steps backward. "I'm sorry if I worried you, but it's not as if we're a couple. I assumed you wanted me to stop bothering you, so I did."

She peeked at me over her shoulder, but her expression had changed. She no longer seemed edgy. Her eyes had softened, her posture too. "Maybe I was worried, and I'm glad you're not quitting."

Before I could formulate a response, she rushed toward me, captured my face in her hands, and crushed her lips to mine. Right about the time my shock wore off and I was about to haul her body into mine, she pulled away.

"Seattle might be fun," she said. "I've never been there before. Have you?"

My mouth opened, but I couldn't speak. The lass had kissed me, and now she casually talked about our business trip. She was the most confounding woman I'd ever met.

"I've never been to Seattle either," I finally managed to say. "At least we don't have to travel commercial. Evan's jet is much faster and more comfortable."

"Yeah, I've been on it before."

Evan would have flown her to Scotland for the family events she'd attended. I should've guessed she'd been on the jet before, but my brain had stopped functioning when she kissed me.

What on earth was happening to me? Speechless over a kiss. Me. I'd seduced my fair share of women in the line of duty, and for personal pleasure, but Serena stole my voice and my good sense.

The elevator doors opened. We had reached the ground floor.

I gestured for Serena to exit. "Ladies first."

"This isn't my stop."

"Why did you ride down to the first floor if you didn't need to?"

She nibbled on her bottom lip but said nothing.

I stepped out of the elevator. "Where are you headed?"

Her shoulders hunched, she curved her lips into a shy smile. "Third floor."

The doors glided shut while Serena and I regarded each other.

For a minute or two after the doors closed, I stood there immobilized by the realization that Serena had taken the elevator to the ground floor, instead of getting off at the third floor, simply to be with me. She must have. Why else would she seem embarrassed when I asked? The facts led to one conclusion.

She liked me.

And worse, I liked her.

Bod an Donais.

Chapter Fourteen

Serena

The doorbell rang while Chase and I were carrying the remnants of our dinner into the kitchen. My son had volunteered to wash the dishes. A teenage boy. Voluntarily doing chores. Well, I'd always known my kid was no average boy. I supposed growing up without a father had made him feel obligated to lend a hand, since I'd worked crazy hours as a nurse before taking the job with Evan.

The old guilt rose up inside me like a monster crawling out from under my bed. I should've gotten a different job years ago, so I could spend more time with Chase. But nursing was what I'd trained for before Rob died, and I hadn't known what else to do.

At least the chiming doorbell distracted me from the guilt.

I left Chase to start washing, though he reminded me, "They have these machines that wash dishes for you, Mom. It's not the Stone Age anymore."

"Sure, but—" I cut myself off before I said those machines were too expensive. Evan paid me enough that I could afford one. So maybe I should get a dishwasher. Christ, it was hard to give up the penny-pinching mindset after living that way for over a decade. I settled for telling him, "I'll think about it."

Then I hurried to the front door and pulled it open.

Isla MacTaggart smiled. "Serena, I was hoping you'd be home. Am I imposing? I don't want to be a bother, but I thought you and I should have a good blether."

Luckily, I'd spent enough time around the MacTaggart clan to know she was suggesting we have a chat. In this case, a woman-to-woman chat. Did I want to have this kind of conversation with Isla? She seemed nice, but if she wanted to talk about me and Logan, I wasn't sure I was up for that.

"Donnae worry," she said. "I'm not here to interrogate you. Whatever you and Logan do together is your business, not mine. But since my brother clearly likes you, I wanted us to get to know each other better. Logan told me the two of you are flying to Seattle early in the morning, so I won't keep you long, I promise."

Isla wore an outfit similar to the one she'd had on the day we met at Evan and Keely's house. The choker with a large jet stone at its center still encircled her throat, but her dragon earrings had been replaced with silver pentacles.

"Come in," I said, swinging the door open and moving aside. "We can talk in the living room."

She crossed the threshold, and when I pointed toward the doorway to the living room, she headed in that direction.

I closed the door, feeling a little weird about chatting with Logan's sister, and followed her.

We both sat on the sofa, Isla at one end and me at the other, and angled ourselves so we could see each other. Logan's sister looked chic in a Gothic way and very put together, but I was wearing sweats and an old T-shirt with well-worn mule slippers on my feet. Mismatched slippers. Unconsciously, I reached up to feel my hair and… I don't know. Try to fix it? That was a hopeless task. I needed a shower.

"Relax," Isla said. "I'm not here to judge you, Serena. You should see what I look like when I'm at home. You wouldn't recognize me."

"How did you know I was thinking about my crummy clothes?"

"I'm psychic." She maintained a serene expression for about two seconds, then burst out laughing. "I'm having you on. You were touching your hair and looking at your slippers. I love mules, don't you? They're so easy to slip on and off."

"Sometimes they fall off my feet."

"Oh, I hate when that happens." She scooted a little closer. "You must think we're off our heads, my sisters and I. But we're not as eccentric as you might think."

"I don't mind eccentric. Actually, I admire that about you three. You don't care what other people think and do your own thing, which seems to make you happy. That's all that matters."

She nodded gravely. "Aye, but I cannae say the same for Logan. His time in the military and the SIS has made him so closed off."

"He was in the military?"

The revelation shot a cold spike through me. I'd loved one military man and wound up devastated by losing him. I wasn't in love with Logan. Wasn't even sure I liked him. But the thought of developing a relationship with another man who put himself in harm's way on purpose... I wasn't sure I could go through that again.

Logan wasn't in the military or the SIS anymore. Did he still crave danger? Did he need to be a hero, even as a civilian?

"Logan was in the army," Isla said. "I don't know what he experienced during those years, since he won't talk about it, but I know it changed him. Joining MI6 changed him even more. He's afraid to trust anyone."

"I get the feeling you're trying to tell me something, but I don't know what."

She inched closer still. "Logan is a good man. He was a sweet and loving lad, and I know he can be that way again. Maybe not exactly like he was before, but happier than he is now." She touched my knee. "And I'm positive you'll be the one to show him the way."

I opened my mouth, but no words came out. Show him the way? I wasn't a swami or a guru or whatever. If Logan needed way-showing, he wouldn't get that from me. Even if I could figure out how to loosen him up, I wasn't sure I wanted to do that. It would mean getting involved with him. Seriously involved. Relationship involved.

"You're conflicted," Isla said. "But you want to give it a go with him, I can see it in your eyes."

"Are you sure you're not psychic?"

"No, just very perceptive." She folded her hands on her lap. "I have to be. As the oldest child, it's always been my responsibility to look after my sisters and brother. Our parents never forced me to do it, but I wanted to. I love them all so much, and I want them to be happy."

"What about you? Who looks after your happiness?"

She averted her gaze. "We're talking about you and Logan."

"There is no me and Logan. We work together." And occasionally had sex in inappropriate locations. Sure, we'd had lunch together once. And maybe I'd stayed in the elevator instead of getting off at the third floor so I could hang out with Logan a little bit. None of that meant anything. Pathetic excuses, I knew. "Look, I think Logan is nice enough, but I'm not the one to set him straight. Honestly, we don't get along that well."

"Nonsense." She touched my knee again. "I can tell from the way he talks about you, and the way he looks at you, that the two of you get on very well. You're compatible, in the opposites-attract way. He's the rough and tumble sort. You're the nurturing type. A perfect complement to each other."

Rough and tumble? Oh, I definitely could not get involved with a man like that.

I winced, because I had to admit a part of me liked his bad boy side. A somewhat large part of me that kept growing every day. Sex in the copy room? Not my style at all, but when Logan suggested it…

Heat tingled over my skin at the memory.

"The spell should be working by now," Isla said. "Things will be better between you two."

"Spell? What on earth are you talking about?"

"My sisters and I cast a wee spell to make Logan more receptive to the idea of falling in love."

Great, his sisters put a spell on him. Even if I believed in that stuff, I wouldn't want him to develop feelings for me because of a magic incantation. "Does Logan know about this spell?"

"Oh, he knows."

Even better. I couldn't believe Logan would buy into their magical powers, but he must've been less than thrilled with their meddling. If anything, their "spell" had probably made him less receptive to the idea of love.

"Look, Isla," I said, "you're sweet, and I appreciate that you want Logan to be happy, but you've really got the wrong idea about us."

Isla's lips parted, but she didn't get the chance to speak.

"Wrong idea about who?" my son asked.

My focus swerved to the doorway where Chase stood. I swore he hadn't been there a second ago, but there he was now. He must not have heard much, based on his question.

"Oh hello," Isla said, beaming at my son. "It's so nice to see you again, Chase. I'm Isla. We met at the brunch on Saturday."

"Yeah, I remember. You're Logan's sister." Chase rushed over to shake Isla's hand. "Logan's awesome. Are you, like, a witch or a sorceress or something?"

"Yes, I'm a Wiccan."

"Awesome!"

"Chase," I said, "eavesdropping is rude."

"I didn't mean to do it. This house isn't that big."

"Yeah, I know." But I was on edge thanks to my conversation with Isla and all her suggestions of something brewing between me and Logan. "Sorry, honey. I shouldn't have snapped at you."

"It's okay. Were you guys talking about Logan?"

"Aye," my guest said.

Chase aimed his excited face at me. "Are you and Logan, like, dating now?"

What could I say to that? What should I say? *We argue a lot, and sometimes we screw, but I have no fucking idea what we're doing.* No, not an appropriate parent-to-child conversation. I struggled to come up with some kind of response, but I failed.

"They're friends," Isla offered, with a furtive wink at me. "And it's their business. We should leave them to figure things out on their own, don't you think?"

"Sure, yeah," Chase said.

The look on his face told me he really, really wanted me to say I was head over heels for the cool ex-spy, and the wedding would be in two weeks.

Isla clapped her hands on her thighs and got up. "I'll say good night. Serena, please call me anytime you want to talk. I'd like us to be good friends."

"I'd like that too," I said, rising to show her to the door. "Thank you for stopping by, Isla. Maybe we can have lunch sometime."

"That would be lovely." She glanced back at Chase. "Good night, dearie."

Chase said good night too, and Isla left.

The instant I shut the door, Chase rushed up to me. "Are you dating Logan? It would sooooo cool if you were. Logan's awesome."

"Uh-huh." I ruffled his hair, earning a whiny groan from him. "I have to pack for my trip. Remember, Evan will be here at five thirty to pick us up, and after you guys drop me off at the airport, you'll go to Evan and Keely's house for the weekend."

"I know, Mom," he said in a long-suffering tone. "I'm not brain damaged. I can remember things for more than five minutes."

"Just making sure. It's a mom's job to be a pest, you know."

He snorted out a laugh. "Duh."

I tousled his hair again. "I love you too, sweetie."

"Mom," he whined. "You're so embarrassing."

"There's nobody else around, so you can't be embarrassed."

He rolled his eyes.

"Better go pack," I told him. "Scoot."

He rolled his eyes again but hustled to his bedroom.

Chase would have fun with Evan and Keely, but I faced a weekend alone with Logan MacTaggart. Either we would murder each other, or we'd wind up getting it on in the most inappropriate places in Seattle. Evan had insisted Logan and I have hotel rooms right next to each other. At least there was no adjoining door. I thought. I hoped.

Me and Logan. All weekend.

What had Isla called us? The perfect complement to each other. I wanted to dismiss the idea out of hand, but something inside me wouldn't let me do that. Maybe we could be more than fuck buddies. Maybe...

No, no, no, I did not have feelings for Logan.

While I retreated into my bedroom to pack, I couldn't help wondering if Isla's instincts were right. And if Keely was right about why I insisted I hated Logan. And if maybe, possibly, I should try to see past my fears and give him a chance.

Chapter Fifteen

Logan

My sisters showed up at the airport to say goodbye. Evan had meant to simply drop off Serena, but her son insisted on saying hello to me, so both Chase and Evan joined us on the tarmac. With Evan's jet behind us, we talked for a few minutes about banal things, until my sisters arrived. They descended like a plague of locusts—smiling, cheerful locusts dressed like folk-rock singers—and hugged me and Serena so fiercely and so often that I felt sure we both were suffering from lack of oxygen.

When Isla hugged me for the last time, she whispered into my ear, "The spell is working, I can feel it. You are open to the possibility of love. Show Serena who you really are, don't be afraid."

Isla and Elspeth, who had been hugging Serena, switched places. Elspeth threw her arms around me and murmured in my ear, "Serena's wonderful. I'm so happy you finally have a girlfriend."

"Serena is not my girlfriend."

"Donnae ruin it and chase Serena off, Logie."

"Never call me that again."

Elspeth pulled back and pointed at the right side of her head. "What did you say? I didn't hear you. Bad ear, remember?"

"That's your other ear, Elspeth."

"Oh, is it?" she said with a grin.

Isla collected up Kirsty and Elspeth, and the three of them left.

Chase had gone too, to spend the weekend with Evan and Keely.

Serena and I boarded the jet alone.

I dropped onto a sofa and propped my feet on the table in front of it, but Serena gingerly lowered herself onto a chair, gripping the armrests and clamping her teeth over both her lips. Her gaze flitted here, there, and everywhere.

"Something wrong?" I asked as I linked my hands behind my head.

"No…" She hugged herself, one foot tapping furiously.

I should've enjoyed watching her, enjoyed the view of her delectable body swathed in pale-pink trousers that hugged her thighs and a blouse that clung to her torso, not to mention the bra that cradled her breasts, the ones I'd often fantasized about licking and nibbling and squeezing. I couldn't enjoy any of it, though, not with the anxiety evident on her face and in her posture.

"Are you a nervous flyer?" I asked. "You've flown to Scotland several times, so I assumed you were a seasoned veteran."

"Doesn't matter how many times I fly, I'm always like this for takeoff and landing." She glanced out the window. "Once we're in the air, I'll be okay."

"But until then, you'll be a mess? That's not acceptable. I won't watch you squirm until the jet reaches altitude."

She flashed me a scowl. "So sorry I'm ruining your flight experience."

That wasn't what I'd meant, but I decided not to argue with a woman in distress. Her anxiety bothered me more than it should have. I'd traveled with nervous flyers before, but I'd never suffered an overpowering need to ease their anxiety. I should let her deal with it on her own.

I couldn't.

"All right," I said, getting up. "I'm coming."

"You're what?" Wide-eyed, she tracked my movements as I headed toward her. "What are you going to do? Hit me over the head? Or give me the Vulcan death grip?"

I chuckled, kneeling in front of her. "Vulcan death grip? It's a myth. Spock invented it to trick the Romulans into believing Kirk was dead. I think you meant the Vulcan nerve pinch, which knocks you out."

Serena stared at me. "You're a *Star Trek* fan?"

"Oh, aye. My mother loves it, so we grew up watching the show. I've seen dubbed versions of it in several countries, but you haven't lived until you've heard it in Russian."

"I—" Her brows cinched together, making a wee crinkle above her nose. "You are the most confusing man I've ever met."

"Because I like *Star Trek*?"

She chewed the inside of her lip. "Because every time I think I've got you figured out, you throw some new surprise at me."

The engines started up, and the jet rolled across the tarmac toward the runway.

Her fingers clenched the armrests hard enough to turn the knuckles white. She glanced from window to window while gnawing on her lower lip.

I pried her fingers away from the armrests and clasped her hands. "Easy, *gràidh*. Look at me, not the windows. Come on, Serena, look at me."

She swiveled her gaze to mine.

"Tell me how you met Keely," I said. "You've known each other for a long time, haven't you?"

"Are you shitting me? You want to hear my life story when we're about to d—" She froze when the engines revved up, their high-pitched whine growing louder as the jet's speed increased. "Can't talk."

"On to Plan B."

"Plan what?" Her voice had become a high-pitched whisper.

"Donnae worry, I always have at least three backup plans."

I lunged up to mash my lips to hers, thrusting my tongue deep without waiting for her to give me a tacit invitation to ravish her mouth. She could barely speak, much less focus on what I was doing. Not yet, anyway. I slid a hand behind her nape to tip her head back a touch, so I could forge deeper into her mouth. She tasted like sweet coffee and cherries. I scraped my tongue over hers, tickled the roof of her mouth with the tip, groaned when she began to respond with ravenous swipes of her own tongue.

Somewhere in the back of my mind, I noticed we had lifted off the runway.

Not that takeoff stopped me. I'd meant to kiss her only enough to short-circuit her anxiety, but I couldn't stop. Her velvety tongue demanded a response, and I gave it, relishing the odd combination of flavors in her mouth and the pinch of her teeth nipping my bottom lip.

My wits reassembled themselves about the time my cock roused.

I sat back on my heels, the taste of her lingering on my tongue. "You'll be fine now."

Serena gazed at me, her eyes glossy with desire. "Huh?"

"We're in the air." I patted her thigh. "You survived."

The lass blinked several times until she'd regained her senses, then slapped my arm. "That was a dirty trick."

"No trick. I distracted you."

She puckered her lips, but then sighed and slumped into her chair. "Thank you. I guess."

"You're welcome. I guess." I ran my tongue over my lips. "What did you have for breakfast? I tasted cherries and coffee."

"I ate a light breakfast."

"Of what?"

She screwed up her mouth. "Cherry Pop Tarts."

I stifled a laugh. "What will you have for lunch? M&Ms?"

"No," she said, sticking her tongue out. "For your information, I was in a hurry this morning. Besides, Pop Tarts have vitamins and stuff in them."

"You should try a hearty Scottish breakfast. Now that's a meal to get you ready for the day ahead. What you had at brunch on Saturday was only a sampling."

"Oh no, I've heard about the full Scottish breakfast." She wrinkled her nose. "It involves sausage made from pig's blood."

"If I feed you blood sausage, you'll be able to call me disgusting again. I know how you enjoy that."

She hadn't called me disgusting, or any of its synonyms, in quite a while. How strange.

Giving her thigh one more pat, I returned to the sofa. Ankles crossed on the table, I leaned my head back and closed my eyes. A wee nap sounded good.

"May I sit here?"

I opened my eyes to find Serena standing at the other end of the sofa while pointing at it.

"You don't need my permission," I said. "Sit on the sofa, sit on the floor, stand on your head, whatever you like."

She settled her bonnie erse onto the sofa and clasped her hands on her lap. "I thought we should have a conversation."

"We had one a minute ago."

"I mean a real conversation."

Groaning, I shut my eyes again. "When a woman wants to have a real conversation, it means we'll be discussing feelings and all that barmy nonsense."

"It's not crazy to talk about feelings." She cleared her throat. "Isla paid me a visit last night. After talking to her, I realized I'd like to know more about you."

Opening one eye, I peered at her. "Why?"

"I guess being suspicious comes with being a spy, hey?" She shimmied her bottom, inching backward until her back met the sofa. "I want to understand you. We can at least try to be friends."

I glanced at her with both eyes this time. "Friends? We've had sex twice. I don't become mates with women I've fucked."

"Friendship is a starting point."

"What exactly are we starting?"

She huffed, slapping her palms on her thighs. "For heaven's sake, Logan,

I'm trying to be nice. Naturally, you have to turn friendliness into a capital crime. I want to get to know you, that's all."

"You don't want to know me better, lass." I closed my eyes again. "Trust me on that."

"Do I have to smack you to get a straight answer?"

I bit back a Gaelic curse. "Why don't you get to know the pilots better? I'm sure they'd love to have a beautiful woman haranguing them."

The sound of her clothes rustling told me she was moving around, but I had no illusions she would go to the cockpit to have a blether with the pilots or that she would leave me alone. The scent of her drifted to me, infiltrating my senses. She smelled of powder and flowers and indefinable womanly things. Christ, how could she smell like pure woman but taste like Pop Tarts?

And why did that make me want to bend her over the table and shag her until she screamed?

"I'm not going away," she said in a sing-song voice. "I have a teenage son, so you'll have to do a lot better than surly and childish to run me off."

"Childish?"

"Playing possum is juvenile, at the toddler level."

I had no bloody idea what she was talking about, so I looked at her. "Since I've never seen a possum, I can't pretend to be one."

"Playing possum means you're pretending to be asleep."

"Give me one minute of silence and I won't be pretending."

"Logan."

"*Mhac na galla*. Why don't you go back to calling me disgusting and storming out of the room?"

She half turned toward me, her fingers tapping on her legs. "It's been suggested to me that I've been a bitch to you because I'm afraid I might like you. A little bit. Not hate you, at least."

Realizing I couldn't get out of this unwanted conversation, I rubbed my eyes and sat up straighter. "Keely told you that, I imagine. Evan and his wife have become the worst meddlers on any continent."

"It wouldn't actually kill you to be honest with me."

"You want honesty? I'm not the relationship sort, much less the marrying sort. In fact, I am the last man on earth any parent would want their daughter to get involved with."

"Please. You are not the worst man on earth. I can think of three or four who are worse."

I arched one brow. "Three or four? You aren't very good at comforting me."

"Do you want me to comfort you?"

Why had I said that? I hadn't needed or wanted anyone to comfort me in years, not since I was a starry-eyed lad who still believed in happy endings.

Serena tucked one leg under the other. "Isla mentioned you were in the military."

"Yes."

"And?"

I shrugged and rubbed my neck.

She made a disgusted noise. "Trying to have a conversation with you is like talking to a fish."

"Fish don't speak."

"Exactly." She faced forward, drumming her fingers on her thighs. "You are the most infuriating man on the planet. If I knew how to hire a hitman, I'd have you whacked."

"Come on, lass. If you want me dead, at least do me the courtesy of whacking me yourself."

She growled. Loudly.

Making her angry seemed like the only way to stop her from asking questions I didn't want to answer. Maybe I should have told her anything she wanted to know, but I couldn't. If Serena found out about the things I'd done, the men I'd killed, she wouldn't want me anymore.

Why did that matter? I wasn't the man for her anyway.

"You need to talk to me, Logan."

"Only if I want a relationship with you, which I don't." I turned sideways, resting my arm on the sofa's back. "Let's join the mile-high club."

She snorted. "You already blew any chance you had to get in my pants when you refused to talk to me."

"I don't need to share my past with you when all I want is to fuck you on every surface in this jet, starting with the table." I leaned over to skim a hand along the table's glossy surface. "Your scent and your cream will be all over this."

Her cheeks had turned pink, and her pupils had enlarged. But instead of admitting what I'd said made her randy, she curled her lip at me. "I was right the first time we met. You are the most disgusting man on earth."

She slapped me. Hard.

I chuckled, though even I noted the dark edge to it. "You're finally catching on. I'm a right bastard, and I always will be."

Serena stalked down the aisle to the chair farthest from me, one that faced the opposite direction, and flumped onto it.

I had a view of the back of the top of her head.

Maybe I had gone too far in making her angry. She'd thank me for it later, when she finally gave up her fantasy that I might be a decent bloke underneath the surface. I was sparing her from making an enormous mistake. Getting friendly with me would bring her nothing but misery. A woman like Serena Carpenter deserved a good man.

No one with a past like mine ever got a happy ending.

Seducing her was out of the question. Leave the lass alone, that's what I needed to do. Leave her alone and hope she gave up on her fantasy of who she wished I was.

I stretched out on the sofa and tried to sleep, but I only ended up playing possum.

Chapter Sixteen

Serena

Logan and I did not speak for the rest of the flight, or on our way to the hotel, or in the hotel. He walked me to my room—since it was next door to his, that wasn't much of a sacrifice—and then retreated into his own room. Our rooms turned out to be adjacent suites. He said precisely five words to me: "See you in one hour." That was all I'd gotten from him since the moment I'd slapped him.

Why had I let him goad me into getting mad?

Nobody knew how to push my buttons the way he did. Ticking me off hadn't been that hard for him to do, but I couldn't fathom why I'd let his taunts get to me. I didn't want a relationship with him. Did I? No, of course not. Logan didn't want that either. I never should have listened to Keely and let myself believe for even a moment that Logan and I could be anything other than casual lovers.

I couldn't do that anymore. Sex with him confused me even more than his evasions did. I needed a clear head to get through three days with James Bond MacTaggart. If I could avoid him during the daytime, I could slip away to my suite and order room service in the evening. No need to leave my room. No need to see Logan.

First, I had to survive an afternoon with him.

But I had a plan for that.

An hour after he'd skulked off to his suite, Logan knocked on my door.

"The conference is starting," he said. "We need to check in."

He turned on his heels and stalked toward the elevators.

I grabbed my purse and spiral notebook, then hurried after him.

Logan did not speak another word while we exited the hotel or during our cab ride to the conference center. It was two blocks away, and I would've liked the fresh air and exercise of walking there, but I decided not to argue with him anymore today. We registered at the conference and sat through the introductory boringness, all without speaking to each other. I kept glancing at him, but he acted as if I weren't there.

His behavior might have indicated he was still angry about our argument on the plane, but I didn't really believe that was the case. I had the strangest feeling he was ashamed for some reason. I couldn't explain why I thought that. Something in his demeanor, something in his eyes, something intangible and indescribable. He'd transformed into an ass when I asked about his military service. Rob hadn't liked to talk about his tours in Iraq, so I wondered if Logan had served in a war zone too.

I wouldn't find out today.

Logan took me back to the hotel and scurried into his room without so much as saying good night, leaving me to order room service and ponder the mystery that was him. I'd wanted to get away from the man, to hide in my suite and avoid him as much as possible. Now that he'd made the decision for me, I felt weird about it. Three times I picked up the phone in my suite and started to dial the number for his, only to hang up before I finished punching in the digits. Several times I grabbed my cell phone and almost texted him. After that, I tried to sleep.

At two a.m., I finally gave up and resorted to flipping through the TV channels. Since it was the middle of the night, I came across a dirty late-night cable movie. Watching naked people getting it on made me think about Logan, which made my eyes burn for some strange reason, so I switched to a nature documentary. Lions chasing down cute little gazelles didn't bother me half as much as thinking about Logan naked.

Not that I had any idea what he looked like in the buff. But I had a vivid imagination.

I fell asleep at some point but didn't realize it until three confident knocks on the door roused me. Groggy and cotton mouthed, I crawled out of my enormous, very comfy bed and stumbled to the door. When I pulled it open a few inches, Logan smirked.

"Still sleeping at eight o'clock?" he asked. "You can't blame jet lag with a one-hour time difference."

"Didn't sleep well, like that's any of your business." I rubbed my eyes and blinked until at least I could see him clearly. As for thinking clearly, I hadn't achieved that level of wakefulness yet. "Why are you here?"

"The conference starts at nine. It's eight o'clock."

"What?" I flung the door wide open, spinning around like I could summon more brainpower with kinetic energy. "Shit. I have to shower and—"

I froze when I caught sight of Logan.

He was staring at me. At my body. At the skimpy nightie I wore.

"Better hurry," he said, running a hand up and down his clean-shaven jaw while he continued ogling me. "I'll order breakfast while you get dressed."

I ran to my suitcase and dragged it toward the bathroom.

Logan rushed over and snatched the suitcase away from me, picking it up like it weighed nothing instead of the five thousand pounds I was sure it did weigh. He carried my suitcase into the bathroom, then strode over to the phone on the bedside table.

"Thank you," I said.

He mumbled something.

I slammed the bathroom door shut and showered in record time. For my next amazing feat, I got dressed, put on makeup, and blow-dried and styled my hair, all in ten minutes flat. When I ambled out of the bathroom, I looked entirely presentable. Yeah, presentable was all I could manage this morning.

Logan was sitting at the foot of the bed looking delicious, as always, in his gray suit with no tie.

His gaze veered to me, and a slow smile warmed his expression. "You look as beautiful as ever."

"Thanks. You look pretty damn good yourself."

"Breakfast should be here any minute."

I sat down at the foot of the bed a few feet from him. "I'm starving. Hope you ordered a good meal, and not one of those light, nutritious breakfasts that comes with green goo that's supposed to be a drink."

"No goo." He angled toward me. "I ordered pancakes, bacon, sausage, eggs, and waffles with plenty of butter and syrup."

For a couple seconds, I could do nothing but stare dumbly at him. Then I grinned and laughed. "You really do know how to please a woman."

Before our budding conversation could wilt into uncomfortable silence, the food arrived. We moved to the table by the window and dug in. God, it was so good. I hadn't eaten much last night, despite ordering room service. The silent treatment from Logan had left me a bit nauseous. Arguing with him might be a great tool for dieting, but I didn't like the way we'd left things.

I didn't get a chance to bring up the topic of yesterday. He beat me to it.

He stabbed his fork into a waffle and tore off a piece, peeking up at me through his lashes while he consumed the food. "About yesterday…I'm sorry."

"Me too. I shouldn't have slapped you."

"I deserved it. Today will be different. I've come to a decision, and I know what I need to do to set things right."

"That's it? You're not going to explain your behavior?"

"Later. We need to eat and head to the conference."

We ate in silence, rode to the conference center in silence, and didn't speak to each other again until we had entered the venue. I stopped us partway across the cavernous lobby.

He arched a brow at me.

I handed him a piece of paper with handwritten text on it. "I worked out which seminars and workshops we should attend." I pointed at the paper. "The ones written in blue are yours, the red ones are mine."

"What do you mean yours and mine? We're attending these torture sessions together."

"It's more efficient to split up. We'll get more done."

"Evan was very clear when he said I'm to attend the seminars and workshops with you."

"This way is better."

"No, it's not." He angled toward me, his expression one of mock seriousness. "You can't leave me all alone."

That humor, the snarky kind that always made me want to hit him or kiss him or both, had returned to his voice. Whatever had spurred his behavior yesterday, he'd clearly gotten over it this morning.

"Let me guess," I said. "You'll be lost and confused without me."

"Aye."

"You're a big boy, Logan. I think you'll survive."

He moved closer, dipping his head to whisper in my ear. "Are you willing to risk it? If I get lost and starve to death because you weren't there, you might feel guilty."

"Uh-huh." I fought to sound calm and unaffected even while his breaths tickled my earlobe. "Maybe you need therapy. This fear of getting lost seems to be worse than before."

"Let's stay together, Serena. For safety's sake."

"Fine, whatever." I fiddled with my notepad as an excuse to step away from him. "Let's go."

We walked down the hall to the room where our first seminar would take place and strolled down the aisle that bisected the rows of plastic chairs set up inside the room. I planned on sitting in the front row, in the hopes that might deter Logan from trying any hanky-panky, but he seized my hand and half dragged me down the third row from the back. We wound up in the corner farthest from the aisle and from the podium where the speaker would stand.

Logan gestured for me to sit down.

I plopped onto the chair.

He started to move like he was about to sit on my lap.

"Hey!" I gave him a solid shove. "Get your own seat."

"But I need comforting. This room is so large and confusing."

"Honestly, Logan." I pointed at the seat beside mine. "Sit down. In your own chair."

"If you insist." He settled onto his chair. "I can see why Evan likes Keely to talk to him in her schoolteacher voice. The way you spoke to me just now makes me want to do all sorts of filthy things to you."

"No sex talk. No flirting. No anything that might in any way, shape, or form resemble dating behavior." I crossed my legs and clenched my list of seminars so tightly the paper crinkled. "Neither of us wants a relationship."

Why did I feel slightly nauseous when I said that? It was crazy. My need to get to know him had evaporated after his performance yesterday. Yes, one hundred percent gone. I did not want more than sex with Logan, and I didn't even want that anymore.

Okay, maybe I *wanted* it. But I would not indulge my lust.

"Are you sure about that?" he asked.

For a second, I thought he'd read my naughty thoughts. But of course, he was talking about the relationship issue. Had he changed his mind about that? No, he wouldn't.

Had I changed my mind? Again? Vacillating had become my default state these days. Logan confused the fuck out of me.

I laid the paper on my thigh and flattened my palm over it. "Let's focus on the seminar, please."

"But I like talking about sex with you. It makes your cheeks turn a bonnie pink."

"Shush. I said no flirting, so do what I tell you."

He leaned toward me, not quite close enough for his breaths to tickle my ear. "Aye, there's definitely something to the schoolteacher voice."

For the rest of the day, we attended workshops together. Logan flirted, in his odd way, and I ignored it. If he wanted me to act like Keely and keep telling him to behave, I was not going to indulge that fantasy. After the last seminar at four o'clock, Logan and I walked back to the hotel. When we reached our adjacent suites, he informed me he needed to "take care of a few things" and disappeared into his room.

I retreated into mine and kicked my shoes off. I had just stripped down to my slip and underwear when a strange noise drew my attention to the door.

Someone had slid an envelope under it.

Yanking the door open, I stuck my head out and checked left and right. Nobody there. I shut the door and snatched up the unsealed envelope, which had my name written on it in a confident, elegant hand. The envelope held a single sheet of thick ivory paper. Sliding it out, I unfolded the sheet.

"Be ready at eight," it said. "Wear something nice."

Logan had signed the note.

Part of me wanted to stomp over to his suite, bang on the door, and demand he explain. The rest of me, the much larger part, wanted to find out what he had up his sleeve. The idea of a mysterious assignation was exciting.

He had told me to wear something nice. I hadn't brought anything other than conference-appropriate clothes, all slacks and sensible shoes. The hotel had a boutique downstairs, but since Evan had set us up in the swankiest hotel in Seattle, I knew anything I bought here would cost a fortune. Well, Evan had finagled this weekend with Logan. He could pay for me to buy a new dress.

I called Keely to confirm it was okay. She said, "Spend an obscene amount of money. That's an order. We have billions of dollars, honey, go wild." The question of whether Evan would've agreed with that order was answered when he hollered in the background, "Aye, go wild." I couldn't fathom what it would be like to be married to a billionaire. Being the friend of one was bizarre enough.

At three minutes to eight, I sat in my room dressed in a new, outrageously expensive outfit and waited for Logan.

Precisely at eight o'clock, he knocked on the door.

I swung it open, and almost tripped over my own feet, even though I hadn't taken even one tiny step.

Logan wore a kilt, fashioned from the blue MacTaggart clan tartan, with black boots and socks. From the waist down, he was all Scottish. From the waist up, he was modern chic, with a black suit jacket and crisp white dress shirt, and a tie to boot.

Holy heaven, he looked incredible.

Logan offered me his hand. "Come, lass. We have a reservation."

"Where? Why?"

He smiled and chuckled. "At a restaurant, for our first date."

I gazed into his hazel eyes, my body suddenly warm and relaxed and tingly. A date with Logan? We'd both said we didn't want that. Yet here, tonight, I wanted it more than anything.

"For one night," he said, "can we not overanalyze? Let's enjoy spending time together and let the rest work itself out. If after dinner you don't want to be with me, I won't ask you for a date again."

He was still holding his hand out.

I laid my palm in his.

"You look stunning, Serena," he said as he clasped my hand and led me down the hallway. "You're the most beautiful woman on earth, and that's not a line. It's the truth."

I couldn't think of a damn thing to say, so I gave up on trying and let him lead me away.

For our first date.

Chapter Seventeen

Logan

The maître d' escorted us to a booth in the far corner of the restaurant, a secluded spot where no one would notice or disturb us. I'd asked for this sort of table when I made the reservation earlier today. I wanted Serena all to myself. Never in my life had I eaten at a five-star restaurant where the prices had more zeroes in them than my paycheck. My old paycheck. I hadn't worked at Evanescent long enough to have received my pay yet, so I'd been forced to ask Evan if I could use the company credit card and pay him back later.

"Don't worry about it," he'd said, sounding almost offended that I'd asked. "It's a business expense."

"But this is a personal dinner, not business related."

"You and Serena work for me, and you're in Seattle on business. Charge it to the company account."

That seemed wrong to me, but then, Evan had more money than any normal human could imagine having, and so did many of his clients. A business dinner that cost a small fortune might not raise any red flags with the tax authorities. I decided to accept the CEO's decision and move on.

I had more important things to focus on tonight. One thing, actually.

And she was just sliding into the semicircular booth across from me.

When she'd opened the door to her suite earlier and I had first glimpsed her, the sight had robbed me of any capacity to form meaningful sounds. I was fair certain I'd mumbled nonsense while my chin dropped to my chest and saliva dribbled from my lips. Maybe it hadn't been quite that bad. She had taken my breath away, though.

Her black lace dress clung to every curve on her body but flared out into a flowing skirt beneath her hips. The neckline plunged far enough below her breasts to be tantalizing, though not so much that it would raise eyebrows among the stuffier crowd. The dress left most of her shoulders bare yet somehow held the dress up, and the semitransparent sleeves extended all the way down to her wrists. Other parts of the dress seemed semitransparent too, like the fabric that covered her belly. Her black shoes featured heels so high and slender I wondered how she managed to stay upright.

And her hair. It flowed over her shoulders in golden-brown waves and curled around her face in a way that made me imagine brushing those locks away from her face while I buried myself inside her lush body.

Bod an Donais. She was a vision of sensual beauty. A goddess come down from Mount Olympus.

I'd never been poetic, but I was afflicted with a sudden urge to blether romantic nonsense about her creamy skin and her stunning gray eyes.

Now, ten minutes after I'd first seen her in that dress, she had decided to sit on the exact opposite side of the round table instead of next to me.

"Why are you over there?" I asked.

"So we can look at each other while we're eating and talking."

I shook my head, petting the curved bench beside me. "No, lass, you belong over here. Where I can touch you and smell you. This is our first date, after all."

She seemed to think about that for a moment before she slid across the bench to sit an arm's length away from me.

Like hell I'd let her get away with that.

I slung an arm around her waist and dragged her closer. We were inches apart. Much better. I nuzzled her hair, sucking in a deep draft of Serena-scented air, and moaned. Fuck, she smelled good. Always.

"What are you doing, Logan?"

Reluctantly, I pulled my face away from her hair. "I love the way you smell."

"I don't use perfume or scented oils or whatever."

"No, it's your natural scent. All woman and sex and everything else that drives men wild."

"Never thought I'd see the day Logan MacTaggart gets mushy."

Was I mushy? I had no idea. I hadn't waxed poetic about her eyes or her hair, so she must've been exaggerating. A mushy man would've written a sonnet or…something. I had no clue how to romance a woman.

I settled a hand on her thigh. "That wasn't mushy, lass. It was seduction."

She turned her face toward me, her lips curving into a sweet, sexy smile. "Don't get ahead of yourself. I haven't decided if I'm sleeping with you tonight."

"You will." I draped an arm across the bench behind her. "We want each other, Serena, and there's nothing stopping us tonight. This isn't the office. It's not someone else's house. We have two suites at our disposal, and I intend to take advantage of that fact. You can say no, but we both know it would be a lie. Do me the courtesy of telling the truth when I ask you to spend the night with me."

"Honesty goes both ways, you know." She tapped a finger on my chest. "And you haven't exactly excelled at telling the truth. Whenever I mention your military service or your time with MI6, you do whatever it takes to end the conversation. Last time, you got so obnoxious that I slapped you."

"I remember." And I had deserved it.

She angled toward me, her breaths reflecting off my face. "If you really want to date me, start talking. Conversation is how people get to know each other. It's an integral part of the process." She sank back against the bench. "Or that's what I hear. I haven't dated in a really, really long time."

"Neither have I. The last time I took a lass out on a date, neither of us had a mobile phone in our pockets."

"It was the Stone Age, eh?" She nudged me with her elbow. "You're not that old. Me, I was born before the wheel was invented."

The sparkle in her eyes assured me she was having me on. No one who saw Serena Carpenter would describe her as old. Vitality poured out of her. Still, it was possible our age difference made her uncomfortable.

"Does it bother you that I'm younger?" I asked.

She made a dismissive noise. "I'm not Keely. I don't have a hang-up about age. Besides, I've been with men younger than you."

"They were wee bairns, then?"

"Ha-ha. Last year I had a brief thing with a twenty-year-old."

Part of me wanted to ask what sort of "brief thing" they'd had, but it wasn't my business. Not yet. Before I could ask her questions like that, I needed to reciprocate the honesty she'd given me, tonight and that day when I'd bought her lunch and she'd confessed to being melancholy because her son wanted to visit his grandparents for the summer.

"When does Chase leave for Vermont?" I asked.

"Tuesday." She stared down at her lap, her fingers moving restlessly over the fabric of her dress. "I agreed to let him stay there for two months."

I brushed a curl of hair away from her cheek. "You'll miss him."

"Of course I will. He's never been gone for more than a few days before. When he was twelve, he begged me to send him to summer camp, but after three days, he was begging me to let him come home."

"Did you?"

"Yes. I missed him then too." She snatched her napkin off the table and focused intently on spreading it over her lap. "Not sure he'll miss me this time."

"He will."

"We'll see." She took a deep breath and raised her face to me. "Your turn. Why don't you want to talk about your past in the army and MI6?"

"Those are serious topics, and I was hoping we could save the serious discussion for after."

"After what?"

"Dinner, dancing, and sex."

"Okay, we'll put a pin in that." She hesitated, eying me for a moment before asking, "What about your sisters? I'd love to hear about them."

An image of Elspeth flashed in my mind, a memory of a day long ago, of her pallid face and brave smile. I grabbed my water glass and gulped down half its contents, but the tightness in my throat lingered. "That would also be part of the serious conversation we'll have later."

"You can't use that excuse for everything I ask you about."

"I won't. Just…pick another topic. Please."

"All right." She scrutinized me for a moment, her attention making me squirm like I hadn't done since I was a teenager and my parents had caught me sneaking a girl into my bedroom after midnight. Fortunately, Serena gave up her scrutiny, sighed, and smiled. "Tell me about your cousins, then. That can't be serious territory. You cousins are some of the happiest people I've ever met."

"Every single one of them is completely insane."

Her smile broadened, and her eyes sparkled with humor. "You can't fool me, Logan MacTaggart. You like your cousins. Evan is your best friend."

My best friend? I didn't remember ever having one of those. Wasn't it something people only had in movies? Serena and Keely were best friends, but it was different with women. Wasn't it?

Serena touched her fingertip to the spot above my nose, between my eyebrows. "You've got a little divot there, which means you're confused. You shouldn't be. It's obvious you and Evan are best friends."

"Bollocks. I hardly know him."

"You're in America now, and we say bullshit instead of bollocks." She traced a line down my nose with her finger, tapping it on the tip. "No bullshitting, Logan. You were Evan's best man when he married Keely, you flew all the way to America because he asked you to, and you took a job he offered you even though you're sure it was just a matchmaking scheme. Why would you do that unless you're very fond of Evan?"

"Maybe I did it for Keely. It's hard to say no to a pregnant woman." We both knew that was bullshit, but after years as a covert agent, my default response in uncomfortable situations was to lie and evade. When Serena opened her mouth, I held up a hand to silence her. "I'm overflowing with shit, I know. Maybe I do like Evan, but I have no bloody idea if he's my best friend. He should have a say in that, shouldn't he?"

"Let's call and ask him."

Her cheeks dimpled when she said it, and I knew she was teasing me again.

"Go on," I said. "Call Evan."

"Is that a dare?" Her lips cinched into a tight pucker, but they twitched as if she struggled not to smile. "I can't call him. I didn't bring my phone."

"You can borrow mine."

"That won't be necessary." She picked up a menu, flipped it open, and froze. "Are these prices in American dollars or Indian rupees? I've never seen this many zeroes on a menu."

"Don't worry about the price. A billionaire is paying for our dinner."

"Right. Okay." She blew out a breath. "Oh, lobster sounds fabulous."

We both ordered the lobster and talked while we waited for our meal. I told Serena stories about my barmy cousins, and she told me about how she met Keely and some of the things they'd done together to entertain themselves in Carrefour, Utah. During dessert, she asked me about the MacTaggart clan's love for the Highland games.

"Not every MacTaggart enjoys sports," I said. "Ask Evan about shinty, and you'll get an earful."

"He had fun playing it last summer."

"Aye, but he refuses to admit he doesn't hate shinty anymore."

"Do you like it?"

"Yes." I swallowed my last bite of dessert and leaned back, aiming my most devilish smile at her. "I like any chance to batter someone. The Buchanans can attest to that."

"Come off it, Logan. You are not a bad man." She patted my cheek. "You are the strangest MacTaggart I've met, though."

"You must not have met Rory or Iain."

"Oh, I know them both. They're odd, but you're weirder."

I didn't know whether to be offended or honored she'd given me the title of oddest MacTaggart. "What about Evan? He's strange too."

"Sure, but you're the only one in your family who wants everybody to think you're a villain."

The tack of this conversation had shifted, and I didn't like it. We were veering dangerously close to the serious topics I'd wanted to put off until later. All through dinner, I'd listened to her talk about her friendship with Keely, and I'd been entranced. Her face lit up when she told me about the people she loved, and every time that happened, all I could think about was taking her upstairs and making love to her.

"Have you been to the Highland games?" I asked. "The MacTaggart version, that is."

"Not yet. I hear Rory's hosting them behind his castle again this year."

"Aye, Rory loves to show off for his wife. He says she gets very randy when she watches him toss cabers."

"Guess you ought to toss a few around for me."

"I don't need cabers to make you randy."

"That's true." She settled her hand on my thigh. "Let's go upstairs."

"Not yet." I got up and offered her my hand. "It's time for dancing."

"I thought you were joking when you said that."

"No, *gràidh*, I want to dance with you."

She looked mildly startled for a moment, but then switched her attention to my hand, regarding it with suspicion. "I don't know how."

"Neither do I." Bending over, I leveled our gazes. "Can you shuffle your feet?"

"Yeah, but—"

"Let's shuffle together." I straightened and offered her my hand again. "Please."

She settled her palm on mine.

I led her out onto the dance floor, where couples engaged in various versions of dancing, everything from regal ballroom style to foot-shuffling worse than mine. I held Serena close, one hand on her back, the other clasping hers. We moved across the floor with our gazes bound to each other while a small band played a romantic melody, but I paid no attention to the music. My focus stayed on her, on those beautiful gray eyes that studied me in a different way now, a softer way, and I found myself entranced by this woman, the only woman who'd ever made me want to romance her. And I did want to do that. As much as I'd enjoyed arguing with her, something had changed between us. I'd fought it for days, even trying to make her angry so I could avoid confronting whatever this was that she made me feel.

Last night, while I lay awake contemplating my bad behavior, I'd come to a realization. I wanted more with Serena. Forget rude, disgusting Logan. Tonight, all I wanted was to give her what she deserved.

Which was everything.

The song ended, and we wandered back to our table so I could sign the credit card slip, then we hurried to the elevator. Four people piled into the car with us. I silently cursed their presence, because I needed to kiss Serena this instant.

I needed to have my hands on her sensual body and to taste her mouth, and to not give up that pleasure until the elevator stopped on our floor. I couldn't do any of that. The two men and two women who'd joined us in the car all knew each other and seemed to have started their partying already, based on their overly boisterous laughter and the way they kept stumbling into each other.

I settled for holding Serena's hand.

One of the men pointed at me and laughed a bit too vigorously. "Look at the guy in a skirt. Do you wear a bra too?"

I ignored the drunken eejit. Worse men had lobbed far worse insults at me.

The eejit staggered toward Serena, and his gaze swerved to her breasts. "Whoa, you look like a real girl—a real hot one. What are you doing with a guy in a skirt? If you want a real man, I'm available."

"No thank you," Serena said coolly. "Real men wear plaid skirts."

She turned to face the doors.

The eejit swung an arm up, intent on grabbing hers.

I seized his wrist, nailed him with my coldest stare, and spoke in a deceptively hushed tone. "Best think about that, laddie. I could separate your shoulder with one small movement. Is harassing my woman worth the agony?"

The laddie stared at me, his eyes bulging and his face going pale. "I-I was only fooling around. Sorry."

I released his wrist. "Don't try it again."

He staggered backward, shaking his head.

The elevator stopped. The second the door slid open, the eejit and his friends rushed out.

As the doors glided shut, Serena turned toward me. "Wow, you really scared the living daylights out of them. I've seen steely glares before, but yours is the best by far."

"It's easy to scare off a drunk eejit."

"He was an idiot, for sure." She ran her tongue across her lip in a sensuous glide. "But I got a tingle down my spine when you told that toad to buzz off."

"I didn't tell him to buzz off. I told him I could dislocate his shoulder."

"Yeah, I know." She moved closer and skated her hands up my chest. "Never knew threats of violence could make me so hot, but I want to shove my head under your skirt and do filthy things to you."

My cock twitched, roused by her offer, but I couldn't let her do it. I meant to seduce her the right way, not the way I'd done twice before. Take my time. Make love to her slowly.

She bent her knees, lowering her face closer and closer to my kilt.

I grasped her shoulders and urged her upward. "I want to kiss you, *lean-nan*."

Now I was calling her sweetheart in Gaelic. Maybe she was right, and I had gone mushy.

Her lips kinked into a naughty smile. "A kiss? That's what I was trying to give you."

"No, Serena." I pushed her back against the wall and molded my body to hers, caging her there. "On the mouth. That's how I mean to kiss you."

I caught her lower lip between my teeth and released it little by little.

She sucked in a breath.

And I kissed her.

Chapter Eighteen

Serena

Logan kissed me like he'd never kissed me before, with a tenderness and gentleness that stunned me, and yet somehow made it even more sensual. He savored my lips for the whole ride to our floor, never taking the kiss deeper, seeming satisfied to simply revel in the feel of my lips. I reveled too, in the way he swept his lips over mine, back and forth, and sneaked his tongue out to taste my skin. I sampled his flesh too, licking and nibbling until he groaned long and low.

When the elevator doors opened, we couldn't stop kissing.

He thrust a hand out to prevent the doors from closing, and without separating his mouth from mine, he wrapped an arm around me and guided us out of the car. We stumbled down the hallway toward our adjacent suites. Our kissing grew more passionate as our tongues delved deep and twined around each other, our hands groped each other's bodies, and we both grunted and moaned from the sheer pleasure of devouring each other.

Logan pushed me up against a wall and pulled his head back.

Breathing hard from our kiss, I glanced around and gradually made sense of our surroundings. "This is my suite."

"Aye. It has a larger bed than mine. It's bigger overall."

"Why didn't Evan give you the bigger bed? You are more sizable than me."

"Evan and I agreed you should have the larger room." He stepped back a few inches, enough that he could rake his molten gaze over my whole body. "Where's your keycard?"

I shoved a hand inside my bodice, under my breast, and retrieved the keycard I'd taped there. I offered it to Logan. "Here you go."

He smirked as he took it and noticed the two strips of clear tape dangling from it. "That's an interesting place to keep your room key."

"No pockets in this dress, and I didn't want to carry a purse. This was a practical solution."

"It's still warm." He pressed the keycard to his cheek, then held it to his nose so he could sniff it. "And it smells like you."

"Open the damn door already."

He grinned, the expression so wickedly erotic it made my sex throb. "I love it when you're ravenous."

Before I could swear at him again, he unlocked the door and ushered me inside.

I'd left a lamp on, the one on the bedside table. It provided the only illumination, since I'd shut the drapes to cover the floor-to-ceiling windows. Logan ambled over to the table by the windows and switched on the lamp beside it. The bulbs of both lamps provided a warm glow that spilled out around us, a sensuous kind of light that seemed to caress my skin.

He held out his hand to me.

I took his hand, letting him usher me toward a chair by the windows.

"Sit," he said. "Please."

"Why? I want to undress you. Been waiting a long time to see you naked."

"The wait is over." He gestured for me to sit. "But I want to take it slow with you tonight, and feeling your hands on me will destroy my willpower."

Destroy his willpower? No man had ever claimed I affected him that powerfully.

Logan certainly shattered my willpower, for reasons I still couldn't understand. Maybe I didn't need to. He made me feel things I hadn't experienced in a long time, and some things I'd never experienced before. Maybe all I needed to know was how good he made me feel.

He sauntered to the bed, pulled something out of his inside jacket pocket, and dropped it onto the table. As he turned back toward me, I saw what he'd left behind.

Condoms.

Oh yes, a man like Logan would never forget protection.

Logan perched on the bed's edge, removing his big black boots and his socks. Rising, he moved past the foot of the bed to take up a position directly in front of me but a couple yards away. He was granting me a perfect view of him from head to toe, with the lamplight spilling over him. The canny Scot had chosen the perfect spot to stand in, so I would have the best view of his nakedness. He knew how much I wanted to see him, and he always gave me what I wanted.

In terms of sex.

And at dinner tonight. He'd been the perfect date, sexy and charming, considerate and exclusively focused on me.

Logan shrugged out of his jacket, folded it over, and tossed it with a seemingly careless movement. The jacket landed on the chair across the table from mine, draped over it like he'd planned for it to end up like that.

I had no doubts he had planned it. Logan MacTaggart had skills, and I'd only scratched the surface of his many hidden talents.

He tugged his shirt hem out from under his kilt and the belt that held it in place, then removed his tie. He tossed it away as expertly as he had gotten rid of his jacket. One by one, he unhooked the buttons of his shirt, revealing his muscled chest a little at a time, teasing me with increasing glimpses of his toned flesh. Once he'd undone the last button, he slid the shirt off his shoulders and let it fall to the floor.

My God, the man had a gorgeous chest. His years of working outdoors, as a bricklayer, had sculpted his body into a masterpiece of Classical beauty. With my gaze, I traced the lines of his pectorals, then followed a path along the center of his well-defined abs straight down to his kilt. His skin was smooth, with only the barest hint of fine, dark hairs that tapered down to the region below his kilt, where he hid the rest of his manly treasures.

Oh yes, I knew without any doubt he kept a priceless treasure down there. I'd glimpsed it, felt it inside me, and come with my body clenched around it.

Logan unhooked his belt, slowly, deliberately, his gaze on me the whole time.

I glanced up at him twice, but I couldn't keep my attention away from what he was doing. His strong fingers eased the leather out of the buckle millimeter by millimeter, and I knew he was teasing me in a different way now. No humor, just pure sensual determination.

He ditched the belt, and it thumped down on the table. He held his kilt in place with one hand, the plaid clenched in his fist.

My pulse raced. I couldn't catch my breath, overcome by a ridiculous anticipation. I'd seen men naked before. Lots of men. Well, maybe not *lots*, but more than a few. The realization I was about to see Logan naked for the first time shouldn't have set my tummy to fluttering and my sex to tingling.

He dropped the kilt.

My jaw crashed to the floor. It was a moronic response, to be slack-jawed and speechless, barely able to breathe, because I'd gotten my first good look at his dick. I couldn't help it. If I'd thought his upper body was gorgeous, it had nothing on his nether regions. Men's penises had always seemed to me like rather silly looking appendages. I mean, they just hung there most of the time, like limp bananas. Not that I'd ever told a man my opinion of their most treasured body part. Not even Rob knew. Some things a woman had to keep to herself.

But Logan… Holy shit, the man had a beautiful cock. Long, sleek, and thick, it hung between his legs in a manner I could only describe as majestic. It sounded stupid, and there was no way on earth I'd ever tell Logan that, but it really did seem like the best description. He also had the most muscular thighs I'd ever seen, with defined sinews I could imagine flexing with every thrust.

I licked my lips, my mouth watering.

His majestic cock twitched.

Logan strode up to me and knelt at my feet. With warm, sure hands, he slipped my high heels off my feet, letting his fingers trail down my inner ankles and along the sensitive skin on my soles. I shivered when he did that—twice, once for each foot. Two little shivers of heat and hunger. He did this to me so easily, with such skill and patience and single-minded focus.

He stood, gesturing for me to do the same. "Your turn."

Stripping for Logan? The thought of it made me instantly wet, instantly desperate to have him inside me. But he'd undressed for me, so I owed him a striptease of my own.

And God, I wanted to undress for him.

I moved to the spot where Logan had stood a moment ago.

He lowered his naked body onto the chair I'd vacated. A slow and lascivious smile spread across his lips. "The seat is still warm. From you."

My nipples had already gone hard, but the dirty way he spoke those words made the tips ache and harden even more.

I reached behind my neck for the zipper on my dress, but I couldn't quite get it. My fingers were trembling. Logan's striptease had gotten me so excited I couldn't grasp the tiny zipper. Great. I'd managed to get into the dress, but now I couldn't get out of the damn thing.

"Need a hand?" Logan asked.

"Um, yeah."

He crooked a finger.

I heeded his come-hither gesture and approached his chair, turning around to give him my back.

He pulled the zipper down inch by inch, letting his fingertips brush my skin, leaving a trail of electric pleasure in their wake. Cool air kissed my back, from my shoulders all the way down to my waist, and I knew the dress hung wide open now. I hadn't worn a bra, since it would've shown through the sheer back of my dress.

I was about to move away when his lips touched my skin. Warm, sensual lips. He kissed his way up my spine, over my shoulder, and pressed an open-mouth kiss to my throat. His tongue flicked over my flesh, damp and velvety, and my breathing grew heavier. Desire settled low in my belly, making my clitoris pulsate.

Logan pulled away. "Finish."

His voice had gone rough.

I walked back to the stripping spot and pivoted toward him.

Eyes half closed, he drank me in while stroking himself with one hand, the movements measured and unhurried.

I eased the dress off my shoulders, letting it slide down until I'd exposed all of my breasts except for the nipples. Then I waited.

Logan hauled in a deep, ragged breath and released it in one big gust. "You're a vixen, aren't you? Teasing me with your body."

"You like it." I let the dress slip down to my waist, my arms still caught in the sleeves. "You teased me, so I'm teasing you."

He stopped stroking himself, though he kept his hand around his erection. "I don't have your self-control. I might come before you get your dress off."

"Self-control? I have none of that where you're concerned."

I wriggled my arms free of the sleeves and let the dress tumble to the floor to pool around my feet, leaving me in only a pair of sheer black-lace panties. I hooked my thumbs inside the panties, about to shove them down.

Logan held up a hand. "Let me do that."

He unfurled that big, beautiful body and strode toward me.

Standing face to face, inches apart, we gazed into each other's eyes for several seconds in silence, the sizzle between us so intense I expected to see waves of heat curling up around us. The green flecks in his eyes seemed darker somehow, probably thanks to the subdued lighting. The golden brown of his irises lured me in like he'd cast a spell over me to make me pliable to his will and his alone. What was it about this man? How did he mesmerize me without speaking a word or even touching me? I lost control with him, every time we were alone. That used to scare me.

Tonight, I luxuriated in the freedom of it.

He slipped his fingers inside the waistband of my panties and tugged them down so very slowly, bending his knees to lower his body in sync with the speed of his fingers. They grazed my skin and elicited tiny shocks of pleasure that made my skin tighten and my sex grow slicker and hotter. He drew my panties down over my hips, then let them go. They fluttered down to my ankles.

I stepped out of them.

Logan sat back on his heels, his face level with my mound. "*Mo gaol,* you're beautiful. Even better than I'd imagined." He glided his hands up my thighs, over my hips, and splayed them over my belly. "Every inch of you is perfect."

If anyone else had said that, I would've dismissed it as part of the seduction. With Logan, the tone of his voice told me he meant it.

He swept me up in his arms and carried me to the bed, managing to hold on to me while he flipped the covers back. When he laid me down on the mattress, with my head on the pillow, he kissed me sweetly. I held his face in my hands, skimming my thumbs over his lips, gazing into his eyes and wondering how I'd wound up here, with this man. I'd thought I hated him. Tonight, I couldn't for the life of me remember why.

Without looking away from me, he levered his body over mine, poised on all fours. He nuzzled my throat. I arched my neck and grasped his arms. He kissed, licked, and nibbled his way down my throat and past my collarbone, where he paused to marvel at my breasts like he'd never seen a woman's tits before. Carefully, he placed his hand over one breast, curling his fingers around it.

"I was right," he murmured. "They do fit in my hands like apples."

"When did you think that?"

"The first time I saw you, and every time since."

He shifted his hand to expose my nipple and the areola, then sealed his mouth around them. The moist heat of his mouth penetrated my skin, seeming to dive straight down to my core. He lapped at my stiff peak, suckled it gently, and grazed his teeth over it, repeating the actions over and over and over until I was gasping and clenching the pillow.

Then he switched to the other breast.

I was writhing and moaning by the time he lowered his body onto mine and slithered down, down, down until his face hovered over my mound. He swirled his fingers through the hairs there, obsessed with his task, and didn't stop until I spread my legs, desperate for more, for everything. Still, he toyed with me, parting my folds with two fingers and blowing a stream of air over my swollen flesh, then gliding his fingers down and up, nudging my taut nub.

"Please, Logan," I moaned.

He closed his mouth over my clit and sucked.

My hips bucked up off the bed.

With both hands, he grasped my ass before it hit the mattress again, elevating my hips to give him better access. He swirled his tongue around my nub, scraped his teeth across it, teased it with the tip of his tongue, and lapped at it tenderly. Finally, he began to swipe his tongue back and forth, up and down, varying the speed and the space between each stroke until my body went rigid and the breath caught in my throat.

He stopped lapping at my flesh but kept his mouth over my clitoris.

For what seemed like forever, I hung suspended in that moment before climax, desperate for it to happen but wishing this maddening bliss would go on and on. I couldn't breathe, couldn't move, couldn't think about anything except Logan and his incredible mouth.

With one swipe of his tongue, he sent me hurtling over the edge.

I cried out as I plunged my hands into his hair, clinging to him through every spasm of my climax, while he lashed his tongue over my flesh to draw every ounce of pleasure from my body. When the orgasm finally faded, I lay limp and panting.

He rose onto his hands and knees again as he reached for something on the table.

My hormone-drenched brain couldn't process what he was doing. I heard the rip of foil, but even that clue failed to register. Only when he pushed inside me did I rouse from my haze of bliss, amazed by how gently he entered me and how completely he filled me. Once he'd gone in as far as he could, he hesitated, his gaze searching mine.

"What is it?" I asked.

He shook his head. "I don't know. This is so… Are you sure you want to be with me?"

"Yes, I'm sure." I gripped his biceps. "I want you, Logan. Only you."

How could he doubt that? Maybe he was as stunned by the way our relationship had changed as I was. Tonight, we'd behaved like a normal couple on a date.

And it had been wonderful.

"I want only you, Serena." He kissed my forehead. "Only you."

He pulled his hips back and thrust into me, the pressure unyielding and delicious. I grasped his arms tighter, loving the firmness of him inside me, loving the way he withdrew almost all the way only to plow into me again, lost to the storm of sensations he evoked with every movement. He kept his gaze on mine the whole time, and I couldn't look away. While he pumped faster and harder, I was entranced by the need that tightened his features and darkened his eyes, even as the pleasure mounted inside me. After the way he'd made me come earlier, I didn't know if I'd survive another climax. He might blow me apart from the inside out, and I wouldn't give a damn.

To die with Logan inside me… That would be the ultimate bliss.

Maybe that thought was a bit morbid, but in this moment, it seemed right.

He bent his arms until his full weight rested on his elbows.

I locked my legs around his hips and latched my arms around him.

"Serena, *mo gaol*," he said as he dropped his head onto the pillow beside mine. His thrusts grew wilder, penetrating deeper, until our bodies bounced on the mattress and we clung to each other like we might spin away into the depths of outer space without our bodies bound to each other. "*Mo leannan*, I—"

He came with a strangled shout.

To feel his release pulsing inside me, it set off my own climax. I clutched him with my whole body, from my arms and legs to the muscles deep inside me, and buried my face against his neck as I cried out again, louder than before, while my nails dug into his flesh.

We lay there for a moment, wrapped around each other, without speaking or moving. I couldn't budge a muscle, couldn't think, spent in body and mind. His big body on top of me should've felt heavy and crushing, but instead, the weight and heat of him felt like the sweetest bliss I'd ever experienced. In a few seconds, maybe another minute, he'd move off me, for sure. I didn't want him to. I loved this intimacy, this moment, this night with the last man on earth I thought I'd ever want to cuddle with or sleep with all night, and certainly not to date or dance with or any of the other things couples did together.

But I did want it. All of it.

With Logan MacTaggart.

Chapter Nineteen

Logan

I rolled off Serena to lie next to her on my side, suddenly cold from the loss of her body heat. I scratched my chest, but the strange feeling there wouldn't go away. What was happening to me? I'd never had an epiphany in my life. Other people talked about them, some even claimed to have experienced such a thing, but I always dismissed it as their imaginations. What was an epiphany, anyway? A moment of clarity? A sudden realization? No one should need a proverbial light bulb to pop on and show them the way. It was ridiculous.

Yet here I was, gazing at Serena like I'd never seen her before, overwhelmed by the strangest sensation that something pivotal had happened tonight. Everything had changed.

No, it was nonsense.

I'd made love to Serena. I had taken her to dinner and danced with her. That didn't mean my life was irrevocably altered by one evening with a beautiful woman. But when I looked at her and witnessed the softness in her eyes and her expression, the lovely way her lips curled up at the corners, my chest ached.

Maybe I was having a mild heart attack.

You're so full of shit, MacTaggart. It's not a heart attack.

Serena lay naked beside me, relaxed and sated, but a few goose bumps had cropped up on her arms. I tugged the covers over her, up to her neck.

The lass laughed, a gentle, affectionate sound that made my chest ache again.

"You've covered me up like a mummy, Logan," she said, pushing the covers off her shoulders and wriggling her arms free of them.

"I didn't want you to be cold."

"Thank you." She reached out to lay a hand on my cheek. "You're so sweet."

"What happened to disgusting and loathsome?"

"Changed my mind." She smiled again in that endearing way, still holding her palm to my cheek. "But now I see the real you. Isla's right. Underneath that steely mask, you are sweet and kind."

My mouth might've fallen open in that moment. I stopped blinking, for certain. No one had called me sweet or kind in years, not since I'd been a naive lad at school. Well, my sisters occasionally called me those things. No one else did.

Until tonight.

"Don't look so shocked," Serena said. "You let your guard down and let me see the real you. I feel like I'm finally getting to know you."

"Twice you've said you finally see the real me, but I haven't changed. You've seen who I really am since the day we met." I peeled her hand away from my face, but couldn't quite give it up yet, so I held her hand between both of mine. "I'm a bastard, Serena. That's who I am. Even if I want to be the kind of man you need, it's not possible."

She trailed the fingertips of her other hand over my cheek. "You can't fool me anymore. The man who just made love to me feels more than lust, and the man who took me on a romantic date wants more than a quickie in the copy room."

"We had sex a minute ago. You're suffering from a hormone-induced fantasy that I'm a normal human being." I set her hand on her belly, on the blanket that covered her. "I stopped being normal or human a long time ago. You can't do and see the things I have and keep your humanity intact. You have to cordon off those parts of yourself, or you'll go mad."

"That's crap, Logan. You are human, through and through." She sat up, and the covers slid down to her waist. "I get that you've been through awful stuff I can't even imagine. But stop trying to make me hate you. It won't work anymore, I'm wise to your game."

"It's no game." I sat up too, but even the sight of her naked breasts couldn't arouse me. "You need to walk away from me, for your own good."

She lifted her chin, giving me the haughty look that usually made me want to bend her over a piece of furniture. "You don't tell me what to do. I decide that."

"But you keep making the wrong decision."

The woman studied me with narrowed eyes for a moment that seemed to last forever. My skin began to itch, and my throat went thick.

"Oh, I get it," she said at last. "You're panicking, Logan style, because we shared an incredibly intimate experience. It was more than sex. We talked and danced and flirted and then we made love. Now you're scared."

I started to speak, meaning to deny everything she'd said, but I was paralyzed. Was she right? Was I panicking? I'd faced down terrorists and double agents, but a woman who wanted more than sex scared the hell out of me? No, it couldn't be that. It couldn't be.

"You know I'm right," she said, laying both her hands on one of mine. "It's okay to be scared. I am too. I haven't wanted more than sex with any man since my husband. Flings were all I thought I needed. One-nighters, maybe the occasional week-long thing. Nothing more. But with you, with the man I thought I hated, I suddenly want everything."

"Not sure I can give you that."

"I believe you can if you want to, but I'm not proposing marriage. Let's get to know each other, really get to know each other, and see what happens."

Serena Carpenter was the most beautiful woman I'd ever seen, and the most exciting lover I'd ever had, but she was more than that. She had a keen mind, a soul-deep compassion, and a strength of spirit that made her even more enticing. I shouldn't have been surprised. She had lost her husband and raised a child on her own.

I looked down at our hands, both of hers covering one of mine, and carefully threaded my fingers with hers. "Why would you trust I'll keep being this way? I changed rather suddenly."

"You haven't changed at all. I've seen glimpses of the good man underneath the obnoxious exterior before tonight." She hooked a finger under my chin and urged me to look up at her. "Even that day in the copy room, I saw it. When the lid slammed down on my hand, you were very concerned."

"It was my fault."

"That was an accident, but you took the time to make sure I wasn't hurt. That's not a bastard thing to do."

"But—"

"No, Logan. You are a good man. Accept it." She feathered her lips over mine. "Just don't get obnoxious again when I ask about your time in the military and MI6."

The time had come to tell her what she wanted to know. I'd said I would tell her after dinner, dancing, and sex. This was after. I didn't want to do it, but I always kept my word.

"To tell you about that," I said, "I need to explain about my sisters first. No one in the MacTaggart family is what most people would call normal, but my sisters have reasons for their odd way of life."

"Normal is overrated. I happen to like strange people." She tapped my chin with one finger. "Which explains why I'm in bed with you."

"I suppose it does." I glanced down at our hands and our intertwined fingers. "Elspeth is the baby of the family, eight years younger than Kirsty and eleven years younger than me. Isla is the oldest, and I'm two years younger than her. What I'm trying to say is that we've always felt differently about

Elspeth since she's so much younger."

"The rest of you look after her, the way Lachlan and his brothers looked after Jamie."

"Aye, she's the youngest in her family too. But it is a bit different with my family." I inhaled a long breath, letting it out gradually, but even that couldn't lessen the tightness in my throat when I allowed the memories to flood in. "When Elspeth was nine, she contracted bacterial meningitis. We didn't realize how sick she was at first, because she tried to hide it so we wouldn't be upset. That's how Elspeth is. She thinks of everyone else first, even when it puts her own health at risk. Finally, we realized how ill she was and took her to the hospital. For a while, we weren't sure if she would make it."

Serena clasped my hand to her chest.

"I remember one day," I said, "when I was sitting beside her hospital bed. She couldn't breathe on her own, so there was a tube going down her throat. She looked so pale. I wanted to pick her up and hold her, but I couldn't. Instead, I prayed. Had no fucking idea if anyone was listening or if praying would do any good, but it was all I could do. She didn't wake up right then, of course."

"But she pulled through."

"Aye. The next day, they removed the breathing tube. We were all there when she opened her eyes." Had my voice cracked slightly a second ago? I didn't get choked up about anything, not anymore. But I hadn't thought about Elspeth's illness in a very long time. I hadn't let myself think about it. I rubbed my eyes with one hand, but let Serena keep hold of the other. "After that, my sisters gradually became more and more interested in Wicca. I think it's their way of dealing with all the parts of life they can't control, because casting silly spells and wearing talismans makes them feel they have some measure of control over the unknowable."

"Did Elspeth fully recover? She seems pretty healthy these days."

"The only after effect was partial deafness in one ear. It was a miracle she didn't have anything worse."

"Maybe your prayers worked."

I met Serena's gaze, and my throat constricted again when I saw the compassion in her eyes. "Maybe it did work, maybe it didn't. But I made a promise in those prayers, and I always keep my word."

"What did you promise?"

"That if Elspeth lived, I would join the army and help my country fight the evil forces in the world. It sounds moronic now, fighting evil, but that's what I promised in my prayers." I lay back on the bed, suddenly exhausted. "So that's what I did. When I was twenty, I joined the army and became a military intelligence officer. Served three tours in Iraq."

Serena crawled to the headboard and leaned against it, gazing down at me. "Is that how you got into the SIS? They recruited you from the army?"

"You are a clever woman. Yes, that's how it happened."

"My husband served in Iraq too, for the US Army." She rubbed her arms, her gaze going distant. "It changed him, the things he saw and the stuff he went through. I'm sure it changes everyone who serves in combat."

She was giving me an excuse for my behavior with her and giving herself a reason to forgive me. I understood that, but I wasn't sure she ought to do it.

I tried to pull the blanket over her, but she shrugged it off. "I'm not cold, but thank you for caring. You really are sweet."

A sour taste invaded my mouth every time she called me sweet. I grunted something resembling words that wasn't actually words.

Her mouth crimped like she was trying not to smile. The expression carved out dimples and made me want to drag her into my arms just to hold her.

"You think I'm scarred by combat," I said. "Maybe that's part of it, but the worst things I've done didn't happen on a battlefield."

"I get that." She'd stopped rubbing her arms but kept her hands on them. "And I understand you might not want to talk about this stuff, but I hope sometime you'll tell me a little about those things."

She deserved to know, so she could make an informed choice about whatever we were doing together. Even my family didn't know what I was considering telling Serena.

I pushed up into a sitting position, leaning against the headboard. "You need to understand that most of what I did in the army and in the SIS is still covered by the Official Secrets Act. And for the things I can tell you, I can't share all the details."

She reclined against the headboard, gazing at me with that same empathy she'd shown earlier. "I was married to a military man, Logan. I know sometimes a soldier can't talk about what he's seen and done."

"But you said you don't like secrets."

"That's why I don't like them, because I've lived with them before. But I understand sometimes secrets are kept for a good reason." She sighed heavily. "Doesn't mean I have to like it. Knowing someone must've been through hell but not being able to help them, not even knowing what they went through… It's hard."

"You're talking about your husband."

She nodded. "He was special forces. Rob went on some classified missions that he never could talk about, but those seemed to be the experiences that traumatized him the most. He never had PTSD, but I knew he'd been through something I couldn't understand, something bad."

"Why would you want to be with me? I have even more secrets, worse ones, and I can't tell you everything."

"Before I answer that, would you answer one question for me?"

"All right."

She was silent for a few seconds, considering me in a way that made my skin itch again. "What have you done that makes you think you're a horrible person?"

And there it was. The question I'd hoped I would never need to answer, but that I'd known would come up eventually. If I didn't answer, she would be upset. If I told her the truth, I might lose her.

Did I have her now? We'd spent one evening together, on a date, but that didn't give me leave to assume she was signing on for a relationship. I still didn't know if I wanted that.

I shut my eyes and let out the breath I hadn't realized I was holding. Of course I wanted that. Why else would I have gone through all this rigmarole to give her a real, romantic date?

With my eyes still closed, I told her the truth. "I've killed men, Serena."

"Am I supposed to be shocked? You served in a war zone."

"I'm not talking about enemy combatants, though I took out some of those too." I forced myself to look her in the eye. "I've killed men, some of whom were unarmed, because they had the power to blow my cover and expose my assets. That means human beings, ones who relied on me to protect them. I had no qualms about eliminating those threats. I am a killer, Serena."

"Bullshit." She gave me her mulish look, the one I'd seen often enough to recognize it. "I notice you call yourself a killer, but not a murderer. Do you even realize you're doing that?"

"What's the difference? A killer is a murderer."

"Not necessarily. Killing can be self-defense, or defense of another person. Murder is cold-blooded." She considered me for a moment, seeming to look for something in my expression. "When you were talking about Elspeth, your face changed. You weren't so closed off, hiding behind that steely mask. And when you're trying to convince me you're a rotten bastard, I can see that other part of you peeking through. If you had murdered people for no good reason, not in self-defense, you wouldn't call yourself a killer. You wouldn't feel the need to explain at all, because you'd be a cold-blooded sociopath."

"Maybe I am."

She slanted toward me, her expression fierce. "Bullshit again, Logan."

"Why do you want to forgive me for what I've done?"

"Because I know you're a good man." She bent even closer, her nose almost touching mine. "You can't chase me off. I'm on to your game, so stop trying to play me. The reason you want to convince me you're a killer is because this thing between us scares you."

I started to object, but like I had earlier, I stopped. Maybe her claim had some merit. I hadn't tried to date a woman, much less start a relationship with one, since before I joined the SIS. Maybe I was afraid she'd eventually realize I was a monster after all, and she'd leave me. Before Serena, I'd never worried I might be a murderer.

"You're right," I said. "I'm a flaming eejit and a coward."

She straightened and smiled. "No, Logan, you're something much worse. You are a typical man."

"Christ, shoot me now and put me out of my misery. No one has ever called me typical before. It must mean I'm turning into a bampot."

"You're not crazy in the head, but you are crazy hot."

This was the kind of conversation I liked, the kind that might lead to more sex. But we had other things to talk about first.

"It's your turn," I said. "Tell me your secrets."

Tell him my secrets. His request sounded like a no-brainer—I didn't have secrets, I didn't like them—but I hesitated on the verge of saying so. Did I keep certain truths to myself? Did I keep them even from myself? What Keely had told me the other day, about me being afraid of liking Logan, had been festering in my mind ever since. Maybe I was afraid of this whatever-it-was between us, and maybe I'd led him to believe certain things that weren't precisely true. Maybe I'd kept secrets from him because I couldn't admit to the real issue.

I was afraid, just like he was.

"You must think I'm a hypocrite," I said. "I've told you I don't like secrets and basically chastised you for keeping stuff from me. Yet I've been doing the same thing."

"Have you?" he said in a casual tone, like he didn't know I had done that. "I suppose we've both been hiding things from each other."

"But you shared your secrets, the ones you won't get executed for telling me." I drew my knees up to my chest and locked my arms around them. "It's time I confessed."

He shifted position, angling his body toward me so we faced each other, but he said nothing. He simply waited for me to start talking.

Though he gazed at me with a patient, almost tender, expression, it took me a minute to muster the confidence to speak.

"I never really hated you, Logan," I said. "But I've known from the start what you've done in your past. Not the details, obviously. Your cousins and Keely told me you'd been a spy and what you'd done for Keely and Evan last year. I didn't know until recently, when Isla told me, that you'd also been in the army."

"Does that make a difference?"

"It shouldn't, but for me it does." I shut my eyes for a couple seconds, biting down on my upper lip. Then I met his beautiful gaze. "I didn't want to get involved with another military man. You remind me of Rob, my husband, in some ways because he wanted to serve his country and protect the world from bad guys. Every time he came home, he seemed a little more different, a little more closed off."

"He was different, I'm sure. My family would tell you the same thing about me. It can be hard to readjust to home life after being on edge constantly for so long."

"I get that, I do. But after his third tour in Iraq, I begged him to get out of the army. He wouldn't do it." I shook my head, remembering those days. "He went back for another tour. Three days before he was supposed to come home, he was killed. Rob survived four tours, a total of more than five years in Iraq, without any serious injuries until the very end. For more than half of our marriage, he was gone. He hated the violence and bloodshed, but he kept going back for more. That has to mean he liked the danger, right? Why else wouldn't he quit?"

"Nothing is ever that simple." Logan rubbed his eyes, his head bowed. "After you've seen war for so long, it's hard to leave that behind. You need the sacrifices to be worth it, and for some, that drives them to keep going no matter what."

Though I wanted to ask him if he'd ever done that, I'd agreed to tell him about me right now. So I forged ahead. "Okay, maybe Rob didn't love the danger. Maybe he refused to quit because he felt obligated in some way, like he owed it to all his friends who had died over there. But if that way of life becomes a part of you…"

Logan cocked his head, studying me. "Your husband couldn't leave the army, even for you and your son, so you're afraid I'm the same. The SIS is a part of me, and I can't ever leave it behind. That's what you think."

"Isn't it true? Being in the military, then MI6…" I hunched my shoulders. "Why would you keep doing that kind of work if you didn't feel a need to do it?"

"You've got it backwards. I quit MI6 because I was tired of the constant stress. After years of living that way, I wanted out."

"But you're fed up with your current job. The civilian life isn't enough for you."

He searched my face for a long moment, his expression difficult to read. Was he annoyed? Confused? I had no idea.

Finally, he scrubbed a hand over his face and said, "You think I want to go back to the SIS, or the military."

"Why wouldn't you? It's not a crazy question. You must've experienced awful things and probably feel that same obligation Rob did, to make the sacrifices mean something."

He blustered out a sigh and glanced up at the ceiling. "Serena, I was a bricklayer for three years. I wasn't bored in that work."

Okay, I'd forgotten about that. Deep down, though, I couldn't believe he'd been satisfied with that job either.

"I know what you're thinking," he said, "but I wasn't frustrated as a bricklayer. It was hard labor, and I didn't have time to feel sorry for myself. The problem with the job Evan created for me is that it's nothing I know how to do. I feel like a fish flopping around on the sand."

"Are you sure it's not the danger you miss?"

He reached out to brush his fingers over my cheek. "No, lass, I don't need to fulfill a misplaced obligation, and I don't miss the danger. I miss the hard work. Being a spy used my brain and my body. Oddly, being a bricklayer did the same thing. I was always calculating what to do and when, and how to do it right. Being head of security at Evanescent leaves me with too much downtime."

I wanted to believe him. I wanted it so badly.

Logan kissed me, softly, sweetly. "The only thing I miss about my previous life is having something to actually do at work, instead of spinning round and round in my desk chair for half an hour."

"You didn't really do that."

His lips twitched up at the corners.

I couldn't help laughing. "You did? You spun in your chair because you were so bored?"

"Why do you think I kept sneaking up on you to steal a kiss? It was the only thing I could think of to keep from going insane from boredom." He ran his hands up and down his thighs. "When I'm with you, I don't feel rudderless anymore, or on the verge of slipping into a coma. You keep me sane and awake, Serena."

"Great. I'm your No-Doz and Prozac combination pill."

"No. You're more than that, much more."

I was more? For so long, way before he'd started working at Evanescent, I'd dismissed Logan as nothing but a cad. He wanted to have a poke, not have a relationship. That's why I'd been able to convince myself I hated him and keep him at a distance. He wasn't the kind of man I could ever fall for, not in a million years.

Except he was. Like Rob, Logan had served his country and lived with the daily terror of being in a war zone. Maybe that explained his behavior. He'd forgotten how to relate to civilians, even his own family. Unlike Rob, Logan seemed to have left the war behind and moved on. He might not have been satisfied with his current job, but he claimed he didn't want to go back to his old life.

Could I believe that? Should I?

I wanted to, desperately.

My hand seemed to move of its own volition, reaching out to touch his cheek, tentatively at first, then caressing his skin. His cheek was smooth, with no trace of evening stubble. He'd shaved for our date. For me. A man wouldn't do that unless he wanted more than sex. Hell, I'd done the deed with Logan before tonight when he had stubble on his face, so he hadn't needed to bother. The fact he had made the back of my throat ache.

"I get it now," I said. "You're still trying to adjust to civilian life, even after three years. It's amazing you're so comfortable telling me about your past considering where you've been."

"Don't pity me for my war experience. I got off much easier than a lot of soldiers did." He rubbed his eyes again, his mouth tight. "I watched friends get blown apart by IEDs. I saw soldiers and civilians being gunned down or killed by grenades or suicide bombers. Somehow, I survived without any major injuries."

"I'm so sorry for what you've been through, but I'm glad you survived." I took his face in my hands and kissed him. "I'm glad you're here with me."

"So am I."

"There's one thing you need to understand. I'm going to worry. I can't help that. I'm going to panic about pretty much everything, at least for a while." I frisked my hands up and down my arms, suddenly chilled by the thought of what I needed to tell him next. "I lost one man I loved, and I'm terrified of going through that again. What I feel for you, it's not love yet. I want to find out where this might lead, but I'm also afraid of what might happen if I fall for you."

"You worry I'll die. Because I've led a dangerous life, and you think I want to go back to that world."

"Maybe. I don't know."

Logan pulled the covers up over me, but they slid back down. He warmed me with his hands instead, running them over my arms, my shoulders, my back. The contact comforted me more than he could possibly know, more than I could've explained. I hadn't received this kind of comfort in a very long time, and somehow, it seemed right for it to come from Logan.

And that realization made me feel like I had been disloyal to Rob.

Tears pricked at my eyes, threatening to stream down my face. I sniffled, determined not to cry.

"It's all right," Logan said. "Cry if you need to."

He pulled me into his arms and held me. His embrace was gentle, and as he stroked my hair with one big hand, I found myself relaxing into him as the need to cry evaporated. My eyelids fluttered shut. The warmth of his firm body suffused me, and I slipped my arms around his waist to cuddle closer. How strange that the man I'd convinced myself I hated gave me more comfort than I'd ever known in my life.

I'd been so wrong about Logan.

Reluctantly, I peeled myself away from his body.

He kissed my forehead, then swung his legs off the bed on my side, seeming about to leave.

I opened my mouth to ask where he was going but froze when I caught sight of the network of scars on his back. They had faded and probably weren't easily visible under normal conditions, but the subdued lighting in this room struck his scars at the right angle to reveal their faint lines. Some formed circular shapes, while others looked like slashes. I wriggled closer to skate my fingertips over the marks.

"How did you get these scars?" I asked. "And how did I not notice them before?"

Logan smirked at me over his shoulder. "I was on top of you."

"Right. I never did get a good view of your backside. But how—"

"I was tortured."

His matter-of-fact statement stopped me. While he stared straight ahead at the windows, his features devoid of expression, I examined his scars. While my mind conjured up horrific images of what might have been done to him, an invisible weight bore down on my chest.

"Jesus, Logan." I wrapped my arms around him from behind, resting my chin on his shoulder. "What happened? You don't have to tell me, but..."

Though his gaze stayed on the windows, his shoulders deflated. "I was a spy, *gràidh*. Twice I was captured and tortured in hopes of breaking me and gaining intel. I wouldn't break, and that...annoyed my captors."

I hugged him tighter and decided not to ask why he kept calling me darling in Gaelic. I'd heard Evan call Keely *gràidh* often enough that I'd asked him what it meant. In this moment, all I cared about was that Logan had opened up to me. "You must have escaped, right?"

"Yes. It wasn't easy."

Something in his voice convinced me he was understating the difficulty. I wanted to know the whole story, but I also didn't want to know.

He levered himself off the bed and turned toward the door.

"Where are you going?" I asked.

"Back to my room."

"If you want to leave, I understand. But I'd rather you stayed."

He moved only his eyes to look at me. "I assumed you'd want me to go."

I shook my head, clucking my tongue. "You really shouldn't make assumptions about what I want."

He smiled a little. "That's a bad habit of mine, isn't it?"

Throwing the covers back, I patted the mattress. "Get that fine ass back in this bed and make love to me again."

"Again?" His brows lifted. "Aren't you tired?"

"Nope."

I stretched out on the bed.

He crawled up it to straddle my body, his face above mine. "You are *nèamh*, for certain."

"What does that mean?"

"Heaven, *leannan*. You are heaven."

I knew *leannan* meant sweetheart. Logan had called me darling and sweetheart and…heaven.

He kissed me, taking his time while he explored and savored my lips before diving deep inside my mouth to intoxicate me with the sweetest, hottest kiss I'd ever experienced. By the time he rolled a condom over his length and pushed inside me, I was already halfway to climax. No one kissed like Logan, and no one made love to me the way he did either.

What was this thing between us? A romance? A love affair? Neither of those adequately described the feelings that overwhelmed me when he lovingly brought me to orgasm again and again. But a word he'd spoken seemed like the perfect definition.

Nèamh.

I'd found heaven in Logan's arms.

Chapter Twenty-One

Logan

Lying beside Serena, I watched her sleep while the light of the rising sun elongated across the carpeting, creeping toward the bed. I'd woken early, feeling better than I had in a very long time. What was it about Serena? How did she make me forget about my past and think of only the things I wanted to do with her? Not just sex. I wanted to take her home to Scotland and show her where I'd grown up.

And introduce her to my parents.

What the fuck was wrong with me? I hardly knew Serena. We'd had our first date last night. It was much too soon to even think about having her meet my parents. She'd met my sisters…

Mhac na galla. I'd been initiated into the love cult by my own doing.

Evan would harass me to no end for this.

I pushed up on my elbow, gazing down at Serena lying on her side with one hand tucked under her cheek. The covers had slipped down to her waist. I couldn't resist drinking in the sight of her bonnie breasts and remembering all the ways I'd loved them last night. With my hands. With my mouth. At one point, with my toes. Aye, Serena inspired me to be extraordinarily creative. She'd been creative too, in ways that left me spent and gasping for breath, and satisfied in every way.

The sun kissed her back, making me want to kiss it too.

But if I touched her, she'd wake. And I loved watching her sleep too much to disturb her. Being with this woman, it was *nèamh*.

Her lids fluttered partway open.

"Good morning," I said, bending to kiss her forehead. "It looks to be a bonnie day."

She rolled onto her back, stretched, and moaned with pleasure. "Good morning. I feel fantastic. How about you?"

"Fantastic, aye. Thanks to you."

She smiled with serene contentment. "Last night was incredible. Not only because of the sex. I loved having a real conversation with you, even when we were ripping open old wounds. I feel closer to you now."

"I feel the same way." And oddly, I didn't mind having opened up to her. Sharing my feelings had never been my strong suit, but I'd gotten much worse about it over the years. Serena had unlocked a vault inside me that I'd kept sealed shut for a long time. "What would you like for breakfast? I'll call room service."

"Mm, something decadent." She sat up and stretched again, smiling, then hopped off the bed. "I need the bathroom. You order for us both."

She sashayed across the room.

The view of her round erse and shapely legs kept me distracted from my breakfast ordering task until she shut the bathroom door behind her. I picked up the phone and ordered the most decadent foods available at this hour. While I waited for Serena to come out of the bathroom, I checked my phone for messages.

I'd gotten three texts and a voicemail from Alex Thorne.

The man was relentless. He wanted an answer about the job he'd offered me, and I had a suspicion he would get more relentless and demanding the longer I delayed giving him that answer.

My attention wandered to the closed bathroom door.

What about Serena? I was pursuing a relationship with her. I couldn't take off to parts unknown without even telling her, but I had no idea how she might react to the news. Not that I'd decided to take the job. It was tempting, though.

Serena ambled out of the bathroom wearing a plush terrycloth robe.

"Where did you find that?" I asked, gesturing at her now-covered body.

"In the bathroom." She stopped a few feet from the bed and fingered the lapels of her robe. "I could get used to this. Complimentary luxury items."

"You should've married Evan, then. I'm not wealthy."

"And I don't care." She settled her bottom onto the bed and twisted around to see me. "What matters to me is the kind of man you are, not how much money you have."

"Evan's a better man too."

"Cut that out, Logan." She scooted closer. "No more trying to convince me you're a cold-blooded killer. I'm not buying it. You're a good man, the kind who's honest with me about what he wants and what he can give. I appreciate that."

Honest? Christ, I needed to tell her about Alex's offer.

"What's wrong?" she asked. "You look like you're either having an attack of irritable bowel, or you're afraid to tell me something."

"You're as canny as a spy sometimes."

"I'm the mother of a teenage boy. I've developed a sixth sense for detecting when a male is holding out on me."

"Of course." I fidgeted where I sat on the bed, my back against the headboard, then cleared my throat. "I, ah, need to tell you something."

"And you think I won't like it." She turned fully sideways to look at me. "Rip off that Band-Aid. You won't know how I'll react until you do."

I hesitated. This was ridiculous. Me, wavering. I'd delivered uncomfortable news many times, and I'd been tortured for information, but telling Serena about Alex's offer turned me into a twisted mass of nerves.

Clearing my throat again, I plunged ahead. "I've had another job offer. It's a limited-time job, but it would require me to travel." I tried not to wince, but my face had other ideas. "Globally."

Her lips warped into a half-repressed smile. "Are you signing up as a stripper on a cruise ship?"

"No, you cheeky lass," I said. "Do they have strippers on cruise ships?"

"Beats me." She clasped her hands on her lap. "Tell me about this job."

"An old acquaintance has asked me to help him out with a small problem." I moved to sit on the bed's edge alongside her. "An item has been stolen, and he wants me to retrieve it."

"How does that involve global travel? Isn't that a matter for the police to deal with?"

"Normally, but there are extenuating circumstances."

She flattened her lips into a slash, shaking her head. "No more hemming and hawing. Spit it out, Logan."

I massaged my jaw. "You've spent a fair bit of time with the MacTaggarts. Have you heard the name Alex Thorne?"

"Don't think so."

"What about the British Bastard?"

Her lips formed a perfect O. "Yeah, I've heard that one. Isn't he the guy who broke Catriona's heart? Lachlan, Rory, and Aidan get very gruff whenever someone mentions the British Bastard. His name is Alex Thorne?"

"Yes." I rubbed my jaw again, realized what I was doing, and cursed under my breath in Gaelic. I was nervous. No one would believe it. "I've worked for Alex before."

"Why would you do that? He hurt Cat."

"I know, but I had just left MI6 and didn't know what the bloody hell to do with myself. Alex had heard about my past and thought I would be the right man for the job." I bent to rest my elbows on my thighs. "Alex is an archaeologist, like Cat, and he's also very wealthy. Family money. He asked me to recover a statute that had gone missing from his private collection. Things did not go as planned."

"Was it dangerous?"

"Alex had...misrepresented the facts about the case. It was much more complicated than he'd let on, and I ran into some dicey situations. In the end, I retrieved the statue and got paid." I studied my hands, running my fingers along the lines on my palm. "I was glad when Aidan offered me a job at his construction company. I shouldn't have accepted Alex's offer. It was too soon after I'd left the SIS, and I hadn't fully recovered from this." I pointed at my back. "Had no business getting into a risky situation."

"But now you're recovered." She toyed with the belt on her robe, winding it around her finger again and again. "You want to take the job Alex has offered you."

"Maybe. Not sure I can trust him to tell me the whole truth about the situation, but the idea of putting my covert skills to use again is tempting."

"You don't trust Alex, but you want to work for him."

"Alex isn't a bad bloke. He can be very personable, and in a pinch, he will come through for you." I lay back on the bed, scratching my head. "But he also likes to exaggerate the positive aspects and downplay the risks. To get what he wants, he will manipulate anyone. I have to admit, though, he never knowingly put me in danger. And he apologized for the trouble I did run into. I believe he honestly felt bad about it."

"Sounds like he's a charming rogue."

"I suppose you could put it that way."

"Listen," she said, planting a hand on the mattress beside me and tipping forward, braced with her straight arm, "if you want to take the job, don't hold back because of me."

"But I don't want to ruin whatever we're trying to build here."

"And I don't want to be the reason you turn down a job you really want to take."

I groaned. "Where does that leave us? I can't turn it down without making you feel guilty, and I can't accept it without abandoning you."

"This is your decision, not mine."

"I won't make the decision without you." I sneaked my hand under her robe to caress her thigh. "Isn't that what couples do? If not, then I learned the wrong lesson from my cousins' mistakes with women."

"Yes, that's the way it's supposed to work, in theory. We hardly know each other, so I can't ask you to include me in your decision-making."

"I need your opinion. I care what you think, what you want."

She chewed on her bottom lip, her fingers drumming on the bed.

While she cogitated, I glared up at the ceiling. Maybe I was expecting her to walk away, but if I was, she proved me wrong.

"There is another option," she said cautiously.

"What do you mean?"

She straightened and set her palms on her lap. "Take me with you."

"Are you daft? It might be dangerous."

"You said Alex never knowingly put you in danger."

"I also said he often misrepresents the truth."

"You're too smart to let him get away with that again." She flapped her robe's belt while she continued. "Last time, you were still shell-shocked from your war experiences and your injuries. This time, you're in top form. Alex Thorne won't stand a chance."

"But—"

She sealed my lips with two fingers. "I trust you, Logan."

I sucked her fingers into my mouth, enjoying the flavor of them for a moment before I took her hand in mine. "I trust you too."

Why did I feel like I'd declared something far more meaningful than my trust in her? I hadn't. Maybe one day I would, but not today.

Someone knocked on the door and called out, "Room service."

"Breakfast is here," I said. When Serena started to get up, I waved her away. "I'll get it."

By the time I'd tipped the cheerful young woman who'd delivered our meal, Serena was walking toward me while re-tying the belt on her robe to make it more secure. I waited at the table by the window, where our breakfast was laid out, though every dish had a half-dome cover on it to keep things warm. I'd ordered every decadent breakfast food I'd seen on the menu, along with plenty of syrup, butter, and jam.

Serena leaned her hip against the table and surveyed the hidden treasures. "What exactly did you order for us? It looks like a meal for ten people."

"Pancakes, waffles, eggs Benedict, bacon, sausage, croissants—"

"Okay, I get it. You ordered the entire menu."

"Not quite. After last night, we both need a hearty breakfast." I slapped her erse. "You wore me out."

She trailed a fingertip along the table's edge. "Oh, that's not how I remember it. You kept seducing me over and over again, and I was too dazed to resist."

"You kept begging me to do it again."

Her grin brightened her face, her eyes, her entire spirit. "Yeah, I did."

I lifted one of the lids to peek at the pancakes underneath it. "Are you sure you want to go with me?"

"Yes." Her fingers crooked on the tabletop, and she glanced out the window. "Before we get too deeply involved, there are a couple things I need to confess. First, I don't want to have any more children. I'm too old for it."

"Keely's your age, and she's having a baby."

"That's not what I meant." She wrapped her arms around herself. "I'm too old to do the whole raising a child thing all over again. I'd be in my sixties when the kid finally goes to college."

"Keely doesn't mind that."

"I'm not Keely." Serena picked up a packet of butter and turned it in her hand, over and over. "The men Keely was with before Evan wouldn't let her have a baby. She's finally getting what she always wanted. I've already had that. So if you've got your heart set on starting a family of your own, I'm not the woman for you."

But she *was* the woman for me. I'd realized that while she was telling me she wasn't the right one.

I took hold of her shoulders and rotated her to face me. "I want you, Serena. Full stop. I don't have my heart set on having children. There are plenty of MacTaggarts to perpetuate the line. My multitude of cousins are seeing to the next generation."

"Okay." She bowed her head, peeking up at me through her lashes only to avert her eyes. "The truth is, I probably can't have children anyway. I had—" She pulled in a long breath, straightened, and met my gaze. "I had two miscarriages before Chase was born and another one after that. A doctor told me I couldn't have children anymore. I got a second opinion and was told I probably couldn't. By the time we'd gone through all that, Rob was deployed to Iraq again, for the last time. We never had the chance to see if the doctors were right."

I got the impression she'd needed to work up to telling me the truth of why she didn't want more bairns. Did she think I'd walk away because she couldn't have children anymore? "None of that matters. Having you is enough for me."

Her eyes grew large and luminous, their gray color mesmerizing.

"Besides," I said, "Chase is a tolerable lad."

She punched me in the chest without much force. "Hey, that's my kid you're talking about."

"I like him. He doesn't assault me with questions and not give me time to answer like Iain's daughter, Malina, does." I took the butter packet she'd been holding and tossed it onto the table, my thoughts returning to Alex's offer. "I need to talk to Evan. I don't even know if he'll give me time off to do the job for Alex."

Serena gave me a look that suggested I was being an eejit.

I sighed. "Aye, you're right. He will."

"Wow, you admitted I'm right. Is that a first in our relationship?"

"Hardly. Last night, I admitted you were right about me being a flaming eejit and a coward."

"You're neither. I said you were scared of this thing between us, that's all."

"Not sure there's a difference, but I won't argue the point."

"Good." She stretched her arms above her head and made a satisfied sound. "Let's skip the conference today."

"But our CEO commanded us to attend."

"We both know this trip was not business. It was a matchmaking ploy." She stretched again, this time leaning backward enough to make her breasts push against the robe. "Keely and Evan will be thrilled if we spend the day getting to know each other."

"What did you have in mind?"

"The usual things, like sightseeing and shopping for useless knickknacks to give to our friends and family. You know, stuff they'll re-gift at Christmas."

"I see." Nodding toward our breakfast, I said, "Should we eat? Sounds like we'll need plenty of fuel to get through the day you've got planned."

She undid the belt on her robe. "How about a poke first?"

"The food will get cold." Not that I cared. The idea of getting her naked again appealed to me much more than pancakes and croissants.

"Make it a quick poke, then," she said, giving me a wicked little smile as she let the halves of her robe fall open.

"Thought you were offended by the term having a poke."

She moved closer, laying her palms on my chest for a moment before she pressed her entire naked body against me. "I have another confession. Every rude, crude word you say makes me want to smack you or rip your clothes off. Usually both. I may have called you disgusting, but that was only to cover up the fact your dirty mouth makes me hot."

"In that case…" I lashed an arm around her waist and spun us around, pinning her to the window. "Let's have a quick poke."

Afterward, I'd worry about whether I was being reckless in letting her go on a mission with me, especially one organized by Alex Thorne. I wanted her with me. Maybe I didn't have serious feelings for her yet, but I knew one thing with absolute certainty.

I could love this woman.

Chapter Twenty-Two

Serena

On the flight home, Logan and I sat on the sofa and talked. Really talked. He told me stories about his cousins that made me laugh so hard my eyes watered and my stomach muscles hurt. I told him stories about the crazy things a little boy will do, making him laugh, though not as hard as I had. The MacTaggarts were a wild bunch, for sure, but they all had hearts of pure, twenty-four-carat gold. Even Logan.

Maybe him most of all.

A few days ago, I'd dismissed him as crude and obnoxious. Today, I had a better understanding of why he was the way he was. Elspeth's illness had clearly changed Logan and his immediate family, but joining the military had been the defining moment in his life. He didn't like to talk about his time overseas, and much of it he couldn't talk about anyway. Still, the bits he'd shared convinced me he was a brave and selfless man who do anything to protect the ones he loved and would lay down his life to save strangers.

How many times had he put his life on the line?

I asked them that as the jet began its descent toward landing.

Logan shrugged one shoulder. "I don't keep count."

"Oh please. You have a photographic memory, but you want me to believe you don't remember the times you almost died saving someone else."

"I was doing my job."

The way he stared out the window, with lines tightening around his eyes, convinced me he was embarrassed to talk about his heroic exploits. I decided not to press the issue.

He propped his ankle on the other knee. "You haven't told me about your family. I know everything Chase has done since he was born, but I know nothing about your parents, or if you have any brothers or sisters."

"Oh, that." I slumped against the sofa. "I haven't talked about it because it isn't very interesting. I get along fine with my parents and my brother, but we're not the close-knit kind of family that you have. My brother Carl lives in Japan with his wife and two daughters. I haven't seen them in years. After Rob died, my family started to keep their distance. I think they didn't know how to handle my grief, and they hadn't known Rob that well, so we kind of drifted away from each other."

"Don't your parents care about their grandson?"

"Sure. They send him cards and presents for his birthday and Christmas."

"*Baothairean*," he hissed.

"What?"

"Your parents are idiots."

The vehemence in his voice made me look at him. His expression evinced a deadly calm that, combined with the harshness of his voice, made my pulse beat faster and my tummy flutter. Maybe I should've found his attitude disturbing, but instead it made me feel safe and horny at the same time. If anyone tried to hurt someone Logan cared about, he would terrify them into submission with one glance. I hadn't totally believed Keely when she'd told me Logan had gotten a sleazy toad to confess his crimes to the cops merely by talking to him. Today, I believed it. That voice. That icy calmness. If I didn't know him, I'd be scared shitless too.

He tilted toward me, his face inches from mine. "Would ye like to teach them a lesson in what family really means?"

A wave of excitement swept through my whole body, hot and sharp and delicious. "That's sweet, but not necessary. They aren't international arms dealers. They're just disinterested parents."

His golden gaze drilled into me for another few seconds before he relaxed into the sofa. "I cannae understand parents not being interested. How could they not know your husband?"

"My parents didn't think I was serious about Rob." I snorted out a derisive laugh. "Maybe they are idiots. I met Rob when I was sixteen. We were high school sweethearts, and we even went to the same university so we could stay together. He asked me to marry him on Christmas Eve during our senior year. Still, my parents thought I wasn't serious about him."

"*Baothairean* of the first order."

"Yeah, maybe. They'd always wanted me to marry someone important, like a doctor or a politician or... I don't know." I let my head fall back against the sofa and focused on the ceiling. "My parents had always been standoffish with Rob, but when he announced he was joining the army, they got positively chilly. They disapproved of the war."

"I didn't agree with it either, but I served anyway. For my country. For my family."

"That's how Rob felt too." The memory of the day he'd told me he wanted to enlist replayed in my mind, and my throat thickened. I shut my eyes. "I wasn't exactly thrilled when Rob enlisted, but for different reasons."

"You worried about his safety."

"Partly, but that's not the main reason." I forced myself to meet Logan's gaze. "Rob and I had planned to get married right after graduation. We'd bought airline tickets for that night, so we could go to Vegas and get hitched. But that afternoon, right after the graduation ceremony, he announced he'd enlisted in the army the day before and he was leaving for basic training in three days."

Logan stared at me blankly for several seconds. "He didn't consult you at all?"

"Nope. One of his closest friends had joined up instead of going to college and had gotten shipped out to Afghanistan six weeks after Rob and I got engaged." I turned sideways in my seat, though I had trouble looking Logan in the eye. "A month before our graduation, Rob's friend was killed in combat. Rob was devastated. I think that's why he enlisted so suddenly and didn't tell me. He was afraid I'd talk him out of it."

"Christ, Serena. I can't imagine... That must've been a powerful shock."

"I felt like he'd punched me in the gut. Making a decision like that without talking to me, it was like he didn't trust me anymore. Of course, later I realized he was grieving for his friend and not thinking straight. At the time, I felt betrayed."

Logan settled his hand over mine. "You don't have to tell me, but I am wondering how you dealt with Rob's decision."

"In a very rational and levelheaded way. I broke up with him." I smiled, though it was more ironic than cheerful. "Rob had hurt me so much by making a huge decision in secret that I threw the engagement ring in his face and told him we were done. He tried to apologize, told me he loved me more than anything, but I didn't believe him. On the day he left for basic training, I told him I still loved him, but I couldn't be with someone who didn't respect me enough to involve me in his decisions. He said he understood, and he asked if we could stay in touch as friends."

"What did you tell him?"

"I said okay."

Logan studied me with his lips working like he wanted to say something but thought he shouldn't.

"Go on," I said. "Speak up."

"I'm wondering how you ended up marrying Rob."

"He was stationed in Virginia, so for a year, we kept in touch by email, phone, even old-fashioned letters. When finally came to visit me, he proposed again—and I said yes." I sank into the sofa, kicking off my shoes and resting my feet on the coffee table, suddenly too weary to stay upright. "I moved to Virginia with him, and we had eight months together before he was deployed for the first time."

Logan moved onto the table. He lifted my feet onto his lap, took my socks off, and began to massage my feet. How did he always know the right thing to do? His big, warm hands soothed me, making it easier to tell the rest of the story.

"I won't lie," I told him, "and say Rob and I had the perfect marriage and never argued. Of course we did. Sometimes, he still wanted to make decisions without consulting me, but we worked through our problems and had a good life together. Nobody's perfect. We all do the best we can with what we've got."

"That's an admirable attitude."

"Uh, thanks." His compliment made me feel weirdly self-conscious again, and I wriggled in place. "Rob got deployed three more times, but when he was home, we made the most of it. He was thrilled when I finally got pregnant, but another deployment took him away. He didn't see our son in person until Chase was ten months old."

Logan rubbed the ball of my foot with his thumbs, circling them around and around until I completely forgot to be anxious.

Eyes half closed, I tickled his arm with the toes of my other foot. "You know, I've never told anyone except Keely what happened back then."

"I'm glad you told me."

"A week ago, I wouldn't have imagined I'd want to tell you all of this." I walked my toes up his arm as far as I could reach. "It seems right that I told you. You're surprisingly easy to talk to."

"I doubt anyone else would agree."

"Oh, I think you'd be surprised by what other people think of you. You're Keely's number two hero, after Evan. Your sisters worship you, especially Isla."

He laughed, though it sounded a touch self-conscious. "Isla worships me? She's always telling me I'm making a mess of my life."

"She wants you to be happy, and she loves you very much."

The jet rolled to a stop.

I hoisted my butt off the sofa to peer out the window. "When did we land?"

Logan smiled. "Didn't even notice, did ye?"

"Nope." I gave him a quick kiss. "You're the cure for fear of flying."

"Maybe I should market that skill and become a billionaire like Evan."

"What would you do with a billion dollars? Or pounds, or whatever."

"No bloody idea."

As the engines wound down, he stood and offered me his hand. I didn't need his help getting up, but I took his hand anyway. I liked the physical contact, with him, the man I'd sworn I would always hate. Today, I couldn't imagine feeling that way ever again, couldn't believe I had ever convinced myself I did feel that way.

While we headed down the stairs toward the tarmac, hand in hand, I said, "Tomorrow, we should both talk to Evan together. We want time off for the same reason, after all."

"I agree. We should tell him together."

I hesitated, glancing at Logan's profile. "I was thinking you should be there when I talk to Chase about this little adventure we're going on."

He stopped on the last step, turning his face to me, his brows crinkled and his lips parted. "Why would you want me there?"

"Because—Well, it just seems appropriate. I mean, we are dating. Aren't we? That means we're a couple."

"I suppose we are," he said slowly.

"So, will you be there when I tell Chase?"

"Yes, I will."

"Good." We stepped onto the tarmac and walked toward the limousine Evan had sent for us. "I think we should do it right away."

"Whatever you want."

The limo driver opened the back door for us, and Logan kept hold of my hand while I climbed inside. Once he'd gotten in, the driver shut the door, and soon the car began to move.

Logan laid his arm across the back of the seat and angled toward me. "You do realize Chase is staying with Evan and Keely. We're going to their house to pick him up. Maybe we should tell all of them at once and have it done with."

"I guess that does make more sense."

He scratched the back of his neck, his expression pained.

"What's wrong?" I asked.

"I need to ask you again." He fidgeted like he was sitting on a pebble. "Are you sure you want to go with me?"

"On your secret mission? Yes, I'm sure." I reflected on our previous conversation about Alex Thorne's offer, and suddenly I understood his anxiety. "Are you afraid I won't like you anymore once I've seen you in your element?"

He swallowed visibly, fidgeting again. "Maybe I am."

"Stop worrying." I kissed his cheek. "I know exactly who you are, Logan, and I'm not going to faint if I see you acting like James Bond. I've already seen your deadly calm stare and your steely-eyed stare, and I've heard your deadly calm voice and your steely voice."

"I'm deadly and steely?" He had a playful glint in his eyes that assured me he wasn't anxious anymore. "That doesn't sound very appealing."

"But it is to me." I laid a hand on his thigh and glided it up to within inches of the bulge in his pants. "It turns me on. *You* turn me on, and nothing is going to change that."

"Good, because you're dangerously close to being ravished right here in this limousine."

I slid my hand a little higher, moving it to his inner thigh. My fingers brushed his hardening cock.

He hissed in a breath, but it wasn't emotional discomfort this time. It was the ever-growing bulge in his pants that made him uncomfortable. "If you're going with me because you're worried I'll be injured during this mission, say the word and I'll turn down Alex's offer."

"Would you really do that? For me?"

"Aye."

He spoke that single word with a hint of surprise and a good dose of sincerity. Logan would turn down a job he wanted to take for my sake. He'd talked about it with me and involved me in the decision.

Rob hadn't done that.

I felt like a traitor for comparing them, but I couldn't deny Logan had done something Rob had never quite managed to do. He had included me in a very important decision, even though that decision was his to make, not mine. For the first time in my life, I wondered if Rob had really been the love of my life, or if I'd polished his memory to a pristine shine because he was no longer here.

Keely's words from the other day echoed in my mind. *Did you ever think you might get more than one love of your life? For different times in your life?*

Maybe it wasn't either/or. Maybe I could have two great loves in my lifetime.

And maybe Logan could be the second.

"Serena, are you all right?"

My focus returned from the past and zeroed in on the man presently observing me with concern in his eyes.

"I'm fine," I said. "Something just occurred to me, and I zoned out for a minute."

"What did you realize?"

"How about I tell you another time?" I covered his erection with my hand, loving that I could feel the heat of his flesh through his pants. "Let's get it on in the limo."

He threw his arms around my waist and hoisted me onto his lap.

Chapter Twenty-Three

Logan

We arrived at Keely and Evan's house somewhat disheveled. I was, at any rate. My clothes seemed determined to advertise the fact I'd enjoyed Serena in the car, announcing the truth with wrinkles that wouldn't smooth out. Serena had reapplied her lipstick and managed to tame her hair, which had gotten very messy. I hadn't been able to resist thrusting my hand into her hair and holding onto it while she rode me with a vigor that had forced me to clench my teeth to keep from shouting. She was the most confident, exciting lover I'd ever had.

Her dress was slightly rumpled when we exited the limousine.

The instant we stepped out, the front door of the house flew open and six people rushed out to hug us and babble greetings I couldn't understand. The noise of their joy was deafening. I'd expected to be met by three people—Evan, Keely, and Chase—but my sisters had joined them.

"What are they doing here?" I growled at Evan under my breath.

"Your sisters? They've been here all weekend." Evan gave me a look of mock chastisement. "You left your sisters all alone in a strange city."

"I knew my meddling cousin would entertain them."

"They entertained us." He clapped a hand on my shoulder. "So, you and Serena…"

"Bugger off, Evan."

He did bugger off for a few minutes, until he and Keely joined me and Serena in the den. We'd left my sisters and Chase in the living room because apparently Isla, Kirsty, and Elspeth had become good friends with Serena's son. The room she and I now stood in was, according to Keely, a den. Evan preferred the term study. It looked like an office to me, but then, what did I know about mansions? I'd lived in a flat in London for years, and before that, army barracks.

"You might call it a McMansion," Keely said when I told her my opinion of the house. "That means it's smaller than a genuine mansion, but bigger than an ordinary house."

"I thought McMansion meant a very large fast food restaurant."

She laughed.

Whenever Keely laughed or smiled, I understood why Evan had fallen in love with her. She was bonnie and sweet.

But when Serena laughed or smiled, I got the strangest feeling in my chest.

Evan took a seat behind the desk, which was much smaller than the one in his office at Evanescent. When he patted his lap, Keely settled onto it. Evan splayed a palm over her very large belly.

Serena and I sat in the chairs on the opposite side of the desk.

Evan smiled at his wife. "Do you think they're about to announce their engagement?"

"It's too soon for that. But maybe they want to thank us for meddling, since it's worked out so well."

I cleared my throat. Forcefully. "Perhaps you'll let us tell you why we needed to talk to you, instead of making barmy assumptions."

"Go on," Evan said. "We're listening."

He glanced at Serena, then aimed a smug smile at me.

"*Thalla 's cagainn bruis*, ye bampot," I hissed at him.

Keely wagged a finger at me. "That's no way to talk to your cousin. Away and chew a brush? Come on."

"Your wife understands Gaelic," I said to Evan. "Why would ye teach her that? Ye cannae curse without her knowing."

Evan grinned. "I started out teaching her dirty Gaelic, but she's a quick study. I had to move on to insulting Gaelic."

Serena jumped in before I could speak. "Logan's been offered a temporary job that's more up his alley than being the head of security at Evanescent. He needs to accept the offer, so he can figure out if working for you will be enough for him, or if he wants to get back in the game."

"What game?" Evan asked.

She flashed me a sarcastically sweet smile. "Being James Bond."

"Ahhh," Evan said, "I see. It's a secret mission."

"Exactly."

"No, it bloody is not," I said. "Al—Someone has offered me a job recovering a missing item. That's all."

Serena poked my arm. "Not quite. You're leaving out the who part of the equation."

"He doesn't need to know that."

"Of course he does. You can't take a job from you-know-who without telling Evan."

I rolled my eyes heavenward but received no divine intervention. "Evan will tell the other you-know-who, and she won't be pleased about it."

Evan's brows rose. "This sounds intriguing. You have to tell us about these two you-know-whos and the you-know-what the first you-know-who wants you to find."

He was smirking, the bastard.

"You need to be honest with your family," Serena said. "I'm sure Catriona will understand."

"Like hell she will." I shifted but couldn't get comfortable in my chair, despite its thick padding. "She still refers to him as the British Bastard and the Limey Louse."

Evan's face blanked for a heartbeat, then understanding dawned. "You're doing this mission for Alex Thorne."

"Who's Alex Thorne?" Keely asked.

"The man who broke Catriona's heart. They met in America when she was working on her PhD there. That's all any of us really knows."

I snorted. "We know she despises him with a vengeance."

"Don't let that stop you," Evan said. "If you want to take the job, take it. If Cat finds out, she'll get over the anger once she's beaten you to death."

"You're hilarious." I squirmed again and resigned myself to telling my cousin the whole truth. "This isn't, ah, the first time I've worked for Alex."

"Really? You'll have to tell us that story sometime." Evan whispered something in Keely's ear, and she nodded. He looked at me. "Take as much time as you need. I'll hire temporary replacements for both of you."

Serena seemed genuinely wounded by that announcement. "Guess I'm not irreplaceable after all."

"Of course you are." Evan kissed his wife's cheek. "But Keely and I want you and Logan to be happy. A holiday filled with adventure sounds perfect. Doesn't it, *gràidh*?"

Keely nodded. "Yep."

Serena had glanced at me when Evan said the word *gràidh*, but she didn't seem confused by it. The first time I'd accidentally called her that, she had been too annoyed with me to notice. The second time, she'd been in the grips of a panic attack thanks to her fear of takeoffs and landings. The third time, she'd seemed startled for a moment.

Did she know what *gràidh* meant? The American Wives had taught her naughty Gaelic, but I didn't know if they'd told her about the affectionate terms.

"Shouldn't you be worried for Serena's safety?" I asked Evan.

"We trust you to take care of her. And besides, you wouldn't let her go with you unless you were certain she'd be safe."

Evan trusted me. How odd.

"Don't look so confused," Keely said. "Evan is your best friend. Of course he trusts you to keep *my* best friend safe."

Was everyone in the family suffering from the shared delusion Evan and I were best mates?

Serena slanted across the space between our chairs and whispered, "Stop fighting it. Having a best friend doesn't make you less of a hot secret agent man."

I grunted.

Evan sighed with a satisfaction that baffled me. "It's settled, then. Let's go share the news."

Serena raised a hand. "Wait. I need to talk to Chase first."

"Wait here, and we'll send him in."

Evan helped his wife dismount his lap, and the pair of them ambled out of the room.

I moved to stand, but Serena waved for me to stay put.

"Are you sure you want me to stay?" I asked, dropping onto the chair again.

"Honestly, we've been through this already. We are dating, aren't we? You should be a part of this conversation. Besides, Chase thinks you're awesome. I want you here because that's what couples do. They talk to the kids together."

"But he's not my son."

"It'll be fine." She grasped my hand. "If you can handle terrorists and double agents, you can handle a teenage boy who worships you."

Chase walked into the room and stopped at the desk, examining it with keen interest. "Hey, can I sit in Evan's chair?"

"Sure," Serena said. "I don't think Evan will mind."

The lad sat in the chair and put his feet on the desk.

"Feet off the desk," Serena said in her stern mother voice.

Chase dropped his feet to the floor. "So, are you guys getting married?"

Why did everyone ask us that?

Serena blushed faintly but maintained her stern voice. "No, we are not getting married. Logan has a temporary job helping an old friend find something he lost."

The boy bent forward, his arms on the desk and his eyes alight. "A spy job? Wicked!"

"Not a spy job," I said. "It's more of a…"

What the hell was it, anyway?

Serena stepped in to explain. "It's like a private investigator job. Logan will find the missing item. That's it." She hesitated, then added, "It will involve travel, though. Possibly outside the US."

"Awesome!" Chase declared. "My mom is dating James Bond. Can I come? A spy job would be waaaaay cooler than Vermont."

"No, you cannot come along," his mother said. "You are going to Vermont. Your grandparents are looking forward to seeing you."

"Aw, Mom."

"You're going to Vermont. No ifs, ands, or buts."

He rolled his eyes and slouched in the chair. With a long-suffering tone, he said, "Fine."

She bit her lip, glancing at me, then faced her son again. "Chase, are you sure you're okay with me and Logan being a couple? It's okay if it bothers you."

"I'm cool with it."

"Are you sure? You're not even a tiny bit bothered?"

"Ugh, Mom. I'm not a baby." He looked at me before rolling his eyes at his mother again. "I mean, it's about time you got a boyfriend. And Logan is the awesomest."

I had no idea how to feel about a teenager calling me the awesomest, and I also had no clue what being the awesomest meant. Did I get a medal for that?

"Okay," Serena said, seeming baffled and relieved at the same time, "let's go tell Logan's sisters the news."

We cut across the hall, to the living room.

My sisters leaped off the sofa shrieking. They rushed at us, Isla and Elspeth flinging their arms around me while Kirsty grabbed Serena. After a moment of blubbering and more shrieking, they switched places, and I found myself being smothered in Kirsty's arms.

"Oh Logan," she whispered in my ear, "I'm so happy for you. Now don't fuck it up. Serena is the perfect woman for you."

She barely knew Serena, so I couldn't decide what criteria she'd used to determine Serena was perfect for me.

Kirsty pulled back enough to see me. "It's because she makes you smile."

I smiled at other times, when Serena wasn't around, but I decided not to mention that to Kirsty. She wanted to believe in the fantasy of my romance with Serena.

"Don't be a grump," Kirsty said. "I see the way you smile at her. You don't look at anyone else that way."

"Are you reading my mind?"

"Maybe I just know you, Logie."

"What way do you claim I smile at Serena? A smile is a smile."

"Oh no, not when you're looking at her." Kirsty pecked my cheek. "You'll figure out what I mean eventually."

Evan clapped his hands to get everyone's attention, and to silence my sisters. "It's late, and Keely and I think everyone should stay here tonight."

"Awesome!" Chase said.

"Wonderful!" my sisters said in unison.

I aimed my best glare at Evan, but it bounced right off him. "There are five bedrooms and eight of us."

"Keely sleeps with me," he said, like I was the daftest dafty on earth.

Well, I was. Christ, even I knew Evan shared a bed with his wife.

"That leaves four bedrooms," Evan said, "and six of you. I'm sure you can work out the math, Logan."

He glanced meaningfully at Serena.

"Kirsty and Elspeth can share," Isla announced.

Elspeth's mouth fell open. "Why do I have to share with Kirsty? She snores."

"I do not," Kirsty snapped. "Any snoring you hear is your own."

"Quiet," Isla said. "I'm the oldest, so I get my own room."

"Where am I to sleep?" I asked.

Everyone stared at me like I was a drooling lunatic.

Chase pointed at his mother. "Duh. You sleep with Mom."

"Yes," Serena agreed. "We can share a bed. Like a sleepover. Two adults can sleep in the same bed platonically."

No one looked convinced by her platonic sleepover claim.

Chase tipped his head to the side, his mouth twisted into a bizarre teenage expression somewhere between annoyance and humor. "Mom, I'm not a baby. I'm fifteen, and I've had sex ed class. You don't need to pretend you and Logan aren't doing it."

Her eyes flared so wide they seemed about to burst out of her head.

"Ahhh," Evan said, "let's everyone else go into the kitchen while these three sort things."

My sisters, Evan, and Keely all fled the room.

Serena collapsed onto the sofa. "I am such a horrible mother."

"Why?" Chase asked. "Because I know about sex? Jeez, Mom, you're so weird."

I sat beside Serena and held her hand. "What's wrong? Chase seems fine with the idea of us sleeping together."

"Yeah," the lad said, "I'm cool with it."

"But—" She leaned in to whisper in my ear so softly I had to strain to hear her. "What if he knows about the one-night stands I had?"

"I doubt he knows that," I said in an equally soft voice. Looking at Chase, I asked, "Is this the first time your mother has had a boyfriend?"

"Oh yeah, she's been like a nun or something until now."

Smiling, I pressed my lips to Serena's ear. "See? He doesn't know."

Her body relaxed as a breath rushed out of her.

Chase trotted to the doorway and stopped to say over his shoulder, "I'm going to find out which room is mine, then I won't leave my bedroom until morning."

He emphasized the last bit while smirking.

The cheeky lad hurried toward the kitchen.

Serena and I regarded each other in silence. Her gaze was tender, and I suspected mine matched it. I'd dated before, though not since joining the SIS, but I'd never experienced this feeling with any other woman. It was…comfortable. Hot and sweet. Soft and strong. Whenever she smiled, a strange sensation gripped my heart.

Laughter burst out from the direction of the kitchen, several female voices joining Chase's.

Serena stood. "We should see what's going on out there."

"Aye."

Rising, I claimed her hand and led her out into the entryway.

Six laughing people tumbled out of the kitchen headed for the stairs. Evan clapped me on the shoulder when he walked by, and Isla stopped to give me a brief hug.

"The downstairs is yours," she said, glancing at Serena and me in turn. "But donnae make too much noise. Elspeth is a sensitive sleeper."

"I heard that!" Elspeth shouted from the top of the stairs. "Make all the noise you want, Logie."

Grinning, Elspeth sprinted down the upstairs hall.

The others had already disappeared in that direction, including Chase.

Serena and I were alone. Again.

A big yawn contorted her entire face.

"You're exhausted," I said.

"No, I'm fine," she claimed, as another yawn overtook her.

I swept her into my arms and carried her upstairs.

She looped her arms around my neck, rested her cheek on my shoulder, and fell asleep.

Chapter Twenty-Four

Serena

Monday, we spent the whole day getting ready for our big adventure. Evan hadn't hired temporary help after all, instead deciding to take a few weeks off and let Vic Bazzoli run things. Vic, who had once been Keely's boss at the electronics store, agreed to take over in Evan's absence. Vic was president of Vic's Electronics Superstores LLC, the sole subsidiary of Evanescent, but now he got to try out being the CEO of a billion-dollar corporation. Logan's secretary, Delilah, would assist Vic.

I'd woken in the morning with Logan's body cradling mine. We both lay on our sides, my backside snuggled up to his front side, his arm draped over my hips with his fingers grazing my belly. His erection formed a hard, thick line against my spine. I knew he was still asleep, thanks to his soft snores, but I wondered if erotic dreams about me had made his morning wood stiffer than usual. He hadn't gotten this hard yesterday morning.

His snores whistled in a steady rhythm.

A little too steady. And too whistly. Too…phony.

I pushed my elbow backward into his gut. "Faker."

He tickled my belly with his fingertips. "I was waiting for you to wake me with your mouth on my *slat*."

"You would have to be asleep for that to happen."

"All right. I'll go back to sleep."

I wriggled away from him and swung my legs off the bed. "No time for blow jobs, I'm afraid. I've got packing to do."

What did a woman take on a mysterious mission, not knowing where she might wind up? Logan didn't know for sure. When he called Alex, while I was packing, the man had promised Logan more details when they met in person tomorrow. Alex lived in Montana, so my first adventure would be visiting a state I'd never been to before, not to mention meeting the enigmatic British Bastard. I had to admit I was curious about Alex Thorne.

After I packed, Logan took me and Chase to his apartment, the one Evan paid for as part of Logan's employment benefits package. It was fancy, with lots of electronic this and that, but it didn't seem like Logan's style. He wasn't the bells and whistles type.

Monday afternoon, I tried to help Chase pack for his trip to Vermont. He needed more suitcases than I did, since he'd be staying two months with his grandparents.

Chase refused my help by rolling his eyes and saying, "Jeez, Mom, I'm not a baby."

"I know that, but you're still *my* baby."

"Go have an actual baby so, you know, I can get a break from your smothering." With a strange kind of gravitas only a teenager could pull off, he added, "Logan would be an awesome dad."

Ohhh-kay. Not touching that one.

That evening, I made dinner for the three of us. We ate it at the same kitchen table where I'd shared so many meals with Chase and Rob. None of the men I'd slept with since Rob had gotten an invite to dinner at my house. I barely said goodbye before leaving them, and I'd never stayed the night with a single one.

Until Logan.

Two mornings in a row, I'd woken up with him. Now, he was seated at my kitchen table eating the meal I'd whipped up for us. I was dating him. Seriously dating. For the first time in more than a decade, I could imagine a future with a man who was not Rob. I felt a little queasy thinking about that, but only for a moment. When Logan slipped his hand into mine under the table, all the anxiety sluiced out of me.

Logan and Chase both offered to help wash the dishes, but I declined their offers. They needed to get to know each other better, so I suggested they go into the living room while I cleaned up.

I wanted Logan to get to know my son. How bizarre.

And yet so right.

When I joined them in the living room fifteen minutes later, Logan and Chase were sitting on the sofa facing each other, smiling and laughing.

Chase jumped up and moved into the armchair beside the sofa.

Logan patted the cushion beside him.

I plopped down right next to him and relaxed into the sofa when he slipped his arm around my shoulders.

"What were you two talking about?" I asked. "Or is that top secret guy stuff?"

Logan aimed a fake deadly glare at Chase. "If you tell her, I'll have to kill you."

Chase laughed. "Logan's awesome, Mom. I'm cool with it if you want to marry him. Moving to Scotland would be totally sick."

My mouth opened, but I couldn't speak. I knew "sick" meant good to a teenage boy, but I couldn't believe Logan would've suggested we might move to Scotland.

"I didn't mention moving," Logan said to me, "or marriage. That's not what we talked about."

"What did you boys chat about?"

"Comic books."

Slack-jawed once again, I gaped at Logan. "You like comic books?"

"I read them when I was a wee laddie, aye."

"Mom thinks comics are silly," Chase said. "She likes goopy romance novels."

Though I heard his statement, it didn't sink into my brain. I couldn't tear my gaze away from Logan, and I wondered whether I would ever fully understand him. My mind cobbled together no words more useful than, "Comic books? You?"

"Yes, *mo gaol.*" Logan nodded toward Chase. "We debated who's the better superhero. Chase claims it's Superman because he can fly and has super strength, but I say it's Batman. He has no powers and uses his wits and gadgets to outsmart the villains."

My jaw dropped even lower, probably nudging my chest. Logan MacTaggart, the toughest guy I'd ever met, talked about comic books with my son.

"What else don't I know about you?" I asked Logan.

"Many, many things." He kissed my temple. "We both have a lot to learn about each other."

Chase was grinning at us. "What does yo gool mean?"

"Not yo gool," Logan said. "*Mo gaol.* It's Gaelic for my love."

My son grinned even more.

Logan had called me his love. I supposed it was nothing more than a generic endearment, like saying "baby," except he'd called me *mo gaol* while we made love too.

We all watched TV for a while until Chase did the fakest yawn I'd ever seen and announced he was "totally trashed" and needed to go to bed. At eight o'clock. Voluntarily. Sheesh, I had trouble convincing him to go to bed at ten and not spend another two hours reading comics under the covers with a flashlight. Tonight, he wanted to go to bed early.

Logan and I watched a Batman movie on TV before we headed into my room to sleep. I didn't know if Batman was the better superhero, but a man using his wits to beat the bad guys instead of superpowers was definitely hotter. When I told Logan that, he got a smugly satisfied look on his face.

For the third morning in a row, I woke with Logan snuggled up to my backside. Rob had never liked spooning, but Logan seemed to love it. I loved it too, with Logan. I hadn't realized I wanted this kind of cuddling until he gave it to me. How odd that a tough ex-spy was the only man who'd ever wanted to spoon with me.

We drove to the airport together, since we would all be flying on Evan's jet. It would've made more sense time-wise to have the jet drop off me and Logan in Montana before continuing on to Vermont, but I didn't want to leave Chase yet. Logan didn't mind that I wanted to fly to Vermont and say goodbye there.

During the flight, Logan and Chase chatted about comic books and played chess. My son had never played that game in his life, but Logan patiently taught him the rules and strategies of the game. I wasn't surprised at all that Logan enjoyed chess. It was an analytical game, one that involved trying to outsmart your opponent. Of course Logan played chess. It made perfect sense.

After their second game, Chase flopped into a chair by the windows and listened to music on his iPod.

I had to tap his shoulder twice and tell him to turn down the volume. Teenagers.

Logan and I curled up on the sofa and took a nap together.

When we reached Vermont, Logan offered to stay inside the jet so Rob's parents wouldn't see him and be upset that I was dating again. I told him not to be a silly goose, which made him shake his head and smile. We walked down the stairs hand in hand.

Chase had already run down the stairs and was currently crushed in his grandmother's embrace. Sylvia Carpenter kept one arm around Chase while she waved and smiled at me. Ed Carpenter ruffled his grandson's hair, which made Chase roll his eyes.

Logan and I stopped in front of Sylvia, Ed, and Chase.

The grandparents both eyed my hand, the one still entwined with Logan's.

"This is Logan MacTaggart," I said. "Logan, meet Sylvia and Ed Carpenter, Chase's grandparents. Logan is my, uh..." *Suck it up and say it, woman.* "He's my boyfriend."

Logan's brows rose the tiniest bit.

Sylvia burst into tears.

Oh shit. What kind of horrible person was I for blurting that out? It had seemed like the right way to break the news, but—

Sylvia dragged me into a bear hug. "Oh Serena, we're so happy for you. Ed and I have been worried you were still grieving for Rob instead of moving on with your life. You're like a daughter to us."

Rob's parents had seemed to be the ones clinging to his memory and to the grief. Maybe I'd been wrong about them. Maybe I'd avoided visiting Sylvia and Ed because I couldn't handle it, not the other way around.

I decided to tell them the truth. "I was afraid you'd be upset about this. You and Ed talk about Rob so much, and you've been wanting to commemorate his passing."

"Oh no, dear, we didn't mean it that way. Of course we want you to find love again. Rob would want it too." She let me go and stepped back to study me. "I'm sorry if we made you feel like that's not what we wanted. Keeping Rob's memory alive doesn't mean you can't start a new life."

Christ, I'd been so wrong about so many things. Sylvia and Ed. Logan. What I wanted.

We all ate lunch at a restaurant near the airport, chatting about nothing much and telling funny stories. Spending even an hour with Sylvia and Ed made me feel…lighter. A weight had lifted off my chest simply because I'd realized, finally, that Rob's parents weren't clinging to the past. Maybe I'd been the one holding on, resisting the chance to move forward into a new and wonderful future. Fear had held me back, fear of loving another man who had a dangerous job and fear of losing Logan the way I'd lost Rob.

Even if Logan and I didn't work out, I owed it to myself to give us a chance. I owed it to Logan too. After all, he'd lifted the bulk of that weight off my chest.

We said goodbye in the restaurant parking lot. Chase hugged me, then he shocked Logan—and me too, for sure—by hugging him.

"Take care of my mom," Chase said. "And make sure she has fun."

"I will," Logan replied. "You have my word."

"Cool."

My son climbed into Sylvia and Ed's SUV.

I watched as the vehicle drove away and waved to Chase. A pang tightened the back of my throat, and tears stung my eyes.

Logan put his arm around my shoulders. "If you've changed your mind about coming with me, I'll understand."

"No, I haven't changed my mind." I wiped my eyes and sucked in a breath, fortifying myself. "It's hard to say goodbye to my baby for so long, that's all. Two months. I know he's fifteen, but still…"

"You'll miss him." Logan gave me a little squeeze. "He'll miss you too."

I gazed up at Logan, marveling at how sensitive and considerate he could be. I probably should've been confused by his frequent shifts between dirty-talking, rough-around-the-edges Logan and the sweet, thoughtful man who wouldn't make a decision without my input. The contradictions didn't bother me, not anymore. Little by little, I was coming to understand him.

And he understood me, more than anyone else ever had.

Logan the sex god I understood. Logan the complicated, real man still presented me with mysteries I intended to solve.

We walked the two blocks back to the airport so we could enjoy the beautiful weather. The sun warmed our faces, and a temperate breeze kissed our skin. By the time we boarded the jet, I had resolved to interrogate Logan, in a polite way, and get to the bottom of the mystery that was Logan the ex-spy, Logan the army intelligence officer, and the most enigmatic part of him too.

Logan the bricklayer.

The two of us settled onto the sofa where earlier Chase had lounged while listening to music on his iPod. He thought I was a fuddy-duddy for making him use an iPod instead of giving him a smartphone. I didn't want my son developing neck or eye problems from staring down at a screen for hours or becoming incapable of communicating face to face because he'd spent too many hours texting.

"What are you thinking about?" Logan asked.

"Oh, just how my son thinks I'm ruining his life by refusing to give him a phone."

"Rae, my cousin Iain's wife, won't let her teenage daughter have a phone either."

I perked up at that revelation. "Really? Here I thought I was the only twenty-first century mom who won't give her kid a smartphone."

"You are not alone. Rae has explained to me more than once that studies have shown using electronic devices rewire children's brains."

"I've met Rae twice, but we didn't get a chance to talk much."

"If you tried to speak to every member of the MacTaggart clan at every gathering, you'd never get any sleep."

"Your family is numerous." I turned partway toward him. "I've been curious about something. Why did you become a bricklayer?"

"I told you. Aidan offered me the job, and after everything I'd experienced in the army and the SIS, I was ready for less stressful work."

"Yeah, I've heard the one-line summary. Now I want the whole story."

He let his head fall back against the sofa and stayed silent for a moment before answering. "It was honest work. I didn't need to lie or worm my way into anyone's trust. I knew what I needed to do every day, and I did it. The physical aspect of the work kept me stimulated, but there's also an analytical side to it. You can't toss a pile of bricks up, slap some mortar on them, and hope the finished wall will stand. There's planning involved."

"You must've liked it, since you stayed in that job for three years."

"I did enjoy it. After a few months, Aidan offered me a promotion. I became manager of the bricklaying part of Aidan's construction projects. I still did hard labor, but I was in charge."

"Everybody had to do your bidding. I can see why you'd like that."

He rolled his head to the side to look at me. "Are you calling me a dictator?"

"No, I'm calling you bossy. In a sexy way, though, like when you tell me what to do in bed."

"You tell me what to do too."

"True." I propped my feet on the table, kicking off my shoes. "The first time we sat here on this sofa, you said filthy things to me."

"And you slapped me."

"You deserved it."

"I suppose I did." He splayed a hand over my thigh. "But you've admitted my filthy mouth gets you excited."

"Mm-hmm." Despite his hand on my thigh making me shiver, I stuck to my resolution to peel back the layers of Logan. "Have you ever been married?"

"No."

"Engaged?"

He compressed his lips. "No."

"Serious relationships?"

"*Bod an Donais.* Must we have another round of the American Inquisition?"

"Yes. Please."

"At least you said please." His mouth quirked in a sardonic expression. "No serious relationships. I was shy in school, and I was in the army or the SIS for most of my adult life. Not many chances for romance in a war zone. Besides, according to my sisters, lasses find me intimidating. They keep telling me to loosen up and open up. They also say smiling like a hungry lion does not qualify as being friendly."

"I'm familiar with that smile." I traced the seam of his lips with my fingertip. "You don't intimidate me. Your feral smile makes me wet."

He skated his hand up my thigh. "Do you remember what I wanted to do the first time we were on this sofa?"

"Yes." My pulse accelerated as the memory barreled through my mind. Logan had told me he wanted to fuck me on the table. I covered his hand with mine and guided it between my thighs. "What will you do after, when my cream is all over the table?"

He tipped toward me, his gaze glued to mine. "Lick it off."

"That's disgusting." Unlike every other time I'd used that word with him, I didn't sound revolted. The words came out husky.

"I like it when you call me disgusting in that sexy, hungry voice. You turn me into a ravening beast."

"Mm, I love your beastly side."

He gave me a crooked smile. "I suppose that makes you off your head, which makes you the perfect woman for me."

For the first time since I'd met Logan, I wasn't afraid to speak the truth. "I think you, Logan MacTaggart, just might be the perfect man for me."

Chapter Twenty-Five

Logan

I slouched on the sofa with my feet on the floor, legs spread and trousers hanging wide open, while Serena knelt between my thighs. Her attention was riveted to my cock. Though it was limp, as spent as I was by all the things we'd done to each other over the past hour, she seemed determined to get me hard again.

Serena lowered her mouth toward my cock, licking her lips.

"That's enough," I said, cupping her cheek. "We're on our way to an important business meeting. If you do that again, I'll be useless."

"I like you useless. It means you're relaxed and satisfied."

"Come up here." I patted the cushion beside me. "I'm in the mood to hold your succulent body against me."

She climbed onto the sofa and cuddled up under my arm, her cheek on my shoulder.

I'd never been one for cuddling, but with Serena, I liked the way it felt to hold her close. The warmth of her supple, inviting body gave me one of those strange sensations in my chest. Not pressure. Not pain. It was more…tender.

Logan MacTaggart having tender feelings? No one would believe it.

"What are you thinking?" Serena asked.

"I'm musing about what an incredible lover you are."

"Bullshit." She traced a line across my forehead. "You've got the crinkle up here that means you're thinking serious thoughts."

A week ago, I would've made a sarcastic comment and offered her a poke. Today, I had the oddest inclination to tell her the truth. "I was wondering what my friends and family might say about me now. I've gone soft in the head and in the heart—for you."

She looked surprised, but only for a moment. Then she smiled with a sweetness that triggered a new sensation in my chest, a pressure that hit me hard but quickly dissolved into something gentler. Her voice was hushed when she said, "I've gone soft for you too."

I decided that was as close as we'd get to expressing our feelings, at least for today. I wasn't at all sure I understood my feelings for her yet, but I knew they wouldn't fade away. They would only grow stronger.

She was watching me again, the way she did whenever she tried to understand me.

"Don't do that," I said.

She pretended to have no idea what I meant. "Do what?"

"You're trying to decipher me. Forget it. I'm indecipherable."

"Nobody is indecipherable."

"You haven't met Alex yet."

"Hmm." She trailed her finger down the bridge of my nose. "Maybe Alex is a mystery, but you are not. You're like that World War II code the Germans had, tough to crack without the right equipment. But I've got the machine that decodes you, Logan MacTaggart." She tapped her temple. "It's right here. Your days as a mystery man are over."

"You are the most intelligent woman I've ever met, so I'll accept that you might crack my code."

"Thank you."

"I'm solving your mysteries too."

She slid her finger down to my lips, her expression turning serious. "I think you might be doing that."

The pilot's voice came over the intercom system. "We'll be landing in a few minutes, Mr. MacTaggart."

I thanked him, even though I had no idea if the man could hear me. I'd never thought about whether the intercom was two-way.

Serena and I lay there on the sofa until the jet touched down, then we got up and reassembled our clothes. Her dress and her underwear had wound up lumped on a chair. I didn't remember which of us had tossed them there. I remembered vividly unbuttoning her dress with my teeth and opening her bra the same way. I loved that she'd worn a bra with the clasps in the front. Otherwise, I wouldn't have been able to pluck those tiny metal hooks apart with my teeth and hear her small gasps every time I did.

"Stop that," she said, though I could tell she didn't mean it. "We are not having sex again until we get to wherever it is we're sleeping tonight."

"Alex will invite us to stay at his house. It's rather large."

"You mentioned he's rich. Is his house a mansion?"

I shrugged, tucking in my shirt.

She rolled her eyes exactly the way her son often did. "You are always so helpful with the details."

Crouching to put my shoes on gave me an excuse not to respond. I didn't like talking about Alex Thorne with Serena. Aye, he was rich. And good-looking. And very outgoing. Women loved him. I did not want Serena to be seduced by his charming-rogue persona.

That wouldn't happen. She was with me.

But I didn't have Alex's easy charm. Maybe sleazy was a better term for it. I groaned inwardly. No, he wasn't sleazy. If he were, I wouldn't be worrying he might sweep Serena off her feet.

"What are you fretting about now?" she asked. "The crinkle is back."

"I'm wondering if Alex is going to tell us the whole truth. It seems unlikely, but there's always a chance Hell will freeze up today."

"That's not what you're really worrying about."

Part of me liked that she understood me so well, but another part wished she'd stop analyzing me.

I made a show of scanning the view out the window, as if I needed to hunt for villains out there, anything to avoid looking at Serena. "Women love Alex. That's how he got his hooks into Catriona, she fell for his roguish persona. He has money and charm and—"

Serena laughed like I'd told a good joke. "That's adorable, Logan."

"What is?"

"You're jealous of Alex because you think I'll fall under his spell." She looped her arms around my neck. "There's no chance of that. I'm completely enthralled by you."

"Of course you are. I've known that since the day I fucked you in the copy room."

"You switch from feeling insecure to being arrogant faster than any human being I've ever met."

"I love to be the best."

She smacked my erse, took my hand, and led me out of the jet.

A Mercedes-Benz waited on the tarmac for us. The driver, a stern-faced gent dressed in a black suit, held the door for us while we got inside. I noticed the familiar bulge under his jacket. He was carrying a gun.

"Uh-oh," Serena said once our driver had shut the door. "The crinkle is deeper. What's up?"

"The driver has a gun." I shifted position but couldn't quite get comfortable despite the plush cushioning of the leather seat. "I suspected it before, but now I'm sure. Alex has kept important facts from us."

"Maybe he always has bodyguards. If he's as shady as you say, he might be security conscious."

"We'll see. One way or another, he is going to tell me the whole story before I agree to take this job."

"Are you going to scare the shit out of him the way you did with that numbskull in the hotel elevator?"

"No. All I have to do is threaten to tell Catriona where he is."

"He's afraid of her? Jeez, what kind of history do they have?"

"I wouldn't say he's afraid of Cat." I stretched my legs out and crossed my ankles. "But Cat did swear vengeance if she ever saw him again. This was eleven years ago. Still, she seems to hold a permanent grudge against Alex. The lass is a spitfire, so who knows what she might do to him."

"Catriona seems like such a sweet person."

"She is, most of the time." I sighed, remembering all the comments Catriona had made about Alex over the years. Nothing concrete, but enough to convince me he'd hurt her badly. "I don't know what happened between Alex and Cat, but she despises him. Not like you thought you hated me, but in a much fiercer way."

"You know what that means."

"She hates him, that's what it means."

"Nope." Serena pressed her lips to mine. "We thought we hated each other, but really, we were fighting our attraction and the possibility of romance. Catriona probably thinks she hates Alex because he hurt her, but she still loves him. It can be galling to want someone who pisses you off."

"You might be onto something."

Our car wended its way down roads less and less populated with houses, heading into the woods of the Montana mountains toward Alex's home. For once, I wasn't contemplating Serena and our fledgling relationship. Instead, I pondered what might've happened between Alex and Cat.

What would she do if she ever saw him again?

Chapter Twenty-Six

Serena

After what seemed like hours but had been thirty-two minutes according to my phone, our car turned down a gravel driveway hemmed in by tall trees. After several minutes more, the woods opened to reveal a structure.

I elbowed Logan. "You rat. That's a mansion by anyone's standards, and you acted like you had no idea how huge Alex's house is."

"Just keeping up my indecipherable front."

The house stretched across the length of a football field, by my guesstimate, and it hunkered three stories high. The facade seemed Victorian, but I was no expert. The sun glinted off the many windows, each one featuring ornate ironwork. At least that's what it looked like as our car pulled into the semicircular drive, stopping directly in front of the main doors. Yeah, the house had double doors at the main entrance. Massive, ornate wooden slabs.

A set of brick steps led up to the doors.

Our driver, who had the face and demeanor of a bulldog, opened the car door for us.

Logan and I mounted the steps to the doors that towered higher than Logan. And he was no shrimp.

The doors swung inward, parting to reveal a gray-haired man who was offering us a polite smile.

"Welcome to Moirai House," he said in his prim British accent, waving for us to enter. "Mr. Thorne is waiting for you in the study. My name is Reginald. Follow me, please."

Logan had reverted to his relaxed but alert and slightly dangerous mode. "Thank you, Reginald."

Something about the butler, or whatever he was, bothered me. I couldn't put my finger on it, but I got the impression Logan noticed it too.

Reginald guided us through a foyer and down a hallway, veering toward a set of less massive wooden doors. He swung the doors inward and waved for us to enter.

We walked into a room lined with wooden shelves that were stuffed with books, many of which looked old, possibly even antique. Two tall windows interrupted the bookshelves and bathed the space in muted sunshine. At the room's center hulked a large but tasteful mahogany desk with a solitary lamp sitting on its surface, casting its warm glow throughout the room. Papers and pens and other office items lay on the desk, everything neatly arranged. But it wasn't the stuff on the desk that grabbed my attention.

It was the man seated in a high-backed, fancily upholstered leather chair.

The desk separated us from him. He had his eyes closed and his chair turned sideways to the desk, but he didn't move or in any way acknowledge our arrival.

"Is he asleep?" I whispered to Logan.

"No, he is not asleep," the man behind the desk said in a husky British accent. "He's thinking."

Logan surveyed the room with his gaze, the way he always did when entering a new situation. "Scheming is more like it. Alex Thorne is always plotting something."

"Am I?" Alex said as he rose from the chair. His gaze landed on me, and he smiled, exposing his perfect white teeth. He had the face of an angel, but something about the glint in his eyes clued me in to his roguish side. The beautiful Brit strode around the desk to offer me his hand. "You must be the woman who's finally tamed Logan."

"Guess I am." I slipped my hand into his, expecting a quick shake, but instead he clasped my hand in both of his. "I'm Serena Carpenter. And you must be the infamous Alex Thorne."

"Infamous?" He chuckled. "That's the MacTaggart family's opinion. I hope you'll reach your own conclusions about me." He raised my hand to kiss it. "I can see why Logan is enamored of you. I'm instantly enchanted by your beauty too."

Oh yeah, he was definitely a font of bullshit. But he did have charm, I had to admit. Gorgeous, sexy, endearing, and polite. No wonder Catriona had fallen for him. Alex's charms made me more curious about him, but I was not enchanted by the man.

Alex released my hand and returned to his chair, waving at the smaller ones on this side of the desk. "Make yourselves comfortable, please."

Logan and I settled into the fancy upholstered chairs.

"May I get you a drink?" Alex asked. He gestured toward a wet bar set into the wall between the bookshelves. "I have Talisker single malt if you'd like that, Logan."

"No," Logan replied curtly.

Alex leaned back in his chair, his elbows on the arms, and steepled his fingers under his chin. "I assume you've decided to take the job."

"First, I want to hear the details." Logan crossed his ankle over the other knee and affected a relaxed, I-don't-give-a-shit pose. "All of the details, Alex. Not the abridged and heavily edited version. Everything. Now."

Despite his casual posture and unreadable expression, his voice had a slight but unmistakable edge.

I glanced at him as desire shimmered through me. Logan the dangerous spy got me so hot.

At the same time, he made me feel safe. That no longer seemed bizarre to me. Of course he made me feel both outrageously turned on and completely safe. That was Logan.

"No pleasantries first?" Alex asked. "Perhaps a finger or two of Scotch? I have several varieties."

Logan spread his hand over his bent knee, curling his long fingers around it. "No. The facts. Immediately."

That edge had sharpened, and his expression had taken on an impossible to describe aura of deadly intent. Nobody messed with Logan.

Except Alex Thorne.

The man smiled, his eyes glittering in the filtered sunlight. The color of his irises reminded me of melted brown sugar. "Always straight to the point, aren't you, Logan?"

"Yes." Logan turned that clipped syllable into a threat simply by squinting his eyes the tiniest bit. Faint lines fanned out from the corners. "I'm not accepting the job without knowing everything. If you lie to me, or hide anything from me, I will be very annoyed with you. And if your obfuscation puts Serena in any danger, I will murder you in the most painful way I can think of." He leaned forward a smidgen. "And I have a vivid, gruesome imagination."

Despite the hot shiver slithering up my spine, I decided it was time to defuse the machismo bomb ticking away inside this room. He had every right to be irritated with Alex, but death threats seemed like overkill.

I studied Logan's face, wondering if he was really as angry as he wanted

Alex to think.

Logan glanced at me, moving only his eyes, and the corners of his lips ticked up ever so slightly, though only for a split second.

The truth hit me then. He wasn't angry at all. This was a ploy to convince Alex the consequences of lying or withholding the truth from us would be serious. I had no doubts Logan would be furious—darkly, calmly enraged—if Alex's games got us into hot water. But right now, he wasn't even annoyed.

I looked at our host. "Logan can be very intimidating, can't he? Better do what he says."

"Logan doesn't intimidate me," Alex said. "No one does. Besides, threats of murder are nothing new for me."

He said that like he was discussing the weather. Was Alex truly fearless? Or had he faked it for so long that even he couldn't tell the difference anymore? Fear was a good thing, in moderation, because it discouraged people from taking unnecessary risks. Logan understood this. Alex... He seemed to have uninstalled the fear program in his brain.

"The facts," Logan said. "Or we walk out the door."

Alex rifled through the papers on his desk, extracted a blue file folder, and set it down on the edge of the desk farthest from himself. With one finger, he spun the folder around. "Here's the dossier on Falk Mullane, a student of mine who pinched three priceless ancient tablets from the university museum."

"In your text, you implied you didn't know who the thief was."

"Did I?"

"You know you did." Logan stretched his arm out to take the folder. While he opened it and perused the papers it held, Alex continued talking.

"Falk wasn't a particularly bright student," Alex said, "but his family are important benefactors of the university, so I was required to take him on as my teaching assistant. A month ago, he broke into my office to download the final exam from my computer. I've been guilty of using 'password' as my computer password, so he didn't need hacking skills to get in. Luckily, I have cameras in my office. I knew it was him. If I'd reported Falk to the dean, he would have been expelled. I offered him a different way to do his penance, by doing me a favor."

"You blackmailed him," Logan said, glancing up from the file he held.

Alex waved a hand, dismissing the idea. "Blackmail is such an unsavory term. I...offered him an alternative."

"What, precisely, did you ask him to do?"

The enigmatic Brit rocked his chair slowly, his hands linked over his belly, and spoke in a tone that implied this was no big deal. "I'm working on a book about ancient writing systems. The museum has several Babylonian cuneiform tablets that would be of the utmost usefulness for my project, but they refuse to let me see them. I asked Falk to sort of…borrow them for me."

Logan closed the file and set it on his lap, keeping one hand on the folder. "You conspired to commit theft."

"Must you be so literal about it? I planned to return the tablets once I was done with them."

"Well, as long as you were going to return them." Logan squinted much harder this time, angling his head down just enough to project a touch of menace. "You are a thief."

Alex harrumphed. "It's no different than borrowing books from a library."

"Do you steal those too? Your definition of 'borrow' seems to be different from the dictionary version."

I put a hand on Logan's arm. "Maybe you should cut him some slack. He is fessing up to his crime."

"Yes," Alex said, "and I'm giving you plenty of ammunition to use against me. If you want to have me arrested"—he picked up the phone on his desk—"I'll dial the number for the police, and you can report me. I'm sure the word of a former MI6 agent will impress them."

Logan glared at Alex.

Our host maintained his genial demeanor, seeming more amused than irritated—and not the least bit cowed.

"All right," Logan said, relaxing into his chair. "What happened to this Falk Mullane? He ran off with your precious tablets, I presume."

"Yes." Alex steepled his fingers under his chin again. "I put a tracking device on his person so I would know where he was at all times. But it went dark ten days ago."

Words tumbled out of me before I had a chance to edit them. "You bugged your student? How? Isn't that against the law?"

"Buying the devices to do such things is not illegal, that's all I know." He scrunched up his face in disgust. "Falk always wears the same hideous baseball cap, can't stand to be without the bloody thing. I planted the tracking device inside the brim."

"Will you be tracking me and Logan too?"

"I doubt that will be necessary."

"And that's vague enough to give you wiggle room to plant trackers on us and claim you never promised not to do it."

Our host stared at me for several seconds, his expression bland, then he broke into a wide grin. "I can see why Logan likes you. Beautiful and clever. It's no wonder you're the woman who finally got under his skin. How old are you?"

"Shouldn't a man as smooth as you know not to ask a woman that question?"

"But we're mates, aren't we? That means I can ask cheeky questions."

I'd never been sensitive about my age, unlike Keely, so I saw no problem with answering. "I'm forty-two. That makes me eight years older than Logan."

"Yes, it all makes sense now." Alex rolled his chair forward and folded his arms on the desktop. "You're mature enough to know your own mind, but still young enough to keep up with Logan."

"How old are you, Mr. Thorne?"

"Dr. Thorne." He smiled with wolfish delight. "But I'd rather you call me Alex."

"Fine." I looked him straight in the eye. "I'm not interested in you, Alex, so you can dial back the charm."

He tilted his head to the side, eying me like I was a strange specimen. "You're really not interested, are you? Beautiful, clever, strong, and loyal. I'm impressed, Logan. You've found a good one." He leaned back in his chair and shook his head. "I never thought I'd see the day Logan MacTaggart fell in love."

Logan did not react to the statement, not in a way anyone else would notice. But I'd spent enough time naked with him, exploring every inch of his body and learning his every response, that I could tell he was startled.

He flipped open the folder and skimmed through the pages inside it. "What else aren't you telling me?"

"You haven't gotten to the last page in the dossier yet, have you?"

Logan tugged the last sheet of paper out of the folder and read it. He raised his brows at Alex. "Your student sent you an email to let you know he plans to sell the tablets on the black market?" Logan glanced at the paper again, this time lifting one brow at Alex. "Unless you pay him ten million dollars."

"That's right." Alex's affable facade slipped for a fraction of a second, exposing something darker, but it faded too quickly to be deciphered. "I don't give in to extortion."

"You blackmailed him, then he tried to blackmail you."

Alex picked at his shirt like he was removing lint. "I suppose you could say that. I know when I'm out of my depth, and that's why I've hired you to find Falk and retrieve the tablets."

"You haven't hired me yet," Logan said. "Not until I agree to take the job."

"Oh, you'll agree. We both know it."

"Are you sure there's nothing else you need to share?"

"I've told you everything I know."

Logan seemed satisfied with that response. He shut the folder and stood, offering his hand to Alex. "I'll find Falk Mullane for you and retrieve the artifacts. Do you want Mullane himself as well?"

Alex rose to shake Logan's hand. "I'll leave that up to you."

"One last thing." Logan speared Alex with a knife-sharp stare. "Why wouldn't the museum let you see the tablets? You're a professor of archaeology and ancient history at the university that owns the museum."

"Well…" Alex shrugged one shoulder in a negligent gesture. "I *was* a professor there. My tenure was denied, and my employment terminated."

"For what reason?"

"Misconduct. It was a false accusation."

"What sort of misconduct?" Logan asked, his gaze sharpening on Alex. "Did you seduce a female student?"

"I have never done anything inappropriate with a student."

"Catriona might disagree."

"You're implying I abused my position to seduce her. But I wasn't her teacher, and besides, the rules are different for graduate students. Things were less strict back then, at any rate."

I got up to stand beside Logan. "What did you do to get yourself fired?"

Alex scratched his chin. "I slept with the ex-wife of one of the university's most important donors. He didn't acknowledge the distinction between wife and ex-wife. She's his forever, or so the blighter thinks."

"If you're unemployed, why do you still need the tablets?"

Logan gave me an appreciative look, one infused with sensuality.

"My publishing contract was rescinded," Alex said, "but I plan to release the book myself. I'm sure I'll find another position soon enough."

I had to ask one more question, even at the risk of sounding like a dunce. "What is cuneiform, anyway?"

"The written language of the Babylonians, and the oldest known writing system. It looks rather like chicken scratches." He gave me a different kind of appreciative look than Logan had, one that seemed more intellectual than seductive. "I love a woman with a strong sense of curiosity. I'm sure Logan values that quality in you too."

Logan said nothing and gave nothing away on his face.

"Why don't you stay here tonight?" Alex asked, fulfilling Logan's prediction about where we would sleep tonight. "I have fifteen bedrooms for you to choose from, and I guarantee they're more comfortable than any hotel in this area. The food and the company will be better too."

He winked at me.

I swore Logan growled faintly, but decided I'd probably imagined it. Probably.

Logan managed a polite smile. "We'll stay here. Thank you, Alex."

"Brilliant," Alex said with a broad smile. "I took the liberty of asking the chef to prepare a meal for three. It should be ready any moment, so follow me to the dining room."

"You assumed we'd be staying here before we even arrived."

"I knew I could persuade you, but honestly, I thought it would take more effort." He shot me a high-wattage smile. "Apparently, Serena has made you less grumpy."

Logan growled, more audibly this time. "I was never grumpy."

"No," I agreed. "He was hard as nails, not grouchy."

"Was?" Logan said, his lips twitching in a teasing smile. "I'm still hard as nails, *leannan*."

I kissed his cheek and murmured into his ear, "After dinner, I'm going to feast on you for dessert."

He coughed into his fist but choked on it, and winced while he discreetly adjusted his dick through his pants.

I grinned.

Chapter Twenty-Seven

Logan

The dining room turned out to be a room as large as half of my apartment back in Carrefour—and that was no tiny space. Evan had insisted on providing me with an apartment as big as a house. What one man needed with so much space, I had no idea. Here in Alex's dining room, I realized my apartment was minuscule. This mansion could've housed my entire family, including all my cousins, their wives, and their children, not to mention their parents and grandparents.

Serena and I sat on one side of the very long table that was made of a reddish-brown wood. Alex had taken a seat on the other side, directly across from Serena.

"What a beautiful table," she said. "What kind of wood is this?"

"Dalbergia from India," he said, running his hands over the polished surface. "It's commonly known as East Indian rosewood, and it's one of the most expensive woods on earth. It's hard to work with too, which makes it even more expensive to have furniture made from it."

I tapped my fingernails on the table. "That explains why you had to have a table cut from this wood. Still obsessed with having the most expensive everything, aren't you? I've never understood the need to show off your wealth."

"To impress the ladies, of course."

No, I didn't believe that. He had some other reason for flaunting his money, but the answer didn't matter to me. I was here to do a job, not plumb the depths of Alex Thorne's soul.

Reginald, Alex's butler or housekeeper or whatever title the lord of the manor had given to the man, poked his head through the open doorway to announce dinner would be served in two minutes. Alex thanked him and looked away. He didn't see the dark sneer Reginald gave him, right before the butler disappeared into the hall.

That man had no love for the lord of the manor, but Alex seemed oblivious of Reginald's disdain for him. Maybe Alex had annoyed Reginald earlier today, or maybe he had other reasons for his display of hostility, reasons that had nothing to do with ill intentions. I decided to keep it to myself, for the moment, but keep an eye on Reginald.

Alex's mobile phone rang. He glanced at the screen, his features tightening for a heartbeat, then he excused himself to take the call in the hallway.

Serena toyed with the silverware laid out in front of her. "Reginald's British accent sounds different from Alex's."

"Reginald is faking his accent." I leaned back in my chair, which was probably made of the same high-end wood as the table. "He's Australian, not British."

"How do you know that?"

"I was a spy, *leannan*. Recognizing when someone is lying, whether with their words or their accent, can mean the difference between life and death."

"That's an impressive skill to have. Can you speak in different accents too?"

"Aye."

The lord of the manor walked back into the room, reclaiming his seat at the table. "What did I miss?"

"Serena was wondering why your man Reginald speaks with a British accent when he's from Australia."

Though surprise flashed on Alex's face, he tamped it down quickly. "You have hidden talents, don't you, Logan? Yes, Reginald is originally from Australia, born and raised in Sydney."

"Why does he pretend to be British?"

"That was his choice. He thinks Americans are more comfortable with a butler who's British." Alex smiled with genuine affection. "When I met Reggie, he was a struggling actor. After twenty years of bit parts and narrating local TV ads, he gave up and started looking for a new life path. We happened to meet, and I happened to need a right-hand man I could count on. Reggie fit the bill."

"Because he's a liar, just like you." Which made me wonder again about the look he'd given Alex earlier.

Alex laughed softly. "Ah, Logan, you have the strangest sense of humor."

"Yes, he does," Serena said. "But you get used to it."

Her dimpled cheeks told me she was teasing.

I loved the way she teased me.

But I could not let Alex off that easy. Not when he kept smiling at Serena.

So I hit Alex with—what had Serena called it?—my deadly calm stare. "Are you aware Catriona has invented several colorful, insulting nicknames for you?"

"Has she?" He affected an air of disinterest, but I wasn't convinced.

"Aye. She calls you the British Bastard, the Limey Louse, the Soulless Sassenach, and several other things I won't repeat in front of a lady."

"I see." Alex braced his elbow on his chair's arm and scratched his cheek with one finger. "How enterprising of her."

Two women bustled into the room, one pushing a cart. They went to work setting our meal on the table and serving each of us before they bustled out again.

Serena took a bite of food before she asked Alex, "What does the name of your house mean? Moirai, is it? That sounds Greek or Latin or something."

"You're correct. It's Greek." He pushed the food around on his plate but didn't eat it. "The Moirai were goddesses who set each mortal's fate at birth. Essentially, we're all fucked from the moment we crawl out of the womb."

The bitterness in his voice surprised me, but I decided his attitude toward fate was irrelevant to the mission.

Alex regained his annoyingly cheerful attitude within minutes, and throughout dinner, Alex and Serena blethered about things of little interest to me, like archaeology and home decor. Serena laughed at his jokes and smiled at him often. I tried to remember she was being friendly, nothing more, but the way Alex looked at her made my shoulders bunch up and my hands curl into loose fists.

If he didn't stop smiling at her, I might throw my plate at his head.

To stave off an assault charge, I sneaked my hand onto Serena's thigh and massaged her flesh.

Her breathing grew uneven.

I watched Alex, my lips curving into a self-satisfied smile, and kept massaging her thigh.

She slapped her hand over mine, but instead of peeling it away from her leg, she guided my hand down to the hem of her dress and slipped it underneath the fabric. When she pulled her hand away, I eased the dress up until my fingertips brushed her panties.

They were damp.

I swallowed a Gaelic curse. She was ready for me, right here, right now, in front of Alex Thorne. A fleeting thought tormented me, that maybe she was aroused for him and not me, but then I realized how daft that idea was. Though he'd been flirting with her all through dinner, she hadn't reciprocated. Her laughter and smiles had been friendly, not seductive.

Besides, I was the one currently sliding my fingers inside her wet panties.

Serena jerked, though only a little. Her pupils had enlarged, and her cheeks sported the faintest speckles of pink.

And Christ, she was getting wetter by the second.

I sneaked a finger between her folds, stroking her up and down, slowly and deliberately. I wanted my head between her legs, but for now, this would have to do.

Our host made a bad joke, and Serena laughed with a hint of panic in her voice.

Did she mind me touching her this way in this setting? With Alex talking to her? She had put my hand under her dress, so I decided she liked what I was doing.

She took a sip of her wine and spluttered when I pinched her clit.

"Are you all right?" I asked calmly, despite the fact my cock was getting harder by the second. "Maybe you drank your wine too quickly."

"No, I'm fine." She spread her thighs, giving me full access to her body. "Alex, tell me more about those cuneiform tablets. It sounds fascinating."

He launched into a mini lecture about the tablets.

I moved my whole hand between her thighs, rubbing the heel against her hard nub, curling and uncurling my fingers to tease her folds. While she pretended to be engrossed by Alex's lecture, I thrust my middle finger inside her.

"How fascinating," she said to Alex, though I was fair certain she had no fucking idea what he'd just said.

Thrusting my finger in and out, rubbing her with the heel of my hand, I watched her expression. When I added a second finger, her eyes flared wider for a second. Her body tensed.

She was about to come.

In front of Alex.

"Suddenly, I'm in the mood for Talisker," I told him. "Would you mind getting that bottle?"

"Happy to."

Alex got up and left the room, though the door stayed open.

I laid a palm on Serena's cheek and turned her face toward me, taking her mouth in a hard, hot kiss while I worked her body with my fingers and palm. My mouth muffled her cry when she came. Her entire body went rigid and jerked with every spasm, but I kept rubbing until her climax faded.

When we pried our lips apart, her mouth curved into a dreamy smile. Her cheeks were flushed, her lips swollen.

My cock was stiff as steel.

Alex sauntered back into the room carrying a bottle of Talisker single malt Scotch whisky and three glasses. He sat down and poured two fingers of whisky into each glass, then handed one to me and another to Serena.

She swigged hers in one gulp—and promptly started coughing.

I patted her back. "Easy there, *gràidh*. Whisky is for sipping, not pouring down your throat."

Alex observed her like he couldn't quite figure out why she'd done that.

"My fault," I whispered into her ear. "I shouldn't have done that to you, but I couldn't resist. You are so fucking beautiful when you come."

Alex observed us with his brows furrowed. "Did I miss something?"

"Nothing that's any of your business," I said.

Serena picked up her water glass and took a dainty sip. "I could really go for something sweet."

Alex's gaze darted between me and Serena, but then settled on her.

Would he figure out what we'd been doing? He was clever...

His lips crept into a knowing smile.

I might've been smirking.

Serena affected a look of innocence that was not at all convincing. "So, is there dessert?"

"Yes," Alex said, "there is. Shall we have it in the living room?"

While we trailed Alex down the hall, with a few meters between us and him, Serena tucked her arm under mine and pressed close to my side. She spoke in a voice too soft for Alex to hear, unless he had unnaturally sensitive hearing like Superman, which quite frankly wouldn't have shocked me, knowing how strange and secretive the man was.

"You looked kind of testy for a while there," Serena said. "Jealous?"

"No," I hissed, sounding like the jealous man she was accusing me of being. Calming my voice, I added, "I didn't like the way he was looking at you."

She clamped her teeth down on her lips to stifle a laugh, resulting in a soft snorting noise. "That's the definition of jealousy, Logan."

"No, it's called guarding what's mine."

"Uh-huh, sure." She looked up at me with her lips tight from the smile she was struggling not to show. It twinkled in her eyes anyway. "Whatever makes you feel better."

"You like Alex."

"Sure, he's fun to talk to. But don't worry, I'm interested in only one man." She craned her neck to peck a kiss on my cheek. "That's you, in case there was any doubt."

I sighed with mock disappointment. "Guess I won't have to murder him, dismember his body, and bury the pieces across the State of Montana after all."

"Nope." She rested her cheek on my arm. "You're not fooling me. I know you like Alex."

"He's an erse and a *bod ceann*."

"Come off it, Logan. You may not trust him a hundred percent, but he is your friend."

I made a rude noise.

She tipped her head back to aim a tender smile at me. "You won't admit Evan is your best friend. You won't admit you like Alex. I remember a time when you thought I was a raging bitch. At least now you admit you like me, but you really should cut Alex some slack. He's still in love with Catriona."

I didn't have the chance to ask how she arrived at that conclusion, because we had reached the living room. Serena was right about Alex, I was sure of it, but I wanted to know how she'd figured that out. I had years of experience in ferreting out secrets.

The three of us enjoyed a pleasant conversation over dessert. Afterward, Alex announced he was "retiring for the evening," which I took to mean he was off to bed. As he headed for the stairs, he told us, "The servants are asleep, so you have the house to yourselves. Explore, if you like."

"You call them servants?" Serena asked. "Isn't that kind of outdated?"

He paused at the bottom of the stairs. "Would you prefer I call them employees? Either way, they do my bidding."

She gave him that skeptical look I knew so well, having been on the receiving end of it many times. It translated roughly as *you're blowing smoke up my erse, but I'm not having any of it.* "Thank you for a lovely evening, Alex."

"You're welcome." He waved for us to follow him. "Come, I'll show you the room I think will work best for the two of you. I'm assuming you want to sleep together."

"That's very considerate," Serena said.

He showed us to the room farthest from where he slept. It was enormous. The massive bed seemed small in the cavernous space, and I swore my breathing echoed off the high ceiling. While Serena went into the attached bathroom to get ready for bed, I poked my head in to tell her I was going downstairs to get a glass of water.

"You're going to snoop," she said, glancing at me over her shoulder.

I should've known I couldn't fool her. "No, *leannan*, it's called reconnaissance. But only if you're an ex-spy. For average people, it's called being nosy."

"Have fun being nosy, then."

"Cheeky lass." I slapped her erse. "Stay here. I won't be long."

Before she could complain about my command that she stay put, I hurried out the door. What I expected to find, I had no idea. Alex was hiding something, probably several things, but I didn't know if those secrets affected the mission I'd agreed to undertake for him, or if they were unrelated and therefore none of my business.

I was examining a locked door across from the dining room, mulling whether to break in, when I heard the stairs creak.

A soft "shit" followed.

Chuckling, I walked back to the stairs.

Serena had just reached the bottom, hunched over in some sort of attempt to be stealthy. When she saw me, she grimaced. "Busted, huh?"

"Where are you going?"

She hunched her shoulders.

I took in her appearance—a knee-length satin robe and nothing else. "You're barefoot. Are you at least wearing something under that robe?"

"Nope, I'm naked as a jaybird."

Her statement both irritated and aroused me. She was the only woman on earth who could do both to me at the same time.

"What are you doing?" I asked.

"Snooping. Like you."

"You're bloody awful at it. I heard you coming down the stairs." I tried to frown at her but couldn't quite pull it off. "Shouting 'shit' isn't very stealthy."

"I did not shout. I hissed."

"Whatever you say."

She glanced around, looking for all the world like a cartoon character making sure the villains weren't lurking nearby. Then she took my hand. "Come on, let's go to Alex's study."

"Why?"

"To snoop."

I let her lead me off toward the study, enchanted by her excitement over the prospect of rifling through Alex's desk. Had I corrupted the lass? If I had, I couldn't regret it. She was endearing as a somewhat bumbling would-be spy.

Light spilled out of the study into the hall.

Serena stopped us at the edge of the light. She tiptoed sideways, dragging me by the hand, until we could see into the room without moving into the glow the lamp inside cast out here. Alex was reclining in his chair, facing the doorway, his eyes closed. A half-empty bottle of Talisker sat on the desktop beside an empty glass.

Serena gave me a puzzled look. She mouthed, "Asleep?"

I shook my head.

"Not asleep," Alex announced, opening his eyes. "You might as well come in. Sorry to interrupt your plans to… What were you wanting in my study? A shag on the desk?"

Now that he mentioned it, aye, that would've been perfect.

Serena dragged me into the study. "We were planning to snoop. You know, go through your desk drawers and stuff. Since you're not in your bedroom, maybe we'll start there instead."

"Logan, you are one lucky bastard. Serena is delightfully naughty."

Aye, she was. But I didn't like hearing *him* say it.

"Why aren't you in bed?" I asked. "You said you were retiring."

"I needed to think, and I do that better here."

"You mean you wanted to get drunk, and your liquor is in here."

He lifted one shoulder.

Serena moved closer to the desk. "Why did you want to get drunk?"

Alex picked up the empty glass and turned it in his hand. "I'm a British Bastard, remember? We Limey Louses tend to do things like that."

Serena and I exchanged glances.

Looking into her eyes, I knew she'd come to the same conclusion I had. Despite his flippant response when I'd told him about Cat's nicknames for him, the truth had knocked him back on his erse. He might have said Cat despised him, but he hadn't really believed it until tonight.

"Never mind," Alex said breezily, getting up from his chair and wobbling the slightest bit. "The study is yours, to do with as you please."

He hurried out of the room. His footsteps clomped on the stairs, fast and loud enough to echo down the hall.

At least he wasn't drunk enough to fall down the stairs.

"That was odd," I said. "Alex Thorne upset? I've never seen it before."

"He's still pining for Catriona." Serena turned toward me and undid the belt on her robe, letting it fall open to reveal all of her creamy skin. "But let's not talk about that anymore."

"Aye, let's not." I slung an arm around her waist and pulled her snug against me. "Let's defile Alex's desk."

Chapter Twenty-Eight

Serena

We didn't see Alex at breakfast. We didn't see him when we left for the airport. On our way out the door, we asked Reginald where Alex was and if he was all right. The butler almost sneered when he told us, "Dr. Thorne is indisposed." I wondered if Reginald's opinion of his employer wasn't a good one, despite the fact Alex clearly thought of him as a friend. Logan and I agreed "indisposed" meant Alex had a hangover. Jeez, he must've gotten drunker after he went upstairs last night. Hearing the nasty nicknames Catriona had given him must've upset the man a lot more than he wanted us to know.

Once we'd boarded Evan's jet, which our CEO had given us permission to use for as long as we needed to go wherever we wanted, Logan and I settled in on the sofa. He slipped his arm around my shoulders, with his fingers trailing down my arm.

"Where are we going?" I asked.

"Cairo."

"Egypt?"

"Yes, *gràidh*. Alex gave me all the information about the tracking device he planted on Falk Mullane. The last ping came from Egypt."

"Why would Falk take Babylonian tablets to Cairo?"

Logan brushed his fingertips up and down my arm. "To sell them, no doubt. Mullane must have underworld connections, and he's found a buyer for the tablets. The lad has a record, for petty crimes like shoplifting and vandalism. He's also spoiled. To excess. His parents aren't billionaires, but they are upper middle class—very upper. They've bought Falk everything he wanted, from a Mustang convertible to a small house near the university."

"Why would a man who's sitting pretty risk everything by committing crimes?"

"Boredom." He traced circles on my arm while he gazed straight ahead at nothing in particular. "I've seen it many times. A prince will become a terrorist because he has nothing better to do, and what the hell, he might get into heaven sooner and have a harem of women at his disposal for eternity. Falk Mullane isn't likely to get a harem, but he will have the thrill of doing something dangerous and clandestine."

"Do you wish for the same excitement? Even a little bit?"

"No." He turned his face to me, his features tight. "Do you believe me?"

"Yes. If you say it, I believe it."

The tension eased out of him, and he sank back against the sofa. "I've sent Evan all the information about the tracking device. He's offered to check it out for us. The device isn't one of a kind, it's an off-the-shelf model, so he should be able to get an identical one and deconstruct it."

"Will that help us?"

"It might. Or it might not."

"Pretty handy to have a billionaire tech genius as your cousin, and your best friend."

Logan threw his head back and groaned. "*Mhac na galla.* Will ye ever stop pestering me to admit Evan and Alex are my friends?"

"Afraid not." I tickled his lips. "And in case you've forgotten, I know what your Gaelic curse words mean."

He hissed something under his breath that I couldn't quite make out.

"What was that?" I asked.

"Russian." He kissed the tip of my nose. "Since you know Gaelic, I'd better start cursing in a different language."

"Stick to Gaelic. It suits you."

"In that case, let's test your knowledge." He pulled me close, our noses touching and our gazes locked. "*An toir thu dhomh pòg.*"

The smoldering heat in his voice set off a matching fire between my legs.

"Sorry, I don't know that one," I said. "But it must be about sex. You've got that lusty look in your eye."

"*An toir thu dhomh pòg* means give us a kiss."

"Us?" I glanced around like I was searching for other men. "Do you want to have a foursome with the pilots?"

"No. I'm wanting you to kiss me."

"Why didn't you say that? The word us implies—"

He covered my mouth with his.

When he pulled away, I was breathless from the intensity of his kiss. This man had skills, in kissing, in bed, in detecting fake accents, everything. I was sure Logan could do anything he wanted and do it very, very well.

"It's a long flight," he said. "Get some rest."

"Not tired. I only woke up a couple hours ago. If we had a deck of cards, we could play poker."

"You know the game?"

"Don't look so shocked." I prodded his chest. "I beat your cousin Rory at it, and I've been told he's the family expert, unbeatable."

"When did you play poker with Rory?"

"A few months ago, when he brought his wife and kids to Carrefour to visit Keely and Evan. Keely's a poker demon too, but she rarely beats me."

"No one's as clever as you." He studied me with a look of amused fascination. "What are the stakes in these poker games?"

"Food. Candy, usually. Butterscotch is my favorite."

"How many butterscotch candies did you win from Rory?"

I raised my chin like the haughty bitch he'd once thought I was. "I'll have you know, I won a whole package of them. One of those family-size bags, not a piddly little thing."

He braced his head on one raised hand, his arm on the sofa's back. "You surprise me constantly, Serena. It's…refreshing. Not many people can do that to me."

"I don't think I've ever surprised anyone before." I pretended to think hard, squinting my eyes and squishing my lips. "Actually, I surprised Rory when I beat him at candy poker. He's very good at the game."

"Aye, Rory's good." Logan caught the back of my head in his big hand and tugged me closer. "But I'm better."

"You mean at poker?"

"At everything."

We moved into comfy chairs on either side of a small table. A deck of cards lay on the table's highly polished surface. Logan had found a hidden compartment under the sofa that held all sorts of games, from checkers to cards. He insisted we play strip poker, but I reminded him there were other people on board.

"Do you really want the pilots and the flight attendant to see you naked?" I asked.

"No," he replied, "especially since the flight attendant is a man. But it would be you they'd see naked, not me. I'm going to win."

"Overconfident, hmm?" I picked up the deck of cards and shuffled it. "I beat Rory, remember?"

"If I'd ever played with him, I would have beaten him soundly. And for more than candy." He watched me shuffle the deck again. "What are the stakes, *mo leannan*?"

God, I loved it when he called me his sweetheart. "Let's play for kisses."

"Kisses? That might lead to fucking, ye know."

"Oh darn." I dealt the cards. "The winner gets the first orgasm."

"I'm liking these stakes better than candy or money."

We played for an hour, each of us earning kisses, each kiss more heated than the one before. I beat Logan, though I suspected he'd lost on purpose. And yeah, I got the first orgasm—first of several. After that, we got dressed and watched movies on the built-in big-screen TV, ate a gourmet meal served by Evan's chef, and played another round of poker.

I let Logan win that time.

And after that, we both needed naps.

We arrived in Cairo in the evening, a little after sunset. Just as the plane was landing, Logan received a call from Evan. They talked for thirty seconds at most, which had me wondering what on earth they'd been conferring about. While we exited the jet and tromped down the stairs, I asked Logan about it.

"Evan examined the tracking device." Logan lifted me off the last step by grasping my waist. "He found a way to ping the tracker even if it's turned off. Don't ask me how. He explained, but technology isn't my strong suit. I can use it, but don't expect me to understand it."

"Don't feel bad. I wouldn't understand what Evan said either. That's why he's the tech genius, and we're the grunt workers."

"I love grunting with you."

We drove a rented car, an average-looking, nondescript vehicle that wouldn't stand out like the uber-luxury model Alex had wanted to give us. When he'd told us his plan last evening, before the drinking-alone-in-the-study incident, Logan had told him we needed to blend in, not advertise our presence.

"That's why I hired you," Alex had said. "No one knows how to be sneaky better than you."

It was true. Logan drove—he'd been here before and remembered the layout of the city—while I watched out the windows to get glimpses of Cairo. I would've loved to see the sights, but we weren't here on vacation. Logan needed to hunt down Falk Mullane, and I relished the chance to see him in action. Knowing he'd been a spy was different from experiencing that side of him. We were in a relationship now, so I needed to know all of him.

And I loved that he wanted to show it to me.

Evan had sent Logan an app for his phone that showed us the current location of Falk's tracking device. Logan gave me his phone, saying I would be his navigator. I got a glowy feeling in my chest knowing that he wanted to include me as more than window dressing or a silent passenger. He talked to me while he drove, about nothing important. To keep me relaxed, I realized. Not knowing what we might be walking into had me on edge.

Not because I felt endangered. As long as I was with Logan, I knew nothing bad would happen to me. I had a normal amount of fear, of course, unlike the apparently fearless Alex. But I trusted Logan to watch out for our safety, mine and his. Mostly, I was excited. We were on a spy mission. Together.

The blinking green dot hadn't moved since we'd first activated the app.

While Logan steered the car around a corner, I asked, "Is it a bad sign that the dot hasn't moved?"

"Not necessarily. Mullane could be sleeping."

"This early in the evening? It's barely past seven."

"Maybe he's exhausted from pinching antiquities and selling them to illicit collectors."

The green dot on the screen flashed red for a second. Two words appeared onscreen: "Tracker active."

"What does this mean?" I asked as I tilted the screen so Logan could see.

He glanced at it and frowned. "That's not good."

Yanking the steering wheel, he swerved over to the side of the street to park.

"What's wrong?" I asked.

Logan took the phone. "Someone turned on the tracker."

"It couldn't have come on by itself? Like it had a weak signal and now it's getting a strong one again?"

"Since the tracker hasn't moved, that wouldn't make sense. Besides, Evan told me the device couldn't be turned off, it could only be disabled permanently. For it to come on again…"

"That's bad. Really bad."

"Aye." He squinted at the screen. "This might be a trap."

Before I could express my confusion, he dialed a number on his phone and held it to his ear.

"Are you calling Evan or Alex?" I asked.

He held up a finger to silence me.

I watched him and waited.

"Evan," he said, "can the tracker turn itself back on spontaneously? That's what I thought. Are you sure? Thank you." He disconnected the call. "It's what I thought. The device must've been shielded so it wouldn't be able to send a signal. That's a purposeful act, not a fluke. Evan says someone was blocking the signal, and now they've let it through again."

"To trap us."

He nodded, looking very unhappy with the situation. "I'm taking you to a hotel, then I'll find Mullane."

"No. I'm with you all the way."

"Serena—"

"That was the deal. We do this together."

"It's too dangerous. I won't put you at risk."

"So don't." I grasped his face with both hands. "I trust you, Logan. And I'm a big girl, I can handle myself. Before I became an executive assistant, I was a nurse. If you get injured, I can patch you up. You need me."

He glowered at the steering wheel, clenching it with both hands. "Fine. You're coming with me, but you do exactly as I say. Understood?"

"Yes, sir, secret agent man."

"This is not a game."

"I know, and I'll do what you say, unless I have no choice but to do something else instead."

"Agreed." He steered the car back onto the street. "I'm glad you wore jeans and walking shoes. If you need to run, you're dressed for it. If anything should happen to me, head for the US embassy."

My mouth went dry. He was worried, more than I'd realized until this moment. But I couldn't leave him to walk into possible danger alone, not knowing if he would live or die. I wasn't there when Rob died. At least this time, I would be at Logan's side if anything did happen. I would know exactly what went down and why he was taken from me.

I shut my eyes and said a prayer. *Keep Logan safe. Please, God, don't take him away from me too.*

Chapter Twenty-Nine

Logan

It was fully dark by the time we found the location of the tracker's ping. I tried again to talk Serena into going to a hotel, but she refused to do it. Maybe I should have pushed harder, driven her to a hotel and locked her in the room, but I couldn't make myself do it. She wanted to stay with me. I understood she was worried about what might happen, and she had good reason to worry after the way she'd lost her husband. Maybe I should've pointed out she had a son at home, and she shouldn't put herself at risk. But I couldn't make myself do that either.

Whether it was reckless and irresponsible or not, I let her come with me. I wanted her with me. No woman had ever asked to accompany me on a mission.

Serena wasn't an average woman. She was…extraordinary.

The location turned out to be a small, dilapidated warehouse on the outskirts of Cairo, situated barely off the Nile flood plain. Of course, the Nile didn't flood like it used to before the construction of the Aswan High Dam.

Aye, a dam was what I should be thinking about right now.

I drove past the warehouse, not even pulling into the driveway, and circled back around on narrow streets until I found a good place to hide our vehicle.

"We'll need to walk," I said. "About two blocks, that's all. But we have to be quiet and inconspicuous."

"No whooping or shooting off fireworks. Check."

"This is serious, Serena."

She squeezed my hand. "I know. Inappropriate humor is how I'm dealing with the fact I'm terrified."

"You're not terrified, you're excited. Which is worse."

"Don't worry, Logan. I'll follow your lead. I trust your instincts and your expertise with this spy stuff. I trust you, period."

She trusted me. She would listen to me.

I looked into her eyes, and pressure gripped my heart. Not a bad feeling. A strange and unprecedented feeling that my life had changed more than I'd realized until this moment.

Serena got out of the car first, and I followed, heading for the trunk. Our bags were inside. I retrieved the item I needed and showed it to her.

"That's a gun," she said. "Is the situation that bad?"

"I hope not, but I believe in being prepared."

"Where did you get a semiautomatic handgun?"

"Alex gave it to me last night. I didn't bring my own weapon, since I had no idea how serious the situation was." I ejected the magazine and checked it was full, then snapped it back in. "Naturally, Alex neglected to mention a few things. Like the fact Falk Mullane has a record and has underworld connections."

I strapped on the shoulder holster Alex had also given me. Why an archaeologist needed a gun and a shoulder holster should've confused me, but knowing Alex, I hadn't been surprised at all. The man had a tendency to get himself into trouble.

"Do you know how to use a gun?" I asked Serena.

"Yes. Rob taught me how to fire and clean a semiautomatic pistol. I still have his service weapon, though I haven't used it since he passed away. But I remember everything he taught me."

"Good." I grabbed another item from my bag.

"Zip ties?" Serena said. "What are those for?"

"Restraint." I stuffed the bundle of zip ties into my pocket and brought out the last item I needed, a flat rectangular box the size of my palm that resembled a tablet computer. "This is a thermal imaging device, created and patented by Evan. It will let us see into the warehouse before we go inside and tell us how many live bodies are in there."

"Live bodies? You mean people."

"Could be animals too."

"Oh. Right."

Stowing the thermal imaging device in my shirt pocket, I shut the trunk and took Serena's hand. We slunk down the dark road toward the warehouse. My eyes adjusted to the darkness as we moved, so by the time we reached the warehouse, I could see well enough. The half-moon glowing above us helped too. We dropped into a crouch as we turned onto the driveway, where tall reeds lined one side, giving us decent cover.

We stopped halfway up the drive and huddled there.

I brought out the thermal imager, switching it on. The screen managed to be readable while giving off very little light. Only viewing the screen head-on could I see the image on it. I had no idea how Evan managed that, but then, he was a billionaire for a very good reason. The man was a genius.

And according to Serena, my best friend.

Thinking about that would have to wait until later. I needed to focus on the little screen displaying heat signatures as multicolored shapes. I moved the tablet slowly, panning over the warehouse, counting the bodies and noting where they were.

Serena pressed her mouth to my ear and whispered, "How many?"

I held up five fingers.

We continued toward the building in a crouch. I would've preferred to belly-crawl, but I wouldn't do that with Serena here. Not that I was sorry she'd come. Having her with me felt...right. If I'd asked her to belly-crawl with me, she would've done it, but I wouldn't be able to keep an eye on her as easily if we did that.

Ten meters from the warehouse, I stopped us again and checked the thermal imager. Still five bodies. One of them was probably Falk Mullane, which left four hostiles. Assuming Mullane wasn't a hostile. Maybe he was, considering he'd tried to blackmail Alex. I couldn't assume he wanted to be rescued, when he might have joined forces with whoever else hid inside the warehouse.

From this distance, I could see more details on the building. Most of the windows were smashed or missing altogether. Where a set of large doors had once been, there was a gaping maw of darkness. One of the old doors lay on the ground a couple dozen meters away, like it had been thoughtlessly discarded when the owners abandoned the place.

I didn't like this at all.

An abandoned building. In the middle of nothing. Four hostiles and one unknown quantity holed up inside it. Mullane had a criminal record—petty stuff, but still a record—so I had to assume he was in there with other criminals, possibly ones more dangerous than he was.

Keeping Serena behind me, and her hand in mine, I crept toward the building and sidled along its wall until we reached the gaping maw that had once been a doorway.

I glanced at Serena.

She nodded.

We tiptoed through the massive doorway into the unknown.

The thermal imager had shown targets to the right. I could make out a hallway in that direction. I turned down the hall, keeping my back to the wall. Serena did the same as she gripped my hand more firmly. I gave her hand a light squeeze, my attempt to reassure her. I had no idea what we might find, but I didn't want her terrified. Alert and aware, that was the right mindset. I had no doubts she could manage it.

Our shoes made no sound on the concrete floor.

Voices drifted to us from further down the hall. I couldn't make out the words, but I had the impression they weren't speaking English. As we neared the source of the voices, I noticed a room at the end of the hall, directly in front of us. It either had no door or the door was open all the way. The room inside was gloomy, with only ambient light from a window to illuminate it.

I pulled out the gun Alex had given me.

Serena stuck close behind me, her body almost plastered to mine, as we edged closer and closer to the doorway.

The voices grew louder, and I paused to listen. They alternated between Russian and English, as if they were explaining what they'd said to someone who didn't know Russian. Another voice occasionally spoke Arabic. I couldn't quite make out the words, but I recognized the accent and the cadence of each language.

Enough waiting for these bastards to reveal themselves.

I slipped the gun into Serena's hand.

She didn't balk, didn't react at all other than to close her hand around it.

Wonderful lass.

I took a slow, deep breath.

And I charged into the room.

Chapter Thirty

Serena

Logan bolted into the darkened room like an avenging angel, though he had no divine powers to protect him. He'd given me the gun, which meant he was unarmed. Why bring a gun if he wasn't going to use it? The truth hit me as Logan rammed into a shadowy figure inside the room, seemingly in slow motion, though I knew it was adrenaline altering my perception of time.

He was trusting me to not do something stupid. And to realize he didn't need a weapon to take down bad guys. He was also trusting me to know when he might need the gun and to give it to him at the right moment.

Logan trusted me. And I trusted him.

Inside the room, Logan tackled a man to the floor and punched him three times, until the man stopped fighting.

Another figure separated from the shadows and headed straight for Logan. Though Logan had jumped to his feet, he was facing away from the onrushing attacker.

"Behind you!" I shouted from the doorway, where I hugged the jamb.

Logan spun around and dealt with the attacker, knocking him out with two swift punches and a wicked blow to the groin delivered by his knee.

Peripherally, I noticed something on the opposite side of the doorway, close to the jam. Could it be a light switch? Did this place have electricity? Would more light help or hurt Logan?

Another figure rushed at him, landing a nasty wallop to his gut before he had time to react. Logan doubled over and stumbled backward. He recovered from the blow quickly, but not quick enough. His new attacker grabbed something off the floor, a pipe or a length of wood, and swung it back as if preparing to strike.

I couldn't stand here doing nothing, and I didn't think I could hit a shadowy target with the gun. I needed light.

Without a clue what I might find, I pushed away from the jamb and rushed across the doorway. My fingers found the object I'd seen—a light switch, thank heaven—and I flicked it.

Light flooded the room, blinding me for a second.

It must've blinded Logan's attacker too, and Logan.

My vision cleared right as the attacker, a burly man with a scarred face, swung his pipe at Logan.

Logan caught the pipe and rammed his knee up into the man's groin. He tore the pipe from the villain's grasp and swung it like a baseball bat, whacking the creep in the gut.

The bad guy staggered backward, but he didn't stop.

Logan wielded the pipe with both hands, ready to strike again.

A fourth man loitered on the other side of the room, which looked like an old office, along with a fifth man who was tied to a chair.

I didn't have a chance to take in more details. The fourth bad buy whipped out a large knife and tossed it to the thug Logan had walloped with a pipe.

The villain charged at Logan, knife in hand.

No time to think. I reacted on instinct.

I raised the gun and fired.

The shot hit the thug in the shoulder. He dropped the knife, lost his balance, and stumbled into an old metal desk. Dazed, he slumped to the floor.

"Get the bitch!" the thug shouted to his cohort, his voice thickly colored by what sounded a lot like a Russian accent.

The only man left standing abandoned the guy strapped to the chair and whipped out a gun, aiming it at me.

Logan catapulted over the desk to tackle the man. The gun went spinning across the concrete floor.

The thug staggered to his feet, glaring at me with murder in his eyes.

I aimed my gun at him. "Stop right there."

Logan grabbed the zip ties out of his pocket. He roughly shoved the man who'd formerly held a gun into a dilapidated but sturdy wooden chair, securing his wrists by looping the zip tie through a spindle in the chair's back. That creep would not be running away, at least not fast enough to escape. Logan proceeded to secure two of the other men where they lay on the floor, but for the big thug he used four zip ties to secure the man's wrists and ankles, tying him to the old metal desk that I noticed was bolted to the floor. He wouldn't be escaping either. Not that I believed for one second any of these guys had a chance in hell of getting away from Logan even if he hadn't tied them up.

He approached the man who was tied to the chair.

I hurried over there too. The man looked young, twenties by my estimate. He had dirty blond hair that needed a trim and an angular face. I'd seen that face before. Alex's dossier on Falk Mullane had included a photo of the grad student.

We'd found Falk. But where were the tablets?

Falk stared blankly at us for a couple seconds, then burst into tears.

Well, he burst into sobs. I didn't see any actual tears. I exchanged glances with Logan, who seemed equally unimpressed by Falk's display. The kid was faking it.

He wasn't a kid, though. He was an adult. Much younger than I was, but a grown man nonetheless.

Logan barred his arms over his chest as he aimed his patented scary-calm glare at Falk. "Terrified are ye?"

The words conveyed no concern or empathy.

Falk faked a few more sobs. "Oh, th-thank God. P-please get me out of h-here, whoever you are. These m-men kidnapped m-me and threatened to k-kill me."

"I see," Logan said, tipping his head side to side while squinting at the man tied to the chair. "Afraid you're overdoing it, laddie. A few too many stammers in your plea for help."

Falk's eyes bulged, and his lip quivered.

Quivered too much. He was in no danger of winning an Academy Award for his performance.

The supposed prisoner bowed his head and let out a loud, not-the-least-convincing sob. "P-please, I d-don't know wh-what you m-mean."

Logan laughed, though the sound was menacing rather than cheerful. "I've seen drunk prostitutes put on a more believable performance." He ambled behind Falk, studying something on the back of the chair. "If you were a genuine prisoner, those scunners over there would have tied you up better than this. You can slip out of this rope anytime."

"Are you serious?" Falk said with too much relief and excitement. "Thank God those guys didn't tie the rope right."

"Oh, they tied it correctly." Logan reached down, flicked something, and the rope around Falk's wrists fell to the floor. "Your men made sure you could easily get yourself free, the way you instructed them to do."

Falk rubbed his wrists like they hurt, but given how easily Logan had released the restraints, I doubted Falk had any rope burns.

"What do you mean?" Falk asked. "You can't seriously think those guys work for me. I was kidnapped."

Logan moved in front of the supposed prisoner, standing inches from the man, and planted his shoe on the chair between Falk's legs. "You are a liar."

"Please, you gotta believe me."

"No one has to believe anything. And I donnae believe a word that's come out of your mouth." Logan bent his raised knee and leaned into it. "Try again, laddie."

Falk clamped his lips shut, flattening them. His gaze skipped around the room as he took in the sight of the four burly men Logan had defeated single-handedly. Falk's attention shifted to me, and his brows squished together. "Who's the chick?"

Nobody had ever called me a chick before, not even when I was a teenager.

Logan snapped his fingers in front of Falk's eyes. "Look at me, laddie, not her. I'm your entire world right now, so forget about everyone else in this room and *look at me*."

If he'd spoken those words to me, in that icy tone, I would've obeyed him.

Falk had at least that much sense, since he swerved his gaze back to Logan.

But of course, he couldn't keep his trap shut. "Why'd you bring your girlfriend? She's a potential hostage."

"Hostage?" Logan chuckled with such dark intent that a thrill rippled through me. "Think again, Mullane. Do yourself a favor and start telling the truth. Why did you hire those men?"

"What? I didn't—"

Logan transferred his foot to Falk's chest and leaned in close enough his breaths fluttered Falk's hair. Their noses were almost touching. "No more lies, no more evasion. The truth. Or I might need to resort to digging the facts out of you."

I had no idea what "digging the facts out" meant, but I was positive it wouldn't be pleasant. Logan would never take it too far, of that I was certain, but I had no doubts he knew every possible way to get the truth out of someone.

Falk's eyes widened. "Shit, man, you're seriously whacked, aren't you?"

Logan gave Falk's chest a shove with his shoe. "Stop yer blethering, ye *cacan*. You have five seconds to confess. One, two—"

"I don't—it's not—"

"Three, four—"

"Okay-okay!" Falk threw his hands up in surrender but made the mistake of glancing at me. "Jeez, lady, can you get your pit bull off my chest? He's speaking in tongues or something."

Logan backhanded Falk, making the twerp yelp and flinch. "What did I say about looking at her?"

"Not to do it."

"And will ye be doing that again, ye *cacan*?"

Falk shook his head. "No. But, uh, half of what you say sounds like gibberish."

"It's Gaelic, laddie. I called you a wee shit, which is what you are. A *cacan* and an eejit." Logan raised his hand as if to backhand Falk again. "Start talking."

"Yeah, sure, yeah." Falk squirmed, turning his face away but peeking at Logan out the corner of his eye. "Did Alex send you? I only ask 'cuz it'll make this easier to explain if you already know what he made me do."

"Alex Thorne didn't make you do anything." Logan folded his arms over his raised knee, his foot still pinned to Falk's chest. "He offered you a job, and being a larcenous little *bod ceann*, you took it. And then you blackmailed him."

Falk looked confused but had enough sense to not ask what *bod ceann* meant. Logan was calling Falk a dickhead, and I had to agree the term was fitting.

"Look at me," Logan said.

The *bod ceann* faced Logan again, swallowing hard. "Yeah, I blackmailed him. Alex deserved it, though. He's such a prick and thinks he's always right, and how does he get all those women to sleep with him? That asshole gets more tail than any—"

Logan seized Falk's nose and twisted it, letting go as soon as the twit flinched and said ow. "Focus, laddie, and forget about Alex. Your petty jealousy is not illuminating. Start with the thugs you hired."

"Oh, them." The twit shrugged, managing a sheepish smile. "I hired them over the internet. A friend taught me how to get on the dark web, and I found a site where you can hire anybody to do anything. So I did."

I couldn't resist speaking any longer. "Did you pay by Visa or Mastercard? Probably got double cash back for a bulk purchase. Or maybe the dark web has a four-thugs-for-the-price-of-two deal."

Logan threw me an amused look over his shoulder, one that Falk couldn't see.

"Sorry—" I cut myself off before I said *sorry, honey*. Logan was in a groove with the badass spy routine, and I didn't want to ruin the mood. "I'll be quiet."

Falk seemed to have run out of common sense, because he sniggered at Logan. "You whipped or what? Maybe your girlfriend should do the interrogating." He sneered at me. "Gimme a blow job and I'll tell you everything. With that mouth, I bet you suck guys off real good."

A muscle pulsed in Logan's jaw, and his eyes narrowed to slits.

Oh no, Falk, you moron. Biiiig mistake.

Logan slugged Falk in the stomach. "Never look at her again. Never speak to her. For you, she does not exist. Understand?"

Wheezing, his face flushing crimson, Falk nodded.

"Good." Logan removed his foot from the other man's chest and took half a step backward. "You think you're a criminal mastermind, but you are a fucking eejit. Why did you hire those men?"

Falk was still trying to catch his breath, but he managed to speak, albeit haltingly. "I found a buyer for the tablets on the dark web, but I figured I'd better bring some muscle with me in case the buyer tries to shaft me."

"Or kill you, which is more likely. After five minutes with you, I'm plotting various ways to murder you and dispose of the body."

Falk gaped at Logan, too flummoxed for words.

"Something went wrong," Logan said. "Your hired thugs turned on you."

"Yeah, they decided keeping the money for themselves was a better idea. When you two showed up, they were talking about who should shoot me in the head." Falk rolled his gaze toward the man tied to the desk. "Sergei was really jonesing for it. He's a total psycho."

"Aye, that's what you get when you buy thugs over the internet."

The use of his name seemed to rouse Sergei. He blinked rapidly, lifting his head, which had lolled onto his shoulder. His attention landed on me, and he snarled, "You bitch, you shot me."

"Haud yer wheesht," Logan snarled back.

Sergei shut his mouth but scowled at Logan.

"Where are the tablets?" Logan asked Falk.

"Cyprus."

"Why would you hide the tablets on Cyprus?"

A few beads of sweat dribbled down Falk's temples. "My parents have a vacation house on the island. Since they're in Japan for the month, I figured I could stash the tablets at the Cyprus house until I meet with the buyer and get my payment."

"Then why are you in Egypt?"

"Because Leonid over there"—Falk pointed to the first man who'd attacked Logan—"thought we should lure you here, since I knew Alex sent somebody after me. It was a trap, and you walked right into it."

"We knew it was a trap, ye *cacan*." Logan studied Falk for a moment, the intensity of his stare making the younger man cringe. "How did you know Alex sent someone after you?"

"I paid off the butler to get info. You know, that dude Reginald."

Alex couldn't have known about that, I was sure of it. He trusted Reginald. Of course, Logan had deduced the fact the butler was faking his British accent. If he faked one thing, he could fake another—like loyalty.

"Where is your buyer?" Logan asked.

"Milan. He's a mondo collector of really old crap."

I had to ask. "How did you ever make it to grad school? You're not that smart."

"No, I'm not," he admitted with a rueful smile. "I cheated. Lots. And my parents bribed some people too."

Logan seized Falk's shirt and hauled him out of the chair. "We're going to retrieve the tablets, and you're coming with us." He glanced at the goons. "Without your mates."

"You're leaving them here? I mean, they'll be real pissed about that."

"*Da*," Sergei said, "we tear his head from his body. The tablets belong to us."

The man who'd previously guarded Falk bounced his chair across the floor, eliciting a sound like the scraping of nails on a chalkboard. "No, it belongs to my country."

He spoke with a different accent from the other three goons.

"Your country?" Logan said. "You're Egyptian. Babylon is in modern-day Iraq."

I sidled up to Logan. "What are you going to do with them?"

"Leave them here, for now. But don't worry, I have plans for them." He grabbed Falk's wrists and bound them with a zip tie. "And I need to call an old friend."

Chapter Thirty-One

Logan

Maybe I had suffered a wee attack of anxiety about how Serena would react when she saw me in my element, as she'd phrased it. I shouldn't have worried. Even while I interrogated the *cacan* Falk Mullane, I'd kept an eye on Serena, and she had been fine. The wonderful lass seemed to enjoy our adventure in Cairo, but I knew she'd come down from that adrenaline high sooner or later, and then she would realize she'd shot a man.

To protect me.

Other men might've been upset if they needed a woman to save them, but I loved her strength and bravery.

Serena must have wondered about my plan for the hired thugs Falk had ordered over the internet. Her unspoken questions were answered when my contact at the Egyptian version of MI6 walked into the office in the old warehouse. Serena cocked one hip and set her hand on it, her brows rising, when she saw the attractive woman dressed in a sleek black pantsuit and sensible but stylish black shoes.

I may have rushed too much to introduce the women.

"Serena," I said, "this is Nadya Zaman. She's with Mukhabarat, the Egyptian intelligence service. We worked together a few times. Nadya, this is Serena Carpenter. She's my, ah…"

"I'm his girlfriend," Serena said with a cool smile.

Why hadn't I been able to say the word girlfriend? It sounded strange, considering who we were. Not teenagers. Not even in our twenties. To refer to a forty-two-year-old widow and single mother as my girlfriend was odd, to say the least. What else could I call her?

Serena's smile had an edge to it, as did her voice, when she shook Nadya's hand and said, "It's a pleasure to meet one of Logan's spy buddies."

"Are you with the CIA?" Nadya asked, and I was sure the question was not a joke.

"No," Serena answered. "I'm the executive assistant to a Scottish billionaire."

"My cousin Evan," I said, as if that mattered. For some reason, this conversation made me uneasy. Tackling four brutes hadn't bothered me, but this did.

"How interesting," Nadya said, then she turned to me. "When you called, you mentioned something about illegal antiquities?"

"These men attempted to coerce this one here"—I hooked a thumb toward Falk, who was slouching in a chair with his wrists zip-tied—"into handing over priceless Babylonian tablets that he was transporting for Dr. Alex Thorne, a professor at a university in Montana. These charming lads over here"—I indicated the four thugs—"abducted the other one."

I had decided to go along with Mullane's ridiculous story, at least officially. I needed Nadya to take these men into custody but leave Mullane with me, and though I doubted she was buying the lie, I knew she would cooperate. Giving her a narrative to share with her superiors would smooth the way for all of us. We needed Mullane to take us to the tablets, after all. And we needed him to take the fall for stealing them.

Maybe I should have felt bad about that, but the *cacan* deserved what he got. Every time I experienced a twinge of guilt over it, I reminded myself the bastard had laid a trap for us and had hired four thugs to do who-knew-what to us.

"Antiquities crimes are punished severely in Egypt," Nadya said to the men. "Do you enjoy prison? I'm sure our facilities will be to your liking, if you like sand flies and scorpions, and if you enjoy daily beatings."

I liked the way the Russians squirmed, those scunners. The Egyptian man, whose name I hadn't bothered to wring out of him, seemed even more disturbed than his cohorts. He'd probably spent time in an Egyptian prison and knew what it was like.

"My men will be here soon," Nadya told me. "I can handle these four until then. I'm sure you need to be somewhere, Logan."

"Thank you, Nadya."

She kissed me full on the mouth—thankfully, not with tongue—and smiled. "It's good to see you. Have a safe journey."

I seized Mullane by his bound wrists and grasped Serena's hand. We exited the warehouse, trudging down the road to where I'd parked our car. I considered stowing Mullane in the trunk, but decided Serena might not appreciate that, so I shoved him into the backseat. Serena took the passenger seat while I got in on the driver's side. Once we were on the move, driving toward downtown Cairo, Serena spoke.

First, she sneaked her hand onto my thigh.

"You could've locked Falk in the trunk," she said. "I wouldn't have minded."

"Hey!" the *cacan* said. "I'd mind."

"Haud yer wheesht," I told him. "No one wants to hear anything you have to say."

Mullane sulked, but kept his mouth shut.

"Did you sleep with Nadya?" Serena asked.

It was my turn to squirm. "Yes. It was a long time ago."

"Business or pleasure?"

"A bit of both." I glanced at her sideways but couldn't gauge her mood. "Nadya and I worked together on various assignments, and we shagged a few times. That's all."

"Are you saying Nadya was your spy fuck buddy? She kissed you, Logan."

"Yes, but, ah… That's the Egyptian way of saying hello."

A laugh spluttered out of Serena. "Really? That's what you're going with? Egyptians say hello with a big sloppy kiss. Looked like she had her tongue in your mouth."

"She didn't."

"Nadya said it was good to see you, which is code for 'please fuck me, Logan.' Right?"

Mullane snorted as if he were trying not to laugh.

I glared at him over my shoulder. "I told you to haud yer wheesht, ye *bod ceann*."

The *cacan* bowed his head and stopped snorting.

Serena was giving me a crooked smirk.

We drove to the hotel in silence. Alex had made the reservation, so naturally, it was posh and expensive and had a view of the Nile River. While we'd waited for Nadya to arrive, Serena had gone outside to call Chase and I'd called Alex to update him, while I kept an eye on our prisoners. Alex wasn't happy to hear Falk's claim that Reginald had betrayed him, but he didn't answer when I asked what he meant to do about it. I suggested he find some way to make sure Falk hadn't lied about Reginald. I even offered to interrogate the twat some more, but Alex told me not to bother. He said only, "I will deal with it in my own way."

He'd insisted we spend the night in Cairo and fly to Cyprus in the morning, so we'd be well rested. I had to agree with him. After our long flight from Utah and the trouble in the warehouse, Serena and I needed a good night's sleep.

A good poke first, though.

But Alex had reserved one suite. With one bed. How could I make love to Serena with Mullane in the room? The snickering twat would ruin the mood.

Luckily, Alex had booked us the Royal Suite at the Conrad Cairo, a luxury hotel. The suite had one bedroom, but also a spacious living room. I'd brought ropes in the trunk, though I'd decided I wouldn't need them at the warehouse. Now, I used them to tie Mullane to the sofa in the living room. I also sealed his mouth shut with duct tape I'd found in the warehouse.

Serena studied my handiwork. "You really know how to restrain someone, don't you?"

"Aye."

"You've got impressive skills." She grabbed my hand and towed me into the bedroom, slamming the door. "Fuck me, Logan."

"What?" I'd been hoping for this, but her bluntness stunned me speechless, more so this time than on that morning at Evan's house.

"I said fuck me." She whipped off her shirt and bra, flinging them across the room. "Watching you handle the bad guys made me want to rip your clothes off."

She removed the rest of her clothes while I stared dumbly.

"Get naked," she said with a hint of annoyance.

"This is probably adrenaline talking," I said. "Wait until it fades—"

"Screw that." She took hold of my shirt and yanked it up and over my head. "I need your cock, Logan. Inside me. Now."

"But—"

She unbuttoned my trousers and shoved them down to my ankles. "Why are you arguing? I want sex, and you're acting like you've never done this before."

Why the bloody hell was I arguing?

I shed the rest of my clothes and dragged her toward me, our bodies crashing into each other at the same instant our mouths did the same. Our tongues tangled, the hunger that burned in us both making our kiss wild and raw. I tried to maneuver us toward the bed, but she pushed me backward toward the balcony.

"Outside," she mumbled against my lips. "I want you outside."

Take Serena outside? On a balcony? In the middle of a crowded city? Fuck, I wanted that. I wanted her, like I'd never wanted any woman before.

Somehow, I managed to open the sliding glass doors while stumbling backward with my eyes closed and a ravenous woman glued to my body. I ran into a chair and cracked my eyes open enough to see the table near the chair and avoid toppling us into it. My erse smacked into the sturdy railing.

Her hand found my cock.

I spun us around, pinned her wrists behind her back with one hand, and thrust deep into her. Her head fell back, her mouth open, her eyes closed. She was stunning, her expression full of lust and hunger. I let go of her wrists to hold her with one arm around her waist while I held on to the railing with the other. She locked one leg around mine. I plowed into her hard and fast, gasping for breath, already on the edge.

"Come for me, Serena," I growled. "Do it now."

"Logan," she moaned. "Oh God, yes, do it harder."

I bent to suck her nipple into my mouth and scrape my teeth over it, and I fucked her harder. She threw her arms around my neck and shackled both legs around me, while I slammed her into the railing. In the back of my mind, I worried I might be hurting her, so I flipped us around to lay her across the table, pumping into her all the while, spellbound by the look on her face and the sensation of her body tightening around me. The first spasm of her release gripped me, while I pounded into her with brutal thrusts.

She cried out, her entire body bowing inward.

I threw my head back, a hoarse shout exploding out of me when I came inside her. She screamed while her climax intensified, and I kept pumping until I'd spent myself inside her completely.

She went limp on the table, one arm dangling off the edge. Her breasts heaved with every breath she hauled into her lungs.

I couldn't speak until I'd caught my breath, which took a few minutes. While we both recovered, we stayed where we were. Serena laid out across the table, me bent over her with my elbows on the glass surface. Her legs stayed lashed around me, and my cock stayed buried inside her incredible body.

"Mm," she hummed with satisfaction, running her fingers through my hair. "That was unbelievable."

"Adrenaline," I said, and kissed her forehead. "It heightens the senses and makes for fantastic sex."

"So this was nothing special for you."

I drew my head back to see her face. "Is that what you think? Oh aye, I've fucked loads of women on the balconies of top-floor suites at luxury hotels all around the world. Being with you is nothing special."

She smacked my chest with the back of her hand. "I'm serious."

The look on her face convinced me of that.

I brushed hair away from her eyes. "No, Serena, I've never experienced anything like this before. Making love to you is a revelation."

"Then why did you say adrenaline always makes sex better?"

I had said that, hadn't I? "No, I didn't mean it that way. I've gone on dangerous missions and had sex while adrenaline was burning through my veins, but it was just sex. What we've done can't compare to anything else."

"For me too."

Reluctantly, I pulled out of her body and carried her into the bedroom. With one arm, I cradled her to me while I tossed the covers aside. Then I laid her on the bed with her head on the pillow.

"Are you hungry?" I asked. "It's late, so I don't know if room service is available. But I'm sure I can find you something."

"Not hungry." She ran her palm over the sheet beside her. "Lie down with me, please. I need to tell you something."

I crawled across her body to lie down beside her, turning onto my side and bending my elbow to prop my head on my hand. "You can tell me anything, *mo gaol*. I hope you know that."

"Yes, I know that." She trailed a fingertip over my lips. "You're amazing, Logan. I've seen you in action, and I'm not terrified or intimidated. I love your badass side, your sweet side, and especially that dirty mouth of yours. You are the second relationship I've had in my entire life."

"Being with you is the only real relationship I've had with a woman."

"I figured, based on what you said about dating." She turned onto her side and tucked her hands under the pillow. "I convinced myself I hated you because I wanted you so much, more than I ever wanted Rob. Even back when I called you disgusting, deep down I knew I liked you. It was terrifying. Partly, I was afraid I was betraying Rob. Mostly, I've been afraid you'll die like he did. I mean, you're ex-military, ex-MI6..." She looked straight into my eyes. "Today, I prayed that nothing would happen to you. I prayed harder than I ever have before."

"Serena..."

"You don't have to say anything, just listen. Keely told me something that's been banging around in my brain for a while. She suggested that maybe I could have more than one love of my life, one for each stage of my life. Rob was that person for me, in that time."

She couldn't mean to imply what I thought she was implying.

A thump originated from the living room, followed by a crash.

"Mullane," I hissed.

"Better go check on him."

"I don't want to."

"Would you rather I checked on him?"

"No, I would not." I heaved myself off the bed. "Stay here. We'll finish this conversation as soon as I get that *cacan* sorted."

I threw the bedroom door open and stalked to the sofa, where Mullane lay half off it, his head on the floor. A lamp had fallen off the table beside the sofa, accounting for the crash. The thump would've been his worthless head hitting the floor. I ripped the tape off his mouth.

"Are you all right?" I asked, probably sounding annoyed, since I was.

"Yeah, I'm okay." He wriggled. "Could you help me up? The blood's all rushing to my head and making me woozy."

I hefted him off the floor and back onto the sofa.

As I was about to reapply the duct tape, he said, "If you guys are gonna hook up again, could you at least get me some earplugs?"

"No."

I slapped the tape over his mouth and strode into the bedroom.

Serena lay on the bed, asleep.

The mystery of what she'd been about to tell me would have to wait.

I slipped into bed with her and pulled the covers over us.

Chapter Thirty-Two

Serena

I woke in the morning feeling fabulous, physically, but less than spectacular on the inside. Nightmares had tormented me while I slept, and I knew Logan must have noticed my tossing and turning. Once, I'd bashed my elbow into his chest. Instead of grousing or snapping at me, he'd pulled me against his big, muscular body and murmured soothing sounds until I fell asleep again. When I woke this morning, he was gone.

But I heard his voice in the living room. He sounded annoyed, so I assumed Falk was being an ass again. Did the twerp know how to be anything else?

I crawled out of bed and got dressed.

The nightmares replayed in my mind, despite my attempts to forget about them. I got queasy thinking about those images of pain and death and sorrow. It was like being thrown back in time to eleven years ago, when I'd been informed of Rob's death, except in the dreams I witnessed all of it. They didn't afford me any distance from the pain, and I didn't know if I could handle it in real life. Not again.

Yes, I'd dreamed of Logan dying. Over and over and over. The images wrenched my stomach into knots and poisoned my mouth with a sour taste.

While I pulled on some clothes, I reflected on yesterday and the thrill of going on an adventure with Logan, witnessing a side of him I was pretty sure his family and friends had never seen. His spy buddies had seen his lethal side, but only I truly knew that part of him. Logan was the most capable, intelligent, determined, and trustworthy man I'd ever met.

So why did I feel sick when I thought about our relationship?

Maybe it was the aftermath of a thrilling experience. I'd come down from the adrenaline high, and it had left me drained.

I wandered into the living room to find Logan looming over Falk, who lay on the sofa with his hands still bound but the tape removed from his mouth.

Logan glanced at me. "The *cacan* won't stop whining."

Falk whimpered with exaggerated agony. "I'm starving. This must be some kind of violation of the Genevieve Convention, holding me against my will and not giving me food or water."

Logan rolled his eyes. "It's the Geneva Convention, ye eejit, and it doesn't apply."

"Why not?"

"Because we aren't at war. Nobody knows I've kidnapped you, anyway."

I came up beside Logan. "I'm hungry too. If you don't care about our prisoner, at least feed me."

That ended their argument. Logan ordered breakfast, and even cut the zip tie off Falk's wrists so he could eat more easily. The second the twerp was done, Logan cinched the zip tie around his wrists.

We took Evan's jet to Cyprus, flying over the Mediterranean until we touched down on the island. Logan rented a car at the airport and threatened to stow Falk in the trunk but relented when the idiot wised up enough to realize he ought to stop complaining. The house owned by Falk's parents turned out to be a large villa perched atop a jagged cliff with a stunning view of the aqua-blue waters of a small bay. The sun beamed down on us as we got out of the car in the semicircular gravel driveway.

At the large front doors, we waited while Falk searched every planter on the porch for the spare key. He'd managed to lose his key, naturally. Some criminal mastermind he'd turned out to be.

I closed my eyes and tipped my head back to let the sun warm my face. Even that couldn't melt away the unease that lingered inside me.

Did Logan and I belong together? Or was a little while all we could have?

Those thoughts popped up out of nowhere. I turned my face away from the sun, wondering why the hell I'd wondered such a thing about my relationship with Logan. The obvious answer was that I worried something might happen to him. Yes, of course I worried about that. But could there be something else, something I hadn't consciously realized yet?

The inside of the villa featured that modern, industrial style so many people liked these days. I hated it. The sterile white walls and concrete floor seemed cold and soulless. The stainless-steel accents gave it the aura of a meat locker. Everything in this place sent a chill through me, one so bone deep I couldn't shake it.

Logan hooked an arm around my shoulders. "Are you feeling all right? Maybe you've come down with something."

"I'm fine, I swear." Physically, I was.

Falk led us into a bedroom—the one reserved for him, as it turned out—and pulled a storage trunk out of the closet. He opened it up, carefully withdrawing three objects the size and shape of letter-size paper, though they were thicker than any paper sheets. They were fashioned from clay and stamped with chicken scratches.

The cuneiform tablets.

At the airport, Logan had bought a hard-sided suitcase and a bunch of cotton gauze. Now, he and Falk wrapped the tablets in the gauze and stowed them in the suitcase. Falk tried to take the case, but Logan hit the twerp with his coldest glare and Falk gave up.

Half an hour later, we were back on the jet and taking off.

I tried to admire the scenery as the plane lifted off and soared over the Mediterranean. Even the crystal-clear aqua waters of the bays around the island couldn't interest me. I kept glancing at Logan, and every time I did, my chest hurt.

He made numerous attempts to engage me in conversation, but I wasn't much use for that. Saying "uh-huh" or "uh-huh" hardly qualified as talking. Finally, he gave up and coaxed me into lying on the sofa with him. I fell asleep for the rest of the flight.

Two state troopers met us on the tarmac as soon as the jet landed. They took Falk into custody, along with the tablets. Those would be returned to the museum once Falk had gone to trial or pleaded guilty. Logan suggested, in that frighteningly calm voice of his, that Falk should "make the right choice" and enter a guilty plea. Considering how terrified he was of Logan, I had a feeling Falk would sign a confession as quickly as possible.

When we reached Alex's house, the sun was setting.

Before Logan could push the doorbell, the doors swung open.

Alex hunched at the threshold, his posture and facial expression exuding contained fury.

For a second, I thought he must have a twin brother and that's who had opened the door. But no, it was Alex. His charming-rogue persona had disintegrated, replaced by a murderous expression that seemed to darken his eyes. He wore rumpled jeans and a rumpled T-shirt, and even his hair was a mess. Dark circles discolored the skin under his eyes, while a shadow beard speckled his face.

Logan eyed Alex like he hadn't seen the man before. "Is everything all right, mate?"

"Yes," Alex said, drawing the word out almost like a snake hissing. "Everything's fine. Reggie and I had a nice long chat."

Alex sounded as edgy as he looked, his voice rougher and lower, and he spat the butler's name.

I suffered a fleeting thought that he'd murdered Reginald, but I dismissed it right away. Alex didn't seem like a killer. He was angry, for sure. Seriously angry. But homicidal? No, I couldn't believe that.

"What did Reginald say?" Logan asked.

Alex stepped aside so we could go into the house. He shut the door and rubbed his jaw. "Reggie admitted to taking a bribe from Falk. He said he's bloody sick of taking care of a narcissistic arse, and the money Falk gave him will buy Reggie a first-class trip back to Australia."

Logan's gaze flicked around the foyer before settling on Alex again. "Where is Reginald?"

"The state police have him. He confessed to aiding and abetting Falk." A ghost of Alex's old smile made his lips twitch at the corners. "I hope they wind up in the same cell block. Good old Reggie will get bloody sick of listening to that whingeing little wanker and beg me to get him out so he can clean my toilet with his tongue."

Even Logan seemed to have no clue how to respond to that.

I supposed we had to cut Alex some slack. He'd found out last night that his longtime employee, someone he'd clearly thought of as a friend, had sold him out.

"Come," Alex said, almost snarling the word as he waved for us to follow him down the hall.

Logan and I seated ourselves in the chairs across the desk from where Alex normally sat, but our host didn't sit. He leaned against the windowsill, gazing out at the ever-deepening twilight.

"Alex?" Logan said.

He jerked like he'd forgotten we were in the room. Forcing a smile, he shuffled to the desk and retrieved a thick envelope from one of the drawers. Alex held it out to Logan, stretching across the desk. "Your payment. I added a bit extra for the trouble Falk caused you."

Logan rose and accepted the envelope. He slid it into the inside pocket of his jacket without bothering to open it.

"Don't you want to count it?" Alex asked.

"I trust you."

Had he paid Logan cash?

"I'm exhausted," Alex said, rubbing his neck, his face pinched. "If you don't mind, I'll have dinner in my room tonight. Please stay. You've had a long trip, and I'd like to speak to you both in the morning when we're all well rested."

Logan and I assured him that was fine.

Alex told us to eat anything in the kitchen that we wanted, then he left us.

We ate a quiet meal in the kitchen, seated on stools at the island, making ourselves ham sandwiches from the ingredients in the refrigerator. Alex had bought the most expensive version of everything. The food was delicious, but I still endured that lingering melancholy. It had softened a bit, becoming a background unease rather than a cold knife-edge of fear.

Logan watched me like I was a suspect under surveillance.

I supposed that was how he showed his concern.

We went upstairs a little while later, to the same bedroom where we'd slept the night before last. Jeez, we'd taken a whirlwind international holiday, and I'd barely seen Cairo or Cyprus. I mumbled something to that effect, not really expecting Logan to hear or respond.

He did, of course.

Grasping my upper arms, he asked, "What's wrong, *leannan?*"

"I don't know. Maybe I'm wiped out from double jet lag. I never got used to the time zones over there, and now I'm back here but still not in my usual time zone."

He kissed my forehead. "You need rest. Let's get in bed."

Despite his statement, he didn't look like he thought a good night's sleep would cure whatever bothered me. We undressed and climbed into bed naked. I fell asleep within seconds.

But I woke in the middle of the night, afflicted with a sudden need to feel Logan. Sure, his body was spooning mine, but I needed more.

I flipped over and peppered kisses on his face and lips until he woke up.

"What is it?" he mumbled. He squinted into the darkness broken only by the faint glow from the windows.

"Make love to me. Please."

"Now?"

"Yes. Please, Logan, I need you."

He rolled me onto my back, with his body on top of mine, and made love to me. Sweetly. Slowly. Like he was memorizing my body, my responses, the sounds I made. The feel of him inside me, the pressure of every leisurely thrust, distracted me from everything else in the entire world. When Logan loved me, nothing else mattered.

My climax swept over me like gentle swells on the ocean. I gasped and clung to him, reveling in the sensations of the sweetest release I'd ever known. He pushed inside me twice more before sagging on top of me, his face in my hair.

I debated whether to speak but decided no words could do justice to the way he'd made love to me tonight. It meant everything, feeling him fill me, wrapping myself in the warmth of his body, knowing he wanted to be here, now, with me.

But for how long?

He turned onto his back and pulled me half on top of him, his strong yet tender fingers caressing my hair.

I drifted off again, but that single thought gnawed at me in my dreams.

For how long would I have Logan?

Chapter Thirty-Three

Logan

In the morning, Alex joined us for breakfast in the dining room. He had made the food himself. I hadn't seen any of his "servants" since we got back from Cyprus, but I didn't ask what had become of them. Not my business. I did wonder if he'd hired those people strictly to convince us he was fine. Still, Alex seemed himself again today. He blethered with us about nothing of importance, and of course, flirted with Serena.

Let him flirt. Serena didn't want him.

After breakfast, we left. On the flight home from Montana, I showed Serena what Alex's envelope contained. Her eyes flew wide, but she regained her composure swiftly and didn't even gasp when I handed her one of the hundred-dollar bills from inside the envelope.

She held the bill between her thumb and forefinger and sniffed it.

"What are you doing?" I asked with a chuckle.

"I've never seen a hundred-dollar bill before, much less touched one. I wondered if it smells different from a ten or a twenty."

"Does it?"

"Not really." She held the bill out to me.

"It's yours. You earned it when you shot Falk's low-rent thug." I took out a stack of bills and offered them to her. "Actually, you earned half of my fee. I couldn't have accomplished my mission without you."

"Oh please." She thrust her hundred-dollar bill in my face. "Take it. The money is yours, Mr. Bond. I came along for the ride, that's all." She craned her neck like she was trying to peer inside the envelope. "I'm feeling very nosy, so I'm going to ask. How much did Alex pay you?"

"Twenty thousand dollars."

"Holy shit." She ripped the stack of bills out of my hand and stuffed it, along with the first bill, into her bra. "I'll take your money after all. You can afford to pay me."

"But you're priceless."

"You're sweet even when you're full of shit."

I kissed her. "Take a moment to count your money while I use the bathroom."

Setting the envelope on the table, I headed for the lavatory. When I came back a few minutes later, Serena was lying on the sofa, asleep. I could use a lie-down too, but I'd settle for a chair. Disturbing Serena just so I could sleep beside her wouldn't be right.

I picked up the envelope I'd left on the table.

The flap was up, and I could see the bills inside it. Some were crumpled.

Serena had returned the bills she'd stuffed in her bra.

I dropped onto the chair beside the sofa and propped my feet on the coffee table. My gaze gravitated to her, lying there asleep, her lips forming a faint smile. She'd been agitated yesterday, but today she seemed like her usual self. I slouched in my chair so I could rest my head against its back, and I watched her sleeping.

We went home and went back to work. Monday morning, I wore a kilt as usual, and Serena aimed a sexy smile at me when I strode up to her desk. Though we talked for a few minutes, I still had the feeling something was bothering her. I asked, and she avoided answering. The lass was clever at evading my questions, but she had to realize I was even better at figuring out what she was doing. That probably explained why she never lied to me outright.

Every day, we would have lunch together, sometimes at a restaurant, sometimes at her desk or mine, sometimes in Evan's office. He had taken an extended leave of absence so he could spend more time with his wife, since Keely would have the bairn any day. After that, Evan planned to stay home with his wife and child for six weeks, possibly more. He was a billionaire, after all, and didn't need to work. Taking care of his new family would give him plenty to keep himself busy.

As for me, I was bored out of my skull again.

I liked the company, and I liked the other employees, but I still couldn't figure out what on earth I was meant to be doing. The guards kept watch. A complex, state-of-the-art security system—designed by Evan, of course—monitored everything the guards couldn't and hunted for unusual signals or whatnot. I didn't even try to understand it. I was a hands-on sort of man, not a circuits and code sort.

What was left for me to do? I'd asked myself, and Evan, that question ever since the day I'd agreed to work at Evanescent.

One thing made the tedium worthwhile. I could see Serena anytime I wanted.

Several times a day I told my assistant, Delilah, that I was going on a "security survey" of the building. I doubted she believed my story for one second, but nonsense was the only excuse I could think of to get out of my office and visit the top floor. I usually found Serena at her desk, scrutinizing papers or emails on her computer screen. Occasionally, she wouldn't be there. After a few days, she stopped getting irritated when I would call her mobile phone to find out where she'd gone. One day, I was leaning my hip against her desk, the one she wasn't sitting at, when I called her.

"Yes, I'm alive, Logan," she said before I could utter one syllable.

"Where are you, Serena? I need to kiss you. Or shag you in the copy room. Your choice."

"This is a workplace, Logan, not a brothel," she said. "I'm in the building, and that's all the information you're getting out of me. If I tell you exactly where I am, you will run down here and seduce me."

"You love it when I do that."

"True, but it cuts into my work productivity rating."

"Fuck productivity. My cock is so hard I'm in agony. You'd be doing a good deed by tending to my medically necessary needs, Nurse Carpenter."

She laughed loud enough anyone around her must have wondered if she'd lost her mind. She lowered her voice to a whisper. "Honestly, Logan, stop saying things like that when I'm with other people."

"Cannae do that. Besides, aren't you the lass who ordered me to fuck you on the balcony of the Conrad Cairo hotel? Anyone could've seen us there, and Falk Mullane heard us."

"Yes, I did that," she said, still whispering. "And I don't care if strangers see or hear us, but having my co-workers know is another thing altogether."

"Where are you? I need to see my woman, and feel you, and taste you."

She hesitated for only a second. "Accounting."

Aye, she always gave up and told me.

"They have a file room, don't they?" I asked.

"Yes. But why—Ohhh no, Logan. Absolutely no, no, no."

"Absolutely yes. Stay there. I'm on my way."

I sprinted to the elevator, but it was grinding its way up from the first floor. Since accounting was only two floors below me, I sprinted down the stairs instead, taking them two at a time. When I burst through the stairwell door, breathing hard and sweating, three women who were waiting for the elevator gawped at me. One yelped. I smiled and slowed to a fast walk as I rounded the corner into the hallway that led to accounting.

When I pushed through the glass double doors, I was still breathing rather hard.

A wall separated the waiting area from the employees behind it. A waist-high counter let the woman seated behind it see and talk to anyone in the waiting area, but I was headed for the door that said "employees only." The woman behind the counter shouted something when I barged right through the door.

Serena was standing next to one of the dozen desks in the room, talking to the gray-haired woman seated behind it. When Serena noticed me, her face took on the exasperated but aroused look she reserved for me alone.

To the gray-haired woman, I said, "Melody, love, you look bonnie as ever."

Melody smiled and shook a finger at me. "Don't sweet talk me, Logan MacTaggart. I won't give you any of my homemade potato salad today. It's all for me."

"Keep the salad. I have other needs at the moment." I nodded toward Serena. "I'm borrowing Serena for a few minutes. We need to evaluate the security features of the file room. Evan's orders."

My cousin had ordered no such thing, but the good part about working for family was that they'd let you get away with murder. Not literally.

Well, maybe under the right circumstances...

"Go on," Melody said. "We were just gabbing, anyway."

I bent to kiss her cheek. "If I weren't already taken, I'd be asking you for a date."

She pointed at me while looking at Serena. "You've got your hands full with this one, don't you?"

"I sure do," Serena said. "But I can handle him."

We made it halfway to the file room door when Serena's phone rang. Someone needed her help. Someone always did. With Evan on leave, Serena had taken over many of his duties, becoming a sort of substitute CEO. She couldn't do everything Evan did, but she filled in on as many tasks as possible. Evan was busy worrying about his wife.

After finishing her call, she told me, "I have to go. Sorry, but how about a rain check on the file room sex?"

"You can't leave me. I'm bored to tears."

"I don't see you crying."

"They're stealth tears." I slung an arm around her waist and pulled her close, ignoring the raised eyebrows from everyone in the vicinity. "Don't leave me to do paperwork. I'll get cuts all over my fingers."

She bit her lip. Her face, her entire body, seemed to wilt. "You really don't like your job, do you? I suppose after Cairo it's hard to go back to a mundane life."

"What are you on about?"

"Nothing." She pretended to shake off her dark mood with a smile, but I wasn't convinced. "It's fine, never mind."

She kissed me and walked away.

I gave up and went back to my office, where I pretended to know what the fuck I was doing. Mostly, I tried to figure out what Serena had meant by going back to a mundane life. Had she meant she missed the excitement of hunting down antiquities thieves? Or did she think I missed it?

As the days went on, Serena's melancholy moments became more frequent. I tried to pretend I'd suddenly decided to like my job, but Serena didn't believe me. I was an expert at deception, yet somehow, I couldn't fool her. So I stopped talking about work at all, which left me with not much of anything to say.

My sisters went home a week after Serena and I came back from our adventure. We said goodbye to them at the airport, in front of Evan's jet.

When Kirsty hugged me, she whispered into my ear, "Don't let Serena get away. Whatever trouble you're having, work it out."

If it was that obvious we were having trouble, I'd better do something drastic to fix things with Serena.

"Don't worry," I whispered back to Kirsty. "I have no intention of letting her go."

"Good." She pulled back and kissed my cheek. "See you soon, Logie."

"What makes you think it will be soon? I live here, in America."

"Either way, I'll see you soon. And the answer will be yes."

Days later, I was still trying to puzzle out my sister's meaning. Kirsty and Isla loved to put on mysterious airs, but Kirsty also had an uncanny knack for guessing what other people would do, especially with family. Sometimes, I almost believed she could read minds.

Two weeks after we'd come back from our adventure, I reached a decision. Serena *would* tell me what was wrong. I drove to her house after work, like I did on every weekday. We spent weekends in my apartment, because she loved having sex in front of the big windows and in the enormous shower. I let myself into the house with the key she'd given me. With Chase away visiting his grandparents, we had the place all to ourselves.

I found Serena in the living room, sitting on the sofa with her legs tucked under her, sipping a glass of what looked like whisky.

"When did you start drinking alone?" I asked, sitting down beside her.

She shrugged.

I stretched my arm across the sofa behind her. "Are you missing Chase? Is that why you've been unhappy lately?"

"No. I mean, yes, of course I miss him. But no, that's not the reason."

"What is it, then?"

"I don't know. I feel like I'm…" Her gaze darted to me, and her eyes glistened with fresh tears. "Never mind."

"You can tell me anything." I took the glass from her and set it on the coffee table, then pulled her snug under my arm. "Please tell me what it is, *mo chridhe*."

She froze, not blinking for so long that her tears dried. "Why did you call me that?"

"*Mo chridhe*? You know what that means, I gather." I hooked a finger under her chin. "You *are* my heart, Serena."

"You mean it, don't you?"

My first impulse was to make a sarcastic joke, but her stricken expression changed my mind. "Yes, I mean it. I love you, Serena."

"I love you too. Never thought I'd feel this way again, but I do."

"Why does loving me make you sad?"

"That's not the reason. Loving you is the best thing that's ever happened to me." She snuggled closer, looping an arm around me and pressing her cheek to my chest. "What we have, it's better than what I had with Rob. At first, I felt horrible for thinking that. But I've realized it's okay to love you more than I loved him. It doesn't diminish what I had with Rob. I'm sure he's up there in heaven thanking God I fell for a military man, not some pasty-faced wuss."

"But I'm not the sort of man any woman wants to marry."

"Yes, you are." She raised her head to gaze into my eyes. "You're no killer. You do what's necessary to protect the world from creeps like Falk and his henchmen. You're a hero, Logan."

I grunted. "That lot was hardly a threat to global security."

"No, but they were bad guys. Alex needed your help, and you saved him from a bad situation."

"That's not heroic."

"I think Alex would have a different opinion. When I talked to him yesterday, he said how grateful he is that you got the job done."

"You've been talking to Alex? Do I need to go to Montana and batter him?"

She laughed, without much enthusiasm. "No. He's lonely, especially since he found out about Reginald, and I think he needs a few friends. Like you and me."

Alex had known Reginald for a long time and trusted him. Betrayal from a friend… Aye, that had to be a hard blow.

"You should call him," Serena said. "Invite him to visit us."

I almost balked but realized she might have a point about Alex. "Maybe I will sometime. Tonight, I'm more concerned with you."

"Think I need a few days off. We both went back to work the day after we got home from Cyprus."

"Aye, we need a change of scenery." And earlier today, I'd suddenly had an idea that seemed like the perfect solution.

She sat up, pulling away from me. "What scheme are you concocting?"

"No scheme. A plan, that's all." I turned toward her. "Let's go to Scotland on holiday."

"Scotland? For how long?"

"As long as it takes. I've already cleared it with Evan. He's having Tamsen Spurling come over to fill in for him and for you. She shares vice president duties with Stewart Atkins, so he can handle things at Inverness while Tamsen is here."

"Okay," she said, sounding uncertain. "But I don't know about going on an extended vacation to another continent without my son."

"Chase can come along. I'm sure he'd love Scotland."

"I promised Sylvia and Ed they could have Chase for two months."

"We'll invite them along too. Make it a group holiday."

Her eyes went wide while she made small gasping noises.

I caught her face in my hands. "Say yes, Serena. This will be good for us."

She clamped her teeth over her upper lip, letting it slide free gradually. "Okay. Yes."

We both grinned. I threw my arms around her, and our mouths collided.

My phone rang.

I kept kissing her.

Serena's phone rang while mine was still ringing.

We broke our kiss and answered our phones.

"It's happening," Evan said, his voice higher pitched than usual. "The bairn's coming. Right now."

Serena and I looked at each other and said at the same time, "Keely's in labor."

"I cannae drive," Evan said. "Keely's in pain and—"

He spewed a long string of Gaelic curses.

"We're on the way," I told Evan. "I'll drive you to the hospital."

Their house was five minutes from Serena's, but tonight, I'd break the speed laws to get there faster. Evan might have a panic attack if I didn't.

I jumped up and hoisted Serena off the sofa. "Come on, the newest MacTaggart wants to meet the world."

Chapter Thirty-Four

Serena

Evan seemed on the verge of a nervous breakdown when we arrived at their house and I told him it wasn't time to go to the hospital yet. He worried because he loved Keely so much, and because this was the first pregnancy for an over-forty woman. I'd been a nurse in my previous life, as well as a mom, so I knew all about the stages of labor. Logan had resorted to giving Evan a big glass of single malt Scotch to keep him calm.

Keely was serene. Glowing, actually. She couldn't wait to meet her baby.

Until early labor ended, and the real work began.

Logan and I stayed with Evan and Keely throughout the early stages, taking care of them both in their home. Forty-nine hours after Keely had called me and Evan had called Logan, we drove them to the hospital. The main event had finally begun. Logan and I stayed in the waiting room while Evan went with Keely.

Seven hours later, she gave birth to a beautiful baby girl.

Evan shambled into the waiting room looking exhausted but happy, his grin lopsided. I hugged Evan, crying while I congratulated him. Couldn't help it. Keely had waited a very long time for this, and I'd been there through both her previous marriages and a third failed relationship, all of which had left her demoralized and feeling like happiness wasn't possible. She finally had everything she wanted.

Logan hugged Evan too, though he didn't cry.

Evan took us to see Keely and the baby. She had pale blue eyes like her daddy. The color might change later, but I had a feeling it wouldn't.

"Her name is Joy," Keely told us, looking even more tired than her husband but just as happy. "Joy Serena MacTaggart. It seemed like the right name for a baby who'll be so loved by so many people. It took a lot of miracles to get here, but we made it."

"Her middle name is Serena?" I said. "You didn't have to do that."

"Of course we did. You encouraged me to give Evan a chance, and we might never have gotten married if you hadn't done that."

I started crying again, which made Keely cry too.

Keely and Evan's happy ending had required a lot of miracles, for sure. I'd watched her try to push Evan away, only to fall hopelessly in love with him. Their love story was a miracle in itself, two wounded people who met once and lost each other, then found each other again through a coincidence that felt more like fate.

Then there was Evan's parents. Samuel Drake had been imprisoned for thirty years for a murder he hadn't committed, and Evan had known nothing about it until last year. He hadn't even known his father's name. Today, Sam was free, cleared of the murder charge thanks to his determined son. Evan had been born after his father went to prison, but today, his parents were as happily married as he and Keely were.

If Evan and his mom could overcome obstacles that seemed insurmountable, maybe Logan and I could do the same.

He'd been so patient with me, with my mood swings and my inability to explain what was bothering me. Maybe a vacation in Scotland would clear my head and help me figure out why the thought of being with Logan for good made me want to cry. I worried for his safety, sure, but that wasn't the whole problem.

I told Keely I'd stick around to help her with the baby, but she wouldn't hear of it.

"Go to Scotland with Logan," she said. "You've never spent more than two days there, and I know you never took the time to really see the place. Popping over there for the occasional family gathering isn't a vacation. Take Chase and Rob's parents and *go*. That's an order."

"But you just had a baby."

"And I have a brilliant, highly capable husband who can help out. My parents are coming too, and so are Evan's mom and dad." She shooed me away, even while cradling her daughter with one arm. "Get out of here. Have fun in Scotland with your unbelievably hot boyfriend."

Logan had stepped into the doorway and must've heard Keely's description of him, though he didn't let on he had.

"Are we away yet?" he asked.

"Yes, we're leaving." I kissed baby Joy's head and then kissed Keely's cheek. "I'm so happy for you, sweetie. Send me lots of pictures."

"I will." She switched to a secretive murmur when she added, "Go get yourself happy too. You deserve it."

Logan claimed my hand and led me away.

Wow, Scotland. What could I say? It was beyond beautiful. I'd seen it before, but only small parts of the country. We traveled in Evan's jet, picking up Chase and his grandparents along the way. Before our stop in Vermont, though, we'd made a detour. Logan had balked when I suggested it right after we boarded the jet in Carrefour. I waited until we'd both taken our seats on the sofa.

"Ye cannae be serious," he'd moaned, slipping into casual Scot-speak like he did anytime I made a suggestion he thought was ridiculous. "You're wanting me to show up in Ballachulish with Alex Thorne? Catriona will have me castrated."

"Since when is Logan MacTaggart, lethal secret agent, afraid of his wee lassie cousin?"

"Wee lassie? Ye havenae seen her angry. She's like the Incredible Hulk, only red instead of green."

"You've been hanging out with Chase too much."

Logan dropped his head back onto the sofa and groaned loudly. "If I invite Alex on this holiday, half the family might excommunicate me. Besides, do we really want Alex following us around?"

"What's the real reason you don't want to invite him?"

"He's bloody irritating."

I punched his arm, though not hard. "You like Alex. He's your friend. And the poor guy is all alone since the Reginald thing. I feel bad for him."

"Aye, he has been sounding a bit off lately."

"You've called him every day for the past three days. Obviously, you're worried about him too." I wriggled to get closer to Logan, laying a hand on his chest. "If you convince Alex to come with us, I will do anything you want."

One side of his mouth kinked upward. "You already do anything I want."

"True. What else can I do to entice you?"

"I'll have to think about that." He stretched and got up. "Right now, I'd better tell the pilots to update the flight plan. We're stopping off in Montana first."

When we arrived in Montana, Alex was waiting on the tarmac for us. Well, waiting inside his very expensive car, the one he'd sent to pick up me and Logan the first time we'd flown here. Back then, a chauffeur had driven the Mercedes-Benz. Today, Alex sat behind the wheel, looking like his usual self. Logan and I met him at the car and escorted him to the plane. Alex seemed fine—cheerful, charming, roguish as usual. He flirted with me shamelessly, but Logan didn't mind anymore. He realized I wasn't in the least interested, and that Alex wasn't interested either. He was just being Alex.

During the flight to Vermont, the three of us chatted. Logan and I relaxed on the sofa, side by side, with his arm around me. Alex took the chair beside the sofa and set his feet on the table. We laughed, a lot. It turned out Alex was not only gorgeous and charming, but hilarious too. I could see why Catriona had fallen for him. But I wondered what drove them apart, what exactly he'd done that had been so awful she cursed him to this day.

It would've been rude to ask him about that, so I squelched my curiosity, for the time being.

Alex surprised me by bringing up the Catriona issue himself.

He sighed, linking his hands behind his head and leaning back in his chair. "I probably should have said no when you invited me on this little holiday. The two of you won't be popular with the other MacTaggarts for this."

"Logan invited you," I said. "Not me."

He smiled with a touch of smugness. "Ah, but you pull his strings. He told me so. 'Serena ordered me to ask you,' he said, 'and I can't say no to her.' Sad, really, when a man hands his testicles over to a woman."

"Trust me, Logan has kept all his manly bits. And I wanted you to come with us because you've been through a lot lately, what with Reginald turning on you and Falk Mullane's blackmail nonsense. You need to be with friends."

He raised a single brow. "So this is an 'Alex is pathetic and needs our meddling to set him right' sort of holiday?"

"Exactly."

"I see." He grabbed a bottle of water off the floor, where he'd set it earlier, and swigged it. "You'd better prepare for a blood bath when Cat sees me."

Since he'd brought up the subject of Cat, I took that as permission to butt my nose into his business. "What did you do to make her hate you so much?"

He turned the water bottle in his hand, staring down at it. "That's a long story. Let's hold off on it until another day."

Rats. I'd really hoped he would tell me. My curiosity was clamoring for an answer, but I had no right to push for one.

The silence dragged on for a very long moment.

Until Logan cleared his throat. "Catriona isn't the only MacTaggart who might beat you bloody. Her brothers are extremely protective of their sisters."

"Ah yes," Alex said with feigned wistfulness. "The Three Macs. A Scottish brotherhood as ruthless as the mafia."

"How do you know that's what my cousin Iain calls them? You've never met any MacTaggarts other than me and Cat."

"But she loved to talk about the family. I know more about you and your clan than you realize." Alex slid his feet off the table. "Logan, why would you risk alienating the rest of the MacTaggart clan simply to cheer me up?"

Since Logan's expression had blanked, I answered. "He's doing it because you two are friends."

Alex got that devilish glint in his eyes and a devilish slant to his lips. "Friends? Me and Logan? Serena, you are beautiful, but you're also clearly insane."

"Come off it. You and Logan are friends."

"Maybe." He screwed the cap back on his water bottle, seeming absorbed in the task. "I still think bringing me along was a bad idea. Luckily, I like bad ideas. They make life more interesting."

The conversation devolved into good-natured jibes after that. Eventually, we all decided to play poker. It was Alex's idea, naturally. He suggested strip poker but rescinded the offer when he realized he had "no desire to watch Logan get his kit off." We played regular poker instead.

I won. Twice.

After that, the men lost interest in the game.

We picked up Chase, Sylvia, and Ed in Vermont, then took off for Scotland. Chase was thrilled to meet a "real, live British guy," and he wound up talking comic books with both Alex and Logan. Logan announced British superheroes were all bampots, and Alex countered by stating Scottish superheroes were so pitiful no one even knew their names. Chase had a ball listening to their good-natured argument, and I loved seeing Chase and Logan, the two men I loved most in the world, having such a great time.

Sylvia, Ed, and I got reacquainted during the long journey "across the pond," as Alex called it. I'd forgotten how nice it was to have parents, even if they weren't my actual parents. Sylvia and Ed felt more like Mom and Dad to me than my own family.

The mood on board sobered when the pilot announced we would land at Inverness in fifteen minutes. I'd told Sylvia and Ed about the Cat and Alex situation. They agreed it sounded like Alex needed a vacation with friends, but none of us was excited about the moment when Catriona and Alex would meet again for the first time in eleven years.

Once the jet had landed, Logan positioned himself in front of the door. "I think Alex should stay on board while the rest of us greet whoever is out there waiting for us. I hope it's my sisters and parents, and only them, but I can't guarantee it."

Alex smiled with devious amusement. "Am I meant to hide in here until the way is clear and then skulk out of the plane?"

"No. But let me assess the situation before you come out."

"Should we have a secret signal? You tap your nose or whatever?"

Logan scratched his chin like he was considering the problem. "Why don't I shout your name? 'British Bastard, get your erse out here.' Would that work for you?"

"Yes, that sounds lovely."

The rest of us headed down the steps to the tarmac.

Luckily, we didn't have a horde to deal with. Logan's parents and sisters had come, but the rest of the clan had stayed home. After his family greeted me and Logan with hugs and joyful cries, we introduced them to Chase, Sylvia, and Ed. They treated my family like long-lost members of the Mac-Taggart clan, not like strangers they'd just met.

God, I loved these people. All of them.

After the hellos were done, Logan whistled to get everyone's attention. "We have another guest with us. Please keep an open mind about this."

"About what?" Isla asked.

"You'll see." Logan shouted toward the jet's open door, "You can come out now."

Alex strode down the steps toward us.

"Who is that?" Kirsty asked. "He's beautiful."

Once Alex reached us, Logan introduced him. "This is my friend, Alex Thorne."

At the mention of his name, Logan's parents and sisters froze. Five pairs of eyes were locked on our guest.

Isla spoke first. "Alex Thorne? As in the man who shattered Catriona's heart? The British Bastard?"

"Yes," Alex said, "that's me. Though I'm partial to the Limey Louse."

All the MacTaggarts except for Logan exchanged baffled glances.

Finally, Kirsty stepped forward to offer Alex her hand. "I'm Kirsty, Logan's sister. Welcome to Scotland."

He stared at her hand for a moment, seeming baffled himself. Then he shook it. "Thank you. Believe it or not, this is my first time in Scotland."

Elspeth hurried forward. "Really? You've never been? We'll have to show you the sights."

"Aye," said the third sister, Isla. "But only if Catriona says it's all right. She is our cousin, after all, and you are a stranger."

"I understand," Alex told her. "Please don't feel obligated to be nice to me. I expect to be assaulted repeatedly by various MacTaggarts."

We all piled into the limo Logan's cousin Rory had hired for the day, to bring the gang to the airport and to ferry us back to the home of Logan's parents. I wouldn't see Rory or any of the other MacTaggarts until tomorrow. It was getting late, and we all needed a good night's sleep before dealing with the rest of family.

Logan's parents assumed we would share a room, but I had to make sure Chase was okay with that.

"Duh, Mom," he said when I asked. "I told you, I know about sex. And I like Logan. He's the awesomest."

Yep, I was sleeping with the awesomest guy on earth, and my son wanted me to share a bed with the man who was James Bond and Superman wrapped up in one kilt.

"Besides," Chase added, "you'll sleep in the same room after you get married."

Ohhh-kay. I did not want to go anywhere near that discussion. Not yet.

As I lay in Logan's arms, listening to his soft snoring, I tried for the umpteenth time to figure out why I couldn't shake this feeling I wouldn't have him for long. Was it plain old fear? Was it something more?

Maybe this vacation would help me answer those questions.

Chapter Thirty-Five

Logan

No gathering of the MacTaggart clan ever went as planned or ever stayed low key. My parents and my sisters liked Alex, but they held off final judgment until they saw how Catriona reacted to his presence. Our extended family had arranged—what else?—a day of sports and revelry at Dùndubhan, the castle owned by my cousin Rory. It was now a museum run by my cousin Jamie and her husband, Gavin, but Rory reserved the right to take over the estate whenever he liked.

No tourists were allowed today. Dùndubhan was hosting a private party, with outlandish games and sports.

Jamie and Gavin met us in the courtyard, greeting us as we climbed out of the car. Everything was fine until Alex stepped out.

"Who is this?" Jamie asked.

"Yeah," Gavin said, "you didn't tell us you were bringing somebody else. Is he Serena's brother?"

"No," I told him. "This is Alex Thorne."

Jamie frowned at me, then at Alex. "Cat's Alex? The British Bastard?"

"Aye."

My wee cousin marched straight up to Alex, pulled her arm back like a baseball player about to pitch a ball, and smacked him in the face. The sound of her palm striking his cheek reverberated in the walled courtyard.

Alex massaged his cheek. "It's a pleasure to meet you too."

"You've got some nerve coming here," Jamie said. "Catriona will be here for the games, you know."

"I assumed as much."

Jamie moved closer, hoisted herself up on her toes, and tipped her head back to glare at Alex. "So will my brothers."

Her tone transformed those words into a threat.

Alex was not impressed. "I look forward to finally meeting them. I'm sure we have a lot to talk about."

"There won't be talking. There will be blood." Jamie whirled on me, thrusting a finger in my direction. "How could you bring him here?"

"I thought it was about time everyone buried the hatchet. We're all adults, and Alex isn't the devil incarnate. He's a friend."

Jamie squinted at me, her lips pursed, and growled just like her brother Rory. "Fine. Have it your way, but mark my words, you will regret this once Cat gets here."

"We'll see."

Gavin took his wife aside and calmed her down with hushed words I couldn't make out and several long, lingering kisses. Jamie agreed to give us a tour of the castle, though she refused to speak to Alex. Cat was her sister, and I couldn't blame her for being upset. But Serena had been right. Alex and Cat needed to confront the ghosts of their past and lay them to rest once and for all.

Jamie and Gavin showed Serena, Chase, Alex, and Chase's grandparents around the castle while I made my way through the garden to the door hidden behind a flowering bush. I shoved the old wooden door open and marched onto the green. The grassy area offered a perfect place to hold any sort of festivities anyone might want to have. It had hosted Highland games several times. The first games held here had been for a singular purpose. Rory had wanted to force Gavin to break free of his past and finally commit to a life with Jamie, and nothing cleared a man's head like hurling tree trunks.

Would caber tossing be on today's schedule?

The answer was yes, which I found out a few minutes later when more of my cousins arrived. The Three Macs—Lachlan, Rory, and Aidan—arrived with Iain and their respective wives and children. The women and bairns went inside, though Iain's daughter, Malina, would've complained if I'd called her a bairn out loud. She was fourteen, after all. Chase might like having another teenager around.

My four cousins cornered me against the wall.

And every last one of them wore a kilt. No one had told me this was a plaid festival. Wearing kilts meant caber tossing was on the agenda.

They should've known better than to try intimidating me, but then again, I rather doubted they had any hopes of accomplishing that.

Iain, the always calm cousin, leaned against the wall near me, arms folded over his chest. He aimed his famous Buddha smile at me. His wife had named that expression after the Buddha. Until we'd met Rae, the rest of us had simply called it Iain's smile. He never got upset about anything, at least not the way some of my other cousins did.

Lachlan, the oldest of the Three Macs, folded his arms over his chest too. His younger brothers, Rory and Aidan, did the same.

I leaned back against the wall but felt no compulsion to cross my arms. "All right. Have your say."

Rory smacked his fist into the other palm. "You brought the British Bastard here."

"No, I brought Alex Thorne."

"Why would you do that? Unless you're itching for a skelping."

"Go on and try that," I said, staring right into Rory's eyes. "I'd love a good laugh."

Iain pushed away from the wall and moved to stand beside me, though he spoke to the Three Macs. "Let's not turn this into a medieval battle, eh? The lasses won't be impressed by the three of you getting battered to a bloody pulp by Logan. And besides, you should really leave that for Catriona to do."

Lachlan squinted at Iain. "You're assuming we can't take Logan."

"Aye, Lachie, that's right. I'm assuming the facts."

I somehow kept my impassive expression when Lachlan scowled at Iain over his use of the hated diminutive Lachie.

Aidan lowered his arms. "Iain's right. Logan would fair trounce us in a fight."

The rest of my cousins raised their hands in surrender.

Everyone who'd gone inside the castle walls began to pour out through the garden doorway. My cousins wandered off to find their wives, and I waited for Serena to emerge. She was the second to last person to walk onto the green, and she came up alongside me.

Alex walked out last.

When he saw the Three Macs, he stopped.

They saw him too, and rounded on him in unison, stalking toward him like a line of Celtic warriors determined to corner the enemy. All they needed was blue face paint, since they already had the kilts.

"You've got nerve," Lachlan said. "Showing your face at a MacTaggart family gathering."

Alex raised one brow. "How do you know who I am? We've never met before."

"Jamie rang Rory to warn him you were here, and Rory rang me." Lachlan raked his slitted gaze over Alex, and his lip curled. "You are the only one here I don't recognize, and the only one who's dressed like a Sassenach."

"How exactly does one dress like a Sassenach?"

Aidan chuckled darkly. "Ye wear posh clothes and prance around like a numpty."

"He's not wearing a kilt," Rory said. "That's how we know he's a Sassenach."

Alex Thorne might have been a Sassenach, an Englishman, but he was hardly dressed like a moron. Not that I knew how morons clothed themselves.

I grasped Serena's hand. Together, we headed toward the disaster in the making, aka Alex Thorne, and positioned ourselves next to him.

"Kilts are the litmus test, ye say?" I asked. "Well, ahmno wearing one either."

Lachlan rolled his gaze toward me and sighed. "You're family, Logan. We forgive you for neglecting to dress appropriately."

More MacTaggarts had arrived while my cousins had cornered me, right before they ganged up on Alex. He didn't seem perturbed by their display of Scottish machismo, or by the throng of cousins and other relatives swarming the green. I spotted my parents and my sisters, along with the parents of the Three Macs. Iain's parents were here too, but Evan's mother and father had flown to America to see their new granddaughter. They would miss whatever battle seemed destined to take place here.

We might give Robert the Bruce a run for his money today. The Battle of Dùndubhan might prove more vicious than the Battle of Bannockburn, but unlike that historic fight, there would be no victor here. One Englishman against a horde of Scots? Alex had no chance of leaving the battlefield without blood being spilled.

"So, you're siding with the British Bastard," Rory said to me. "Are you wanting a beating, Logan?"

"No one will beat anyone today." I took a moment to consider my cousins, and an idea came to me. "You lot believe in second chances, don't you? Your wives gave you another go even after you fucked up badly. Rory, Emery took you back in spite of everything you put that poor lass through with your daft marriage of convenience idea. Lachlan, you told Erica you could never love her and then you walked out on her, but she forgave you. Iain abandoned Rae for thirteen years, and she took him back. So before you start planning a royal rammy, remember you lot aren't much different than Alex."

My cousins aimed their best cold stares at me, but theirs couldn't compete with mine. I was about to strategize how to take them out one by one when they exchanged glances and nodded.

"That's a fair point," Lachlan said. "But we're not the ones you have to convince."

Fate seemed to have a twisted sense of humor today, because at the precise moment Lachlan spoke those words, the crowd separated to let a solitary figure pass. Even the Three Macs moved aside.

Catriona halted a few meters from Alex.

She looked him up and down, her face impassive but her eyes glinting with the fire of fury.

Everyone had fallen silent, turning the green into the eeriest stretch of grass in Scotland. No one moved. We all watched Cat to see what she might do.

"You bastard!" she shrieked, and bolted for Alex, roaring like a she-demon.

He didn't move, though his eyes widened a fraction.

Cat was considerably shorter than Alex, but she'd accounted for that. She swung her fist back and punched him in the gut.

My God, the lass was strong.

Alex gasped, doubled over, and stumbled backward two steps.

Then he straightened, cleared his throat, and faced her again.

He was going to let her punch him a second time. Had the man gone barmy? Catriona was on a rampage.

She pulled her fist back for another blow.

When she swung out, he caught her fist.

Cat howled.

"Now, now," Alex said in a sarcastically patient tone, "let's behave like adults, Catriona. Did you honestly expect I'd let you hit me again? One punch, I deserve. Two is a bit much."

She kicked him in the shin.

He winced but held on to her fist. "If I let go, will you promise to end the violence?"

"No, you *bod ceann*, I will not." She tried to wrestle free of his hold, but he was the stronger of the two. Her wild fury had dwindled to a simmer, but her face was red. "How do you expect me to feel when you turn up in my country? You had me arrested."

"No, I didn't. The police arrived at the wrong conclusion, but that's hardly my fault. I got you out of jail, didn't I?"

"You're a bloody liar, that's what I know. Didn't I tell you not to come within five hundred miles of me?"

He shrugged one shoulder, giving the illusion of being unaffected by his reunion with Catriona. "Logan invited me. Why don't you lay one on him, Cat?"

She veered her attention to me, baring her teeth. "You did what, Logan?"

"I invited Alex, like he said. Don't you think it's time you and Alex bury the hatchet? You've been hating him for years. Letting go of the past might be good for both of you."

"Now you're a bloody therapist?" She jabbed a finger in the air in my general direction. "I will deal with you later."

She seized Alex's arm and dragged him through the garden door, then slammed it shut.

Iain tipped his head to the side, peering at the garden door. "Donnae ye think someone ought to keep an eye on those two? A murder would dampen the mood during the games."

"Serena and I will do it," I said. "I'm the ersehole who brought Alex here, so it's my responsibility to thwart a murder."

I guided Serena toward the garden door and pushed it open with a gentle shove. It made a noise when it popped open, but the pair arguing in the garden wouldn't have heard it.

They were going at it like mortal enemies.

Chapter Thirty-Six

Serena

I spotted Alex and Catriona near the arbor. They were arguing, but not screaming at each other, their words hard to make out from this distance away and with lots of greenery between us and them. Logan led me over to the side, behind a well-manicured hedge that camouflaged us. We could see the couple through a gap between the hedge and a flowering bush.

"We're eavesdropping?" I whispered.

"No, we're the emergency referees. If necessary, we'll intervene."

Cat kept jabbing her finger into Alex's chest. He threw his arms up, then spread them wide when he bent to level their gazes and said something that made her squeeze her eyes shut.

"What the fuck do you want from me?" he shouted loud enough that his voice echoed off the walls of the castle compound.

"Nothing!" she shouted back.

I snuggled closer to Logan. "Wow, these two have a lot of passion."

"Yes, you were right."

"Was I? About what?"

Beyond the hedge, Alex shoved both hands into his hair, head bowed, shoulders caving in. Catriona wiped at her eyes with the hem of her shirt. Her lips moved, but I couldn't make out the words.

"You were right," Logan said, "about them. They're still in love with each other."

"I thought I hated you, but I didn't react to you the way she does to

Alex. Whatever he did to her must've been a doozy."

"An enormous doozy, from the looks of it."

Cat said something that made Alex lift his head and scowl at her. She hurried out of the garden, onto the green.

He shambled over to a concrete bench and collapsed onto it. With his elbows on his knees, he let his head fall into his raised hands.

I glanced at Logan. "Should we…"

"No, leave him alone. He wouldn't want to be consoled."

"That's such a guy thing to say." I gazed at his profile, suddenly struck by a realization. "You love this cloak-and-dagger stuff. Even eavesdropping on your cousin and her ex-lover makes you come alive. Spying is in your blood."

He jerked his head to look at me. "I'm not a spy anymore."

"Yeah, I know. You quit MI6."

But maybe he shouldn't have. Was I holding him back? If we hadn't gotten involved, would he go back to that life? He wasn't happy in his new job. Maybe I was making excuses to end things because the thought of losing him any other way terrified me, but his boredom with his current job was real. And I still could not shake the chilling fear that we wouldn't be together for long.

So, I distracted myself.

"We should talk to Alex," I said. "Come on, the poor man is miserable. Catriona has her brothers and sisters to help her, but Alex only has you and me."

Logan groaned, making an exasperated face. "Fine. We will talk to Alex."

He clasped my hand, leading me out from behind the hedge.

Alex raised his head and screwed up his mouth.

Near the bench, we stopped.

"Did you enjoy the show?" Alex asked.

"We couldn't hear what you said," Logan told him. "Speak up next time."

I slapped his chest. "No teasing. Can't you see he's in pain? Alex, we wanted to make sure you and Catriona didn't do anything stupid, like bludgeon each other to death with garden trowels."

He turned his gaze up to the heavens. "This is perfect. While Cat tells everyone out there what a vile bastard I am and gets drowned in sympathy, I have you two to tell me to buck up."

"We're not telling you that. We want to make sure you're okay."

"I'm right as rain. A good sucker punch is exactly what I needed today."

Logan squeezed my hand. "He's fine. Let's leave him be."

"No, he is not fine." I yanked my hand free of his and sat down beside Alex. "It's not hopeless, you know. What's broken can be mended."

He gave me a look that epitomized sarcasm, humor, and self-loathing in a way only this man could've pulled off. "You're a lovely woman, Serena, but being with Logan has turned you into—what do the Scots call it?—a bampot. Catriona despises me."

"You two had a rip-roaring argument. That kind of passion doesn't come from hate. It comes from repressed desires and fear."

He held perfectly still for several seconds, his gaze on me.

Logan gave me an exasperated look, which I ignored.

Alex made an irritated grumbling noise that matched his hand gesture. "Cat doesn't want me anymore. She'd sooner tear my balls off, grind them into paste, and shove it down my throat."

"Logan and I thought we hated each other," I said. "It was only recently that we took a hard look at ourselves and realized the antagonism was a cover, and we were fighting the inevitable out of fear. Logan told me once that passion and hate often go hand in hand. What he didn't understand at the time, what neither of understood, was that desire can be disguised as hate."

"I'll take that under advisement."

Logan shook his head, his mouth twisting into a half-suppressed smile. "He means he thinks you're full of shit, and he's going to ignore everything you just told him."

Alex adopted a look of totally convincing feigned innocence. "I have no idea what you're talking about. I always listen to advice, especially when it comes from a beautiful woman."

"You're a liar, Alex. It's who you are. But you ought to know by now you can't fool me."

"No, I never could. Which begs the question of why you take the jobs I offer you."

Logan shrugged. "I like a challenge."

"You like a mystery. You're a spy, Logan. That's who you are."

A lump hardened in my throat. Logan was and always would be a spy. Even Alex understood that. But Logan would give up what he really wanted to make me happy. Which was worse? Losing him to resentment because I made him take a boring job, or losing him in the most permanent way imaginable because he went back to his old life as a spy?

Those scars on his back…

I swallowed hard, but the lump wouldn't budge.

"Let's go out there," Logan said, nodding toward the garden door, "and see if things are as bad as you think."

Alex nodded and got up, running his fingers through his hair. "I ask only one favor of you two. If one of Cat's brothers kills me, make sure they don't cut me up and have me for dinner."

Logan sighed and shook his head.

The three of us walked back out onto the green, where the rest of the MacTaggarts were busy setting up for the Highland games.

Rory and Lachlan approached us. They each held small packages wrapped in plain brown paper.

Lachlan offered his package to Logan. "You'll need a kilt to compete in the games. We thought you might've left yours back in America."

"I did." Logan accepted the package and unwrapped it. He held up the kilt made from the blue-and-green tartan of the MacTaggart clan. "Thank you."

Rory held out his package to Alex. With a sly and slightly feral smile, he said, "We let Cat pick one for you."

"Hmm, that sounds rather dangerous." He removed the brown paper and held up his kilt. "Ah well, at least she still has a sense of humor."

The kilt was fashioned from pink plaid, and it had sparkly flowers sewn onto it.

Logan narrowed his gaze on Rory. "How did you happen to have a pink kilt large enough for a man to wear?"

"Catriona made it for me as a joke. I handed it off to Gavin, because apparently Jamie loves to see her husband in ridiculous outfits."

Chase came running up to us, grinning like it was Christmas morning and he'd gotten the life-size space shuttle he'd asked Santa to bring him. He held up his own kilt, in the MacTaggart tartan. "Look, Mom, Lachlan made me an honorary MacTaggart. I get to compete in the games. Isn't that wicked awesome?"

"Yeah, wicked awesome." I glanced at the cabers stacked on the other side of the green. The large cabers. Tree trunks, really. "Lachlan, are you sure it's safe for a child to compete? I've heard about how zealous you guys are when it comes to winning."

"Donnae worry," Lachlan said. " We have wee cabers for the wee laddie."

"Hey!" Chase said. "I'm not a baby. I'm fifteen."

Rory chuckled. "You sound like Malina. She's always reminding everyone that she's not a baby, she's fourteen."

"Yeah, I thought I was the only one who gets treated like a baby by my mom, but Malina has all these grown-ups who keep talking like she's a kid."

I ruffled his hair. "Because you are kids."

"Mom, stop that. You're soooo embarrassing."

Chase trotted off to find Malina, whom he called "the only person around here who's not way old and totally weird." I was glad he'd made a friend, but I still had qualms about the caber tossing thing, even with "wee cabers."

Logan and Alex ducked into the garden to don their kilts. When they returned, everyone stared at Alex and his pink, sparkly kilt. To his credit, he stood tall and proud, eying everyone like he was daring them to ridicule him.

Was it strange that I felt proud of him?

The MacTaggarts started the games with the hammer throw. I'd known this family was competitive, but I'd never witnessed their Highland games before. The Three Macs announced the combatants—yes, they actually used that word—would be split into pairs who would face off against each other. The winners of each round would be split into new pairs, and so on until only two remained. The ultimate champion would be determined in the final round.

Rory and Lachlan argued over whose hammer traveled the farthest, demanding that Iain re-measure the distance three times. Their throws had come within a few inches of each other, but finally, Iain declared Rory the winner. Logan and Alex were paired in the first round. I had a feeling Logan held back, since he knew Alex had never done this before. Logan lost, and Alex advanced to the next round.

When Logan came over to me, I asked him, "Did you let Alex win?"

"That's an insulting question. A MacTaggart never throws a match."

"I heard a rumor Rory threw a match to let Gavin win once upon a time."

"That was never proved."

By the time they got down to the final two, it was Rory against Alex. I couldn't decide whether every other MacTaggart had let Alex win, or if he had skills nobody realized until today. Either way, the final round pitted him against the toughest of the Three Macs, the man known as the Steely Solicitor.

Rory grasped the four-foot-long wooden pole, which had a metal ball attached to the other end, and swung it around and around. When he released it, the hammer soared through the air. It whumped down a long ways from the starting line.

Alex acted disinterested. What a load of bullshit. Inside, he must've wanted to win so badly he could taste it.

The MacTaggarts cheered.

Despite my love for the MacTaggarts, I found myself rooting for Alex.

He spun around with the hammer's handle in his grip and sent it sailing. It whumped down a good three feet past where Rory's throw had landed.

Silence descended. It was the kind that made you look to the sky to see if demons were about to touch down and start Armageddon.

I clapped and cheered.

Dozens of Scots stared at me, along with some Americans.

Logan gave me an appreciative, if amused, look. Then he started clapping. "Good show, Alex!"

One by one, so gradually it was like cold molasses dripping down a windowpane, the MacTaggarts began to clap. The American Wives Club cheered, led by Emery and her piercing whistle.

Catriona moved to the front of the crowd, no more than a dozen feet from Alex.

He went stone still, his gaze glued to her.

She glanced at his pink kilt, her lips ticking up at the corners. "Congratulations, Alex. But don't expect the winning streak to continue."

With that, she whirled around and disappeared into the crowd.

The stone put began. Brawny, sweaty men heaved enormous rocks in a manner reminiscent of the shot put. Alex didn't make it to the final round this time, but Logan did. I clasped my hands under my chin, bouncing on my toes while I watched him face off with Iain. Logan's cousin was a good twenty years older, but he had the MacTaggart muscles and the MacTaggart virility. Not a wrinkle on his face. What was in the water here? I needed some of that.

Iain went first, hurling his stone across the green.

Logan stepped up to the mark and hefted his boulder, testing its weight. When he glanced at me, I gave him a thumbs-up signal. He smirked and flung the stone.

The rock sailed through the air. Going, going, going. Down, down, down, and—*whump*. The stone struck at least five feet past Iain's throw.

I jumped up and down and whooped. "Go, Logan!"

Damn. I'd turned into one of the American Wives.

What the hell. I adored Logan, and my man had just beaten the reigning champion of the stone put at the MacTaggart Highland games.

Logan sauntered up to me, pulled me into his arms, and kissed me like a man who meant it. Really meant it. The American Wives Club cheered while their husbands made catcalls.

The caber toss came next.

I watched with my eyes half shut, my face scrunched up, while Chase tossed a caber with instruction from Lachlan. Visions of my son getting impaled by a caber tormented me, and even though I knew a tree trunk couldn't do that, I squeezed my eyes shut and prayed. Only when I heard the cheers and knew he'd thrown the caber without getting hurt did I start breathing again.

"Relax," Logan said, his arm around me. "It's over. You can look."

A breath rushed out of me as I opened my eyes. I spotted Chase, grinning and pumping his fists in the air, and I cheered. My kid had tossed a caber. It was oddly invigorating to see him participate in a manly sport with the manly MacTaggarts. Chase fit right in here.

Maybe caber tossing wasn't such a dangerous sport after all.

In the first adult match, Alex was paired with Rory.

The Steely Solicitor tossed his caber first, and Iain measured the distance.

"Sixteen point one meters!" he called out. "That's about fifty-three feet for you Americans."

Alex, who had received tips and a lightning round of training from Logan, raised his caber by walking his hands up it until the thing stood tall in front of him. Keeping the caber upright, he walked his hands down the tree trunk until he could grasp its bottom. Then he hefted it up.

His gaze darted to the crowd, where Catriona stood in front observing without expression.

Alex looked away too late. His grip on the caber slipped, and the thing wobbled. He tried to firm up his hold on it, but its teetering put him off balance, sending him staggering sideways.

Logan and Rory both ran toward him to help, but they didn't get there in time.

He tripped and hit the ground on his back.

The caber smacked down on his right shoulder. His face contorted with pain. A shout exploded out of him.

A frigid chill ripped through me. What if he was crushed? How heavy was that caber?

Catriona raced toward Alex. She got there before Rory and Logan and fell to her knees beside him. "Someone help! He's hurt!"

Her panicked expression was unmistakable as she cradled his face in her hands.

Rory and Logan carefully lifted the caber off Alex.

He massaged his shoulder. "That bloody hurt."

"Somebody call for an ambulance!" Cat shouted.

"That's not necessary," Alex said, pushing up into a sitting position. His face contorted when he used his right arm, but the fact he could use it suggested he hadn't broken anything. He looked at Cat when he said, "I'm fine, don't worry. It is nice to see you don't want me dead after all."

I hurried over to inspect his arm. "I used to be a nurse, so I'm the only one here qualified to check you out."

Alex nodded.

"No bones were broken," I said after I'd examined him. "You didn't dislocate your shoulder either, but I'm sure you'll have some nasty bruises later. You were lucky."

"I always am." He grabbed Catriona's hand, and in a voice rife with sarcasm, he asked, "Would you be my physical therapist?"

She yanked her hand free. "You're still a bastard, and I still despise you."

Cat jumped up and bolted for the garden door.

The games went on after that, though Alex didn't compete anymore. He'd wanted to, the idiot, but nobody would let him. I threatened to have Logan hogtie him if he tried to get back out on the field. After the games, once everyone else had left and Jamie and Gavin had gone into the castle with Chase, Logan and I sat down on the concrete bench in the garden.

He sandwiched my hand between both of his, the chill of my skin lessened by his warmth. "This was an unusual day."

"No kidding."

"Tonight, we'll be sleeping in a castle. I've never stayed at Dùndubhan before."

His voice retreated into the background of my perception as he went on talking about the history of the castle. The day's events replayed in my mind, ending with Alex getting smacked down by a caber. If that caber had been a little bigger, if it had struck a little further to the left, he might've died. I didn't love Alex, but I'd grown fond of him. The thought of him dying stabbed a pain through my chest. But when I imagined anything like that happening to Logan...

Cairo. The thug with a pipe. Logan. A gunshot.

My chest constricted, like a giant boulder had settled onto it. I couldn't catch my breath, couldn't stop my mind from conjuring up a different scenario. I fired the gun too late. It missed the thug, and the pipe slammed into Logan's skull.

Can't breathe, can't move, can't breathe.

"What is it?" asked the Logan in the present, the one sitting beside me, alive and unharmed.

His voice dragged me out of the memories. I gazed down at his hand wrapped around mine, his fingers threaded through mine, and that lump re-formed in my throat. Could I live with the constant fear that something might happen to him? It was too much. Too hard. Too...real.

"I love you, Logan. But this isn't going to work."

"What isn't going to work?"

"Us. This relationship." I should've pulled my hand away from his, but I couldn't do it. Somewhere between whooping because he'd won the stone put and watching Alex almost get crushed by a caber, I'd realized something important. "I'm terrified you'll die, and I can't live like that, constantly worrying something will happen to you because you have a dangerous lifestyle."

"How is sitting at a desk all day dangerous?"

"That's not what you want to be doing." My hand had grown cold again, so cold that the chill seemed to seep into my blood. "You hate your job at Evanescent. The only reason you're staying with it is because of me. Being a spy is who you are. It's in your blood. Even Alex knows that. You come alive when you do that covert stuff, and I can't watch while you shrivel up inside from boredom and start to resent me for being the reason you're not doing what you were meant to do, what you want to do. That would almost be worse than if you died."

"You have no idea what I want."

"I'm holding you back from your true calling." My eyes burned, tears welling in them. I sniffled and wiped at my eyes, but I couldn't stem the flow. The tears rolled down my cheeks. "I won't sit by and wait to lose you, either because you get yourself killed or because of the resentment that will come. It has to. Better to end this now, before we hurt each other."

"That's bollocks, Serena." He grasped my shoulders and forced me to turn toward him. "You aren't afraid of resentment. You're looking for a reason to walk away because you're afraid I'll go back to the SIS and die like your husband did, die in a faraway country and for reasons you can't understand. That's why you want to push me away. It has nothing to do with my job or my previous career."

I leaped up and stumbled backward a step. "I'm scared shitless that something will happen to you, because you like dangerous situations. But you will come to hate me for holding you back from what you really want. It'll happen, I know it. That's why we can't be together."

He sprang up off the bench, towering over me. "I want you. That's all. I want a life with the woman I love, and that's you. Donnae tell me what my true calling is, or what makes me feel alive. It's you, Serena, not dangerous situations. I come alive when I'm with you."

Tears streamed down my cheeks, the salty tang of them leaching into my mouth. I wanted to throw myself into his arms and tell him to forget everything I'd said, but the frigid, gnawing fear wouldn't let me. "No, I'm sorry, no. I can't do this."

He caught my face in his hands, stilling my movements. In the softest, gentlest voice, he said, "This has been a stressful day, and you're exhausted. Take the night to think it over. I'll stay at my parents' house. You stay here, and in the morning, we'll talk again."

"There's nothing left to say. I'm sorry I led you on—"

"You did no such thing." He kissed my forehead. "Take the night. Rest."

He ran his thumb over my lips, smiled sadly, and left.

Chapter Thirty-Seven

Logan

Did I sleep that night? Of course not. I lay in the bed I'd slept in as a lad, in my parents' house, staring up at the ceiling where the moonlight spread across it. I should've been at Dùndubhan, making love to Serena in a medieval castle and begging her to marry me. Then she'd gone off her head and announced she was leaving me.

Like hell she would.

She couldn't honestly think I'd accept her excuses for breaking off our relationship. Everything that had happened lately, from realizing we didn't hate each other to going on an adventure to Cairo and the danger I'd brought into her life, it had been too much. She'd handled herself brilliantly that night, but once the adrenaline wore off, the reality of it all had sunk in. I should've realized, when she'd been afraid to watch Chase toss a caber, that she wasn't quite herself. Like a dolt, I'd ignored the signs.

Until she threw me over.

I must have fallen asleep eventually, because I woke to find three witches perched on my bed. My sisters had dressed already, in their typical Gothic fashion. Isla sat the closest to me, while Kirsty and Elspeth had settled onto the foot of the bed.

"Wakey-wakey, Logie," Isla said. "It's time to go get your woman."

Yawning, I levered myself up to sit with my back to the headboard. "What are you on about now, Isla?"

"We know Serena broke up with you. There's no time to waste, so get out of bed and get dressed." She studied my open bag on the floor and the clothes lumped inside it. "Elspeth, pick out something nice for Logie and go iron it."

Elspeth followed Isla's orders, grabbing clothes from my bag and hustling out of the room.

"What is going on here?" I demanded. "How do you know Serena broke up with me?"

I hadn't told anyone. Though I'd eaten dinner with my family, I hadn't spoken a word during the meal except to make the excuse that Serena wanted to spend more time with her son, alone. Isla had called me "Logie the Stone Man" and tried to wheedle me into telling her why I was "a wee bit more taciturn than usual." I'd scowled at her, and she had given me a tight-lipped but knowing smile.

"Kirsty told us," Isla said. She leaned closer, adopting a serious but slightly sarcastic expression. "She has *da-shealladh*, ye know. The gift of second sight."

"I know what the Gaelic word means, but it's nonsense."

"Maybe it is, maybe it isn't." Isla tapped my forehead with one finger. "Donnae be such a grump. Your woman left you, but she hasn't left Dùndubhan yet. I talked to Jamie earlier. She says Serena is still in her room and wouldn't eat breakfast."

She wouldn't eat? The daft woman. She'd starve because she was afraid to love me.

"Away and boil your head," I told Isla, getting out of bed on the other side since she was in the way.

Kirsty clucked her tongue. "So this is the rude, obnoxious Logie that Serena keeps mentioning. Away and boil your head? Is that the way to speak to your sisters?"

"You lot are in my way. I need to get to Dùndubhan before she leaves."

"Relax," Isla said. "We've taken care of that, with Jamie's help. The lock on the door to her room has gotten…slightly jammed. She won't get out of there until you rescue her."

"What?" I stopped at the foot of the bed. "You locked her in her room? Aye, I'm sure that will put her in the right mood to change her mind about us."

"Drastic times and all that." Isla rose and made a flourishing gesture with her hand. "It will all work out. Go and get her, Logan, or we might have to put a spell on both of you."

I growled under my breath.

Kirsty hopped off the bed and hurried over to whisper in my ear. "Remember, the answer will be yes."

She and Isla left, giggling as they shut the door.

Half an hour later, I was stomping down the hallway of the guest wing at Dùndubhan, wearing the clothes Elspeth had chosen for me. Chase had gone into the kitchen with Jamie and Gavin, where they all promised to stay until further notice. The kitchen was at the far end of the main hall, but I'd gone through the dining room door into the guest wing hallway, straight to Serena's room at the end.

A key stuck out of the door's lock.

I yanked the key out and knocked.

"Who is it?" Serena called.

"Me. Open the bloody door or I'll do it."

"It's jammed. Can you call a locksmith? My phone won't work in here."

"The castle ramparts block it. But the door isn't jammed anymore. You can open it and talk to me."

Silence followed for several seconds. "No, Logan, go away. I said everything I have to say last night."

"The conversation is not over."

I twisted the knob and thrust the door inward. It bumped into the wall.

Serena hunched a few meters away, wringing her hands, with the tracks of tears visible on her cheeks. She'd startled when I shoved the door open, but now she was shaking her head. "There is nothing left to say."

"There's plenty." I leaned against the jamb. "I love you, Serena. My life is with you, and I'm not running away because you invent an excuse to leave me."

"You still don't get it." She spread her hands, new tears rolling down her cheeks. "I can't do this. It's too much."

"Everyone dies eventually. I can't promise to live forever, and neither can you." I took two steps toward her. "You are not a coward. You're a strong, resilient woman who faces life and deals with it. You've raised a son on your own, without even your family to support you. For Christ's sake, Serena, you convinced Alex to take a chance and come here to see Catriona again. You convinced Keely to give Evan a chance when she was afraid to love him. You fight for everyone else, why won't you fight for us?"

She huddled there for a moment, looking at me with a pained expression. Her hands fell to her sides, and her shoulders caved in. "God, Logan, why can't you just give up? You're so much younger than I am, young enough to start a family, you should be with someone who can give you that, someone who's not messed up inside."

"I thought you didn't care about our age difference."

"That's not the point. I'm damaged. I don't know if I can ever get over the fear of losing the people I love." She squeezed her eyes shut. "I couldn't even watch Chase throw a caber because I was terrified he might get hurt."

And then Alex had gotten hurt. Suddenly, her change in mood yesterday made sense.

I came closer and clasped her hands, holding them between us. "Of course you're afraid. You lost your husband in a brutal, senseless way. Since then, you've only had flings with men, until you met me. Now, your whole life is different. Your best friend, who's like a sister to you, got married and had a baby. Your son is growing up. And being with me can't be easy. My past isn't the sort likely to give you comfort, and I've got physical scars to remind you of how dangerous my life used to be."

She raised her face to me, her eyes red but dry, and there was something in her gaze that gave me hope I might get through to her.

"That's the point, though," I said. "My life *used* to be dangerous. I'm not a spy anymore, and I have no desire to ever go back to that life. Yes, I liked our adventure in Cairo, but not because of the danger. I liked the challenge of finding Falk Mullane and the tablets, and I liked having you there with me. You've seen every side of me, and I thought you accepted all of it."

"I did. I do." She hauled in a shaky breath. "I love you, all of you, even the deadly secret agent part. You're right about my fear of people dying, but I don't know if I can get over it."

"You can, and you will." I cradled her face in my hands, caressing her skin with my thumb. "It will take time, Serena. You've avoided facing the fear for a long time, but you can get over it. I'll help you."

"What can you do? It's inside me."

"I'm going to teach you something I learned years ago on the battlefield." Keeping hold of her face, I inched even closer until our breaths mingled. "Life is precious. You can't think of it as a path to death, but only as a winding road full of life and love and opportunities. Every road reaches its end eventually, but you can't focus on that. Focus on life, Serena. On the future, the possibilities, the happiness you can have now—if you take the risk."

Her mouth opened, but she seemed unable to speak.

That was fine, because I had something else to say. "I talked to Evan last night, and we came up with a plan. You're right about the job at Evanescent. It bores me out of my skull. Evan and I agreed I'll stay on as head of security, but I won't man a desk anymore. My job will be to keep an eye on the other employees and run regular tests of the physical security measures, to make sure no one can circumvent them. Evan's people know how to deal with digital incursions, but I know more about the old-fashioned, hands-on sort. I'll offer the same service to the company's clients."

I waited for her to say something, but she hadn't regained her voice yet. Honestly, I needed a moment too. Never in my life had I delivered such a long speech, and I wasn't done yet.

So I got back to it. "I'll also occasionally travel to Evanescent's global headquarters at Inverness to perform the same sort of tests there and at the factories in Wales and Cornwall. But I will be free to take freelance security jobs, like the ones I've done for Alex."

Though her mouth had fallen open again, her tears had faded away.

"In case I wasn't clear enough," I said, "this means that I'm not going back to MI6 or the military. Not ever. I don't want to. This arrangement eliminates the boredom, and it will let us have a holiday in Scotland whenever we like. The only unknown in this equation is you."

"Why would you do that? Why change your whole life?"

"For you, because you mean more to me than any job. Can you handle having me around every day, permanently?"

She gazed at me with eyes that had become clear and bright, full of the life I'd always seen in them, the life that made her so beautiful and wonderful. "Yes, Logan, I can handle it. I want to be with you, I want to take the risk."

"Good, because I have something else to say." I dropped to one knee. "Maybe I shouldn't do this yet, but you might've noticed I'm not the sort who waits for the right time."

"You always pick the right time. I just couldn't see how right you were." She brushed her fingers over my cheek. "I see it now. And I'm ready, so go on."

I took hold of her left hand. "Serena Carpenter, will you be my wife?"

She laughed, almost giggling. "That's it? No romantic, soppy speech?"

"You also might've noticed I'm not one for speeches. The one I made a minute ago is all I've got in me today." I kissed her hand. "Well, will ye have me?"

"Of course I will. Yes, Logan, yes."

Was this what Kirsty had meant? The answer would be yes, she'd told me twice. No, second sight was a myth.

I rubbed Serena's third finger. "Sorry I don't have a ring yet. This proposal was spontaneous."

"That's the best kind." She knelt and looped her arms around my neck. "A bone-melting kiss will do for today, to seal the deal. Are you sure you don't mind being a stepdad to a teenage boy?"

"Chase is the least annoying child I've ever met, even if I did watch him stuff an entire Scotch egg in his mouth at Aunt Aileen's birthday party."

"He did what? Oh, he'll be hearing about *that* when I see him."

"Later. Right now, I need to kiss my future wife."

"Yes, you do."

I tugged her close. "Your lips won't be leaving mine for a long, long time."

Epilogue

Alex
Five Weeks later

Human bodies filled the great hall at Dùndubhan, humans full of life and revelry, men and women dressed in elaborate costumes and wearing masks to conceal their identities. Colored lights cast a muted glow on the cavernous room, with delicate strobes occasionally flaring across the space. Only Aidan MacTaggart would turn his birthday party into something naughty and for adults only. Earlier today, he'd held a party with the children, his and the ones belonging to his siblings and cousins. Tonight was for the rest of us.

Trying to identify the partygoers proved a challenge, with their faces mostly or fully covered and only their eyes and mouths visible. I recognized Aidan's wife, Calli, by her red hair and striking green eyes. Evan's wife, Keely, had even more striking green eyes and raven hair that made her stand out from the crowd. There was no mistaking Evan either, with his eerily pale blue eyes that seemed almost silver. As for Logan, I knew him by his stance and the way he seemed to always be watching for trouble. With a beautiful wife like Serena, I didn't blame him for keeping watch on the other men in attendance.

I weaved my way through the throng of dancing couples to get to Logan and Serena.

"There you are," Serena said, smiling. "We wondered where you got to."

"Just taking in the party." I took in her costume, a scrap of black fabric with fringe that shimmied whenever she moved. A cap with a red feather attached to it covered part of her black wig. "What are you again?"

"A flapper." She twirled around, making the fringe dance. "You know, from the Roaring Twenties."

"Right. Well, you do look ravishing, Serena. If you ever tire of Logan, let me know." I smiled and winked. "Or if you fancy a shag on the side."

"I don't sleep with men who are in love with someone else."

Logan strapped his arm around Serena's waist. "Stop flirting with my wife, Alex, or I'll have to take you outside and beat you with a caber."

"Just having a bit of fun. Your wife is, sadly, devoted to you and you alone."

It was charming how in love they were, but sometimes watching them together gave me heartburn.

Glancing around the room, I said, "This is quite a party. I'm surprised Aidan invited me, but then, you and Serena probably harassed him until he agreed to do it."

"We invited you to our wedding. That makes you family."

Yes, I remembered the wedding. Catriona had glared daggers at me through the entire ceremony. Hot, serrated daggers dipped in poison. During the reception, she hadn't deigned to speak to me.

But she had looked at me. Often. Stared, actually.

I hadn't seen her at this party yet, but her costume might have fooled me.

"What does Cat do for a living these days?" I asked, for reasons I couldn't explain even to myself.

Logan answered. "She teaches the occasional class at the Loch Fairbairn school."

Catriona had been the cleverest student I'd ever known, but now she worked part-time at a school for children. She should've been a tenured professor at a university by now, conducting her own digs and making archaeological discoveries.

"She's over there," Serena said.

I swung my gaze back to her. "What?"

"Catriona. She's over there." Serena raised her arm and pointed one outstretched finger toward the other end of the great hall. "She's the one dressed like a pirate wench. Or is it a hot peasant girl? Not sure, but it's something from ye olden days. Either way, you can't miss her. She's standing at the wall."

Against my will, my attention swerved to the sexy female leaning against the far wall. I couldn't make out her costume from here, not with the dim lighting.

"Go on," Logan said. "You want to see her, so get your eejit erse over there."

"That would be a bad idea. Waterloo bad."

Logan slapped a hand on my upper arm and shoved. "Get your erse over there before I have my sisters cast a love spell on you."

I started to walk away, then paused to tell Logan, "For the record, I am not doing this because I'm terrified of your sisters. They're odd, but hardly frightening."

Serena laughed. "Of course not."

Why did she sound sarcastic when she said that?

I wended my way through the crowd of dancers again to reach the far side of the great hall. The woman leaning against the wall had her eyes closed, but I would've recognized her even if Serena hadn't pointed her out. That silky, cinnamon-colored hair. Those sensuous lips. Those legs. I remembered vividly how it felt to have her thighs gripping me while I fucked her.

Cat's costume was…incredible. She wore a pink, mini-skirt version of a peasant frock from medieval times, with tiny sleeves that hung low off her shoulders and a plunging neckline. Knee-high boots covered her calves, but most of her thighs were bared. Red velvet gloves stretched down her arms from her elbows, though they left her fingers exposed. Her mask was crimson, and its color accentuated the shimmering highlights in her hair. The luscious locks cascaded over her bare shoulders, teasing the slopes of her breasts.

She opened her eyes and blinked at me.

Did she recognize me? I was in costume too, wearing something Logan had picked for me—a black-and-red kilt and a loose-fitting white shirt with billowing sleeves. It gaped open in front, revealing everything down to my waist. I'd told Logan this was not historically accurate clothing, but he only clapped me on the shoulder and said, "But the lasses will like it." He had insisted I wear large black boots too, along with a sporran and a cutlass. I felt like a Scottish pirate who had taken a job at a male revue, the sort where the blokes stripped naked for a slavering crowd of women.

"Are you a friend of Aidan's?" Catriona asked.

I started to speak, then closed my mouth. She hadn't recognized me yet. If I spoke, she might realize who I was. Since I'd come over here to see her, why was I worried she might recognize me? Perhaps because she'd punched me in the gut not long ago, and to this day she refused to speak to me or be anywhere in the vicinity of me, except at Logan and Serena's wedding. After glaring at me throughout the ceremony, Catriona had brushed past me but hadn't deigned to glance in my direction.

The fact she didn't recognize me tonight offered an opportunity, if I were the sort of man who would take advantage of the situation. If I were the rake everyone thought I was.

Yes, I was that kind of man.

I braced a hand on the wall beside her, slanting in to whisper in her ear, lowering my voice and speaking more roughly, like the Scottish pirate stripper with a rakish soul that I was pretending to be. I even tried for a Scottish brogue, though I ended up sounding a bit like a drunken Highlander who had a cold. "You are the most ravishing lass in the room. How about a wee bit of the old hochmagandy?"

"No one says that anymore. You're as Scottish as a burrito, and your accent is horrible."

"Maybe, but you want me anyway."

"I don't know who you are."

"That makes it more exciting, doesn't it?" I dragged the back of my hand down her arm. "A forbidden liaison at a naughty birthday gala. I bet the thought of it makes you wet."

"Excuse me?" Her breathless, husky tone shot lust through me. "I donnae have sex with strangers."

We aren't strangers, I thought. But I said, "Ahm going to kiss ye now."

She hadn't looked at me yet, not since I'd come closer to her.

I trailed a finger along the neckline of her frock. "Ye want me to kiss ye, donnae ye?"

Maybe I was laying on the Scottish a bit thick, but I didn't care. To be this close to her, near enough to sniff her womanly scent and see the pulse throbbing in her neck, it was better than all the fantasies of her I'd enjoyed over the years. This time, I meant to come inside her delicious body instead of my own hand.

I touched my lips to her cheek. So fucking soft. I traced a line across her skin with my mouth, down to the edge of her lips.

Her breath hitched.

"You are stunning," I murmured. "The most beautiful creature ever molded by the angels."

She turned her face toward me. Our lips grazed each other, and our gazes met.

Her eyes widened.

Oh fuck. She'd recognized me.

Cat smacked her palm on my chest and shoved me away. "Alex Thorne, ye bleeding ersehole. What are you playing at?"

"I was chatting you up, wasn't I? You used to love it when I'd do that."

Her lip curled. "I used to love you, but I recovered from that disease."

"How about a relapse, then? Just for tonight."

She bared her teeth at me, like a she-wolf chasing away an interloper. "I'd sooner bathe in scalding acid than have a poke with you. I don't want to see you, I don't want to hear your voice, I don't want to be in the same room with you. Make that the same country. Stay in America, or better yet, move to the middle of the Sahara Desert."

Cat shoved me again with much more force.

I stumbled. Christ, but that woman was strong. "All right. If not a poke or hochma-whatever, how about your mouth on my cock? You used to love doing that."

She raised her hand in preparation for a sound slap but froze. Her hand hung there, caught mid-swing, for several seconds while we stared at each other.

"You're not worth it," she said.

Then she spun around and stomped away from me.

Logan and Serena hoped I might reconcile with Cat. Even if I wanted to reconcile with her, Catriona would never forgive me for the things I'd done. I couldn't blame her for that. Still, part of me wanted to win her back, or at least fuck her again. I'd have more chances to seduce her, since Logan and his wife both seemed determined to invite me to family gatherings.

I could've said no whenever they asked me. Why did I keep accepting their invitations?

Across the hall, I spotted Cat in her sexy little outfit.

Yes, I wanted her. Maybe I still loved her too. But I knew myself well enough to realize a good woman like Catriona MacTaggart deserved better than a rake who had a shaky relationship with the truth.

I said goodbye to Logan and Serena and left the party.

On the way back to my hotel, I wondered if I had it in me to be honest with Cat. Completely honest. The entire truth, unvarnished, no evasion or glossing over the facts.

Where was the fun in that?

Logan had told me Cat worked part-time at a school. She would, I was sure, jump at the chance to have a real job in archaeology. Since I'd gotten my job back, I now had a certain measure of influence again. I could arrange something for her.

She would never accept a position I'd found for her.

I wouldn't tell her I'd done it. Honesty? I'd give her that later, much later, after I'd pulled her into my world again. This would be a secret. An underhanded, rotten excuse to get her back in my life by any means necessary. The truth was overrated, anyway.

An itch started behind my ribs, a deep and unscratchable one that had sharp claws. My conscience again, niggling at me.

I ignored it, again.

Alex Thorne returns in *Irresistible in a Kilt*.

Love the

Hot Scots

series?

Visit

AnnaDurand.com

to subscribe to her newsletter
for updates on forthcoming books in this series
&
to receive a free gift for signing up!

Anna Durand is a bestselling, multi-award-winning author of contemporary and paranormal romance. Her books have earned bestseller status on every major retailer and wonderful reviews from readers around the world. But that's the boring spiel. Here are some really cool things you want to know about Anna!

Born on Lackland Air Force Base in Texas, Anna grew up moving here, there, and everywhere thanks to her dad's job as an instructor pilot. She's lived in Texas (twice), Mississippi, California (twice), Michigan (twice), and Alaska—and now Ohio.

As for her writing, Anna has always made up stories in her head, but she didn't write them down until her teen years. Those first awful books went into the trash can a few years later, though she learned a lot from those stories. Eventually, she would pen her first romance novel, the paranormal romance Willpower, and she's never looked back since.

Want even more details about Anna? Get access to her extended bio when you subscribe to her newsletter and download the free bonus ebook, Hot Scots Confidential. You'll also get hot deleted scenes, character interviews, fun facts, and more!